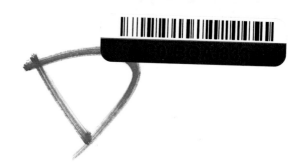

DEFYING GRAVITY

Walter D. Ward

To GALIEN
LIB –
Enjoy Walt

CHICAGO SPECTRUM PRESS
LOUISVILLE, KENTUCKY 40245

CHICAGO SPECTRUM PRESS
12305 WESTPORT RD. STE. 4
LOUISVILLE, KENTUCKY 40245
502—899—1919

To purchase additional copies of this book,
go to: www.defyingG.com

Printed in the U.S.A.

10 9 8 7 6 5 4 3 2 1

Perfect Bound
ISBN: 978-1-58374-253-2
Case Bound
ISBN: 978-1-58374-273-0

A portion of the proceeds from the sale of this novel will be used to improve the lives of disadvantaged children.

I dedicate this work to all the people, known to me or not, who have lessened my burdens, provided guidance, and brought pleasure into my life—family, relatives, friends, and in particular my parents, Norris and Pauline (Burkert) Ward, and my wonderful wife Jane.

These many kindnesses, the compassion I've been shown, can never be adequately repaid. It is my hope that this book passes along to others, at least in part, some of what has been so graciously given to me.

DATE DUE

JAN 1 8 2013			

CONTENTS

Chapter 1
DELIVERANCE

The twin strips of gleaming white concrete stretched on as far as one could see. Slicing irreverently through the gently rolling Midwestern countryside, they left a checkerboard patchwork of pastures, recently harvested fields and oddly shaped woods in their wake. The maples, oaks and hickories, some still ablaze with color, stood in testament. It was autumn's last gasp. It was late October, October 26th to be exact.

Dave sat passively in the back seat of the red 1956 Ford. The scenery slipping past his window, awash in sunlight here, obscured by shadow there, should have set his imagination racing. He slid forward to get a better view. For the most part it was a meaningless gesture. The backdrop, albeit compelling, made no impression. He was lost in thought, consumed as though in a trance. He hadn't heard his parents discuss their first new car's many refinements or marvel at the ultramodern Northern Indiana Toll Road they traveled on. Both would normally have piqued the interest of an inquisitive 13 year-old. Neither did. A mind in the grip of strong emotion simply wasn't open to the sights and sounds of the moment.

Dave hated these trips they made to Chicago. He'd curl up in a ball and close his eyes the minute the car left the curb. Seeing landmarks wasn't necessary. He knew where they were by the car's motion and the sound the tires made. So long as a monotonous whine filled his senses time remained before he had to face the inevitable unpleasantness that lay ahead. Even now when they were on their way home, his stomach ached. All he wanted was to be back in South Bend, back on North O'Brien Street, back with his friends.

"David, are you hungry?" The question, barely audible, came from a long way off.

"Huh?" he responded.

"Are you hungry?" his mother repeated, in a more deliberate tone.

"Aw, not yet," he replied.

"We'll wait a while then. It's a little early for supper."

"Fine," he answered, only half aware of what he said.

With that exchange, conversation ended. Except for a sportscaster pre-viewing collegiate match-ups on the radio and the whistling wind, the Norris family traveled on in silence.

Dave's parents, Dewitt and Lillian, both nearing 50, were short and wore bifocals. Mr. Norris, who always drove, was stocky with a round face and receding hairline. It was easy to tell when you were around him because he invariably had a fat, foul smelling cigar in his mouth. Mr. Norris had strong opinions about lots of things, particularly smoking, which he saw as a right not to be infringed upon. Dave detested cigar smoke and constantly gave thanks that cars came equipped with small triangular vents. If his dad didn't habitually click open the one in front of the driver's window, Dave was sure he'd have been asphyxiated some cold winter day, years earlier.

Dave's mother, a slender, even thin lady, was much quieter and more reserved than her husband. Always dignified and graceful, she had shoulder-length brown hair and on special occasions wore a hat. Like the majority of women in his neighborhood, she tended to the house while the men worked, most in factories around town.

"Mom! Mom!" It was Dave's six year-old sister Ann bouncing up and down on the seat next to him.

"Is that snow?" she asked excitedly.

"Sure looks like it," Mr. Norris replied.

Seconds later the car plunged headlong into one of the streaky snow laden clouds that menace counties south of Lake Michigan when cold north winds blow over the warmer water. This phenomenon, peculiar to the area, could leave one community completely buried while another, just down the road, escaped unscathed. The instant blizzard dropped visibility to near zero; Mr. Norris momentarily took his foot off the gas.

"So soon?" Dave groaned, as he watched waves of flakes stream furiously toward the windshield, then arc abruptly over the roof.

"Not really," Mrs. Norris remarked. "We usually get a good snow or two by now. It is almost November, you know."

Dave folded his arms on the back of the bench style front seat, plopped his head down on his wrists and stared straight ahead. All of nature fas-cinated Dave. A vast ocean, majestic mountain, he didn't need these to

8

appreciate its wonder—just one breathlessly delicate, gone-in-a-flash ice crystal, would do. Where did they come from? How were they made?

"Is it true?" he asked. "Are all snowflakes different?"

"As far as I know," Mr. Norris replied.

Amazing, how could it be? he wondered.

Ahead, isolated shafts of sunlight found rifts in the clouds. Soon they'd be in the clear again. Dave looked at his sister, a cute little girl whose irresistible dimples immediately caught your eye. Her face filled with awe, she was bewitched by the glistening landscape. He hesitated momentarily, then, not wishing to break the spell, turned back toward his window.

"BURMA SHAVE! BURMA SHAVE!" he cried, as the car whizzed past a sign posted along the fence row.

Everyone looked right, straining to read the next phrase in the series.

"If Daisies are your
Favorite flower,
Keep pushing up those
Miles per hour.
BURMA SHAVE"

"BURMA SHAVE jingles are neat," Dave said, with emotion heretofore absent. "Hey, Dad," he continued, scooching up against the front seat, "How fast we goin'?"

"We're moving right along," came the response from Mr. Norris whose face filled the rear view mirror.

Dave noticed his mom and dad glance at each other. Mom's smile and the twinkle in her eye confirmed what he'd suspected all along; she was the real speed limit. It was a valid observation to be sure but, in this case, one he'd misinterpreted. His parents were worried about him. Each trip to Chicago seemed to extract more of a toll. Now that he was active, talkative, and had questions, lots of questions, they knew he felt better. This particular twinkle, one of those private marital signals spouses exchange on occasion, was an expression of both pleasure and relief.

"I'd say it's time for supper," Mr. Norris remarked cheerfully. "How about Stan Leonard's?"

Everyone responded in the affirmative.

Another twinkle from Mrs. Norris.

Wow! What a treat, Dave thought. Leonard's was a high class place, not the kind of restaurant his family could afford to visit very often. And he was hungry, even if he hadn't realized it before.

"Shall we stop at your mother's first?" Mr. Norris asked his wife.

"No, it's been a long day. Let's just have dinner and go on home."

Stan Leonard's was in LaPorte, where most of Dave's relatives lived; both sets of grandparents, three aunts and uncles. Mr. and Mrs. Norris had met there in high school. They married in 1929, shortly after Mrs. Norris graduated, then moved to South Bend in 1940 when a better job became available for Mr. Norris. Their roots, however, remained firmly planted in LaPorte, a rural community encompassing a number of small lakes and a large Allis Chalmers tractor factory. There was nothing much to distinguish LaPorte from other towns its size except maybe for baseball. LaPorte had a special love of baseball.

Before long Mr. Norris eased the car onto the exit ramp's sweeping curve and pulled up to the toll booth. Dave couldn't remember his parents ever having to pay to drive on a road before.

"Dad, have ya talked ta Meyer lately?" Dave asked.

"That's Mr. Abrams to you," Mr. Norris corrected.

"Oops. Sorry. Think maybe he'll be at Leonard's? I'd sure like ta get some more books from 'im."

"He does eat there often, but I don't know; his Sabbath starts at dusk today."

"How do ya know when that is?" Dave puzzled.

"Remember the Epstein's who lived next door to Grandma and Grandpa Norris?"

"Yeah," Dave answered.

"They were Jewish, too, and I asked Reuben that very same question many years ago. He said the Jewish sabbath starts Friday evening when there isn't enough light to tell a white thread from a black one."

Dave eyed his dad with consternation. He was being fed a line sure, but then, when somebody said something that crazy, often as not it was true.

"Sooo, ya think he'll be there?"

"You'll just have to wait and see," Mr. Norris replied. "It depends on how observant he is."

Leonard's occupied a prime spot on the south side of Clear Lake, a half-mile or so northeast of down town. A low modern building with expansive windows to accommodate the discriminating, in LaPorte, it was the place to be. Food was definitely on Dave's mind now, along with two more immediate concerns. The flurries had returned. An ominous glaze covered the pavement. Dave was on alert. He'd taken more than a few nasty spills in the past and was wary of slippery walkways.

"Need a hand?" Mr. Norris asked, once they'd parked.

"Yes, I do," Dave replied.

The dry carpeted foyer brought a sigh of relief. One down, next stop the bathroom. Dave always required more bathroom breaks than anybody else. His dad, for instance, hardly ever needed one and didn't like stopping when they were on the road. Often, while he agonized, Dave wondered if his dad didn't have a spare tank.

The booth Dave's family occupied provided a terrific view of the lake. Cozy cottages lining the eastern shore, Fox Park's Grecian pavilion among the grand oaks in the distance, lacy ribbons of light dancing on the water, shimmering reflections: an impressionist masterpiece—this was living.

Next question, what could he order? He wasn't exactly sure on that but when his dad selected a steak, he went for the shrimp dinner. Mom still had that twinkle in her eye. This day was turning out a lot better than he had any right to expect.

A parting nod, a quirky flip of its cover and the waitress' check pad disappeared into an apron pocket. A second later she was gone. So was Mr. Norris, to visit some men two tables away.

Dave's attention drifted back to the captivating panorama framed by the casement on his right.

Suddenly, his dad and friends were there next to him. They all wanted to know how David was doing. Was he getting around O.K.? How was school going? Did he feel good? And, of course, was he behaving himself?

Those first questions were easy enough. That last one though, about behaving, was always trickier. He shifted his eyes toward his dad before saying he thought he was.

Dave didn't much like it when Dad's friends inquired as to how he was getting on. Being singled out was embarrassing, even if they did mean well. Dinner, on the other hand, was great. *Now,* he thought, as they got up to leave, *a nice contented snooze in the car...*

"David, how ya doin'?" It was Meyer's booming voice.

"Oh, hi Mr. Abrams. I didn't see ya come in," Dave said excitedly. "Could I get some new books from ya, mechanics and science ones, ones with rocket stuff?"

"Whoa there, slow down," Meyer chuckled, raising a hand. "I'll need a list to keep all that straight."

The Norris' sat back down. Meyer and his wife took the next booth. Mrs. Norris dug through her purse for paper. Mr. Norris produced a fountain pen. Dave wrote furiously then leaned across the table and whispered to his dad. "When ya think he'd have 'em?"

"Meyer, are you coming to the game Wednesday?" Mr. Norris asked.

"I hadn't—sure, I could make it. I'll see what I can round up by then."

Dave was aglow.

"Gee, thanks Mr. Abrams!" he exclaimed.

Now, if he could just talk his parents into letting him go with his dad to LaPorte on a school night.

Chapter 2
THE PARROT

Morning found Dave buried under his covers with only a portion of his face exposed. He was in his own bedroom, in his own bed. The books for the moment forgotten, he lay there half-awake, listening to his mother work in the kitchen and the washing machine churn on the other side of the curtain that served as the door to his room. The intrusive sounds, an annoyance at another time, were curiously reassuring at the moment. The curtain swung open.

"Roll out of there," Mr. Norris ordered. "I need you to help me start Will's car."

"Be there in a minute," Dave replied.

That minute turned into ten. Dave's legs were stiff and they itched. He rubbed them, then worked his joints for a time. While he did, he looked out his window. The dusting of snow that seemed to have followed them home from LaPorte had melted. That was good. He got dressed, washed his face and brushed his teeth. A quick breakfast and he was out the back door rearing to go.

The souped-up '39 Ford hot rod with distinctive dull gray primer paint job, belonged to Dave's older brother Will, an army private stationed at Fort Bliss, Texas. Will was cool, very cool. A talented swimmer and gymnast, he wore white T shirts with a pack of cigarettes rolled up in one sleeve and his jet black hair slicked back in a D.A. Girls adored him. The car was fast, too, maybe too fast. When Will was in high school it got him in trouble more than once, but Dave didn't know the details on that because every time things got interesting in his house, he was shooed out of the room. From what he gathered though, that car could really go. Will didn't get home much, which meant the Ford just sat at the curb on Vassar Street, and the longer it sat, the harder it was to start.

"David, when I tell you, squirt some of this starter fluid into the carburetor."

Dave took the can, aimed it and waited while his dad climbed in behind the wheel.

"Now! Give it a shot," Mr. Norris said, stepping on the starter button.

Dave fired a stream into the opening. The starter groaned. Some of the vapor, caught up by the fan, flew into his face. His stomach lurched. He pulled back, grabbing hold of the fender as he did.

Mr. Norris leaned out the window. "What's wrong?" he asked. "Are you all right?"

Dave shook his head, "I think I'm gonna be sick."

Mr. Norris exited the car and helped him to the curb.

"Whew—that smell—my stomach," Dave sputtered, cradling his head in his hands.

Mr. Norris, not certain how to respond, stood by silently.

"Just let me sit here awhile," Dave coughed. "I'll be O.K."

"You go on then," Mr. Norris said. "Your mother can help with the car."

When Dave's mom appeared he knew he had to leave. Another whiff of that stuff and he'd puke sure. He wiped his face, stood up, steadied himself then angled across Vassar Street to O'Brien. Four houses south toward Lincolnway and he was at Ralph's house. Ralph Scanner was one of Dave's best friend's and had been since the Scanner family moved into the neighborhood a year earlier. Known as "Rafe," he and his older brother George "Gunner" were what made the ten and eleven hundred blocks of O'Brien Street come together. Until they arrived there weren't enough kids Dave's age to make playing sports fun. Now, it was lively competition year around. Rafe was gregarious, with a quick, often biting wit that kept you on your toes. As Dave turned onto the short walkway that connected the house to the sidewalk, Rafe came out the front door and sat down on the porch steps to tie his shoes.

"Rafe," Dave called out smiling.

"Hey, what's the haps?" Rafe said, returning the smile.

"We gotta talk."

"'Bout what?" Rafe asked, banging dirt off his sneakers.

"'Bout Wednesday."

"Still set on the plan aren't we?"

"Well, sorta. See I forgot Wednesday was Halloween and asked if I could go with Dad to the football game in LaPorte."

"So, tell 'im ya changed your mind."

"Can't. We're meetin' somebody there and he's comin' ta see me. But look," Dave added quickly, "we can still do the switch on Tuesday."

"S'pose," Rafe said, snugging a pair of laces.

Halloween was always a big deal. Kids could trick-or-treat not just that night but also the one before. The plan Dave and Rafe had cooked up was simple enough: identify houses where the best treats were given out, switch costumes, and double back for a second pass.

"Your sister's not taggin' 'long this year, is she?"

"No way," Dave exclaimed. "I told Mom we might ride over a couple blocks. Anyway, she's afraid the older boys will run by and steal her candy, so Dad's takin' her out awhile Tuesday 'fore it gets dark."

"Try ta scare her with that, did ya?"

"Me?" Dave grinned sheepishly, "wouldn't think of it."

"Gotta go," Rafe said, hopping on his bike. "Gettin' my hair cut at eleven. Catch ya later."

If you lived in South Bend, Indiana, Saturday afternoons in October were reserved for Notre Dame Football. Dave didn't find the games all that interesting. Spending hours in front of a T.V. when you could be outdoors seemed like a big waste of time, especially since Notre Dame was up against number two ranked Oklahoma. Oklahoma had a power house. Still, unless he wanted to stay home and rake leaves all afternoon, there wasn't much else to do. So after a dismal lunch of hash, which had almost the same effect on him as starter fluid, he trekked back to Rafe's. Dave thought Oklahoma would win all along and they did. Unleashing a barrage of four touchdowns before half time, they completely outclassed the Irish. Rockne would've had tears in his eyes. By the end of the third quarter Dave couldn't take any more. He went home. Raking wasn't all that bad; actually, it was kind of fun.

"Dewitt, are you coming out soon?" Mrs. Norris called to her husband.

"In a minute," he responded.

Mr. Norris was busy taping another "Eisenhower for President" sign in the porch window. Dave couldn't see why. There was already a big one on the front lawn and his dad had been wearing an "I like Ike" button for weeks.

Since the Norris' lived on a corner lot it took longer to gather the leaves into a great heap at the end of the driveway next to where the alley joined Vassar Street. After that, you could flop on the pile to pack it down. At dusk Mr. Norris started the fire and the classic fall ritual began. Amid the incessant crackling, streams of glowing embers leaped skyward, while others, caught in eddies, swirled aimlessly about. This was the time for parents to recount tales of their youth, for marshmallows on long sticks to be toasted over glowing coals, for great hissing dragons, gruesome goblins and ghouls to come into being, and then, in an instant, take on an altogether different form. As Dave stared at the images, he reflected on what a wonderful place this was to live: great friends just houses away, sports and games to play, science to discover, and, of course, his family. Best of all, you were safe and if you paid heed to the rules, you could do pretty much as you pleased.

"Trying to burn down the neighborhood are ya?" came a voice from the darkness.

It was Mr. Rasco and his son Ron, another of Dave's friends.

"Just keeping an eye on the fire," Mr. Norris replied, leaning on his rake. "Say Chet, did you see the game today?"

"Can't say that I did. The shop keeps me awfully busy."

Mr. Rasco owned a heavy equipment repair service and always worked a lot.

"You didn't miss much," Mr. Norris noted. "Notre Dame got clobbered."

"I heard, 40-ZIP. It came across on the radio while we were driving over."

"They stopped Hornung cold," Mr. Norris added, pushing some wayward embers into the main pile.

"How about Larsen? Did you see him pitch the perfect game in the World Series?"

"Now that I did see," Mr. Rasco answered. "We have a used T.V. in the shop and after Mantle caught Hodges' long drive to save it for him in the fifth, well, we called it a day and watched the rest."

"We saw it, too," Dave interjected. "They took all us older kids down ta the rec-hall, for the whole afternoon. The place was packed. I thought it was cool when the announcer said Larsen's slow ball was so slow it oughta be equipped with back up lights."

"And remember the reporter asking him, 'Is that the best game you ever pitched?'" Ron added in a low voice. "Larsen'll be in the Hall of Fame for sure."

"We'll have to wait and see on that," Mr. Norris said. "Throwing one great game doesn't make you a great pitcher."

By now the marshmallows were gone and despite her complaining, Mrs. Norris had taken Ann into the house. Then, as Dave and Ron knew it would, the subject turned to politics. Mr. Norris and Mr. Rasco were both cut from the same cloth. Staunch Republicans, they had a certain shoot-first-ask-questions-later attitude about the world.

"I don't see the Hungarians holding out for long," Mr. Rasco ventured.

Mr. Norris nodded in agreement. "The Russian's will crush them in days, a week tops."

At the end of WW II when the Soviet Union expanded westward into Eastern Europe, Hungary fell under the Communist yoke. The uneasy peace that followed had been abruptly shattered earlier in the week after a peaceful demonstration turned violent, then, fueled by pent-up frustrations long held in check, exploded into full blown revolt. With pitched battles raging across the country, the competing superpowers found themselves once again at the brink.

"I think we should warn the Commies to back off and blast them if they don't," Mr. Rasco said. "They wouldn't dare challenge us if they knew we meant business."

"Maybe if we load some of our big jets with A-Bombs and park them right at their doorstep—maybe then they'll get the idea," Mr. Norris contended.

Dave and Ron rolled their eyes.

"You can't do that," Dave blurted out. "They've got A-Bombs too and monster H-Bombs. One of those goes off, half a state'd be gone."

"Yeah, and they've got really big rockets to put them on," Ron supported.

"Their weapons are junk," Mr. Norris countered.

"If they tried to use them they'd probably blow themselves up," Mr. Rasco added.

"Just because they don't have telephones or washing machines doesn't mean they couldn't wipe us out," Dave said, holding his ground. "Things are different now."

Mr. Norris and Mr. Rasco were both born in 1907, long before television, jet planes, rockets, most all the exciting new things that made up Dave and Ron's world. To the boys they seemed old fashioned, out of touch, particularly with the profound realities of the cold war.

"*Gunsmoke*. Five minutes," Mrs. Norris called from the back door.

Dave was ready to pack it in anyway. The discussion had slipped into the circuitous, 'chase your tail' faze, and the fire, so comforting only minutes earlier, had gone cold.

Sunday. Church. Another long sermon to sit through. Prayers for world peace. Dave flashed back to Pastor Gray requesting prayers during the Korean War. Why conflicts oceans away scared him so, why he worried about so many things, Dave didn't know.

The doors of the church opened to the last bars of "Onward Christian Soldiers." Brilliant sunshine flooded in. The warming rays struck Mrs. Norris' face.

"Looks like the last nice Sunday," she said, shading her eyes.

"Knew it," Dave muttered to himself.

They were going visiting: another boring afternoon in LaPorte. All Dave's relatives were old, well, except for his cousins and he didn't see much of them. There was nobody to talk to, nothing to do. It was useless to ask if he could stay home. His friends would be having fun. For him, it'd be hours on a dusty sofa or the porch steps counting off the minutes 'til they'd leave. He'd scream if he heard one more comment about the good old days, how soft kids had it now, how movies and T.V. were corrupting the younger generation. That very night, in fact, the Rock & Roll sensation Elvis Presley was scheduled to appear on the *Ed Sullivan Show*. It was all the talk: long hair, suggestive lyrics, overactive hips (that was the main corrupting part). Mr. Norris called him Elvis the Pelvis.

"We gonna getta watch?" Dave asked, holding back a smile.

There was silence as Mr. Norris braked to a stop in front of Grandma and Grandpa Norris' house on Rumely Street.

"Well—I don't—we haven't decided yet," Mrs. Norris said hesitantly.

When they made the rounds to his other grandparents, the Schwark's, and had an early supper at his Aunt Martha's, Dave got his hopes up. He kept his mouth shut on the way home though. *Best not to push it,* he thought. He kept it shut when they got there too.

"What's that smell?" Mrs. Norris asked, when they entered the house.

"I noticed it this morning before church," Mr. Norris commented. "It's much stronger now."

Ann grabbed her nose.

"Yuk, it stinks in here."

Dave stepped through the kitchen door then quickly turned into his bedroom as if he hadn't picked up on it. When he came out the television was on. He took a seat on the couch and pretended to watch. His mom was already on the hunt for the source of the offending odor. Sullivan made his appearance. Elvis made his. The audience went crazy. Mrs. Norris, hearing the roar, temporarily gave up the search and sat down. Elvis sang "Don't Be Cruel" then "Love Me Tender." All the while throngs of teenage girls, their arms flailing wildly in the air, shrieked and screamed. Others, as if in a trance, swayed methodically from side to side, swooning. The camera caught it all. Elvis gyrated into "Hound Dog," not a hair dislodged in the process. More screaming. Hysterical gasps. Dave saw a frenzied girl collapse into her seat. His sister jumped up clapping.

"Settle down," Mr. Norris ordered, "or you're going to bed."

Ann froze then sat down.

"Think I'll go downstairs awhile," Dave remarked casually, when "The Shue" ended.

The basement was Dave's getaway, a retreat of sorts where he wouldn't be bothered, where he could build things, do experiments, mix batches of rocket fuel and gunpowder. It was perfect. With stagnant cigar smoke floating in layers across the living room above, like an the early morning fog, he could light off samples down below to test their rate of burn and nobody upstairs would be the wiser. Any fumes that did seep through the floor went unnoticed. It wasn't like his parents were stupid, though, and didn't know what was going on, far from it. It was just that America was locked in a life or death struggle with the Russians and people across the country were counting on science to save the day. Dave was doing science, so as long as he didn't blow up the house or an enraged neighbor called to complain a blast in the alley had shaken her's, he was in the clear.

"It's back to the books tomorrow," Mr. Norris said.

"That makes this a school night," Mrs. Norris added. "You better not overdo."

Dave went to object but noticed his dad eying him over the edge of the newspaper he was holding, so much for the basement. He watched Hitchcock then went into his room to read. Dave wasn't exactly the world's most voracious reader but after seeing *20,000 Leagues Under the Sea* on Disney, he'd been hooked on Jules Verne. *From the Earth to the Moon, Journey to the Center of the Earth,* he was working his way through the whole series. These weren't science fiction novels to Dave. This 19th Century author foresaw the future and that future was here: electricity at the push-of-a-button, ingenious mechanical devices of every description, atomic powered submarines. Everyone knew an earth satellite was set to be launched the coming year.

Dave thought his current book, *The Mysterious Island,* was the best of the lot. Here, castaways stranded on a Pacific Island had to rely on science and engineering to survive. They smelt iron ore to make tools, used explosives to blast out a cave house inside a cliff face, built batteries to power a primitive telegraph. These men could do almost anything and Dave wanted to know as much about how things worked as they did. That was probably why he got in trouble again the next day with Mrs. Pritchard, his 8th grade teacher.

It all started innocently enough when he asked if he might work on his assignment behind the portable blackboard in the front of the room where he wouldn't get distracted. Until he got to question four that's what he was doing. Then temptation reared its ugly head. Encyclopedias, a complete set, chuck full of information, not an arms-length away, and he hadn't had access to any for months. What would it hurt if he leafed through a couple for a few minutes? Mrs. Pritchard would never know. She was busy with other students and anyway she wore big clacky shoes. The hardwood floors in the old stone castle of a school he attended gave away her location with every step. He debated. *What the heck,* he thought, *why not?* He pulled out the "T" and flipped it open. *Let's see, "Torpedo."* He started reading: propulsion systems, warheads. Then, out of the blue, hands on hips, there she was, not two steps in front of him.

"And I suppose that's for your assignment?" she asked, with as stern a look as he'd ever seen.

"Wha—no, no ma'am, it's not," he stammered. "I was just lookin' up a few things."

"Torpedoes?"

Dave grimaced

"You put that book away right now and get going on those questions. Do both sets," she ordered.

"Both! O.K. I will," he said, quickly slipping the encyclopedia back into its slot.

"At your seat!"

"All right."

How'd she know, he wondered, on the way to his desk. Coke bottle glasses, those clompers on her feet, it was impossible. He hadn't heard a single clack. Irritating her further though, he didn't dare do that, not after the incident with the snorkel pen the previous spring. His dad had had to make a trip to school on that one.

"See, Eugene—in the next seat over, he got a Sheaffer for his birthday," Dave explained at the conference. "I was just seein' how it worked. Next second, whish, ink came shootin' out the snorkel tube. I didn't mean for it ta happen, honest. I barely touched the plunger."

The offending stream left blue splotches on his notebook, the floor, and, unfortunately, the blond girl in front of him. Her parents weren't at all pleased and didn't exactly look impressed by his explanation. Dad and Mr. Lesher, the principal, weren't happy either. It was pointed out that if he'd been working on his lesson at the time like he was supposed to be, instead of fooling around, nothing would have happened in the first place, that he should have known better, that patience with his shenanigans was wearing very thin. Finally, after Mr. Norris assured everyone nothing of the sort would happen again, things got smoothed over. Dave hoped that would be the end of it but when he got up from supper that night Dad pointed to the bedroom.

"In there! Now!"

Dave's stomach did its usual flip.

"Why don't you stop and think before you do these things?" Mr. Norris bellowed. "If you thought about what you were going to say or do ahead of time all this could be avoided."

"I know, I know," Dave replied wistfully. "I'm tryin' hard, really. But sometimes things pop inta my head and I do stuff or say somethin' I know I shouldn't."

"Well, there'll be no more 'popping' or else."

"I have been doin' better, haven't I?"

"Yes, you have, a lot better," Mr. Norris conceded, "but you've got a long way to go and the next time there's trouble like this we won't just be talking."

Dave felt a shiver shoot down his spine. That last sentence was undoubtedly connected to the assurance his dad had given the girl's parents. We won't just be talking. If he kept repeating that to himself he was sure he could keep from messing up again. After all, he hadn't pointed out that the girl's hair would eventually grow back or remind his dad that he once admitted to dunking a girl's braids in an ink well. Wasn't that already proof he could do it?

"David! Are you daydreaming back there?" Mrs. Pritchard barked.

"Huh, no ma'am, no, I mean yes. Sorry."

"That assignment is due tomorrow morning, all of it, first thing sharp."

"Don't worry, it'll be done, promise. Done good too."

"Done well," Mrs. Pritchard corrected.

"Right."

After school Dave grabbed an apple and went straight to his room. The Revolutionary War—who cared about battles fought with muskets and swords? It was ancient history.

"Are you all right in there?" Mrs. Norris asked from the kitchen.

"Yeah, fine," Dave responded glumly. "Just gotta get my social studies assignment done so's I can work on my pirate's costume tonight."

Mrs. Norris' face appeared at the edge of the curtain.

"I'll call you when dinner's ready," she smiled, "and stop that scratching. You won't like it if you get an infection in one of those legs."

"But they itch," he grumbled, struggling to focus on question seven. Who was General Burgoyne and what happened at the battle of Saratoga?

It seemed hours passed before he heard, "supper time, wash up."

"What we havin'?" he asked, as he slid into his seat.

"Pork chops and sauerkraut."

"Thought so, great."

Dinner time at Dave's house was five-thirty. That way Mr. and Mrs. Norris could catch the evening news off the T.V. in the living room while they ate. After grace was said Mrs. Norris made up a plate for Ann then Dave filled his.

"A little more sauerkraut, please."

"Studying must have made you hungry," Mr. Norris said.

"It did."

"Your mother tells me you've been in there hitting the books all afternoon," Mr. Norris remarked. "That's good. You can't get by in this day and age without an education like you could when I was young. Everything's more complicated now. You have to use your head all the time."

Mr. Norris was always talking up education. The two years of college credit he'd earned during his sports playing days in the early thirties were more than most adults in the neighborhood had. Unfortunately, with the depression and a family to support, he wasn't able to complete his studies. He did talk about graduating though, from some school called "hard knocks," whatever that meant.

"Say Dad, how do ya force yourself..."

"Quiet!" Mr. Norris ordered. "Sports."

In the Norris house you couldn't talk when the sports report was on. Mr. Norris wouldn't allow it. If you wanted the bread passed or another glass of milk you had to motion or point. Even Mrs. Norris usually went along.

"Now, what was that question?" Mr. Norris asked, when a commercial came on.

"How do ya force yourself ta study things you're not interested in?"

"That's tough—you just have to do it."

"We can't always do what we want," Mrs. Norris added. "You should know that better than most."

Dave did know that, all too well. He just hoped there might be a way around the hard work, a trick of some sort he hadn't heard of.

"Quiet!"

The news bulletin logo appeared on the screen.

"Early reports indicate Israel has attacked Egypt in the Sinai peninsula. It is feared Britain and France may soon enter the fray—updates as they are received."

Mr. and Mrs. Norris looked at one another. Dave felt the apprehension their eyes couldn't conceal.

"I don't see why they can't settle things peacefully over there," Mrs. Norris said, "all the senseless killing."

Mr. Norris who sold tools and got around a lot had an "I saw it coming" look on his face. The United States and the Soviet Union squaring off over

Hungary was bad enough. Now their proxies were fighting it out in the Middle East. Dave was scared. Almost anything could happen. What if something went wrong, a miscalculation was made, a minor incident escalated uncontrollably? As his dad would say, all hell could break loose. America was in the midst of a titanic struggle. Reoccurring cycles of normalcy punctuated by intense fear that the country would be obliterated in an immense atomic fireball. For Dave, it's how life had always been.

"Here, I finished your eye patch," Mrs. Norris said, reaching over to the counter. "Try it on."

"You look funny," Ann giggled. "Can ya see?"

"Sure," Dave replied, cocking his head slightly.

Mr. Norris, obviously mulling over the ramifications of what he'd just heard, was staring off into space.

"Can I be excused?" Dave whispered.

Mrs. Norris motioned in response. "But take that patch off on the stairs."

Seconds later, Dave was through the kitchen door and down the steps to his right.

There were two main differences between Dave's basement and those of his friends. Theirs were called full basements because the cellar was the same size as the house. In his, the concrete block walls were inset about four feet and only came up neck high. From there a thin layer of mortar, at ground level, extended to the outside walls where the foundation continued upwards to support the floor joists. The result was a "storage ledge" or shelf that ran across the far end, the front of the house and along the two sides. With white washed masonry, and a dimly lit path through the clutter leading to Dave's lab table and the workbench, you couldn't help but feel you were in a medieval hideaway. Best of all, friends could slip in, unobserved, through the outside door next to his room and take the stairs down without having to go through the house. All in all, it was a pretty slick arrangement.

Dave felt a tap on his shoulder and turned around.

"Whatcha think?"

It was Rafe wearing the eye patch and an ear-to-ear grin.

"Don't do that," Dave scolded. "Ya scared me. I didn't hear ya come in, and take that off, your head's too big. You'll stretch out the strap."

"Ya just startin' on your sword?" Rafe asked.

"Hey, I only been down here five minutes," Dave explained, laying aside the saw he was holding.

"Whew, what died in here?"

"Shhh," Dave gestured, with a finger to his lips. "Come on." He led Rafe back toward the stairs then across to the wall opposite the furnace. "Nobody ever goes here," he said, pulling a rumpled bird carcass from behind a rack of pre-war fruit his mother had canned.

"Where'd ya get that?" Rafe laughed.

"Hold it down," Dave mouthed. "They'll hear upstairs. O.K., look," he continued softly, "Saturday, I went home ta rake leaves 'cause Notre Dame was gettin' slaughtered, right?"

"Yeah, so?"

"Well, the Razyniaks came over ta shoot baskets 'bout when we finished up. Said they'd been busy movin' Mr. R's tools from the garage inta the basement so he can do his taxidermy over winter. That's where the parrot comes in. Somebody had 'im stuff it then didn't pay up."

"Heck, that happens every year," Rafe scoffed.

"Anyway—Pete said all that stuff sittin' 'round went out. Can ya believe it? All I got for a costume is a black bandanna for my head, the eye patch my mom made and this chintzy plywood sword, if I get it done that is. I had ta do somethin'. So soon's they'd gone home for supper, I tore down the alley and sure enough, there he was buried down 'bout a foot in their trash barrel."

"What's the yellow stuff?"

"Part of it's him I think, The rest, I do'no, some kind a mold, I guess. Now the smell, that's 'cause the rain got 'im all soggy, 'specially the excelsior inside. I figured I could save 'im though, so I stuffed 'im under my shirt and brought 'im home. Then I snuck 'im down here and hid 'im behind the furnace where he'd dry fast. That was a mistake, 'cause when the furnace kicked on it spread the smell through the whole house."

"You're crazy," Rafe snorted. "You put that thing in your shirt?"

"Only way I could carry it. I'm dead if Mom finds out. She's been searchin' everywhere since we got home last night, even took the vacuum apart. Thought maybe a mouse crawled up the hose and died in the dirt bag. Tellin' ya, it was way worse earlier."

By now Rafe had tears in his eyes.

"It's not funny," Dave protested. "I couldn't get back down here ta move it. Mom and Dad were afraid I'd overdo, so I had ta sit in my room and read."

"Why didn't ya sneak down? Woulda only taken a minute?"

Dave frowned.

"Oh, yeah—guess ya couldn't do that too easy."

"Guess I couldn't," Dave glared. "One thing though, I'm done doin' research at school. Mrs. Pritchard caught me red handed this time. I got no idea how she knew."

"Rockets again?" Rafe snickered.

"No, smarty pants," Dave grinned. "It was torpedoes this time. And man did she lay the questions on me, practically a whole chapter's worth. I been slavin' 'way on 'em since I got home. You watch though, I get this parrot worked back inta shape, wired up and he's sittin' there on my shoulder, I'll have the best costume goin'."

"I can hardly wait," Rafe coughed.

Three neat pages of homework laid on Mrs. Pritchard's desk and Dave was back in her good graces. A break before lunch where you got to describe your costume (minus the parrot part, of course), treats at the end of the day: sometimes school wasn't half bad.

"It's a little something to get you started," Mrs. Pritchard smiled, as she handed out small bags of goodies, each wrapped and tied with a ribbon.

Dave dropped his into a coat pocket, remembered he'd forgotten his math book and went back to his desk. On the way he overheard Mr. Lesher and Mrs. Pritchard talking.

"Let's hope we don't get drawn into this Hungarian conflict," Mr. Lesher said.

"And to think," Mrs. Pritchard remarked, "not that long ago, we and the Russians were on the same side."

War again. There was no escape. It was the lead story on the evening news: plumes of smoke rising from burning tanks, downed fighters, scattered wreckage, death, despair. Dave was torn. He wanted to know every last detail yet he didn't. He turned away to finish his slice of pie. "Speedy" the Alka-Seltzer character made an appearance. He heard a knock at the back door.

It was Rafe's ta ta-tap tap. Dave handed his dish to his mother and grabbed his foil covered sword.

"Remember now, leaves can be slippery," she cautioned. "And don't forget your eye patch."

Dave shook his head in response and singing, "Pop-pop-fizz-fizz, oh what a relief it is," he was on his way.

"Where's the parrot?" Rafe asked.

"In the garage. I stashed 'im behind Dad's snow tires while Mom was shoppin'. He never puts 'em on 'til the last minute."

"Wanna start on the other sida O'Brien and work down?"

"Not 'til Dad and Ann get back and we gotta skip the Razyniak's end of the block 'cause somebody there's bound ta recognize the parrot."

"Johnson Street then?"

"Let's go two blocks over and hit Brookfield. We did good there last year."

It was agreed. Dave retrieved the parrot, and using the coat hanger he'd fashioned, bracketed it to his shoulder. He hopped on the bar of Rafe's bike and they rode off.

The eleven hundred block of Brookfield had thirteen houses on each side, the same as O'Brien. Like most streets around, it was teeming with excited youth, the sound of leaves being crushed under foot and beckoning lights on nearly every porch.

"Mighta hit a homer goin' here," Rafe said.

Dave groaned. Rafe was Babe Ruth.

"It's at least a triple," Rafe grinned, while he worked to shift a gigantic wad of chewing gum in one cheek to the other side.

"Hope so."

"Got your note pad?"

"Yep, right here," Dave replied, tapping his thigh. "It's one a Dad's pocket ones from work. Oh, and look, found this when I was diggin' through my closet." He turned away then turned back with a rubber Bowie knife clasped between his teeth. "Cool isn't it?" he mumbled.

"You're fearsome, a regular blue beard."

An old world pirate, a baseball great, it was time to cash in.

Trick-or-treat turned out to be more challenging than Dave expected: up one set of porch steps, back down, on to the next house, up again, thick grass to tromp through, the slippery leaves his mother'd warned him about. He had to mark the places they'd return to, straighten the parrot if it slumped fore or aft.

"Polly's 'bout ta lose a wing," Rafe snickered, when they reached Humbolt Street.

"Hey, it's dark out, who's gonna know?" Dave snapped. "Whole bird's 'bout ta fall off. Don't have it braced right. How long we been gone?"

"Umm, say, maybe an hour."

"Gotta get movin' then or we won't have time ta switch. Tell ya what, I'll stick with the bike 'cept where they're givin' really good stuff. That'll speed things up."

It did. Rafe cut across the lawns between houses while Dave walked the bike ahead on the sidewalk. Watching Rafe slip in and out of the shadows, Dave realized just how much he resembled the "Babe." It was amazing: same powerhouse physique, sauntering gait, zest for life, and, when he was batting, same great eye at the plate.

"Dad's not gonna like you going through our trash." It was Luke, oldest of the three Razyniak musketeers.

"Pretty slick isn't it?" Dave grinned.

"It won't be if Dad sees him."

"I thought somebody'd been poking around," Tim, the youngest brother, added.

"Hey, it ain't like anybody's gonna know where I got it. We skipped O'Brien and soon's we're done here we're dumpin' 'im."

"You better," Luke barked.

Dave sighed, shook his head and moved on.

"Guess what?" he asked, when he and Rafe linked up two houses later.

"The Razyniak's just went by."

"Yep," Dave shrugged. "Hey, it's gettin' late. We best whip back ta my house so I can change but cut up an alley first, gotta ditch this bird."

Dave turned the knob on the kitchen door ever so slowly, opened it and looked in. The kitchen was dark. Two rights and he was in his room, certain he hadn't been seen. He felt around, found his Davy Crockett mask and 'coon skin cap, grabbed his B-B gun then, creasing the curtain along its edge, peeked out. The coast was clear. A moment's indecision and he stepped into the kitchen. The light went on.

"It's about time you're getting in," Mrs. Norris said.

"But, we still…"

"You've been out long enough," she said decisively. "You need your rest."

"Mom! Rafe's waitin' for me," Dave pleaded.

Mr. Norris was there in the doorway.

"If your mother says you've been out long enough, that's it. You tell Ralph you're done for the night."

Dave leaned the B-B gun against the door frame and stomped out.

"Can't go with ya," he said, dispirited.

"Get caught again?" Rafe said, emphasizing "again."

"Yes! I got caught 'again,' so what?" Dave grumbled. "Five seconds, that's all I needed, and bang the light comes on. Can't read what's on my treat sheet either, but there's the gray bungalow with the shrubs where the foreign guy lives."

"Milky Ways there, right, middle a the block?" Rafe nodded.

"Yep, odd side, then Nestles at the two houses that share a driveway. Bet those people are related."

"How 'bout the place with straw tied ta the yard light?" Rafe asked.

"Didn't do that one, 'member, too many steps."

"Oh, yeah," Rafe said, flipping on a sheet with eye holes cut in it. "Boo," he screeched, throwing out his arms, "Casper's gonna get ya."

Dave returned to his room, threw the mostly empty bag of treats on his bed, flung the 'coon skin cap against the wall and flopped on the covers. Davy Crockett wouldn't be king of the wild frontier tonight. *What the deal,* he thought. Other kids got to stay out late, why couldn't he? His parents cared about him, looked out for him, he knew that; but why'd they always have to be screwing up his life? He picked up his book then put it back and upended his bag.

Halloween treats broke conveniently into three distinct categories. The good stuff, chocolate and caramels; apples, usually small and sour, Dave figured given by people who didn't much care for kids; and hard candy like jaw breakers. He put those in his coat to trade away at school.

"Better get a move on in there. Mr. Faris will be here any minute now," Mrs. Norris called.

Dave sat up with a start. "Almost dressed," he said, reaching for his clothes.

Stanley Faris was the cab driver who took Dave and four other kids to school each day. A toot of the horn usually announced his arrival. Today he came in for coffee. While it cooled Dave finished his breakfast and loaded his book bag.

"Let's settle down," Mrs. Pritchard directed, "and get your math books out. This is still a school day. I'm going to give you the last ten minutes off this afternoon and no homework but you must stick to business until then."

That wasn't easy, not with some students wearing costumes. Patty, a princess, with gold flecks in her hair, looked prettier than ever.

"Look, Mom!" Dave said excitedly, upon returning home. "I swapped out some of my rock candy at school and Mr. Faris gave us all giant Hershey bars."

"Did you thank him?"

"You bet!" Dave replied.

"Just a little at a time now," Mrs. Norris cautioned. "Sit down a minute."

"O.K.," Dave said, tearing open the wrapper.

"Do you remember Freida Millins, one of the ladies in our sewing circle at church?"

"Um, don't think so."

"She called today."

"Uh, huh," Dave replied, biting off a chunk.

"She lives on Brookfield Street."

"She does?" Dave said, taking notice.

"She does! She said she just had to call and tell me how much she liked your pirate costume with the stuffed parrot sitting there on your shoulder and wondered where you could possibly have found a bird like that."

Dave stopped in mid chomp. "She did?" he gulped.

"Yes, she did," Mrs. Norris said, in a distinctly unpleasant tone. "So where exactly did you find that bird?"

Dave took a deep breath and explained how he'd retrieved the parrot from the Razyniak's trash barrel. You don't lie to your mom, not this Mom.

"Where do you get these crazy ideas?" she sighed.

"My costume was cruddy. Most of the other kids had really neat stuff ta wear. I had ta do somethin'. A pirate's gotta have a parrot. Long John Silver's got one. It's real distinctive."

"Did that bird have anything to do with the horrible smell we had in here?"

"Coulda. See, I put it behind the furnace 'cause it's warm there and I had ta get it dried out fast. I didn't know it'd stink up the house. Then I couldn't get back down ta move it."

"And I spent a whole day searching for that smell. Who knows what you could have gotten from that thing?" Mrs. Norris fumed, with a rare flash of anger. "Where is it now?"

"We dumped it soon's we were done trick-or-treating."

"What am I going to do with you?"

Dave hung his head. Mom hardly ever lost her cool.

"Just go to your room," she said in disgust, "and leave the chocolate out here."

"You're not gonna tell Dad, are ya?"

"Go!" she said, wringing her hands in her apron. "Spotless. That room had better be spotless by supper time or else!" she added, a look of exasperation on her face.

"The whole thing? O.K., O.K., I'll try."

Dave pulled the Electrolux from the dining room closet and dragged it into his room. He could kiss off going to LaPorte. Imagine, a sewing lady living on Brookfield Street, in the eleven hundred block no less. Who woulda thought? As far as he knew, no one from his church lived anywheres' around.

Dave was quiet as a mouse at supper. Had his mom told on him? Was he in for another grilling after dinner or later when Dad got home from LaPorte? Would they just be talking? There was no sign, nothing to indicate one way or the other.

"Been in there studying again?" Mr. Norris asked, while he sprinkled grated cheese on his spaghetti.

"Ah, sorta," Dave replied haltingly, after noticing that his mom was focused on buttering her bread.

His parents looked hungry. The food on his plate didn't look the least bit appetizing. He had to force down every bite, knowing he'd be famished in an hour or two if he didn't.

"Time to get rolling," Mr. Norris said.

Now his mother was stirring her coffee with a deliberate figure eight motion of her spoon.

Dave hesitated, "O.K." he said, getting up.

The stirring continued. Mrs. Norris only looked up long enough to give her husband a good bye kiss.

"Do you have your hat and gloves?" she demanded.

"Yes ma'am," Dave answered. "Sure do." And he scooted out the back door, hoping she wouldn't have a last minute change of heart. Mom was terrific.

Chapter 3
A CLOUD OF DOOM

M r. Norris was an umpire. Initially a side line he took up to stay close to the game he loved, umpiring became a career in 1938 when he landed a job with the semi-pro Northern League. In '39 he moved on to the Pony League (Pennsylvania-Ontario-New York). After that season the sacrifices required to chase a dream were simply too great. The long stretches away from home and family, the money, so enticing up front, barely adequate to cover the additional expenses, Mr. Norris secured a local, more stable job, selling sporting goods. The memories though, the sights, sounds, the many friendships he made—all these were his to keep. In 1943, the year Dave was born, he got his big break. The country was at war and big league ballplayers, along with so many others, had enlisted to fight in droves. With the ranks depleted, suspension of professional baseball for the duration of the conflict was actively being considered. President Roosevelt, knowing people facing long hours in defense plants, and years of struggle, needed something enduring to cling to, was opposed. That led to the establishment of The All-American Girls Professional Baseball League with Mr. Norris as chief umpire. The Norris' were set. Mr. Norris had an enviable position. Only travel to nearby cities was required and this time the pay was excellent.

An experiment from the outset, the good times ended in the early fifties when the league went bust.

"Look Dad," Dave said, as they passed the airport on the way out of town. "That plane, it's got three tails."

Mr. Norris hunched forward against the steering wheel to gaze up through the windshield as the airliner passed overhead. "It's a Constellation," he said. "One of those big four motor jobs like we took to Havana for spring training in '47."

"That's where the ants got me, right?"

"No, that was in Opa-Locka, the next year."

"Oh." Dave didn't remember anything about Cuba or Florida. All he knew was that he and his mom got to go along and that he'd been stripped bare on the spot when the ants attacked. And, that he was a big hit with the young women, a circumstance which sadly hadn't carried over into his teen-age years.

Dave closed his eyes to rest.

"Hold on!" Mr. Norris exclaimed, slamming on the brakes. A rusty pick-up had just pulled out up ahead.

Dave instinctively grabbed for the arm rest and the dash board as he flew forward. His dad's strong right arm forced him back against the seat.

"Crazy driver," Mr. Norris growled, laying on the horn.

The truck accelerated.

"People who don't know how to drive should stay off the road."

Dave's heart was pounding. That was a close one. He heaved a sigh of relief and gave thanks they'd avoided a crash. People sitting next to the driver, in what was known as the death seat, were thrown through windshields every day. He closed his eyes again.

After a time he realized the radio was on. The news wasn't good. The Russians were making their usual threats and the British and French had begun bombing Egyptian positions.

"Looks like ya got it about right, Dad," Dave said in dismay.

"Most of Europe's oil comes through the Suez Canal," Mr. Norris explained. "The canal cuts thousands of miles off a tanker's route. The Europeans depend on that oil. It's their life line. They're afraid the Egyptians will cut off the supply and just when winter's coming on. Control of the canal, that's what it's all about. Eisenhower's a shoo-in now."

Being afraid, Dave knew more than he cared to about that, and he wasn't alone. Just days ago everything was going along normal, now people'd be hoarding food and digging up their back yards to build bomb shelters.

"Is there gonna be a war with atomic bombs?" he asked. "Are we gonna die?"

"Things are pretty rough right now but we'll get through it," Mr. Norris said. "We have the best military in the world and we have powerful friends."

"It's the missiles; there's no way ta stop 'em."

"We have missiles, and a large fleet of bombers. We'll be O.K."

Mr. Norris' assurances didn't set Dave's mind at ease. His brother had actually taken part in an atomic bomb test. The date was May 5, 1955 (5-5-55). The way Will described it, he and his army buddies were crouched at the bottom of a slit trench two miles from a tower with the bomb resting on a platform near the top. When it exploded, he remembered being thrown around like a pebble. And the fire ball—he said his eyes were closed and he had a folded army blanket pressed tightly against his face. Even with that he could see the bottom of the trench as a pool of shimmering, white hot, molten metal.

At first Dave thought that was bunk, but then, why would he lie? Pictures of the doom town they'd built near Ground Zero had been on T.V. He'd seen how structures hit by the intense light instantly burst into flame, then, seconds later, were blown away by the shock wave. The soldiers were protected from that, but once it passed, they had to climb to the surface prepared to fight. That's when they first saw the enormous mushroom cloud churning skyward before them. Its stem, still roiled by primal fire, was a luminous palette of colors. Overhead, the ice capped crown, set aglow by the morning sun, streamed light in all directions. The men, awestruck by the irresistibly beautiful yet terrifying sight, were momentarily overcome. Dave was there with them. His mind's eye had captured the scene intact: the gaping jaws, the tanks advancing in formation as through the world hadn't changed, the thick white frost overhanging the rim above, like ice cream poised to drip. Dave had asked Will what he'd do if there was a nuclear war and a bomb went off in the South Bend area. Will said he'd run toward it, "Wouldn't be much to live for after that."

Dave thought about the movie *Them* he'd seen at the Palace Theater when he was eleven. *Them* were harmless ants living near the Nevada test site that mutated into giant man eaters after being repeatedly exposed to huge doses of radiation. They made shrill repetitive chirps that grew ever louder as they closed in, with massive pincers, for the kill. Dave couldn't get that sound out of his head for weeks. The end for the ants came in an L.A. sewer. It was there, just before the soldiers opened up on the last nest with flame throwers, that Matt Dillon, the marshal from *Gunsmoke*, got it trying to save the boy. Dave wondered, *were these snippets of mayhem and destruction a sneak preview of the future?* How could one know? It was all very disturbing.

"You know, you worry too much," Mr. Norris said, sensing Dave's distress. "Life's full of uncertainties and challenges. Every generation has to face them. We'll get through this."

Dave thought about that. Maybe Dad was right. After all, he'd survived the "Great Depression," two World Wars and Korea, and he didn't seem overly concerned.

"I guess," Dave said, after a minute.

"That's my boy," Mr. Norris smiled. "Just relax. Take it easy. Everything will be fine."

Dave was still trying to sort it all out when they parked in his Uncle Harlan's driveway.

Uncle Harlan, Mr. Norris' younger brother, lived across the street from Kiwanis Field where the LaPorte High School Slicers and the junior high Church League played their football games.

"Haven't seen you in some time," he said, as Dave got out of the car.

"Mr. Abrams' bringin' me books tonight."

"Ah, I see," Uncle Harlan said, with a shake of his head. "Want to give me a hand?"

"Sure," Dave replied.

Uncle Harlan was two steps up a ladder removing the bulb from the overhead porch light.

"Hold this while I put the new one in." he said.

"Why's it so dirty?"

"Halloween is about the only time we use it."

"Have many trick-or-treaters?"

"We had quite a crowd last night and I expect we'll have even more tonight. What's your dad doing back there?" Uncle Harlan frowned.

Dave looked toward the car. "Do'no. S'pose gettin' his game stuff ready."

Mr. Norris filled out his sports schedule by refereeing football and basketball games during the fall and winter months, and was, at the moment, busily "arranging" things in the car's trunk. Mr. Norris did that a lot because the trunk was packed to the very top with tools, brochures, sports equipment, and, it seemed whatever he wanted was never where he could get to it. In this particular case the only thing giving away his presence behind the trunk lid was the occasional swirl of smoke rising above it.

"You're here earlier than usual."

"Dad said they're havin' some sorta parade between games so everything got moved up."

"I did see that, in the paper."

"Kin I use your bathroom?"

"That's usually your first question," Uncle Harlan smiled.

"I held back on the milk at supper."

"Do you need help?"

"Nope."

Uncle Harlan lived in a two story house with the bathroom on the second floor. Dave thought having to climb a whole flight of stairs every time nature called was nuts; course then, tromping down in the middle of the night if the bathroom were on the first floor, that would be nuts too. He liked his house lots better.

When Dave returned to the living room his cousins Gayle and Little Harlan had just come around the corner from the kitchen.

"Bye, David," Gayle said. "Hope the games are good." And she bounded through the door to join a giggling witch on the porch.

Dave went to say "Bye," but didn't get it out fast enough.

"Make anything new lately?" he asked, while he watched the girls through the window.

"I was gonna," Little Harlan responded, "but Dad caught me mixin' gunpowder in the garage and made me throw it out."

"Too bad."

"How about you?"

"Made some sky rockets a while back with fire crackers in the top. One blew up just as it went out of sight."

"Loud?"

"Na, it was up too high, but soon's I get a chance I'm workin' on bigger bombs. Whatcha goin' as?"

"A bum."

"You were a bum last year."

"Hey, I like bums, plus I gotta cool new twist for this time."

"What's that?"

"Come on," Little Harlan led Dave onto the now-vacant porch. A second later he pulled a wine cork and a pack of matches from the box he was carrying.

"What's that for?" Dave asked.

"Just watch." Little Harlan lit one end of the cork on fire, rotated it between his fingers a time or two, blew it out, waved it through the air then began to blacken his face. "Mom would kill me if I did this in the house." He was still touching up his beard when Mr. Norris broke off with his brother behind the car and Dave had to leave.

The banks of floodlights that lit Kiwanis Field pushed back the darkness in all directions. With a marching band stepping off to lively music and twirlers, Halloween at Little Harlan's was much more festive than on Brookfield Street. If Dave had known anybody, if South Bend Central, the high school he'd attend next year, was playing, this would be a great night. The way it was, he found a spot on the fifty yard line, interlocked his fingers behind his head and fell back against the next plank up. He yawned and closed his eyes. *All this for books,* he thought. The players warming up at either end of the field looked like midgets. They'd have to put on a lot of pounds in the next couple years if the Slicers were going to beat any of the other prep schools in the area. Those bigger bombs came to mind. The honor guard with its jerky choreographed motions presented the colors. Dave stood for the national anthem. As the guard withdrew he slumped back onto his seat. One of the midgets, his tiny legs a blur, returned the kickoff to the thirty-eight. Then with the first snap of the ball, stalemate. Maybe his dad wouldn't spot too many infractions. A whistle blew. He'd be here forever.

Foot soldiers facing off across a no man's land, hand to hand combat, strategy sessions behind the lines, movement measured in inches: trench warfare, that's what he was watching. The first period ended. The contenders huddled for instructions on the sidelines with their coaches. Dave searched for Meyer in the crowd but couldn't find him. Down the way Dad was chatting with Arthur Kaufner, a longtime friend.

Mr. Kaufner was nice and Dave wished he'd come visit for a while. Surprisingly he did.

"Your dad said you might like some company."

"I would, but how's come you're not in the press box announcin'?"

"I will be later, but this first game we're breaking in a new man so I'll have a backup next year."

"Yeah, Dad said these were the last games, first ones for me, though. Mey—I mean Mr. Abrams' bringin' me books tonight."

"From the news agency?"

"Yep, and I hope he gets here soon. Watchin' these shrimps play is boring. Nothin' ever happens. I like action."

"Everybody does. Spectacular plays make headlines. When you see one, it's usually a coach taking advantage of an opportunity. It's his job to win ballgames. The players have to win in the moment. There's no grand strategy for them," a now animated Mr. Kaufner explained. "On the field it's a battle of wills. Do you beat your opponent or does he beat you?"

The hand-to-hand combat, Dave thought.

"Pick out a player. Watch him adjust and readjust as the game goes along. See if he finds a weakness to exploit, and remember, for him, each play is a new beginning. If you can see the game from that level you'll get more out of it."

Dave turned, recognizing in Mr. Kaufner the same passion his dad and so many of his dad's friends displayed when they talked sports. Theirs was the small town world of long ago, where outdoor activity was the norm and competitive games a way of life. Love of sport bound these men together then and always would.

"Here, let's get this around you," Mr. Kaufner said and he helped Dave on with his coat.

"Thanks, I didn't realize how cold it was gettin'."

"I hear you're thinking about selling pop at the park during the games next summer."

"I haven't decided on that yet. Baseball's even slower than watchin' this and there's hardly any kids there my age."

"What I said about football goes for baseball too." Mr. Kaufner advised.

"Yeah, Dad's always tellin' me it's a game a inches but I don't know—I could use the spendin' money," Dave said, grimacing as a whistle sounded.

Fox Park curled around the North end of Clear Lake, which separated it from LaPorte's downtown business district. Beautifully wooded with rose gardens along the shore, and a picturesque baseball diamond, it was a haven for families with small children. A tall double slide, picnic area, merry-go-round, monkeys in a big steel cage, plenty of room to roam; once among the stately oaks, away from the traffic and confusion, the cares of the world seemed to melt away.

On Sunday afternoons in the summer, the Northern Indiana Baseball League played games there, with Mr. Norris behind the plate and Mr. Kaufner at the microphone. It was an amateur, extremely low budget, provincial affair.

"I know I'll enjoy hearin' ya next summer," Dave said.

"I do my best to keep things moving."

"You gonna have some new lines for this year?"

"A few," Mr. Kaufner grinned. "You don't dare let your presentation get stale." Mr. Kaufner handed Dave two dimes and two nickel. "Here, buy yourself a coke and a hot dog. These church league games only go two quarters. I need a few minutes to review the between games program. It's called Youth on Parade. Five hundred young men and women will be marching. You'll like it. Remember now, watch the players."

"I'm glad ya came over," Dave said, with a wave. "Oh, and thanks for the money."

As soon as Mr. Kaufner had gone Dave made tracks for the bathroom and the concession stand.

When he got back the parade had started and Dad was sitting next to where he had been.

"I see you and Mr. Kaufner had a nice long talk."

"We did. He knows a lot about sports, almost as much as you."

"Let's watch the parade," Mr. Norris said.

The spectacle was everything Mr. Kaufner said it would be. One group after another marched past the grandstand. Brownies, Scouts, bands, big and small, cheerleaders, Hi-Y, drum and bugle corps, row after row filed by until the brightly lit field was nearly full. Somewhere between the cheerleaders and Hi-Y, Meyer, and a man Dave didn't know, joined them.

"How was the game, David?" Meyer asked.

"The quarterback for St. Peter's is good, the other team's bad."

"St. John's hasn't won a single game this year," Meyer noted. "I don't think they've even scored. Say Gadg, have you met my friend Miklos, Miklos Zavatsky out of Michigan City?"

"Yes, earlier this fall," Mr. Norris replied, reaching to shake hands.

Mr. Norris' nickname was "Gadget." As the story went, an opposing basketball team had a player who was difficult to guard. Mr. Ulrich, LaPorte's coach at the time, said, "I've got a little 'gadget' who can handle him," and he did. Mr. Norris was an excellent athlete. Tough and quick both physically and mentally, effective on either side of the ball, he was a star player who won thirteen varsity letters in high school. Dave had heard him talk about baseball games they played that were delayed just so he could run in a track event.

"It's time for me to be getting back," Mr. Norris said. "The second game's about to start."

"Dad, think ya could call a few less penalties this time?"

The three men laughed.

"We overlook as much as we can," Mr. Norris explained, "but we have to keep the game under control. If we don't, someone might get hurt."

"I've got those books in the truck Gadg. We can make the switch after the game."

Mr. Norris raised a hand in acknowledgment as he walked away. Dave was proud of himself. He'd been aching to ask about the books the whole time, but for once at least, he'd been able to restrain himself.

Mr. Norris and Mr. Abrams, a burly, heavy-set, very friendly man, went way back, but Dave didn't know when or how they'd met. They both smoked cigars though and while Mr. Norris took great pride in gripping his lightly, thereby leaving it undamaged, Meyer chewed the end of his flat and was always spitting out the slimy, disgusting bits of tobacco that fell into his mouth. Dave knew two other things about Meyer. One, when Meyer and his dad got going they monopolized a conversation and he couldn't get a word in edgewise. And two, Meyer owned the City News Agency. That's where the books, mostly magazines, came from. It was Meyer's job to stock drug stores and markets with periodicals and replace those that went unsold or were out-dated. To be sure everything was on the up-and-up he had to send the covers from the ones he removed back to the publishers. The rest he disposed of, or, in Dave's case, presented as a gift. From what Dave pieced together, Meyer's friend was in the same business, though he didn't talk much. Meyer on the other hand bombarded him with the usual questions: was he getting around O.K., how was school going now that he was home, had he gotten lots of Halloween treats and, as usual, was he behaving. Dave replied with his stock answers. They talked about the first game, the halftime show, the enormous crowd, which Meyer estimated at three thousand, the World Series; even Elvis' performance on Sullivan came up. Finally, the second game ended and it was time for the books. Dave and his dad drove to where Meyer's lime green panel truck was parked and the exchange took place, the books, of course, being placed in the car's back seat, the only available spot. Two whole boxes, Dave couldn't believe it. Mr. Norris started the car. As they were about to leave Meyer stuck his head in the driver's side window.

"David," he said, looking across, "you'll be off those crutches and running around the neighborhood with the other boys in no time. Just keep doing what your dad says and everything will turn out fine."

Dave waved politely

Chapter 4
ON THE CUTTING EDGE

The Ford rolled silently down "C" Street. Dave thought he heard Dad say they were low on gas but he wasn't really listening.

"A couple dollars worth of ethyl," Mr. Norris said to the young man at the corner gas station where they turned onto Highway 2, "and check the oil."

"Yes, sir," the attendant answered.

Silence.

"Anything else?" he asked, after he'd slammed the hood.

"No, that'll do it," Mr. Norris replied. He held two one dollar bills out the window. The attendant took them. Mr. Norris rolled it up and they drove away. "A big shindig like that," he said cheerfully, "I'd have thought you'd be asleep by now."

Dave continued to stare out his window and didn't reply. Eventually he spoke.

"Why do people say dumb things like that?" he said angrily. "I'll never be able ta run. I've known that since—since forever."

Dave had polio, Infantile Paralysis, a disease so dread that the very words struck fear in people's hearts. Upwards of twenty thousand youngsters fell victim to it each year; many died. Others, somewhat more fortunate, found their lives reduced to the confines of a large metal tank called an iron lung, their horizons restricted to what they could see above and images reflected off mirrors attached to the finicky machines that made it possible for them to breathe. Those who escaped that fate, perfectly healthy one day, found limbs useless the next. Doctors had no answers at the time. There were no miracle cures or vaccines. During summer months, when most children were stricken, parents often resorted to arbitrary restrictions out of sheer desperation: no swimming or being around other kids on hot days, no sharing food. Long naps were required.

"Just because you're an adult doesn't mean you always know what to say," Mr. Norris consoled. "Maybe Meyer felt if he didn't say something encouraging you would think he wasn't concerned."

Dave felt guilty. He'd never thought much about how his having polio affected the people around him. As they drove along, he wondered why. He knew what had happened on that mid-September day three months after his second birthday; how Dr. Raulston had been called to the house when he tried to stand following a nap and his legs collapsed beneath him, how he'd been hurriedly driven to St. Joseph's Hospital and placed in isolation. He knew his house had been quarantined with a big red sign in the porch window, that his dad, away at the time, couldn't come home, that his older brother and sister couldn't go to school for a time and when they did return, everything in their lockers had been burned. He knew that people, lots of people, left food on their door step and prayed for him.

Of these events, but one image had stuck in his mind, that of his father passing groceries to his mother over the back fence. As she took the bag, their world spiraling out of control, they stole a kiss. He had no idea where that picture came from but it was very clear. Mom had told him she was afraid she wouldn't be able to care for him when he came home. Months later, after the immediate crises passed, she did just that, devoting hours each day to his welfare.

The regimen, repeated each morning, started with Mrs. Norris boiling thick wool compresses in an open pressure cooker atop the stove. Then, using tongs, she ran them through the ringer on the old washing machine next to the sink. From there they'd go directly onto his arms and legs. A technique pioneered by an Australian nurse named Sister Kenny, "hot packs" as they came to be called, minimized the paralyzing effects of the virus. After they cooled, it was time for exercises, then, more hot packs and so on. Dave didn't learn until much later that Sister Kenny had only demonstrated her technique in the United States a few short years before he'd been stricken, or how lucky he'd been that Dad found a workable washing machine when the war was just over and new appliances weren't, as yet, being built.

Maybe the fact that his parents were able to move on with their lives, that they took it all in stride, maybe that's why Dave didn't see it as such a big deal. Another reason might have been that most of his energy went into meeting the challenges each new day presented. Why focus on the past, what might have been? *There's no such word as can't,* Dad would say every time an insurmountable obstacle had to be overcome. Within the physical limits that constrained him, Dave was certain that was true.

"Look how far you've come," Mr. Norris encouraged. "You can walk, something three doctors told me you'd never do. You can climb stairs, go to school."

Climbing the ten steps at Muessel Elementary School when he was seven years old had been Dave's entrance exam to first grade. He'd been so excited. When he reached the top he just beamed, believing, without question, his dad's magic words.

"What's it been, two weeks since your casts came off?"

"'Bout," Dave replied.

"Hang in there, a couple more and you will be able to throw those crutches away."

"I'm still hopin' I can play football with the guys this year, you know, if the weather holds."

"We'll see," Mr. Norris smiled. "That's certainly not out of the question."

Dave had been home five days and as he saw it he'd made the most of them. Sure, he could barely keep his eyes open Thursday at school and his underarms, where the crutches rubbed, were red and raw. Who cared about that? He had catching up to do. His mother hadn't picked up on either of those things at breakfast. That made the day a success before he ever left the house.

"Did you get 'em?" It was Ron Rasco.

"Yep, scads, in here," Dave replied, pushing aside the curtain to his room. "Ya timed it perfect. I just got home."

"I know. I saw your cab leave."

In minutes the two were sitting cross legged on the floor sorting books into piles.

"Where should we put the ones for your mom and Ann?"

"They can go here," Dave said, throwing his pillow against the far wall to make more space on his bed. "Rafe comin' over?"

"I think after practice. How long before you can get back in your brace?"

"Do'no. The stiffness in my joints is mostly gone, but I got a sore."

"A sore?"

"Yeah, here." Dave rolled slightly to his right and pointed to a spot on the back of his left leg just below the hip. "It's comin' 'long fine but that's where my brace rubs and Mom says we can't take any chances. It's not her fault. I did it to myself."

There were two addresses Dave would never forget. One was eleven-o-two North O'Brien Street, his house in South Bend. The other was twenty-two-eleven North Oak Park Avenue, Shriners Hospital in Chicago. Dave's battle with polio hadn't ended with the hot packs and exercises, far from it. Between then and now he'd undergone seven operations, the last six at Shriners, which is where he'd spent the past three months.

The procedure was as follows: You were admitted on a Friday. Monday morning was "rounds." That's where you sat nearly naked in a g-string, scared to death, while the doctors circled your bed to discuss your case like you weren't there. After a week or two when they were sure you hadn't come in with some bug, they operated. Since it was Dave's legs the polio affected, he'd wake up with white plaster casts, usually on both. Two weeks later the stitches came out. Then, when the bones and muscles had healed sufficiently, the process of getting back on your feet began. In most cases a chunk of rubber was attached to the foot of your cast so you could safely put weight on it. Walking, even if cumbersome, helped you regain your strength and balance.

Somewhere in there Dave's leg began to itch and he couldn't reach the spot with his hand. A wooden ruler did the trick. It also deformed the cotton which protected his skin from the rough plaster. Once raised, the lump wore into his leg as he walked. He didn't notice it much during the day when he was active but at bed time when he laid down, he was stuck to the cast. Before he could fall asleep, he'd have to pry himself loose. When the cast came off a week before he was discharged, there it was, a hole about the size of a dime.

"I can feel things in my legs same's you," he said to Ron. "It just didn't hurt much."

"Why didn't you tell the nurses it itched?"

"They couldina done nothin'. Ya had ta tough it out. I tried notta mess with it, but it drove me crazy. When the doctors saw it—heck, I'd still be in there if Mom hadn't convinced them she could handle it at home. She has ta dress it every day. Dr. Raulston checks it too. We're keepin' it real clean."

"Here's a magazine for your mom, but it has bomb shelter plans inside, you want it on her pile?"

"No!" Dave said firmly, "I'll take that one."

"You better do what she says or you'll be back in there."

"Don't worry, I am. I don't ever wanna go back ta Shriner's. Do'no how I made it through this time; I mean it's nice enough, but there's no way out. Mom and Dad tell me ta do what the doctors say, but they're not there. I'm all alone. See, they slap this mask down tight over your face and knock ya out with this stuff called ether. Same things in the startin' fluid Dad uses when he fires up Will's car. It's like you're suffocatin'. They havta hold ya down. Your head's poundin'. It's terrible. When ya wake up, your legs are throbbin' from where they did the surgery. Ya feel it every time your heart beats and you're sick as a dog from the gas. I threw up 'bout twenty times and they can only give ya so many hypos for the pain. It's horrible. They give ya shots too, penicillin. Everybody's scared of 'em. I seen kids, they were shakin'. This one, he cried for like an hour after he got his. I mean, it's for your own good. My folks could never afford ta send me. At Shriners everything's free."

Dave was one of the lucky ones and he knew it. He could walk, though maintaining his balance was always tricky. His right leg was functional even if many muscles didn't work. On his left leg, nothing worked except his two smallest toes and he could only move those down. The main reason he needed a brace was for the knee mechanism. His left knee wouldn't lock and therefore couldn't support his weight. The long leg brace he wore did that for him.

Penicillin was what made it all possible. Before that was discovered and made available after WW II, infection was too great a risk and operations couldn't be performed. Now with a "wonder drug" at hand, they could.

"Let's go back through the ones we sorted first," Dave said. "Maybe there's bomb shelter plans we missed."

"What exactly are the operations for?" Ron asked.

"Mostly it's so's I can walk better. They reattach muscles, if they can, ta replace ones that don't work and—oh, and my right leg was growin' faster than my left so they fixed that."

"I do'no know how I'da made it without Mom and Dad. They came every week, 'cept for two times when the car conked out, even in winter when the weather was bad. It's like an all day thing. They don't get home 'til late. Only adults can visit at Shriners, and only for an hour and a half on Sunday afternoons. It's 'cause they're so afraid a germs. Some kids hardly ever get visitors. They don't say nothin' though and they don't cry. This one boy, he's got this over sized head like a basketball and a really tiny body, nobody ever came ta see him, I mean, not ever. It was hard when your parents did come, musta been awful if they didn't."

"How's come you didn't tell me any of this before?" Ron asked.

"Do'no. No reason." Dave said. "Guess it's just on my mind now. Thought ya said Rafe was comin'?"

"He said he was."

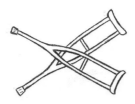

Chapter 5
NORMALCY RETURNS

A "whoop-whoop" and two hands waving wildly outside the back window could mean only one thing.

"I'll get it," Ron laughed.

Dave hurriedly cleared off his bed.

Rafe came in and sat down. "What we got?" he asked, looking over the various piles.

"How 'bout *The Sportin' News,*" Dave answered, "and what's with the tee shirt?"

Rafe grabbed one of the magazines and lay back against the north window sill.

"We were doin' dummy drills and they kept us late. You work up a heck of a sweat. Then I had ta bike over."

"We can tell," Ron groaned.

"Those dummy drills or dummies drillin'?" Dave snickered. "It's cold outside."

"Watch it," Rafe warned. "How 'bout Saturday, everybody playin'?"

"I think so," Ron said, "Not sure about Leon or Mr. Magoo. He might be doing something with his kids."

Mr. Matoszak (Mr. Magoo), a man in his early forties with a pot belly, lived in the fifth house south of Dave's, between Rafe's and Young's.

"Wish I could play," Dave lamented. "I'm gonna miss four months a sports this year."

"Aren't these '57s neat?" Ron said enthusiastically. "I think every new car coming out this year has fins."

"You'll have to break it up in there," Mrs. Norris said from the kitchen. "Supper's early again. Dad has a meeting tonight."

"How are the books?" Mr. Norris asked, after grace was said.

"Great," Dave replied. "We just got done sortin'. There's all kinds, some for Mom and Ann, this one's got bomb shelter plans inside, drawings too. Tells ya how ta build it step by step," and he held up the magazine.

"Not while we're eating," Mr. Norris admonished.

Dave put the magazine aside. Another no-no. He spooned in some stew from his bowl.

"Dad, are we gonna build one?"

"I don't have the time and how would we pay for it?"

"What's a blomb sheller?" Ann asked. "Can you play in it?"

"No," Mr. Norris smiled, "and don't interrupt. Bomb shelters are all the rage at the moment. It's happened before. There's a lot of talk, but it's just that, talk. So far, I don't know of a single shovel full of dirt that's been turned. I already told you, we're safe. There's no need for you to worry."

Dave considered mentioning Pearl Harbor or the current world situation but thought better of it. The news came on. One hundred miners were trapped underground in a coal mine. Mrs. Norris raised a finger. *Now she's gettin' inta the act,* he thought. Dave grimaced and rubbed his underarms while he watched.

"Stop that!" his mother said and before he realized it, she'd stood up, raised his arms and lifted his shirt. "I knew I should have kept you home yesterday. Let me see." She pushed his arms over his head. "How long have they been this way?" she asked angrily.

"Just a couple days."

"There's a Central game Saturday night isn't there?"

"Yes, Ma'am."

"Well, except for school you're off those crutches and if your arms aren't better by then, you won't be going. We're not having any more sores!"

"But it's for the conference championship." Dave looked at his dad and was met with a very stern expression.

"You're grounded. Finish eating, then you're in there," Mr. Norris barked and Dave got the thumb.

In Dave's house you couldn't play one parent off against the other. There went *Dragnet, Gangbusters.* Maybe he should have taken it a little easier. The crutches, he was off those for sure. Nobody in their right mind would miss a Central game. *It won't happen again,* he promised himself. He put a stack of magazines on his bed and lay down. He read about welding titanium in chambers full of inert gas, machines that extruded rocket fuel, stories about space cars, and undersea cities. Even the advertisements were interesting.

Mrs. Norris brought in a snack. "Try to be more sensible," she said. "We know how anxious you are to get back in the swing of things. Just take it a little slower—how's the book coming?"

"I'm gonna read more of it soon's I finish this article on spy cameras."

Dave knew miniature cameras, used for espionage, existed. The big surprise was how many different kinds there were. According to the article, most professionals went with the Minox. Developed in Latvia during the thirties, a Minox wasn't much bigger than a pack of gum and could easily be concealed. What set it apart was its high quality lens and novel, nearly instantaneous, film advancing mechanism. The Germans, after capturing the factory where they were made, used them all through WW II.

Dave put that periodical and the one with the bomb shelter plans on the bookcase under his back window. The other guys would want to see those. He was getting a headache. He took a drink and closed his eyes for a time.

What was behind *The Mysterious Island's* strange occurrences? Why hadn't the castaways perished when the gondola beneath their balloon fell into the ocean? Why did the sea chest they found in the sand at the water's edge contain just the items they needed?

With his pillow behind him, Dave propped himself against the wall at the head of his bed and picked up the book. A ship appeared on the horizon. Would it pass by? Were their prayers being answered? The castaways concealed their presence and waited. The ship moved closer. A spy glass revealed its pennant: the skull and cross bones. Pirates. They were few, the brigands many. Was Union Bay just a temporary port of refuge? Could they avoid detection? Were the pirates planning to make Lincoln Island their base of operation? Night fell. They waited. The sound of anchor chains rattling through hawseholes broke the silence. When dawn broke they would fight, rifles and muskets against cannon. The ship swung around. Shards of stone flew in every direction as cannon balls slammed into the granite wall behind which they hid. Then, suddenly, a deep roar and frightful cries were heard. Cyrus Harding and his companions rushed to one of the windows. The ship, irresistibly raised on a sort of waterspout, had split in two. Seconds later, amidst smoke and flame, it and its criminal crew disappeared beneath the waves. Why? What force, what entity could have wreaked such destruction?

Had they an unknown benefactor? Answers to those questions would have to wait. Dave was done in.

Dave's Friday was measured in steps, actually swings. If you could only use one leg, swinging on crutches was how you got from place to place. With the crutches planted you'd swing both legs forward, put your weight on the good one then do the same with the crutches. Once you got the hang of it, got a rhythm going, you could move right along.

"Mom, can we talk?" Dave asked, after school.

"What's on your mind?"

"Well, bein' cooped up in my room last night, I really didn't do nothin'."

"We're not trying to punish you, but you need to use some common sense. You can't do everything at once."

"I know," Dave acceded. "O.K., at school today," he said excitedly, "I didn't leave my seat once 'cept for at lunch, and last night when I had ta go ta the bathroom, I slid along on my butt instead a usin' the crutches. My arms are much better. They don't hurt at all." Dave pulled up his shirt. "Look—so, could I organize a monopoly game for tonight? Here? In the basement? And tomorrow afternoon the guys are playin' football at Muessel. I think Mr. Matoszak 's gonna play so I could ride along with him. I'd just sit in the car and watch, promise. I wouldn't get out."

Mrs. Norris pondered for a time. "How about your studies?"

"I'm gettin' on ta doing 'em right now," Dave replied.

"All right, but I'm checking. Don't disappoint me," she said, looking straight into his eyes.

"I won't. You can count on me." And Dave went into the dining room to use the telephone.

Everything was set. Dave finished his homework then picked up his book. An investigation revealed that the pirate ship had been sunk by a mine. But how? Who had placed it there? Was it a coincidence? There were too many.

"We are in the hands of a power greater than our own," Cyrus Harding concluded. "And I don't expect we'll discover who our mysterious friend is until he chooses to reveal himself."

The castaways stepped up their exploration of the island, hoping to find answers. Their pace quickened when the dormant volcano occupying its center unexpectedly came to life. Soon after that the telegraph in the cliff house sounded. Come to the corral immediately, Gideon Spilett wrote.

"But we are all here," Ned said.

"The time has come for us to meet our guardian," Cyrus noted.

"Supper time."

Dang, just when it was getting interesting. "Is that apple crisp for us tonight?" Dave asked.

"There'll be some," Mrs. Norris replied.

"Best take ours out first," Dave said. "Rafe and Gunner are comin'."

When Dave heard a knock at the back door, he assumed they'd arrived. He was wrong. It was Luke Razyniak and Leon Cheske. Leon, and his brother Ben, lived five houses down the alley from Dave but their house faced Johnson Street. Leon was Dave's age, Ben two years younger. While Dave watched, they set up a table and chairs in the basement then brought the magazines down.

"Who else is coming?" Luke asked.

"Ron and I'm pretty sure Rafe and Gunner."

"Look," Leon said, holding open a *Science and Mechanics*, "here's the Luger cap pistol that shoots B-Bs."

"I was thinkin' a gettin' one," Dave remarked, "but they're only single shot. Hey—you guys get any further on findin' stuff ta build our own telephone system while I was gone?"

"You're not still readin' that book about those balloon guys?" Leon asked.

"Hey, I been a little busy lately," Dave returned. "Anyway, they didn't have nothin' ta work with when they started out, we could do it. I got the bomber earphones my uncle gave me. You guys got handsets. It's all..."

"Yeah," Leon interrupted, "but we still don't have any wire or a place ta run it."

"I did the calculations," Luke added. "We need half a mile."

"My dad's lookin' for wire," Dave said. "How 'bout the salvage company down town in the old South Shore train sheds? And we could connect it to the trees along the alley. Nobody'd complain," he smiled. "They'd be afraid we'd blow up their house."

Leon frowned. Luke, engrossed in an article on stroboscopes, ignored the comment. It seemed half an hour passed before Ron arrived.

"Sorry. I was waiting for Rafe and Gunner. They got into it again so Mrs. Scanner put them to washing and drying dishes before they could come over."

"Rafe get pounded?" Dave asked.

"I think they were arguing," Ron surmised. "Gunner said Rafe was teasing him."

"What's new there?" Leon laughed. "That happens every day."

"I got no idea how she keeps those two in line," Dave remarked. "Bet she doesn't weigh a hundred pounds."

"Who's banker?" Ron asked.

"We're readin'," Leon replied with a grin.

"Thanks," Ron quipped.

"I can do it," Dave said.

Ron waved him off. "Glad to be of assistance."

The back door slammed. "I'm in." It was Rafe. "Gunner's not comin'. He mouthed off and Mom sent 'im upstairs."

"Him, not you?" Dave questioned.

"I ain't stupid."

After the usual bickering over who got which marker, the action began. Since they'd "revised" the rules by handing out extra money, the game always started with a buying spree. If you landed on a lot of unoccupied properties right off, you were in, if not, too bad. That was Dave's predicament. Two full rounds and all he owned was the electric company and one railroad. "Oh, here," he said, handing Luke the magazine containing the bomb shelter plans. "It's almost the same as the one you guys are plannin' ta build."

"Were planning to build," Luke corrected. "My parents talked it over some more and decided it was too expensive or something."

"Really." *Dad's right again*, Dave thought. But this didn't make sense. Mr. Razyniak worked at Bendix. They made aircraft parts. He knew South Bend was a target and they had the money. He was sure of it. "But, didn't ya get plans from the government and order stuff?" Dave asked.

"We sent it all back. I don't know why. They just changed their minds."

"Hold it," Leon said, putting down the magazine he was reading, "You're on my joint. That'll be six bucks."

"A whole six bucks?" Rafe groaned.

"I wish we was buildin' one," Dave said. "All that goin' on over there, I'm scared."

"Me too," Ron chimed in, "but our dads are still reliving WW II."

"We'd blow 'em ta smithereens," Dave said, holding an imaginary cigar to his lips, "Doubt they'd even get off a shot."

"You're good," Rafe laughed, "oughta go ta clown school."

"My life's work. Ya missed me on Pacific last turn," Dave grinned.

"What! That ain't fair."

"I waited before I rolled," Ron said. "Pay attention next time."

"Hey, I was readin' 'bout the Dodgers. Gotta have somethin' ta do, slow's this game's goin'. Says here they're playin' in Jersey again next year."

"If you're bored, go upstairs and get the snacks. Mom made apple crisp and there's juice. She's got everything ready," Dave said.

"What you guys havin'?" Rafe hooted, as Luke got up to help.

"The Dodgers are moving to California," Ron called, as the two walked away. "Ebbets is falling to pieces."

"They're my favorite team," Dave remarked. "Dad says T.V. money's what's behind it."

When Luke returned, Dave asked him how far he'd gotten on the telescope he was building.

"The mirror's maybe half done. Grinding by hand takes forever, but you can work when it's cold out. I'm machining the metal parts at school. I might have it finished by spring."

"Boy, I'd sure like ta get a lathe," Dave said enthusiastically.

"Dang, that's it. I quit," Rafe snarled. "I'm squallin' outta here."

"Let's see. Park Place. Two hotels, fifteen hundred each, that's three grand you owe me," Luke snickered, as he reached for the shoe ricocheting off the board.

"You win," Ron yawned. "It's getting late."

Dave wanted to finish *The Mysterious Island* before he went to bed but that would have to wait until morning. He didn't dare upset Mom. Plus, Luke's comments about the bomb shelter kept going through his head. He'd already concluded people were a combination of inconsistencies. He didn't know how he knew that but it was true. A person could stake out a position, be cock sure on it one day, then do a complete flip and take the opposite point of view the next. It happened all the time. Problem was, the whole

Razyniak family was cool, definitely not prone to snap decisions. Why would they break off on a project they'd thought through so carefully?

When Cyrus Harding and his band reached the corral no one was there. Instead, they found a wire attached to the sending device. They followed it past the volcano then down the cliff into the sea. "We must wait for the tide to go out," Pencroft the sailor said. When it did, a cave appeared. A small boat was moored at its mouth. The castaways got in and began to row. As the boat crept along they saw light ahead. Rounding a bend they entered a large, brightly lit cavern. In the middle, a huge gray beast lay resting. Without making a sound, they held the wire out of the water. It led straight to the creature. "It's a submarine," Cyrus said in surprise, and so it was. Inside they found Captain Nemo seated on a couch.

"Yes," he said, "welcome to the *Nautilus*. I am its last survivor. It is I who have befriended you."

A long discussion ensued. Captain Nemo explained how the recent Earth tremors had pushed up rock beneath the passage imprisoning the *Nautilus*, how magma within the volcano would soon break through into the cavern, how the resulting steam explosion would destroy the island. The race was on. Could the men build a sea-worthy craft and escape in the time remaining? The rumblings, the eruptions, grew more ominous. Then the island exploded and disappeared.

At this point the book lost its magic. Not only did the castaways survive, but they were picked up by a ship that just happened to be passing by. *No way that coulda happened*, Dave thought.

A peaceful Saturday morning, a good read despite its unrealistic ending, care-free hours — Dave hadn't experienced that in a long time. As he closed the book, one thought stuck with him. Cyrus Harding had asked if the *Nautilus* was powered by the energy of the atom.

"Yes," Captain Nemo replied.

"We must share these wonders with the world," Cyrus said fervently.

"The world you speak of is not ready for such power." Captain Nemo cautioned.

Dave knew the world he lived in wasn't ready for it either.

Meussel Park, shaped like an L with a brewery complex occupying the far quarter, was located five blocks east of Dave's house, on Vassar Street. The neighborhood boys played football there on a strip of land bounded by the brewery fence to the east and a line of trees on the west. Actually it was touch football, two hand tag, because the Scanner boys were bigger than everybody else and no one wanted to get smashed.

When Mr. Matoszak picked Dave up, Rafe, Gunner and Ron were already in the car.

"Doug and the others biked down," Rafe said.

Doug Pilarski lived in the next house past Ron's toward Lincolnway.

"Wow, that means everybody's playin'," Dave remarked.

"Yeah," Rafe said. "After last week, nobody's watchin' Notre Dame."

"'Cept people who love seein' 'em lose," Dave added.

For some reason Dave's comment prompted Mr. Magoo to expound on the various kinds of love. Dave, Ron and Rafe in the back seat looked at one another. That look turned to astonishment when Gunner, sitting in front, entered into the discussion.

"He serious?" Rafe mouthed, clamping a hand over his jaw.

Dave and Ron shrugged then did the same. Moments later, their eyes met again and they exploded into laughter.

"We're only interested in one kind," came a voice through the howls. Gunner and Mr. Matoszak, ignoring the hacks and shrieks, continued their conversation as if no one were around. At the park they joined the bike riders already warming up on the field.

"Can you believe it?" Rafe coughed, as he got out of the car, "Gunner an adult?"

"I didn't know you could laugh that hard," Ron added.

"Man, it's great ta be home," Dave said, wiping tears from his eyes.

Pass ball was loads of fun and Dave wanted desperately to be out there. That said, if you knew everybody, it was still fun to watch Rafe and Gunner going at it, Doug, bolting off the line like a gazelle, Mr. Magoo, panting as he laboriously chugged along, Luke streaking down the sidelines, Pete, with the sure hands. You could count on a variety of plays, spectacular catches, twists and turns to avoid tags and, at some point during the game, Mr. Magoo taking the reins as quarterback. That was one of the fun parts, because, odds on, he'd call his favorite play, a thirty-three, either to the right or left. No deception here. His players would line up on either side of the ball as usual, then, at the snap, converge on a predetermined spot in the flat, down field, overloading a zone. It was a play, that if used sparingly, might be effective, but the defense knew it was coming. So, with bodies crashing together, everyone on both teams leaped for the ball at once. In the process Rafe crumpled to the ground.

"You did that on purpose!" he shouted, grabbing his foot.

"What?" Gunner said, an innocent look on his face.

"You know darn well what! Aw, and I had a clean interception. Why'd ya havta step on the one I always sprain?"

"How should I know where your foot was? You're 'maginin' things."

Rafe hobbled to the sidelines, issuing a deep moan with each step. Dave tapped the horn and pointed to his wrist.

"Be a big crowd tonight," he said, leaning out the window. "We gotta go or we won't get a seat."

If you went to South Bend Central High School, or like Dave, Ron and the two Scanner boys, soon would, Central games weren't sporting events, they were festivals, and you belonged. It was a select group though. The mystique wasn't shared by all. Dave's other friends were Catholic, and thus, would be going to St. Joe. If you went there, you had to get used to losing, because that happened a lot. Central hardly ever lost.

Being from Chicago, Mr. Matoszak wasn't interested in the local sports scene and Mr. Rasco was almost always busy, so the Central boys usually only heard of the team's exploits. Tonight was different. Mr. Norris was available, so they could go.

"How'd you pull it off?" Ron asked as Mr. Norris, Gunner and a tottering Rafe went ahead to find easily accessible seats in the bleachers.

"Do'no. Mom checked out my leg and said the sore was almost healed, so after she bandaged it, I asked if I could wear my brace. Usin' my crutches I can walk without puttin' any weight on it. Guess I been doin' good, 'cause she said yes. I didn't wanna come wearin' a buncha socks on my foot."

Central's performance that night was a disappointment. Expectations of dominance and an easy win, faded into desperate hopes for a comeback, then two interceptions.

"It just wasn't meant to be," Mr. Norris remarked on the way home.

Dave and his friends, who were morosely reliving every set back, couldn't understand how it happened. Other teams got pummeled, never Central.

"I'll drop you boys off at Ron's," Mr. Norris said, turning onto O'Brien from Lincolnway.

As he parked, bright lights shown through the rear window. It was Mr. Rasco.

"Working late again, Chet?" Mr. Norris asked.

"Always," Mr. Rasco replied. "That's the price you have to pay if you don't want to punch a clock. How'd the game turn out?"

"Terrible," Ron exclaimed.

"Got beat twenty-one ta nothin'," Rafe grumbled, "and I use ta think our quarterback was suave."

Mr. Rasco looked puzzled.

"He was intercepted three times," Mr. Norris interpreted.

"I kind of thought Adams would make a game of it," Mr. Rasco said, shaking his head.

"Can't believe we got outplayed like that," Gunner moaned.

"If everyone knew the outcome ahead of time, they wouldn't have to play the game," Mr. Norris remarked.

Dave liked games where Central stomped people. They were less nerve-wracking.

"Say Gadg, did you hear about the car?" Mr. Rasco asked.

"Hardly, I've been on the road most every day lately."

"Some teenagers pushed a fella's car four blocks on Halloween."

"Did they damage it?"

"No, they parked it in parallel next to the curb. He didn't get it back until today."

"That's pretty tame compared with what we used to do," Mr. Norris noted.

Dave turned to Ron with a smirk, then said, "Dad, tell us 'bout tippin' outhouses."

"You too?" Mr. Rasco smiled.

"I did my fair share of prankin' along the way," Mr. Norris said, returning the smile. "Got ol' man Mihlhauser good. Flipped his over with him inside."

Ron looked at Dave, their mouths hanging open.

"I didn't know he was in there until I heard the hollerin'."

A likely story, Dave thought, noting the glow on his friend's faces.

"I wouldina been able ta keep my mouth shut on that one," Rafe burst out.

"Same thing I was thinkin'," Dave added.

"I didn't have a choice in the matter," Mr. Norris said with a grin. "He was one of my teachers."

The boys went into hysterics.

"We might have tipped a few back when," Mr. Rasco chuckled, "but we weren't in your league."

"Ya get caught?" Rafe probed.

"Not that time, but the next year—I just couldn't resist going back."

More laughter.

"Pushing your luck a little there, weren't you Gadg?"

"Probably, but that's easier to see now than it was then."

"So, how'd ya get in trouble?" Gunner asked.

"Well, Mihlhauser's was bolted down. I couldn't budge it, so I went down a block and tipped Niebers'. His was fancy, all painted up. I'd been eying it for some time. Just as it hit the ground he came out the back door and I had to run for it. I would have gotten away again, if it hadn't been for the clothes line. I never saw it. Darn thing caught me right across the chest then slid up under my chin. My feet went out from under me and I landed flat on my back."

"Then what happened?" Ron choked.

"I don't know," Mr. Norris said, scratching his head, "but I must have yelled. I do remember walking to the woodshed with Grandpa. Boy, did he blister my hide."

"Did he find out 'bout Mihlhauser?" Rafe queried.

"I don't know. Doesn't matter though, I paid for both that night."

"Did ya ever tip any others?" Gunner pursued.

"No sir, that wuppin had the desired effect."

"You know, we're putting ideas in these kid's heads," Mr. Rasco said.

Mr. Norris' tone changed completely. "Not if they heard the last part of the story. You did hear that part, didn't you?" he asked, emphasizing each word.

"Yes, sir," The boys replied in unison, the smiles gone from their faces.

"My guess is the Russians will make their move any time now," Mr. Rasco said.

"For the life of me, I don't see how they got the bomb so soon." Mr. Norris responded. "It must have been an inside job."

"There's a lot of talk about bomb shelters just now," Mr. Rasco remarked. "Two of my men were discussing plans for one at lunch yesterday."

"It's all talk," Mr. Norris scoffed, while he angled his watch to catch the porch light. "It's late," he said to Dave. "Get in. Chet, we'll do this again."

Dave got in the car and rolled down the window. "See ya," he waved.

"You're turning out to be quite an instigator," Mr. Norris said, in the tone he'd used earlier.

"Sorry."

Dave was glad he didn't know the whereabouts of any outhouse. One could never predict when a prank might go wrong.

Dave's reintegration into "civilian" life continued. He wore his brace more and more as time went on and used his crutches less. Days were full: there was school, homework, friends who visited, science to do in the basement. It was all a question of pacing himself and getting enough rest. Progress was slow but steady. After school, he'd read or go downstairs and build rockets. He could do those things sitting down. A few pieces of paper wrapped around a pencil and he had a tube. He'd insert a length of fuse in one end, flatten it with his fingers then crimp it in that position with a piece of wire. He'd pour fuel in from the top, cap it tightly and tape a long thin stick to one side. The trick was getting the wire just tight enough and the fuel mix right on. When he did, the rockets leaped skyward and flew elegantly. When he didn't, they fizzled or blew up.

Dave could get around without crutches now so he went to Luke's to get the particulars on the mirror grinding process. Instead of finding him working away as he expected, Luke was sitting a few feet outside the garage in a lawn chair reading. Before Dave could speak Luke motioned with his hand.

"I don't want him to lose count," he said softly.

Through the open door Dave could see Pete leaning over a 55 gallon metal drum. He was moving something on top back and forth in a very deliberate fashion. After a certain number of strokes, he'd move to a new spot around the rim and repeat the process. Dave watched awhile then turned back toward Luke. Luke raised his hand again and held out a *Popular Mechanics.* Dave sat down to read. In a while, Pete stepped out of the garage.

"That's two rounds for me," he remarked.

Luke got up. "Come on," he said.

Dave followed him into the garage. The barrel had a plywood cover with wooden blocks screwed to it that held a thick glass disc in the exact center. What Pete had been holding so tightly was a second glass disc with a vertical round handle attached. Luke pointed out a row of small gray cardboard canisters lined up along the window sill that looked as though they should contain film for a 35mm camera.

"Those hold the abrasives," he explained. "You start with coarse and work your way down to the super fine one on the end. It all comes as a kit."

"They're not very big."

"It doesn't take much. Here, I'll show ya." Luke selected a container from near the middle of the row, sprinkled a few grains of what looked like black sand on the disc and carefully replaced the container's lid. "You can't get even a speck mixed." He worked the abrasive into a soup with a few drops of water and picked up the hand piece. "See these marks," he said, pointing to dots spaced at intervals around the barrels edge. "You work off these." He moved to the starting position, held the top piece with both hands and pushed it across the bottom disc. "You do it with a twisting motion like you're gouging out the middle. The abrasives do that. Then you lift the top piece, bring it back and do it again. After so many passes you move to the next mark. It's all in the wrist motion. I'd say it'll be another month before I get it done. The disc on the bottom is the mirror. The one on top you throw out, but not until you get the focal length perfect."

"When's that?"

"The mirror fits in the bottom of your telescope," Luke explained. "It reflects the light coming in back up to a tiny angled mirror near the front which turns it 90° and sends it out through the eyepiece. The distance between the mirrors has to be exactly 42 inches. You check that every so often at night with a light. When it's just right you send the mirror out and they put the silvering on. That's what makes it shine."

"Why didn't ya just buy one?"

"A mirror six inches in diameter, an inch thick—they're way too expensive."

Since Pete and Tim had disappeared and Luke was anxious to get back to work, Dave said good-by and started up the alley for home. On the way he stopped at Leon's. When there was no response to his knocks, he left.

The door opened. "Hey, hold on," Leon called. "I was downstairs. Nobody's around so I was testing stuff."

Dave went in and joined him in the basement.

"Look at this," Leon said, and he opened the big cast iron door on his family's old coal furnace. The furnace, about five feet across, had a series of large pipes extending up from around its top toward the ceiling. At first sight, it resembled a giant octopus standing on its head with its tentacles reaching out. Leon placed a spoonful of powder on the narrow shelf just inside the door and lit it. The powder burned with a hiss and threw out brilliant white sparks. "It's the aluminum shavings," he grinned, "and all the smoke goes up the chimley. Whatcha think?"

Dave shrugged and shook his head. "It's cool, looks good."

"I'm gonna make ground fountains for New Year's. If I get 'em right, they should shoot up five or six feet. Hey, ya been to Luke's?"

"Just was. He showed me the whole process. It's somethin', but I wouldn't wanna do it. He say's it'll be a month 'fore the mirror's done."

"Yeah, and he works on it all the time. I got somethin' else," Leon said, the grin more devilish, and he took a very large firecracker from inside the bottom drawer of an old Victrola. "I keep stuff like this hidden in there."

"You're not gonna light that thing!" Dave said in disbelief.

Before he could comment further, Leon had stuck a match to the fuse and closed the door.

"Nobody'll hear outside. This old relic really muffles the sound."

Dave backed away in sheer panic, almost falling in the process. He cupped his hands over his ears, opened his mouth and twisted sideways. Seconds later there was a horrific explosion. The heavy cast iron door flew open, swung around and crashed violently into the furnace body. A cloud of smoke and soot shot from the opening. Years of accumulated dust rained down from the ceiling.

"You crazy or somethin'!" Dave yelled at the top of his lungs.

Leon, who had only been feet from the flying door, was thrown back. Once he regained his composure, he ran to see if it was broken. Hacking, coughing, his eyes watering, he was trying to wipe them and wave the smoke away at the same time. Dave, doing the same, tried to help. While Leon feverishly flailed, Dave looked across at the stairs to see if anyone was coming down. When he looked back, Leon, struggling to see, was rubbing his hand over the metal where the door had hit. Dave only saw two small dents and the broken bolt that was hanging from the latch.

"Can ya hear?" Leon yelled.

"Kinda," Dave yelled back.

"I didn't..."

Dave waved him off and started for the stairs. A thin layer of dirt was settling on everything in sight. Leon followed him up to the kitchen. A heavy, noxious odor filled the air. Tiny particles, floating in the beam of sunlight coming through the kitchen window, glinted like diamonds. Leon flung the window open and began whipping a tray through the air to dissipate the cloud. "Get outta here!" he exclaimed. "I'll think a somethin'."

Dave noted the furnace register on the wall next to his foot, pointed out the plume of dirt on the floor in front of it, and dashed for the door.

"Just go! I got it!" Leon yelled.

Dave was out of the house. He tore across the back yard at breakneck speed counting each step, 5-6-7-8. At 13 he was in the alley. At 21 he couldn't be seen from Leon's house. He slowed to catch his breath and noticed he was shaking. Why? He hadn't done anything. No one knew. While he tried to get lunch down he thought about Leon, all that dirt. How he couldn't stay and help. He had to tell somebody what happened. He went to Ron's.

"Can ya believe he lit it in there?" Dave exclaimed. "It was big. Do'no what he was thinkin'." He told Ron about the smoke, the dirt, the blinding flash, how his ears were ringing, how he'd made his get-away. "Couldn't stay ta help. Do'no if he'll get it cleaned up in time or not. Won't be goin' down that way for a while. Hope his parents don't find out."

Ron asked about the furnace.

"S'pose he'll stick a new bolt in the door."

"No," Ron frowned. "The explosion, is it damaged inside?"

Dave shrugged, "no idea. Tell ya though, Leon gets everything vacuumed up, the Cheske's'll have the cleanest house on the block." They both snickered. "And the way I busted outta there, all that walkin' down ta Luke's, my legs didn't hurt a bit. I think I can go the whole game next time we play at Muessel."

Saturday, they did and Dave had a blast. He caught a pass from Tim, threw one to Gunner, neither for much yardage. He lunged to tag a runner and missed, but only by inches. It was wonderful. He was helping his team, making himself useful. That's all that mattered. He spotted openings, helped plan strategy. Sometimes he just stood at the line of scrimmage and watched the action, knowing the man assigned to guard him would eventually get bored. When he did, Dave could step forward and catch a pass, maybe pick up a few yards, even score. If everybody had gone long, he'd lateral back to the quarterback so he could run. Often times, that resulted in a sizable gain. There was always a niche to be found, a way to contribute, if you were alert and willing to work hard. *I'm back,* he thought to himself on the way home. He was jubilant. The long ordeal he'd been through, though never to be forgotten, was finally behind him.

His parents must have felt that way too, because one morning he found a neatly trimmed newspaper clipping next to his cereal bowl. "Elkhart boy blows off three fingers making pipe bomb." A smile grew wide across his face. His recovery was complete. An article such as this would never have appeared if he was in the midst of an emotionally delicate convalescence. His parents weren't worried about his legs anymore, just whether he'd blow himself up. Whew, what a relief.

"Mom, did you put this here?"

"No," Mrs. Norris replied, stepping into the kitchen from the dining room. "It must have been your father. Did you read it?"

"Yes."

"We worry about all this 'science' you're doing," she said. "Look what happened to that boy. He's just your age."

"But Mom, we're careful. We don't do dumb stuff."

Days were shorter now. Rafe, Gunner and Ron started coming over to shoot baskets in the last light before supper. That's when Dave launched his rockets. Not everybody would light fuses. Rafe would. So between games of "horse" or while the others shot around, Dave positioned the rockets' guide sticks, one after the other, in the launch bottle at the edge of the alley next to the garage. If the rockets made it over the trees in the yard past Leon's he deemed their flight a success. Some did, but the fuel rarely burned evenly, so it was a hit-or-miss proposition. The procedure, though, was always the same. Once Dave had things set, he'd hand Rafe the matches and hide behind the telephone pole next to the sidewalk. Ron would stand twenty feet or so away, Gunner a little less. Dave would indicate all was ready and Rafe would light the fuse, back off and turn to watch. A second or two later the rocket would take flight. Rafe would complain the fuse was too short, Dave would say fuse was expensive, and they'd fire another. No matter how often they did it, the procedure was always the same, and it carried over to the court. People were creatures of habit. It was like you played a role.

Ron took longer open shots, Dave, of course, relatively short ones. With the Scanner brothers it was driving, blocking, body contact, always competition and a lot of taunting. Dave wondered, *why did patterns repeat themselves over and over?* Why did people make the choices they did? Why did Rafe and Gunner go at it all the time when other brothers got along?

Something was up at Dave's house. Mrs. Norris was on a cleaning binge. The Electrolux was out. The living room curtains were headed for the washer. The window cleaner was sitting on the dining room table.

"Mom, what's goin' on?" Dave asked. "Is this for Thanksgiving?"

"Well, yes and no," she answered. "Thanksgiving dinner will be here this year but tomorrow I'm having club."

Mrs. Norris was a member of the E. T. Club, a group of ladies who'd known each other since dinosaurs roamed the Earth. They'd palled up at the German Lutheran Grade School in LaPorte eons ago and still got together every few months, to, as Mrs. Norris would say, "keep up on the latest." Mr. Norris called it gossip and got irritated anytime the E. T. Club was mentioned. That's because Mrs. Norris wouldn't divulge what the letters stood for.

"We've made a pact not to tell," she'd explain.

He tried everything to get it out of her, but never could. Frustrated, he'd make for the car in a huff. The wholesale trunk reorganization that followed, was, Dave suspected, his way of letting off steam.

On club day you didn't dare make a mess. You could hang around for a few minutes when the ladies first arrived for the oohs and ahs and the usual questions, then you had to scram. Club meetings were private. Outsiders weren't welcome. The ladies played cards, kept up and ate cake or pie. Dave had no idea why it was such a big deal.

Basketball season began, "Hoosier-Hysteria." Dave, Ron, Rafe and Gunner, still distraught over Central's humiliating loss on the gridiron, had been rehashing the gory details every since. Would disaster strike again? Would history repeat itself? Central's home opener against Gary Roosevelt had all the ingredients. Both teams were rated tops in the state, though Dave thought the last poll placed Central number one.

"I can't believe we get to go again," Ron said, when Dave told him the good news.

"Neat, isn't it? I think Dad worked his schedule 'round just so he could take us."

The atmosphere in the car on this trip was much more subdued than it had been on their last outing. The boys were apprehensive, a little fearful.

"Hey," Ron said, trying to be upbeat, "we went 7 and 2 in football this year, that's not bad."

Nobody commented.

"Don't see why we can't have our own gym," Gunner complained. "Not much fun havin' ta play at Adams'."

"It's money," Mr. Norris remarked, "and there isn't room for one downtown."

Central High School occupied half a city block near South Bend's business district. Adams High School, located in a more open residential area, was newer and had all the amenities. A spectacularly beautiful venue, it was the Central Bear's home away from home.

"Where we sittin'?" Rafe asked.

"What would you say to five seats in the Mezzanine?" Mr. Norris smiled, "right near center court."

The boys looked at one another astonished.

"How'd ya get those?" Dave said. "I heard the game was sold out and they were settin' up bleachers on the stage."

"I made a few calls," Mr. Norris said smugly. "I've got some friends in the business, you know."

"Wow! Thanks Dad! Thanks a lot!" Dave gleamed. His friends were very impressed.

Their seats might have been great, but the game didn't start that way. From the outset Central struggled just to hang on. At half time they trailed 41-29 and spirits had reached a new low.

"Roosevelt's displaying a degree of polish you don't usually see in a season opener," Mr. Norris remarked.

"Yeah, that's gotta be it," Gunner muttered sarcastically under his breath, as Mr. Norris left to visit some sports friends and reporters down on the floor.

"Their big guy's least twenty," Rafe insisted. "Look at the hair on that lip. He's probably married and got kids."

"Maybe grand kids," Dave snickered.

"It wouldn't surprise me if they practiced together all summer in a gym somewhere with the windows painted over," Ron added. "But I still think we'll win. They won't be able to hold the Coleman brothers off for another half."

"S'pose any are on social security?" Gunner asked.

"You're an ignoramus," Rafe belittled. "That's stupid."

Ron put a finger to his lips and motioned toward the line of smiling faces in the row below. A hush fell over the group. Everyone quietly turned their attention to watching people, especially the high school girls.

"Man, see the one 'cross court there by the door, next ta that dopey usher?" Dave whispered.

"Where?" Rafe asked.

Dave extended his arm to give Rafe a line of sight.

"She's really stacked," he sighed, his eyes fixed in a stare. "S'pose I should go down and introduce myself?"

"Go ahead," Rafe snorted. "We haven't had a good laugh, in what, two minutes?"

Dave's attention stayed with the girl until she returned to her seat.

"Looked like you boys were having quite a discussion up here," Mr. Norris commented, upon his return.

"Just talkin' 'bout how old Roosevelt's guys look," Dave explained.

"Big John Coleman's not exactly a kid anymore," Mr. Norris noted.

He didn't look it either when he came out sizzling in the third quarter. From his position at center, he sunk seven shots in rapid succession to give the Bears a momentary one point edge. The lead see-sawed back and forth through the fourth quarter until, with less than a minute to play, he hit two free throws to force the game into overtime. Dave was a wreck, up one minute cheering, in the depths the next. His throat raw, his head pounding from the noise, the tension was overwhelming. Then, as the overtime period started, the crowd, exhausted, went silent. Central added thirteen points in the next three minutes, stunning the Panthers with a 77-68 point win.

"Looks like Central has the powerhouse everyone expected," Mr. Norris said. "They're going to leave a lot of destruction in their wake this season."

Dave and his friends barely heard the comment. They'd joined the joyous throng flowing toward the exits. As the overflow crowd moved along, the band struck up the fight song: "Three cheers for Central High School, Be forever true, Fight for her colors, The orange and the blue." Most people sang along. All Dave could do was hum.

There wouldn't be any attempt to explain John Coleman's scoring prowess, or Central's competitive spirit on the way home tonight. No sidewalk symposiums were in order at Ron's house. Central had survived. That was enough. Everybody was bushed, dead tired. Dave was asleep seconds after his head hit the pillow.

Another unpleasant morning, Dave was sitting with his family in church, not altogether sure how he'd gotten there. He felt terrible. His head hurt. His throat hurt. Maybe if last night's game hadn't been as exciting, if he'd been able to sleep in, if the dreamy girl he'd spotted hadn't been so gorgeous, maybe then he wouldn't feel so rotten. He closed his eyes. His head drooped. Mr. Norris cleared his throat. Dave didn't respond. An elbow caught him in the ribs. Startled, he jerked straight, sure every member of the congregation had their eyes on him. They could have, because on Communion Sundays the Norris' always arrived early and sat in the front pew. Dave wouldn't be confirmed until Easter but could accompany his parents for the blessing when they went to the kneelers. Sitting in the front pew was the only way to insure that Mr. Norris would be there to lend a hand when Dave had to ascend the intervening two steps.

It came time for the collection. The usher handed the plate to Mr. Norris. He fumbled around in his pocket, retrieved a number of coins and deposited them in the tray. As he passed it to Dave, Dave looked in. There, among the others, he saw a coin, that wasn't, as they say, legal tender for payment of debt, public or private. It was a novelty girlie coin about the size of a quarter. Her front exposed, it was obvious what was on the back side.

Dave was flabbergasted. He couldn't have seen what he'd seen, but he had. Fortunately, he'd passed the plate on to his mother before he had time to react. Out of the corner of his eye he glimpsed her reach in and snatch the coin with her right hand while she passed the tray along with her left. Deftly cupping the coin in with the hanky she was holding, she waited an appropriate length of time then inconspicuously dropped both into her purse. It all happened so fast. Was his tired brain playing tricks on him? No. There was a very shapely girl on that coin. His dad had had it awhile too, because it was worn down in a couple places. Dave shuddered, stared straight ahead and didn't move a muscle. Things were very proper in his church. Something like this getting out, when you considered that there was a coin toss on the field before every football game, his family would be ruined. Dave figured some of Dad's pals had given it to him.

"Here ya go Gadg, try flippin' this next time. It'll add some excitement."

What was Dad thinking, carrying a coin like that around? Dave was just glad and more than a bit surprised that he hadn't lost his cool. He took a passing glance at his father and saw that he was still propped against the end of the pew, apparently meditating on the sermon. His mother was looking straight ahead, too. As best as he could tell, no one knew he knew. He'd heard about crazy things happening in other families, but *his* family, and in church. He thought for a minute then grabbed his leg. He was about to bust out. He squeezed as hard as he could, bit in with his finger nails. The moment passed. How long could he hold out. He sat stone faced with his teeth clinched. It was the longest church service he ever attended.

On the way home he marveled at how smooth Mom had been plucking that coin. *Slicker than a magician pullin' a rabbit out of a hat,* he thought. No change in her expression, not a single feather ruffled, now that was being cool, funny too, very funny. There he was, in on maybe the best one ever and he couldn't tell a soul about it. No one could know, not even his friends, especially not his friends. And, oh brother, was Dad in for it. Inevitably, in some private moment, his mom would produce the offending coin, and indicate, in no uncertain terms, her displeasure with his "indiscretion." Dave could see Dad trying to contrive some lame excuse on the fly. There was no chance Mom would go for that. She wouldn't say much, but she'd get her point across.

A smirk slipped out. He turned away toward his window and squeezed his leg again. He thought about Central's amazing victory, the articles he'd been reading. It didn't work. A scene from a Jimmy Cagney movie was stuck in his head. Cagney was a British agent who knew about the plans for the Allied D-Day invasion of Normandy. That knowledge should have prohibited his being dropped into Fortress Europe on a secret mission but his presence was vital to the war effort, so the higher-ups reluctantly gave the go-ahead. Before the objective was achieved the Nazi's caught him. Soon he was strapped to a chair, in the basement of a large building, being "methodically interrogated." Dave could see his dad strapped to that same chair, a bare bulb swinging slowly overhead. A goon would slug Cagney, already battered and bloody. His head would roll to the side. Mom would give Dad "the look." American planes arrived overhead. Bombs began to drop. Cagney smiled wryly then convulsed in laughter as they found their mark. His secret was safe. Dave had no idea how his dad would fare. He just knew it wouldn't be pretty.

"Gonna shoot a couple baskets before we eat," Dave said, as soon as the car stopped.

"Just a few," Mrs. Norris advised.

Dave made it to the garage. How, he didn't know. His jaw hurt awful. His leg, where he'd squeezed it, was bleeding. He didn't care. Eventually, after a lot of deep breathing, he regained his poise. Next challenge, Sunday dinner.

"Dad, whatcha think Central's chances are down state?" he asked, struggling to keep the coin off his mind.

The in-depth analysis that evoked got him through. How was he going to keep a gut buster like this in? Dropping a girlie coin in the collection plate at church wasn't your average, run-of-the-mill, screw up.

Dave had to get out of the house. He called Rafe to see about going to the movies.

Dave loved movies. Where else could the amazing, the impossible, come to life, usually in color and on such a large screen? Movies filled your senses. Science fiction, like *The Thing*, where roles were reversed and plants preyed on people, monsters of every description, space travel, voyages through time, and, of course, irradiated ants. Whether fantasy or reality, movies made you think: *Madame Curie*, the discovery of radium; Audie Murphy's courage in *To Hell and Back;* Gary Cooper, driven by a sense of duty in *High Noon; The High and The Mighty*, about people aboard an ill fated airliner who reorder their priorities when they think death is imminent; the injustice of racism portrayed in *Showboat*. "Ol' Man River"—wow, what a song.

If it was a good movie, there were always things to ponder when you left the theater. Movies expanded your horizons, opened doors into human nature. The good ones helped you grow. It was like going to school, except a lot more fun, because there weren't any tests.

"So, whatcha wanna see?" Dave asked, as he passed Rafe the movie listings.

"Let's do this *Dive Bomber-Ceiling Zero* double feature," Rafe said.

Knew it, Dave thought. Cagney was in the second picture, but how could he say no? There wasn't anything else good showing. At the bus stop, when Rafe had to dig for bus fare, Dave lost it.

"Just thinkin' 'bout Gunner and Mr. Magoo," he fibbed. "Ya know, when we were in the car."

"That was ages ago," Rafe said, a quizzical look on his face.

"Can't help it," Dave sputtered.

Dave kept up the charade at the theater. When a smirk or snicker slipped out, he fended Rafe off with a gesture and a shrug.

Dave was dying to know what happened with Mom and Dad while he was gone. At supper he didn't dare look up even once. He couldn't chance it. He'd had quite enough adventure for one day. His secret though, like Cagney's, was safe, at least for now.

He went to bed wondering. *Maybe someday he'd be as slick as his mother.* That ain't hap'nin, he said to himself.

The next few days were as uneventful as any Dave could remember. If the "indiscretion" had been discussed, no one was letting on. School was going along. He hadn't been implicated in the furnace bomb incident. At home, holiday preparations had progressed to the food preparation stage, well, except for his room. He finally got the O.K. on that then settled in after supper to browse through the last few magazines he'd gotten from Meyer.

There was a knock on the wall next to his bed. He lifted his window to find his friends gathered outside.

"What's goin' on?" he asked.

"We're playing 'capture'," Luke said.

"Tonight?"

"Yeah," Leon replied, "it's s'posed ta snow tomorrow. A big time storm's rollin' in."

"On Thanksgiving? We got relatives comin'."

"Won't have tomorrow," Rafe chortled from the darkness.

"You playing or not?" Luke asked.

"Yeah, O. K., I'm comin'. Give me a minute, I'll be out."

Dave threw on his black jacket then scurried around to find the cork he'd stashed away.

"Be out with the guys awhile," he called, as he swung the kitchen door shut.

"Let's choose up," Rafe said.

"Hold on," Dave objected, raising a hand. "Check this out," and he demonstrated how a burnt cork could be used to blacken faces.

Rafe snatched the cork. "Let me try it," he grinned.

Dave handed over a lighter. "After ya blow the flame out, let it cool a minute," he cautioned

Rafe didn't. "Aw! That burns!" he shrieked.

Dave rolled his eyes. Everybody else laughed.

The cork was a big hit. No more had Rafe passed it along than he tackled Ben around the waist, took him to the ground, slapped it three times and yelled "pin." Dave and Ron had already walked across the yard and were waiting by the alley.

"He got me before you came out." Ron said. "You want to guess what season we're in now?

"I'd say wrestlin'," Dave ventured, with a smile.

"Where'd you get the Zippo?"

"Traded some of the books for it."

"How's come I haven't seen it?"

"I kept it hidden away."

"Why?"

"'Fraid it'd get me in trouble."

"Did it?"

"I—I do'no," Dave replied, after a second. "Dad caught me with it and accused me a smokin' cigarettes. Ya know how much he hates that. I told 'im I wasn't. Then he wanted ta know why I had a lighter. I told 'im the truth, said I was using it ta light off bombs and rockets."

"No way," Ron frowned. "That's baloney."

"Honest."

"You really said that?"

"Yep."

"So, what'd he say to that?"

"Nothin'," Dave shrugged. "He just walked back inta the house. Musta he thought lightin' bombs and rockets was safer than smokin'. He went round and round over cigarettes with Will."

Playing "capture the flag" was about the most fun you could have. To start, you draped a rag over the edge of a trash barrel at each end of the alley: one behind Dave's house, the other behind the next house past Luke's. Then, with an imaginary demarcation line across the middle, you split the block into two equal halves. The goal was to steal the other team's flag and return it to your territory without getting tagged. If you were, you had to stand in a detention area near the opponent's flag and, if not freed by a teammate's tag, you were stuck there for the rest of the game which could be practically forever. Nobody wanted that, so you didn't take stupid chances. You could tear through yards without worrying that an ugly confrontation would take place and not once did an irate neighbor summon police claiming a peeper was about.

The fun was in trying to outwit your "enemy," and you got to sneak around a lot in the process. You could go for a direct assault, chancy at best, use prearranged signals, lure the flag guard away with a decoy, then swoop in. An infinite number of strategies were possible. But you had to play defense as well, or your opponents would make off with your flag, before you got theirs.

Teams usually huddled before a game, but plans fell apart so fast that within minutes an unpredictable offense-defense dynamic by individuals or groups of two or three took hold. Kids in dark clothing darted from shadow to shadow, slipped silently through gates, over fences. Occasionally someone would lay in wait, intent on ambush. Mostly though, everyone wanted to be in on the hunt. Dave couldn't really play capture. He wasn't even fast enough to guard the flag, so after sides were determined, he'd hook on with one just for the fun of it. This particular game he thought he'd see how far down the block he could get without getting caught. Two houses over the line he heard a rustling sound and slid in under a back porch. Two figures jogged past. He guessed Leon and Gunner, but couldn't be sure. He waited awhile, then made for a space behind a row of shrubs further down, paused to listen and moved on to the gap between a trellis and a garage next to the alley. He squeezed in and stood motionless.

A murky outline was moving through the yard across the alley. He waited, straining to see. Eventually the figure disappeared. He peaked around the building but couldn't make out anything. He debated. Luke's garage was only one yard away. Question, where to hide? There were bushes. He'd crawl along on the ground next to them. He took a deep breath and stepped into the open. Light streamed down the alley past him. A car had turned in behind his house. He could see the yellow towel hanging from the barrel up ahead. Doug was guarding the flag. He ducked back behind the lattice work reasonably sure he hadn't been seen. There was a commotion. He heard Rafe shout, "run for it." Two figures tore across the alley through the lights. A third followed. There was yelling. "Gotcha." One of his teammates must have been tagged.

Dogs were barking. The car parked next to a garage. The lights went out. Dave looking through the vines and dead leaves, stayed stone still. Car doors opened then closed. There was more shouting, this time to quiet the dogs. One continued barking. Dave waited.

"Luke, Pete, Tim, it's time to come in," Mrs. Razyniak called.

A dog going berserk, a phone call, that was it for sneaking around, probably 'til spring.

Chapter 6
SCROOGE COMES A-CALLIN'

D ave awoke to howling winds and a room that seemed unusually dark. He propped himself up and looked out his back window. The screen was packed with snow. He lifted the sash and hit it with his hand. The snow fell away, revealing an Alpine scene. Winter had arrived with a vengeance. It was time for heavy coats, hats, gloves, and boots.

On the way to church Dave thought about the school he attended now. Truly a castle, it was Morris School for Crippled Children and it occupied the first floor and basement of the Studebaker mansion, the largest and grandest house in the city.

A week earlier there had been a cold blustery day. Dave remembered watching swirling leaves being whipped into cyclones from the cab's window. He recalled how the wind whistled as it rushed past the building, the shrieks and groans it sent along the paneled hallways and up the wide staircase. Mostly he remembered how quiet it was in class, how his classmates seemed so industrious, so busy. It was an illusion. They were anxious. He was too. During math, the boy behind Patty blurted out, "Snow! Look, it's snowing!" The room instantly came alive with chatter, everybody straining to catch a glimpse of the first tiny flakes. It began to snow hard. Dave noticed that Mrs. Pritchard, busy at her desk, didn't react to the disturbance.

All the kids who attended Morris School were handicapped in one way or another. Most were limited in their ability to get from place to place. Snow and ice would make that much harder, more risky. Mrs. Pritchard seemed to understand and was giving the students time to adjust. After a while she guided them back to their studies. They appeared to comply. Dave knew better. Each was wrapped up in their own thoughts, unaware that those around them were doing the same. Occasionally, a head would bob up, and with a faraway look someone would peer out to see if the snow was accumulating. Dave found himself looking out too. Under the circumstances it was hard to appreciate the beauty of the season. By fifth period the wind had died down and it stopped snowing. They'd been given a reprieve.

Today it was different. There was a wonderland of white outside the Ford's window. Dave didn't much concern himself with that, particularly when he opened the car door at the church's side entrance and heard the organ playing. Somehow the snow biting into his cheeks, the clunky boots on his feet, didn't matter. Today was Thanksgiving, his favorite holiday, and things were going great. Everyone in his family was healthy. The fighting overseas had stopped so you could sleep nights and he was where he wanted to be. He sang: "Come ye thankful people come, Raise the song of harvest home, All is safely gathered in, Ere the winter storms begin." He listened to the sermon. You couldn't know how fortunate you were unless you had something to compare it with. Dave did. No way was he going to be one of the nine who didn't return to give thanks, who weren't grateful. Only once, when the collection plate came past, did he falter, and then only for a moment.

Dave was amazed at what could happen in an hour. As parishioners left the church, ushers were stationed at the doors to pull them shut against the wind. Outside, drifts were beginning to bury the cars. They were in the midst of a blizzard.

Ordinarily, Dave didn't find having polio that much of a burden. He just worked around the limits it imposed, quite successfully, he thought. Today, for a few minutes, as his family made their way home through the driving snow, it got to him. Here he was, barely back on his feet, and now all his travels would be complicated by the weather. Snow brought the difference between him and his friends into focus and drove it into his consciousness. He got hold of his thoughts and put things in perspective. Snow was nothing more than a minor inconvenience. It built character.

The house smelled wonderful when the Norris' arrived home. Mrs. Norris had been up before dawn preparing the feast. The turkey was in the oven. The trimmings were set to go. A plate of cookies, wrapped in foil, awaited on the counter. A linen table cloth and the good china was out. All was ready. Then the phone rang. A few minutes later it rang again.

"It looks like we'll be having Thanksgiving by ourselves this year," Mr. Norris said.

Dinner was still great, but the usual festive spirit was missing. It was strange. Most times, when Dave's relatives were around, he couldn't wait to get away from them and be with his friends. Now that they weren't coming, he missed them.

It was an inside day, a day to rest. Mom and Ann cleared away the dishes. Mr. Norris turned on a football game.

"Dad, Rafe said the Olympics were on today. I told him he was crazy. I was right, wasn't I?"

"No."

"But winter's just startin'."

"It's not the Winter Games, they're in Italy after the 1st of the year. It's the Summer Games from Melbourne."

"Oh yeah, right, Australia's in the southern hemisphere. Can we switch channels?"

"The Olympics aren't being televised. The big shots are fighting over percentages again, so only the highlights are being transmitted. It's not like it used to be. T.V.'s made sports a racket."

Dave and his mother played cribbage that afternoon. Mrs. Norris was a superb card player, lucky as blazes too. She frequently whipped people so handily they wouldn't play anymore. Dave was counting his crib when Mr. Norris unleashed a tirade at the television set.

"Damn thing! Always goes haywire when there's a big play. I've already missed one touchdown pass. This thing has to go."

Mr. Norris stood up and banged on the side of the set. Sure enough, two good whacks in his special spot and the zig-zag lines disappeared. "The heavy weight championship fight's on next week. I'm not missing any more action. We're getting a new one."

"How can we afford that?" Mrs. Norris countered.

"How can we afford not to?" Mr. Norris returned. "As long as I work at Lee's I get my discount, almost down to wholesale. I don't want to pass that up."

"Will a new set make that much of a difference?"

"Definitely, the new models are much more powerful and they come with filters. There will still be some interference when planes come over on their landing approach, but the filters should knock out the rest."

"Well, I don't want another table model. The wires are unsightly and they make it hard to clean. And I don't want a Sylvania. I saw one when we had club at Edna's. The halo light surrounding the picture tube was very distracting."

"It's settled then," Mr. Norris said. "This storm will slow business some so I'll have time to make the arrangements and I can use my Christmas bonus to pay for it."

"Could I—maybe—have the old one in my room?" Dave asked haltingly.

Dave's parents looked at each other.

"My grades are gettin' better," he added quickly. "And I been behavin'."

"We'll see," Mr. Norris said. "But don't get your hopes up."

"Your father and I will have to discuss it," Mrs. Norris added.

Wow, Dave thought. What a switch. The day starts with a blizzard, and by supper time he might be getting his own T.V. He helped clear away the dishes, straightened his closet, worked on his book report. Can't hurt, he reasoned.

Dave's first foray through the snow went well. It packed nicely under foot and wasn't slippery. The sun was shining. The air was crisp. There were three whole days before school started back up, and, he had exciting news.

"Hey! Cut it out," he shouted, when he reached Rafe's and a snowball whizzed past his face. "You'll get the fuses wet."

"I wasn't aimin'," Rafe grinned. "Those rockets ready ta go?"

"Yep, made 'em yesterday. Never guess what's goin' on at my house?"

There was a series of muffled explosions.

Rafe passed off Dave's comment. "It's Mr. Young," he said. "Come on, let's go."

Rafe sprinted through his yard toward the alley with Dave trailing behind.

Edgar Young and his family lived in the middle of O'Brien's ten hundred block. It was Rafe's, Matoszak's, Young's, Webler's then the Rasco residence. Mr. Young was nuts about firecrackers and brought home boxes when he traveled through states where buying them was legal. He went for ones that burst with a loud crack, but weren't powerful enough to blow out windows. As far as Dave knew, he never lit them off on holidays. Instead, he had the odd habit of putting them in with the trash. At first, his wife took out the trash and burned it in the barrel a short ways from the garage. Dave didn't know if she'd ever been close by when one went off, but the trash quickly became Mr. Young's responsibility. He'd stand by, with a rake and watch as a cloud of red embers and scraps of burning paper belched from the barrel's top. Moments later a second blast would eject more. Sometimes there were half a dozen explosions in a row. No way did you want to be walking past when the volcano was erupting.

By the time Dave reached the scene, Tim Razyniak and Rafe were standing at the corner of Mr. Young's garage. He had moved forward to drop in more charges.

"Didn't know you were comin' over," Dave said to Tim.

"I just wondered if maybe you guys were going to," BANG!, "shoot some baskets," Tim explained.

"S'pose we," BANG! BANG!, "s'pose we could," Dave repeated. "Havta shovel off the court first though."

Dave and Mr. Young, an engaging, middle aged man, exchanged greetings. Then, smiling, Mr. Young pointed to the rockets and said, "I see you've been busy."

"Yes sir!" Dave beamed. "Think we could launch 'em here?"

"I can't see what it'd hurt."

Dave stuck one of the rocket's sticks into the snow, got it to where it just stayed upright and handed Rafe the Zippo. He lit the fuse. Wsssh. A rush of smoke and the rocket took flight. When it reached its highest point there was a flash, a small puff of smoke and a pop. Mr. Young shook his head approvingly.

"Didn't know ya had firecrackers in 'em," Rafe said.

"They're just small ones."

Dave positioned the second rocket. Rafe lit it off. Its path was jerky, erratic, nothing like the first one. It didn't fly as high and there was no explosion at its peak. Instead, it rolled over and started down, puffing out bursts of smoke as it fell. Dave glanced across the alley toward the green house that was directly in its path. There was a woman standing in the window next to the back door, obviously doing dishes. The rocket, sputtering as it went, flew past just inches away. The woman gasped, pulled back in a fright. The rocket buried itself partway in the snow, convulsed, threw out one last stream of smoke and soot, then exploded. Bits of black sticky residue mixed with snow and shreds of paper struck the glass and began to run down. The woman was gone. If she'd fainted, they were dead. Nobody made a sound. Mr. Young was white as a sheet. They looked at each other. *So much for the T.V.,* Dave thought.

The door burst open. The woman ran out barefoot into the snow waving her arms in the air and screaming at the top of her lungs. She was headed straight for them. For a split second no one moved, then, Mr. Young, still white, whispered," You boys get out of here! Fast!" Tim took off running down the alley; Dave and Rafe made for O'Brien Street on Mr. Young's driveway.

"Move it," Rafe yelled, out ahead.

"I'm tryin'," Dave replied. "She after us?"

"No, but Mr. Young's gettin' it. Hurry up."

In seconds the boys were in front of Webler's house.

"We can't go home," Dave said.

"Ron's," Rafe pointed, "We can hide there."

Rafe went ahead to knock. Dave hustling along, looked over his shoulder every few steps.

"Don't say nothin' 'bout it," Rafe cautioned, when Dave reached the porch.

Ron answered the door. As soon as Dave was inside he plopped down on the floor to take off his boots. Mrs. Rasco was a stickler on house cleaning.

"Put them on the rubber tray," she directed.

Dave did.

"And what have the both of you been up to this morning?" she asked. "I heard the fireworks."

"Aw—that was Mr. Young," Dave said quickly.

"Yeah," Rafe chimed in. "We heard 'em goin' off 'bout when we were comin' past."

"Poor Beatrice. What that woman has to put up with," Mrs. Rasco lamented. "The man's a pyromaniac."

"I'm gettin' a T.V.," Dave announced. "Well, I might be."

"That's nice," Mrs. Rasco said nonchalantly.

"I didn't hear 'bout that," Rafe complained.

"You woulda if ya hadn't been whippin' snowba..."

"That's 'sensational'," Ron broke in, "just sensational."

"What," Dave said, his face contorted.

"It's my cousin," Ron explained. "We went there for Thanksgiving. It's not far. That's his latest phrase. No matter what it is, 'it's sensational, just sensational.'"

Dave looked at Rafe, both shrugged. "Let's go shovel off the court at my house," Dave said.

Once the three boys were on the front porch and the door was closed Ron spoke. "Let's have it," he said. "What happened? I saw you looking at each other."

Dave and Rafe smiled then burst into laughter. Ron stood there watching with a frown on his face. "I know you were there."

"Us two?" Dave smirked, after a minute—"O.K. It went like this." And he explained about the rocket and the lady.

When they reached Mr. Young's driveway, Rafe stretched out an arm to block the sidewalk then cautiously stepped forward to have a look.

"She's gone," he said. "Coast's clear."

A step further and Ron began to laugh. "I suppose you noticed that your tracks lead straight to my front door."

Now all three doubled up.

"Hey, there wasn't nothin' gonna happen," Rafe contended. "Mr. Young's gotta take the rap. He's the adult. He can't be layin' it off on us kids. We're off the hook."

"Yeah," Dave snickered. "Even if we did do it. I was 'fraid she blacked out in there and somebody'd find her unconscious in a pool a blood."

"Shoulda seen ol' Ed," Rafe mimicked, throwing out his arms. "She was really givin' it ta 'im, I think in Polish. He was just standin' there like a statue takin' it. Bet he didn't understand a word she said."

Rafe's comment provoked another round of laughter. Once it died down he said. "Now, what's all this bunk 'bout a T. V.?"

Dave recounted how his dad had convinced his mom they needed a new television set. "So, I asked if I could have the old one."

"That's crazy," Ron responded. "A lot of people don't even have T.V.s yet. Nobody has one in their bedroom."

"A kid get one? Let's throw 'im in the snow." And Rafe nudging Dave with an elbow that nearly sent him sprawling.

"Listen, I'm serious. Dad works at Lee's Appliance. He sells T.V.s, lots of 'em and he gets a big discount. He has ta have regular jobs. Mom says we'd starve on what he makes doin' sports."

"That don't mean you're gettin' the old one," Rafe scoffed.

"Hey, they didn't say no."

"O.K.," Ron advised. "Here's what you do. Don't ask any questions. Just keep your mouth shut. Adults think you're mature when you hold back."

"Still think we should push 'im in the snow," Rafe said.

Dave spent supper stealing glances at his parents, but like with the coin, learned nothing. First he thought that was a good sign. Then he thought it was a bad one. A moment later he wasn't sure. Then the question he couldn't ask was there on the tip of his tongue. It was torture, way worse than having to clam up for the sports report.

Things were the same when he went to play Monopoly at Luke's the next day. He had to keep his cool. If he mentioned the television then didn't get it, all of his friends would be mocking him, not just Rafe and Ron.

The Razyniaks had the game set up on the carpet in the front bedroom when he arrived.

"We're not playin' in the basement?" he questioned.

"Dad's working on about twenty deer heads," Pete said. "There's not a spot open."

"We're building a dark room too, along the back wall," Luke added, "so I can develop the film from my telescope camera. I've nearly finished the tripod for it."

"Could I see?" Dave asked.

The three brothers laughed.

"Everything's torn up," Pete said. "Mom would have a conniption fit if we took you down now."

Dave was luckier this game than the last. He owned desirable properties and had plenty of money. A few more rolls and he'd win. Or would have, if there hadn't been a squeal of brakes outside followed by a series of dull thuds.

Luke and Pete shared a large paper route. When the delivery truck arrived and the bundles were thrown off, they had to go to work. People didn't care if you were in the midst of a hot game or not, they wanted their newspapers and they wanted them on time. Dave had to settle for almost won. He went home.

First stop, the fridge. As he turned to open it, something in the living room caught his eye, a beautiful new television. He spun around, walked to his bedroom, slipped a finger in along the curtain's edge and looked in. There it was, the 21 inch Philco, on its spindly legs sitting against the wall opposite his bed. He touched it, rubbed his hand along its top. He turned it on. It worked perfectly. He just stood there for a few seconds, then threw up his hands and let out a war hoop. Mrs. Norris walked in. "I see you've found it," she said.

"Thanks! Thanks!" he gushed. "This is great, and it's all hooked up. I didn't think you'd let me have it."

"There are rules that come with it."

"Sure!" Dave exclaimed.

"Your grades will have to improve the next marking period and bed time on school nights stays the same, no exceptions."

"No problem! When did they bring the new one? I wasn't gone that long."

"The truck came about a half hour after you left," Mrs. Norris explained, then she left to start supper.

Dave flopped on his bed, rubbed his hands together briskly and grinned. This was big. He investigated different ways to lay, be comfortable and still see the screen clearly. Occasionally he'd pop up, turn the set slightly to eliminate a reflection then pound his pillow into a new shape and lay back down. The screen was covered with ugly finger prints. Dave got some window cleaner and paper towels. It was more than dirt; a brown film covered the picture tube and the set's cabinet. It was the same gunk that covered the inside of the car's windows. It came from Dad's cigar and it didn't wash off easily. He was glad his room was at the back of the house.

Dave thanked his dad the minute he got home. Mr. Norris repeated the rules. "And remember," he said. "It can be taken out as quickly as it was moved in."

Another little ditty to keep in mind, Dave thought.

Ann was not happy with the new arrangement. "Why does he get one in his room?" she pouted.

Mrs. Norris explained that Dave was older and good things would happen to her when she got older. That didn't seem to help because she came to supper with her lower lip pushed out and a frown on her face. Mr. Norris quickly put a stop to that. Even so, she stayed mad for nearly a week.

During the next few days, all Dave's friends made a pilgrimage to his house. Somehow a television set in a living room was no big deal but the same television, in a kid's bedroom, was. Dave sucked it all up but was careful not to gloat.

During the week a debate arose over what to do on Friday. Central was at home again.

"Thought the fight was Saturday," Dave said.

"Told ya, it's Friday," Rafe insisted. "They're both Friday."

"Man, now we can't go," Dave grumbled. "Dad'll be camped out in front a that new set all night. He's puttin' his money on Patterson."

"Ron's got a radio," Gunner noted.

"O.K., we'll meet up at my house and catch 'em both," Dave replied.

"Sensational idea," Ron remarked, "just sensational."

All of a sudden Dave's bedroom was a gathering spot. Ron brought his radio, the Scanner brothers brought snacks. All four lined up across his bed.

"I listened ta all the Central games when they won state in '53," Dave said.

"How'd ya pull that off?" Gunner asked.

"My crystal radio set," Dave explained. "It's downstairs on the ledge somewhere."

"How's come we're not usin' that?" Rafe asked.

"It's not like a real radio. There's no tuner, no speaker either, and you don't plug it in. It's just a silvery crystal and some wires."

"Yeah sure," Rafe said. "And no one complained when ya stayed up?"

"No one knew. You connect it to a wire aerial on the roof and use earphones. There's barely any power and I could only get WSBT, but they carried the games. It was under my bed for years. It ran all the time. I 'member *Shadow, Lone Ranger, Gangbusters.* I listened ta all the good stuff."

"Enough, already," Gunner said. "They're comin' out."

The two boxers, dancing around, made their way into the ring. Moore wore a flashy black robe.

"S'pose that trim's real gold?" Rafe asked.

"I don't know," Ron replied. "But I hope it's warm because he'll be on a stretcher in a few minutes with it laid on top."

The chatter quieted as a microphone descended from the ceiling.

"And now, from Chicago stadium, what you've all been waiting for. The main event—15 rounds—for the heavy weight championship of the world. In this corner, attempting to become the youngest champion in history, weighing in at 173½ pounds, the challenger—21 year old—Floyd—Patterson!"

A cheer went up from the raucous crowd and Dave's bedroom. "They smell blood," Dave said.

"He'll take Moore in 7," Gunner predicted.

"A knock out in 3," Rafe countered.

"Didn't Patterson win a gold medal in the Olympics?" Dave asked.

"Two years ago," Ron replied, the radio to his ear. "Central's killing Shelbyville."

"In this corner," the announcer continued, "a veteran of 157 bouts..."

"He looks old," Ron whispered.

"Shhh," Gunner said.

"The champ—39 year old—Archie—Moore!"

He was greeted with a much weaker cheer.

Bong! The bell sounded. The first round began. Moore looked dazed, confused. Patterson was all over him. Moore fought him off.

"Look at those jump hooks," Dave said. "He's way faster than Moore."

In the fifth a sharp left dumped Moore. Everyone cheered. A bowl of chips went flying.

"Dad, did ya see that?" Dave yelled.

"Yes-indeedee," came a muffled reply.

"What a shot," Gunner remarked, as everyone reached to clean up the mess.

Dave hoped old Arch would stay down, but he struggled to his feet, eyes glazed, an open cut over his nose. Wham, he took a left. Kablam, a right came across. Down he went, this time for good.

"Let's go see the new T.V.," Gunner said, as Archie, a pile of wreckage, was carted from the ring.

"Wait, how's Central doin'?" Dave asked.

"They're running away with it," Ron replied.

Dave's friends approved of his family's new television set.

"It's a beaut', isn't it?" Mr. Norris beamed.

"Arch really got clobbered, didn't he?" Dave said.

"I haven't seen a fighter get whipped like that in some time," Mr. Norris replied. "That Patterson kid's got class."

Dave noticed that his mother was quietly tending to some mending. She didn't think boxing was civilized. He didn't think it was either. Why would you put yourself in a position where you might be seriously injured, lose an eye, get your brain scrambled? He'd never do that.

Dave accompanied his friends through the house to the back door. Ron couldn't resist pointing out that the new television was sensational. Dave screwed up his face at that and returned to his room. He picked the remaining potato chip slivers off his blanket, got undressed and climbed into bed. Rafe was right. They should have thrown him in the snow. As he turned off his light, he knew he wouldn't even have cared.

Christmas songs were everywhere on the radio now. Most of the time when Dave heard them he sang along. People around the neighborhood were cheerfully greeting each other with handshakes, a friendly slap on the back, a hearty Merry Christmas. Decorations and lights appeared on porches and in windows. Cars with trees strapped on top or hanging out of the trunk regularly passed by. Mr. Norris took a pine needle straight through his unlit cigar when he tried to wedge theirs through the front door.

Dave had missed Christmas the year before last when he was in the hospital and appreciated all the subtleties of the season he'd overlooked in the past.

On the Friday before vacation started, and as Luke reminded him, the winter solstice, there was big news. Two bank robbers had escaped from the dilapidated county jail downtown the night before by hack sawing their way through three bars, wriggling through the opening, then lowering themselves twenty-two feet down a rope made from blanket strips. The update Dave got before school was abuzz with warnings that two fugitives were on the loose. "They are to be considered 'armed and dangerous,'" the report said. Everyone at school knew about the breakout and was nervous. The Studebaker mansion would be a perfect place to hide out. Three floors, two basements, nooks and crannies everywhere; food, water, toilets were available. It was heated. There were telephones and radios; and it was just a few short blocks from the lockup. Mrs. Pritchard even let students go to the restroom in pairs, something she'd never allowed before.

As the morning wore on, Dave lost interest in "criminal activity." His neck hurt. Usually when that happened it meant he'd slept wrong the previous night. Today, for some reason, instead of getting better, it got worse. At lunch he had trouble swallowing. His head ached. Except for turning in his book report, he didn't get much done that day.

When Mr. Faris dropped him off after school, Mr. Norris was rummaging through the trunk and Ron was over. Dave pointed toward his dad. Ron shrugged in response.

"Dad, whatcha doin'?" Dave asked.

"I'm looking for my .38," Mr. Norris replied. "I haven't used it for months. Aw, found it," he said, pulling out a box packed with whistles, running shoes and black and white striped shirts.

Mr. Norris used the pistol to start track meets but was, at the moment, replacing the blanks in the cylinder with live rounds.

"Those jailbirds come anywhere around here, they'll be in for a surprise," he said, clicking the revolver shut. He returned the boxes he'd removed, each to its particular spot, closed the trunk and walked into the house.

"I wouldn't mess with your dad," Ron said emphatically.

"Me neither," Dave agreed. "Man, my jaw hurts," he grimaced, rubbing his neck.

"Your mom O.K. with a gun in the house?"

"Yeah, Dad's real respectful around firearms. You know, 'causea grandpa."

"What's your grandfather got to do with it?"

"Thought I told ya—oh well. It was when Dad was a kid. Grandpa Norris had been out rabbit huntin' and brought his shotgun inta the house. Grandma didn't like it, so ta show her it wasn't loaded he clicked off the trigger and blew a hole clean through the kitchen floor."

"Na, come on," Ron laughed.

"Really. Guess ya could see straight through inta the basement. Dad said after everyone's ears quit ringing it was real quiet around the house, and grandma glared at grandpa for days. Didn't you see Dad check the safety?"

"No."

"Well, he did, twice."

"Did you ever see the floor?"

"Heck, I don't even know where they lived then."

"How about this morning? I came down to see if Mr. Faris took you past the jail."

"Nope, we asked 'im to, but he said they had the area cordoned off and even if it wasn't, they didn't need a bunch a people gawkin' while they were tryin' to investigate. Aw, dang, it even hurts ta talk."

"You are sick!"

"I'm comin' down with somethin' sure."

"You think you'll make the game tonight?"

"Yeah, but hey, don't say nothin' ta nobody."

At supper Dave ate something sour and got a sharp pain from the back of his mouth. "Ow, oh," he said, grabbing his jaw.

"What's the matter?" Mrs. Norris asked, as he rubbed it.

"I bit my cheek," he replied, quickly lowering his head so his mother couldn't get a good look.

"Let's be more careful," Mr. Norris said.

Dave took a lot of razzing in the car for being quiet but stuck to the sore cheek story. When Rafe poked him from the rear seat he angrily turned around and shot back a dirty look.

"That will do boys," Mr. Norris ordered, "not while I'm driving."

"Dad, think they'll catch those crooks?" Dave asked, to change the subject.

"They will. They'll run 'em down," Mr. Norris said resolutely, "and probably when the two least expect it. See, that's the worst part. When you're on the run you have to be on the lookout every minute. You never know when you'll get that tap on the shoulder or that knock at the door. It might be when you're out on an errand, having dinner, at night when you're asleep. It can happen anytime. You never have peace of mind. You're always fearful and that's no way to live. Remember that."

The conversation drifted into speculation. Where might the fugitives be hiding? How could they have gotten through a hole only ten inches square? Who supplied the hack saw blade? Did they have accomplices waiting with a getaway car? Dave just sat listening. What am I doing here, he kept asking himself?

Central's opponent that night was East Chicago Washington. It was another slaughter. Dave hardly noticed, nor did he care that Rafe spent much of the first two quarters carrying on a conversation with Gunner and Ron in sign language. The tip-off that he really was sick came during half time when Mr. Norris was making his rounds. Rafe poked him in the side, "Look," he said.

"What?" Dave groaned, his head buried in his hands.

"It's her, the girl ya saw before."

"Who?"

"The blond," Gunner said excitedly. "You know, the one that's really stacked."

Dave didn't respond. Rafe, Gunner and Ron looked at each other then went silent. When Mr. Norris returned they pointed and nodded their heads.

"All right son, let's have a look," Mr. Norris said, reaching down to lift Dave's chin. "Where does it hurt?"

"Here," Dave muttered, tenderly putting a finger to the back of his jaw.

"A-huh, I see," Mr. Norris analyzed. He rocked Dave's head from side to side. "Both sides?" he asked.

Dave shook his head in the affirmative.

"The game's over for tonight," Mr. Norris said. "Wrap it up boys, we're heading home."

Dave went to protest, "But, Da...," then just reached for his coat.

When Mrs. Norris saw him a second examination ensued. She poked and prodded his neck under his ears. "Where did you bite your cheek?" she asked.

"I didn't," he confessed, hanging his head. "It was the dill pickle."

"I wondered about that."

"What does that mean?" Dave moaned.

"It means you have the mumps. You'll have to stay in the house and be off your feet for two weeks."

"Two weeks?" Dave repeated.

"That's how long it takes before its safe for you to be up and around."

"The whole vacation?" Dave sighed, tears welling up in his eyes.

"I'm afraid so," Mrs. Norris said softly. "You're lucky though."

"How?" Dave barked.

"You have them on both sides so you won't get them again."

"That's lucky?"

"Let's not be disrespectful," Mr. Norris said, with a cautioning finger.

Somehow as Dave shuffled off to his room he didn't feel lucky, not one bit lucky.

The next few days weren't pleasant. It was hard to eat and hard to communicate. To get around he had to slide along on the floor. He objected, but his parents were adamant.

"The mumps are nothing to fool with," Mrs. Norris explained. "You have to be careful or you might not be able to have children someday."

Who cared about that? Still, if his mom said it was important, it must be, so he obeyed.

To occupy his mind, Dave did things he normally wouldn't do. He paged through the stack of newspapers on the end table and found that one of the prisoners dieted before the escape. He studied the picture of a deputy looking up at the makeshift rope hanging against the bricks. Shimmying twenty-two feet down blanket strips knotted together after squirming through a ten inch hole, that was some feat. He read articles about Central, how most sports writers expected them to win state, maybe go undefeated. He watched game shows, played solitaire, cribbage with his mom, finished another Jules Verne book. You had to stay busy or you'd go nuts. And even then, time passed at a snail's pace.

Christmas and New Year's, like Thanksgiving, were somber, rather gloomy affairs. No doubt about it, having friends and relatives around on holidays made a big difference. Dave received a smaller version of the telescope Luke was building as a Christmas present but he missed the fun his friends had lighting fireworks in the alley on New Year's Eve. Watching the flashes and sparks fly from the window of his room wasn't nearly the same as being there.

His only consolation was listening to Mom and Dad play pinochle in the kitchen with his older sister Jean and her husband Robb who lived across the line in Michigan. Dave gathered that the men felt being males made them naturally superior to the women and that, by rights, they should win every game. So far they hadn't won a thing and were both surly. Worse, Mrs. Norris would politely say, "Its O.K., you'll get a hand here in a bit," and, of course, that steamed the two even more. "Hope nothin' 'splodes in here," Dave chuckled to himself.

In the days ahead Dave drew up diagrams in case he and his friends got enough wire for a phone system of their own, and he saw a cool movie. Staying up to watch the late show was one of the neatest things about having your own T.V., though that first Saturday after he'd gotten it his father made him turn the set off.

"But Dad, since there's no school tommor..."

"The noise is keeping us awake," Mr. Norris said.

Dave went to bed with a big smile on his face that night. He might only have a curtain for a door on his room, but he also had a slick pair of earphones his Uncle Wally had given him from a WW II bomber. Once he rigged the television with a jack and connected the two, he could "improve his mind" and not disturb anyone.

The Day the Earth Stood Still helped do that; a flying saucer lands on the mall in Washington D.C., soldiers with tanks take up positions around it. They wait. Eventually a section of the saucer opens. A humanoid alien steps out. Klaatu offers a gift. It is mistaken for a weapon. A nervous soldier fires. Winged in the shoulder, Klaatu falls to the ground. While everyone's attention is on him, a nine foot robot appears. Silvery metallic, it stands mute. Then, the visor across its face rises. Instead of eyes, a death ray targets the soldier's guns. They're instantly illuminated, momentarily glow then disappear. It directs the ray at the tanks and stationary guns. The same thing happens to them. Klaatu calls it off and is "escorted" to Walter Reed Army Hospital for medical care.

As the movie progresses, Klaatu tries to assemble world leaders so he can explain his mission. Deep seated animosities prevent that. As a last resort, he contacts renowned Professor Barnhardt. The professor informs him that a meeting of eminent scientists is about to convene, but cautions that often scientists aren't listened to. He suggests that Klaatu demonstrate his unearthly powers beforehand, but in a peaceful manner. It is agreed. Two days later, at exactly twelve noon, all mechanical and electrical devices across the globe cease to operate: cars, ships, trains, generators, all go dead. There is an eerie silence, yet miraculously, planes land safely and essential services are unaffected. After an interval, everything functions as before. Professor Barnhardt is amazed. At his direction, the scientists gather around the spacecraft. Klaatu explains that he has come to deliver an ultimatum.

"Now that earthlings have developed atomic weapons and will soon venture into space, they pose a threat to others who live there. At one time, we acted recklessly, as do you. We warred against our neighbors, built bigger, more powerful weapons. Only when our civilization was on the verge of annihilation did we recognize our limitations and act to avoid extinction. We created a race of robots, as you see here. We have given them absolute, irrevocable power over us in matters of aggression.

We care little how you conduct your own affairs but once you join the larger galactic family, you, like us, must abide by the agreed upon rules. There are no exceptions. Any nation or planet which does not conform is eliminated. The choice is yours. Live in peace alongside us, or, you and the Earth you live on face certain, swift, annihilation. And let me assure you, such power does exist. We will await your signal but only for so long." At that Klaatu and the robot flew away.

Dave lay on his pillow thinking into the wee hours after the movie ended. The peoples of the Earth were rushing headlong toward Armageddon. There was no doubt about that, but would we foolishly resist like we did in the movie. I mean, a space ship comes from a zillion miles away. A robot vaporizes tanks with a death ray. If the spaceman on board tells you to do something, you should do it.

In a way Dave wished it all were true. If everyone lived by the Golden Rule, even if it had to be enforced, there'd be no war and far less suffering; and the world could live in peace. Why was it we Earthlings could build such miraculous things, yet couldn't control ourselves? Dave didn't know the answer to that question.

The first of the two bank robbers was captured. It was front page news, hilarious and just the boost Dave needed. There was no *High Noon* standoff, no high speed car chase, only a series of miscues the keystone cops would have been proud of. Dave made for the telephone as soon as he'd read the article.

"I had ta call," he told Ron. "They got one of 'em."

"Who?" Ron asked.

"Holloman, one a the jail birds, I just read 'bout it in the paper."

"You're reading the newspaper now?"

"Hey, I'm goin' bonkers down here, it's somethin' ta do."

"So, what does it say?"

"O.K., here's the deal. He and the other guy, Ditmar, made it all the way ta Cincinnati 'fore he got picked up. The police flew him back on a private plane and he told his story to a lady reporter on the way. Musta figured he was done for or he wouldina opened up."

"Probably."

"Anyway, 'cordin' ta him, the two stole a car from the lot next ta the jail. 'Warnt stupid either,' he says. 'We played it smart, checked around careful, so's we gets one with snow tires. Be sure ya get that down. Did a lot of drivin' on back roads ya know.' Then the reporter asks who helped 'em escape and supplied the gas money. Holloman gets defensive. 'Ain't talkin' 'bout nobody but me,' he says. 'What kinda guy ya think I am?' The deputy ridin' along tells 'im ta cool it. 'Wanna hear the rest or not?' he snaps. The lady reporter nods so he goes on. 'Well, somebody musta tipped the law 'cause we was sleepin' one off in the woods when up walks this copper. Had guts too, walked right up ta the car like he's not afraid a nothin'. I don't have no identification so I starts up ta drive outta there, but I drives inta a creek, ditch or whatever 'cause it's dark and almost clips the copper's legs when I tries ta swerve. But now, that was an accident. Then we jumps out. I do'no where Ditmar gets,' he says, 'but he gets away. I make a run down the side a the ravine with the copper takin' pops at me with his gun. I gets away too, but just barely, 'cause it's hard runnin' through the snow—the sticks, ya know, they're sharp and I got no shoes; they're still in the car.'"

Ron started to laugh.

"Hold on," Dave said. "There's more."

"'See, I was sleepin'. I'm real sick, been spittin' up blood for a week, got that nu-monia in my lungs, can feel it down here,' and he rubs his chest. 'I know they're on ta me, so's I keeps goin', makes it to a dirt road and tries ta hitchhike, got a ten dollar bill in my hand and still five cars pass up, go right by. Then one pulls over, but it's another copper so I'm finished. Tell ya though, I wouldn't be on this plane if it warnt for my bad luck.'"

"That is hilarious," Ron said. "And it's in the paper that way?"

"Mostly."

"Anymore?" he asks.

"Well, the reporter asked Holloman if he ever carried a gun."

"'No, never fool with nothin' like that'," he says. "'Already told ya, warnt stupid.'"

"She didn't write it that way?"

"I mighta Keen-tuckyed it up a bit."

"Sounds more like you Hucklberried it," Ron chuckled.

"I just did a book report on Huck Finn," Dave said.

"We had to read it last fall."

"Whatcha think a breaking out of jail where it's warm ta take your chances outdoors in winter when you're coughing up blood?"

"Warnt too bright," Ron snickered. "Some people just don't think things through very well."

"Ya," Dave returned. "I just saw a movie 'bout that."

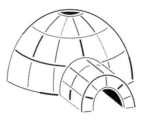

Chapter 7
THE GASSING

D ave's ounce of prevention restrictions were lifted the first Friday in January. He was back on his feet, though this last weekend before vacation ended was unsteady, tiring and altogether wonderful. Holloman was back behind bars. Central had swept victim number ten off the court by 54 points, which Dave thought must be some kind of record. He shot a few baskets then watched his friends play a game on the snow covered court. For once it was other people who lost their footing.

On Sunday the Norris' went to LaPorte. What a thrill, new percolators and electric fry pans to fawn over. One still had a red bow attached to its handle. How exciting. Even going back to school Monday sounded good. When Mom parted the drapes and announced it was snowing, Dave almost cheered. Heavy snow meant they'd leave for home early.

At the edge of town Mrs. Norris took note of the large brick building that was under construction.

"That's the new Castinal plant," Mr. Norris remarked. "I think Uncle Virgil's planning to apply for a job there. They'll be looking for tool and die makers. I'll be in there as soon as the roof's on. You can make some impressive sales when a plant's tooling up. They always need drills and cutters."

After the episode behind Young's garage, skyrockets were passé. Dave had moved on to aerial bombs, or would, as soon as he got the chance. Aerial bombs were small cylinders, essentially gun barrels that shot firecrackers high into the sky, he hoped, more reliably. The trick was finding or making the sturdy cardboard tubes required. They had to fit tightly together and take considerable pressure. If he could get that right he'd try making aerial displays like the ones people flocked to see on the Fourth of July. They had flammable pellets packed in around the firecracker. The pellets had to be arranged just so, hold their shape, and ignite when they were blasted into the air. The brilliant patterns created, the shimmering colors, that's what filled your senses. When you made fireworks you had to solve problems all the way along. There were no books with handy formulas or step-by-step instructions a kid could get hold of. Discovering things was hard, but then that was the fun of it.

Strangely, Dave found the same to be true when he tried building an igloo. No one knew how to go about it. On T.V., cartoon Eskimos cut slabs of snow, magically stacked them one on another and presto, there it was. It took only seconds and the pieces fit perfectly.

You knew that was baloney. Spherical structures were hard, really hard. Nothing was square. Dave thought the slick move would be to start with blocks then fill in around them. He made a mold. It didn't work. Either the snow wouldn't pack or it stuck tight to the plywood and the block broke apart when he removed it. That idea off the table, he went with the simple obvious alternative. Pile snow into a huge mound and sculpt out the inside. A lot of work, to be sure but how many cool things weren't? As best he could remember, he'd never seen an igloo in anybody else's back yard; course then a fresh snow and they were nearly invisible. A cardboard box, deck of cards, a few friends —igloos were toasty warm inside, confining too, like a cozy cave or cramped capsule rocketing through space. Deathly quiet, except for dampened voices, in the dim light, you had to be on the alert every second when you played those games.

On the first cloudless night, Dave and his mother took the telescope out. In the bitter cold their observations lasted only minutes but it was time enough for Dave to know he wasn't interested in astronomy. They brought the telescope back inside. While Dave warmed himself in front of the kitchen register he wondered why he'd wanted one in the first place. Telescopes were expensive. His parents didn't have money for such things. How could he have been so foolish? He'd tried to seem interested, but suspected Mom knew his heart wasn't in it.

The first semester ended. Report cards came out. It was amazing what an incentive a television set could be when viewing privileges were on the line.

Basketball games supplied the action on weekends now. Dave scraped the court down to the pavement every Friday so he could play and was dealing with a stubborn spot of ice when he and Rafe got into it. They taunted each other mercilessly until Dave fired up a rebound that overshot and bounced into the yard.

"Hey, Mr. Hotshot," he said, as Rafe went through the adjoining gate for the ball. "Why don't ya belly in the igloo and I'll set off a stink bomb? Let's see how long ya can take it. I dare ya."

"That's crazy," Rafe scoffed, launching a twenty-footer. "You do it."

"Yeah, well, you're the tough guy around here who's always overheatin'. Nobody else strips down to a tee shirt in this weather."

"All right, I'll do it," Rafe snapped. "Long's I can get out."

"Deal," Dave shot back. "We'll just lay a board loose over the hole."

Dave quickly mixed extra sulfur in with some rocket fuel, rolled a paper tube and folded in a length of fuse. He built up a long thin mound of snow on the ground behind the igloo and rammed a broomstick through it.

"That's so all you'll get is smoke," he said.

Rafe looked skeptical, but crawled in. Dave laid the board across the entrance. He slid the tube into the broomstick hole, lit the fuse and pressed a clump of snow over the opening. He stumbled back against the fence where the rest of his friends were standing. For a moment nothing happened. Then gray black smoke erupted from half a dozen fissures in the igloo. There was a howl of laughter, then dead silence. A second later Rafe burst through the top. Concealed by the smoke, all one could see were massive chunks of snow being thrown out and two arms thrashing wildly through the air. There was a second howl of laughter as Rafe staggered out of the rubble. The laughter turned to gasps when he abruptly stopped and collapsed. Gagging and desperate for breath, he lay there, vapor rising off his head, pieces of snow dripping from his body. Dave, in a fit of fright, stood immobile, then, joined the others, rushing to Rafe's aid. He dropped down next to Rafe and grabbed his shoulder.

"Rafe! Rafe! I'm sorry! I didn't mean—come on! Say somethin'! Please!"

In the background he heard, "Rafe! You all right? You O.K.?"

"He's shivering, run, get his sweatshirt!" Ron yelled.

Dave pointed, "There's a towel, in the garage! Hurry!"

"I'm goin'!" Leon returned.

Rafe hadn't moved. He lay there curled up, hacking, gasping for air.

"Rafe, come on! Say somethin'!" Dave implored. "Dry him off."

"Put this on," Gunner said, holding out the sweatshirt.

Rafe, continuing to cough uncontrollably, got to his knees. He took a swipe at Dave, hitting him in the side. There was fire in his eyes. Dave stepped back, not certain his buddies would pull Rafe off if he got hold of him, even less sure they should.

"M—m—man, I'll—get ya," cough-cough, "I'll get ya for this," Rafe sputtered, in a raspy whisper.

Dave pulled back further, positive he'd be dead if Rafe wasn't incapacitated.

"I didn't mean for ya ta get hurt."

How could this have happened? Rafe was one of his best friends. What if Rafe hadn't been able to get out? He could have died in there. Dave felt terrible. His stomach was all knotted up. This was the dumbest thing he'd ever done.

"Why didn't ya push the board away and come out the entrance?"

"There was smoke," cough, "and flame everywhere. I couldn't see and I couldn't breathe," Rafe choked. "Any more dumb questions?"

"No, none," Dave stammered.

"Then shut up," Gunner ordered. "Or I'll slam ya."

Dave kept his distance while Gunner helped Rafe to his feet. The two walked slowly through the back gate then across Vassar Street, Gunner lending support all the way. Dave's other friends went home. He sat down on the steps outside the back door, cradled his head in his hands. How could he have done something so awful? Where did he get such screwy ideas? Worse, when it got right down to it, he was more worried about his own lousy skin than Rafe. There was Rafe, lying on the ground gasping for air, unable to breathe and he was afraid someone might have seen what happened and he'd get in trouble. He didn't like himself very much at the moment and resolved, yet again, to think before he acted.

Central played an away game that night. Dave holed up in the basement listening. No one called his house. No one came knocking. What did that mean? Rafe and Gunner must have covered for him. Was Rafe embarrassed that he'd been stupid enough to go along with the stunt? Did he know how much Dave regretted it? How guilty he felt? Were the brothers plotting to get him? Could they keep from plotting against each other that long? Too bad Rafe wasn't a girl, then he could spring for flowers and most likely, he'd be off the hook. Flowers almost always seemed to do the trick with them. He was laughing. Rafe didn't look much like a girl. He could plead temporary

98

insanity. How could anyone argue with that? Maybe if he lay low a couple days? Na, his friends already thought he was wacky. What would they think then? He'd have to face up eventually. All he could do was hope Rafe wasn't still smoking hot when he did. The best thing was to do it right away, in the morning, early, about ten, right when Rafe got up. Nobody'd be around then and Rafe would only be half awake.

Dave figured he needed a peace offering for this one and it had to be something good, something Rafe would really like. But what did he have? A few dog eared Superman comics and a ratty stack of baseball cards in a shoe box under his bed, that wouldn't do. Then he remembered there was a bag of hard candy left over from Halloween in his closet. He pulled it out. The pieces were stuck together. He banged the bag against the wall. They broke apart. He hung over the edge of his bed, found the box. It was full of dust. He blew into it. The dust flew back into his face. He coughed and wiped the corners of his eyes.

"How many times ya gonna havta do that 'fore ya learn?" he muttered to himself.

Dave was ready to make his move by nine-thirty the next morning, but waited until ten. As he walked past Babcock's and O'Donnell's houses on the sidewalk, he wondered if this was such a slick idea. When he reached the Scanner's front porch he took a deep breath. "Here goes," he said to himself as he rang the door bell.

Rafe appeared with a look of surprise on his face. "What you want?" he glared.

"Here."

"What's that?"

"It's for you. Real sorry 'bout what happened. I know it was dumb, ya O.K.?"

"Throat's sore." Rafe hesitated. "Come on in," he said.

So far, so good, Dave thought.

"Ya got some nerve comin' 'round here," Gunner threatened. "'Specially when Mom's at the store."

"Came ta see Rafe."

"What's in the box?" Rafe asked.

"Open it."

Rafe slid the lid off and fingered through the contents. "Thanks, but don't get the idea we're even. Ya still got it comin'."

"Only thing I could think of. Had ta do somethin' after what happened. I been worried sick."

"And ya best never do anythin' like that again, or I'll flatten ya on the spot."

Dave could see that Gunner was ready to do it right then. Actually he thought Rafe deserved some of the blame for what happened and considered mentioning it, then he thought again.

"You guys playin' this afternoon?" he asked.

"Might be—do'no yet," Rafe replied coolly.

"O.K., well then, I'm leavin'. Don't wanna get snow all over your rug."

On the way home Dave couldn't decide if he'd gained ground or lost it. He'd gotten by for now, but what about later?

Chapter 8
ICEBALLS

The whole gang turned up for basketball that afternoon. If Rafe decided to take his revenge, it was obvious no one wanted to miss seeing it. There was no indication anything of the sort was on his mind, though Dave made sure they were on the same team and he fed Rafe the ball a lot. Everything was just like always, except it was great packing and after the first game snowballs began to fly.

"Hold it," Leon said. "Let's use what's left of the igloo to make a fort and have a real fight."

"Great idea," Pete seconded.

Dave handed out shovels and the gang went to work. The fort was a waist high wall parallel to the sidewalk along Vassar Street and about fifteen feet inside the yard fence. This was the first snow fort they'd built in a year and except for Rafe and Gunner, the project was alive with enthusiasm. Rafe couldn't stand the leftover sulfur smell so the brothers played one-on-one while the work progressed.

"We'll bury all the stinky stuff," Dave shouted, uncertain if Rafe heard the comment.

"Looks like you got off," Ron whispered in Dave's ear. "They're really going at it."

"Yeah, like I gave flowers."

"What?"

"Nothin', nothin'," Dave said, under his breath. "I was sure I'd catch an elbow in the eye or get smacked inta the telephone pole while we were playin'. Can't figure why I didn't."

"Maybe they're saving up for later," Ron grinned.

"Thanks. That's just what I needed ta hear. Interestin' how everybody just happened ta show up today."

"Right, big secret," Ron smirked. "Wouldn't you want to see you get beat up?"

"Sure, but looks like I won't." And Dave glanced over his shoulder toward the basketball court. "It's 'bout ta blow."

Things always got hot when Rafe and Gunner played one on one. Gunner would dribble in from out of bounds and Rafe would block him. Gunner would turn and fire up a jumper. If it didn't go in they'd scramble for the rebound. When Rafe took the ball out the same thing happened, except Rafe would keep dribbling then give a head fake like he was going up to shoot. When Gunner jumped to block it, Rafe would duck under his arm and lay the ball up. Then he'd ridicule Gunner with a mock response to his head fake and a hokey laugh. That usually went on until enough guys showed up for a real game, or Gunner lost his temper. In the neighborhood that was known as stage four. Stage five was Rafe running for his life or the two punching it out. At the moment they were at stage three, the pushing and shoving phase.

Dave nudged Ron and nodded toward the court again. "A beautiful sight ain't it?" he smiled warily.

"Let's get started," Luke said. "We'll take the street side. Same teams as we had for basketball."

"Yeah," Ben seconded. "We're outside the fence."

"O.K.," Dave countered. "We get the fort, but no chargin' us through the gates or comin' 'round behind through Sinkovics' yard."

"'Fraid we'll get ya in a cross fire?" Pete teased.

"Darn right," Dave replied. "You want in here?"

"Nope."

Pete's reply was accompanied by a flurry of snowballs. One hit Dave in the side. He batted down a second. This was fun. The wall was there to protect his legs, and instead of Rafe zeroing in on him all afternoon, Gunner was out there targeting Rafe. Dave's only real worry was Luke. He made gigantic "iceballs" by packing mounds of snow together super hard on the ground. They were enormous, and came in at terrific speed because he didn't throw them; he flung them with a whipping motion of his arm. An iceball could take you out. You had to keep an eye on Luke every second. That wasn't easy, not with shots coming in from half a dozen angles. Dave imagined Luke's throwing motion being similar to the great pitcher Satchel

Paige, except Satchel came off an enormous leg kick, then threw, where Luke ran up to the fence and whirled around. The word was Satchel's pitches shrunk down to the size of peas on the way in. Iceballs looked like miniature planets coming at you. Satch played for the Kansas City Monarchs in the old Negro League when they barnstormed across America before WW II. Dave was pretty sure his dad had umpired one of their games because he said Satchel scared batters to death, that a lot of the hitters never even saw the ball. And he should know, he had a baseball Satchel autographed.

The action picked up. Dave forgot about unorthodox windups and souvenirs. A string of snowballs came at him. He hunched around, felt them hit his back, ducked down, stood up and fired. It was give and take for the next few minutes.

Gunner got off a shot.

"Gonna havta do a lot better than that," Dave chided, slapping it away.

There was a lull.

"I'm not Mr. Chicken Liver hidin' behind a wall," Gunner said, slipped his hands into his armpits and flapped his elbows like wings. "Baw Ba-Bawk Bawwwk."

With both sides scrambling to rearm, Dave ignored the comment. The melee resumed. The air was full of white streaks, the dull thud of packed snow crashing into coats, trousers, and, on occasion bare flesh. Dave's team forced the attackers back then the tide turned. A snowball hit the top of the wall and broke against his chest. He dodged another. Doug, standing next to him, went to block one with his arm. It hit his wrist and splattered across his face. He stumbled backwards. Dave started to laugh as Doug tried to wipe the snow from his glasses. Thwack—Splat, Dave hit the ground. For an instant he was conscious of only one sensation, a searing pain coming from the right side of his face. It felt like his mouth and eye had been pushed across to his nose. His ear was ringing. There was no other sound. He ripped off his glove in a panic, put his hand to his cheek. It was raw and burned like fire. He felt around his eye, moved his jaw. Both stung like needles had been thrust into them. He couldn't see. He heard laughter. There was a huge, dark figure looming over him. He blinked his eyes but they were watering and wouldn't focus.

"Still gettin' ya for the igloo," Rafe snickered. "Don't get the idea we're even."

Dave dragged himself back from the wall so he wouldn't get stepped on and lay there. An iceball—he'd taken a direct hit, never saw it coming. So much for keeping your guard up. No one seemed to care that he was down. He rubbed his cheek again and worked his jaw. "Aw," it hurt something awful. Chunks of snow hit all around him. His teammates scooped them up, returned fire. He covered his face. The ferocious battle above raged on. He got to his feet and was pelted numerous times. "I'm out!" he yelled as he walked toward the house. A snowball whizzed past his head. He put a hand up to protect his face. "I said I'm out!" He knew his friends thought he'd gotten just what he deserved.

Dave sat down on the steps, exactly where he'd been the day before, vowing never to get into another snowball fight unless he was on Luke's side. His head ached. So did his jaw. Mrs. Norris came out the back door with a clothes basket under one arm. He slid over to let her by.

"What happened to you?" she asked.

"Got smacked—good too."

"You kids play too rough," she said, registering her displeasure.

Dave noticed the basket then he noticed that many of the articles of clothing hanging from the clothes line behind the fort had round white splotches on them. He saw that his mother's free hand was on her hip. There was a frown on her face. That was a bad sign. He got the look he thought his dad had gotten when he slipped up.

"Well," she said, standing there, "What do you have to say for yourself?"

Dave glanced at the clothes again, closed his eyes and shook his head. The action had stopped. The gladiators were watching to see what would happen next. Without a word Mrs. Norris opened the door and disappeared into the house. Dave's buddies took the hint and left. He sat there rubbing his head, not knowing what to do. He was wet and dreadfully cold. Mrs. Norris reappeared and slapped a stiff brush into his hand, he got the look again, and without a word, she was gone. Dave went to work that second. Mom was still angry when she returned and started placing the clothes in the basket.

"Why do you think I waited until today? It's hard on the clothes if you have to fold them when they're frozen."

Dave kept on brushing, "I didn't see 'em," he said.

"Maybe I'll have you hang them out next time!"

Dave didn't reply. He couldn't remember when he'd had such a run of bad luck. The mumps, the igloo, an iceball—a snowball fight was supposed to be fun.

CHAPTER 9
RED DIRT

D ave and his mom took the telescope out again. They found the
North Star off the spoon end of the Big Dipper and looked at the
moon, then used a flashlight and the book that came with the instrument, to
locate the constellations that weren't obscured by trees. Dave hoped some of
Luke's enthusiasm would rub off on him but he knew it wouldn't.

When they were back in the house he started thinking. You had to find
something, at least one thing, you were really interested in, something challenging that made your days enjoyable. If you did, you'd have the world on
a string. Life would be worthwhile and exciting. If not, everything you did
would be drudgery and for work, you'd have to make do with whatever came
along.

The January thaw arrived. For the first time in weeks the sidewalks were
mostly free of snow. Dave was euphoric and off to the Razyniak's as soon
as the cab stopped and he signaled his mom through the kitchen window.
Without boots, his feet felt like feathers. Every step was a delight. *How,*
he wondered, *could people take walking and running for granted?* He sped
along, climbed the sloped driveway at Luke's effortlessly. The paper bundles were still sitting at the curb. That was strange. The "Blue Beast," the
Razyniak's Studebaker station wagon, was gone. The house had that empty
feel about it. The boys must be somewhere with their mom. Dave went
around to the back door anyway and stepped up onto the porch. As he
reached for the doorbell, he stopped dead on the spot. Something wasn't
right. He turned to his right, looked over his shoulder. One of the patches of
snow that still covered the grass, the one next to the drive way, had streaks
of reddish brown dirt on it.

Dave swung off the porch, peeked around the corner of the house, glanced down once more at the dirt then made a break for the garage. He rounded it and was in the alley. Once there he breathed a sigh of relief. It was obvious the Razyniak's hadn't, as yet, discovered what he had, but they soon would. He stepped forward, slipped, fell backwards and caught himself with an outstretched arm. When he straightened up, his hand was covered with freezing cold, soupy mud. The alley was a quagmire, a tangle of ruts. Some areas were frozen, others were boggy. Domes of what looked to be quicksand, pushed up by car tires, lay in wait here and there. He decided to take his chances on the ruts. He inched ahead and slipped again, this time barely saving himself with an awkward step to the left. Slurp, his foot sank deep into a mound of gritty ooze. It rolled over into his shoe. This wasn't going to work. He weighed his options. He was almost a block from home and couldn't go back the way he'd come. Continuing on wasn't a possibility. The only alternative was to cut through Biever's yard across the alley from Luke's and take Johnson Street to Vassar. It was the long way around but he could get home safe on a dry sidewalk and no one would know he'd seen the dirt.

Biever's yard was littered with spent rockets. Some lay decomposing in the grass, others protruded at odd angles from the remaining snow. There looked to be dozens. If someone came out he'd get it for sure. He couldn't hang around to pick them up because his foot was freezing so he went on ahead and hoped for the best. As he made the right turn onto Vassar he saw steely, blue gray smoke ahead on O'Brien Street. The Blue Beast had just gone past.

Dave had no idea why the various bits of information came together like they did while he was there on the Razyniak's porch. Red dirt was subsoil. It was the middle of winter. The ground was frozen. Where had it come from? The Razyniak's basement was off limits because of Mr. R's deer heads and the darkroom they were building for Luke along the back wall. The basement windows were covered with plywood, supposedly to keep out light in case Luke was developing film. All the pieces of the puzzle fit. The Razyniak's were building a bomb shelter, had to be. It was underground next to the house just feet from where he'd been standing. One of the boys had been assigned to carry dirt upstairs, no doubt in buckets, after dark. Along the way some spilled out. Later that night it snowed, so nobody knew. Then today, the bright sun exposed it, coincidentally, just before Dave arrived and on a day Mrs. R was late getting home with the boys. Sure, it was all conjecture but where else could the dirt have come from?

Dave's first stop when he got home was the basement. The metal ankle bearings on his brace were grinding with every step he took. After he cleaned the mud off his shoes and took off his sock he'd have to wash them out with oil. Until he did that he didn't dare go into the house.

Dave could see the Razyniak brothers and their dad hard at work on the shelter. First they'd bust through the basement wall's concrete blocks then they'd go to shoveling. A few feet out they'd shore up the dirt overhead. Working below the frost line would make digging easy and the frozen ground above would lend extra support. Mr. R. could dispose of the debris a little at a time on his way to work each day. Who'd be the wiser?

If you built a bomb shelter, you had to do it in secret. That was the revelation that had come to him on the porch. Not a soul could know you had one. If they did, if the unthinkable actually happened and you had need of it, wouldn't all your neighbors who survived the initial attack want in? With limited space, food and water, what would you do? What would they do? Wouldn't the situation degenerate? Wouldn't primal instincts of self preservation kick in? Would neighbor kill neighbor out of desperation? Would deranged citizens murder their friends to save themselves? Ugly possibilities to be sure, but it could happen. Most humans simply couldn't deal with so terrible a reality. That's why there was a lot of talk but no dirt had been "turned."

If you built a hidden, underground shelter no one knew about, you'd be safe from the radiation and any people left around. That was the connection Dave had missed. That's what, in an instant, had come to him. What his dad had been saying all along suddenly made sense. Now, along with the coin, he had another thing he couldn't talk about.

He had a million questions. Could they really be building one? Was it located where he thought? Would it be made of metal like the culverts alongside roads? Could they get the curved sections down the narrow stairs?

This Boston Blackie gumshoe stuff was fun. Dave debated his next move. He could hide in the bushes after dark, stakeout the Razyniak's back yard. He could try to talk his way downstairs or bide his time until the dark room was finished then look for clues when he got the tour. Whatever he did, no matter how he went about it, he had to play it smart. He couldn't let on he knew. He couldn't betray his friends.

Rafe, Gunner and Ron gathered at Dave's for Central's game against Logansport, the matter of the gassing, seemingly having resolved itself. With Central winning big, as usual, it would have been another heady night if the Norris' hadn't received a bright crimson post card in the mail the week before. It was time for Dave's check-up at Shriners. He knew it'd be about three months from when he got home in the fall, but that was somewhere off in the future, so the anxiety stayed mostly in the back of his mind. As the time approached, it began to slip in whenever he wasn't occupied with something else. Finally, on the Friday in question, the tension peaked and displaced all his other thoughts. He kept reminding himself that nothing bad ever happened on a check-up. It didn't help much. Hopefully that would soon change. Shriners only took kids until they were fifteen. He'd be fourteen in June. If they felt he was doing well enough, the bad times might be over. It was a wonderful thought, but he wasn't chancing being disappointed.

Friday was rough, but not near as bad as he expected. He struggled with breakfast, slept in the car on the way as usual, sensed the roundhouse curve at Michigan City and smelled the stench from the oil refineries when they passed Gary. After that, though, he was awake and mostly O.K.

"What the Shriners do for youngsters, well, it's just short of a miracle," Mr. Norris remarked. "Things no one would have dreamed possible even a few years ago."

"What your father's saying, is that while it's difficult now, you'll appreciate what they've done for you when you're older," Mrs. Norris added.

"S'pose," Dave said. "But if it's so expensive, why they do it?"

"Because of the satisfaction they get knowing they've made a difference in another person's life," Mr. Norris explained. "Think how it must feel to know a young person who has their whole life ahead of them can walk because of what you've done. You're one of those youngsters. I know it's been a rough road, but you keep making progress like you have been and there's no telling how far you can go."

During the examination Dave had to strip down to his underwear and show the doctors what worked on the legs. They checked to see how successful the most recent operations had been; then he had to walk back and forth for them. They knelt down in a line behind and in front, watched his every move intently, contemplated and made notes on his chart. After that they huddled around his X-rays on the light bar while he was out of ear shot. He had no idea what they were saying. They talked to Dad awhile and he was out the door.

"The doctors are very satisfied with your progress," Mr. Norris said, once they'd returned to the car.

"Your next appointment isn't for six months," Mrs. Norris smiled.

"That's—that won't be until almost August," Dave said, surprised.

He was hungry and reached into the cooler for the half sandwich he hadn't finished at lunch. Except for the igloo incident, Dave thought he was doing better, too. He hadn't mentioned a word about the coin or the bomb shelter, not to anyone. School was going good. He was getting on fine.

The Norris' were off for a festive afternoon at the Science and Industry Museum on Chicago's lake front. His check-up only a memory, Dave could hardly wait. The Science and Industry Museum, one of Chicago's finest attractions, was his favorite. It had fighter planes hanging from the ceiling, a captured German submarine you could tour, an underground coal mine and an old fashioned ice cream parlor. Dave and his sister each demolished a dome of chocolate in a waffle cone there. Life was fun when you were in control, instead of when it was the other way around.

Dave had settled on a bomb shelter strategy. He'd just play it cool. There'd be a screw up somewhere along the way. There always was in the movies he watched. If he kept his eyes open he'd eventually have his proof. Course, he'd have to act like he hadn't noticed whatever it was that gave it away. Having the satisfaction of knowing he'd done it by being cagey, that'd be the best part.

It occurred to Dave that the Razyniaks might already have completed the shelter. If that were the case, he was off on a wild goose chase. But they couldn't have. It was simple math. Five people, an extended stay, it all had to do with the dirt. You couldn't build an underground structure until you removed the dirt, even if you built it in stages. He could estimate its size and the amount they'd have to remove, how many bucket loads it'd take, how much time they'd had since they could use the taxidermy and darkroom as cover, the amount the Studebaker could carry at a time without sagging. Fortunately, Dave liked these types of problems, and the way he figured it, they still had plenty of work to do.

January faded into February, February into March. During that time they had another bad snow. Mrs. Norris carried the canister around the neighborhood to collect donations for the March of Dimes, Dave got to see his first Central game in a month and the F.B.I. broke up a Russian spy ring in upstate New York. Dave found that manufacturing aerial bombs was just as challenging as making sky rockets, maybe more. He also found that playing detective was a lot harder than it looked on T.V. A comment Luke made that the cold had cut into his work time on the telescope was the only thing that remotely resembled a clue.

Mr. Norris was grumpy and complained a lot about money destroying the sanctity of sports, though Mickey Mantle's sixty thousand dollar deal with the Yankees didn't seem to bother him. Of course then, the Yankees were his team.

"You watch," he'd say, "the way the West Coast interests are wining and dining O'Malley—they throw enough money his way he'll sell out Brooklyn in nothing flat. Los Angeles Dodgers, huh."

One day Dave got a sturdy brown envelope in the mail. It was from Werner von Braun, the great German rocket scientist who came to the United States after the war. Inside, was an 8 by 10 glossy photograph of him looking up from his desk and an encouraging letter. Dave had written him earlier, after reading about the German rocket program in a magazine he got from Meyer. The picture and letter were a big hit at school, though he was extra careful to see that neither got damaged. After the cab dropped him off and he had a snack, he lit out, envelope in hand, for Rafe's. He'd just crossed Vassar Street when there was a tremendous boom that almost knocked him off his feet. The packet flew out of his hand and came to rest in the gutter near a puddle. He looked up hoping to spot something against the sky then scrambled to retrieve it. This was the loudest sonic boom he'd ever heard. Mrs. Babcock, a friend of Mom's, called from her porch to ask if he was O.K. He held up a hand and said he was. These sudden, sharp claps, similar to thunder, were produced by jet fighters flying at supersonic speeds. The trailing waves, racing along the ground behind, could do real damage. Mostly, they just scared people, angering some, reassuring others. A few people did venture out to see if any of their windows had broken.

Rafe and Gunner didn't respond with that much enthusiasm to his new treasure so he took it down to Luke's.

"Heck, I nearly jumped outta my skin," he said, as he watched the brothers fold newspapers on the front porch. "Bet it was an F-104.They got the new J-79 engine, same's the B-58 bomber."

"I didn't think they were allowed to fly that fast over land anymore," Pete said.

"It was probably a training loop out over Lake Michigan," Luke commented, "and they didn't cut back on their power soon enough."

"'Member, last year on the news," Dave said, "when that guy kicked a can a paint off the scaffolding at the apartment house?"

"Yep," Pete replied, "and some of it splashed on a convertible."

"Corvette," Tim chuckled, "with the top down."

"And the owner flipped out," Dave snickered.

"Wouldn't you?" Luke asked.

"Yeah," Dave replied. "Say, gonna get your telescope done by, when was it?"

"April fifteenth, and it'll be close. That's when the comet will be visible in the Northern Hemisphere."

"Dad's taxes, too," Dave interjected.

It was time for March Madness, the Indiana High School Basketball Tournament. Central was going in with a chance to win its second state title in four years and go undefeated in the process, something that had only been done once before. Mr. Norris was out of town again, working another tournament, so Mr. Rasco filled in. There was something special about going to a big game with friends, even if Rafe and Gunner did lean hard into him every time the car rounded a corner.

"I'd like to stay, but there's business to attend to," Mr. Rasco explained, once he'd stopped in front of Adams' gymnasium where the Sectional was being played. "I'll pick you boys up here when the afternoon session's over then I'll bring you back tonight."

It was the atmosphere, the winning, that made a Central game so great: the band, the cheering, tasty snacks, another opponent biting the dust, the fight song, half the time you couldn't hear yourself think. It was wonderful. When Dave got home he started to tell his mom about his grand experience.

"The games were on television," she said.

"They were?" he exclaimed. Then he realized this was the first time his mother had seen Central in action. "They're somethin' aren't they?"

"Yes, they are," Mrs. Norris replied. "I wonder how far we might have gone if they'd had a women's tournament when I played?"

The evening's challenger went down to defeat as effortlessly as had the afternoons. Central owned another trophy.

The Elkhart Regional, the next Saturday, pitted four Sectional winners against each other. Mr. Rasco planned to accompany the boys at night, and take them in the afternoon, but they'd have to find their own way home between sessions. The search was on. Who did they know that was going? Better yet, who did they know that was going and had four empty seats? That was an altogether different and much harder nut to crack. They weren't even in high school yet and nobody they knew drove.

"Look," Ron said, "if we can't find anybody, Dad's working Saturday. He wants to know one way or the other on Friday so he can tell the mechanics."

The days came and went. The boys didn't have a single prospect. By Thursday, Dave was resigned, then Friday after school, Rafe called.

"I got us a ride," he said.

"Really, who'd ya get?" Dave asked excitedly.

"This kid Lester, know 'im from school. His dad's got a big ol' wagon with extra seats he uses for work, says we can ride along, but he's only bringin' us back as far as town, then we havta take the bus home."

"Ya call Ron?"

"Just did. It's all set."

"Great," Dave said. "Great."

Dave expected that the conversation on the way to Elkhart would center on the upcoming games. It did, but the games were baseball games and the team was the Yankees. Dave supposed that was because the Bears totally outclassed the opposition so far and were favored to win today's games by huge margins.

"Nobody'll beat the Yanks this year," Gunner proclaimed, with an air of authority.

"For sure," Rafe agreed, "not with Mantle and Larsen signed."

Yankees, Yankees, Yankees, Dave was sick of hearing about them. He got it at home, he was getting it here, and opening day was weeks away.

"I hear Mantle's gettin' a bundle," Rafe said.

"Sixty grand," Dave replied in a drawl, "and Larson's gettin' seventeen."

"Selling your services for whatever you can get, that's free enterprise," Mr. Rasco said, thumping the steering wheel. "That's the American way."

Dave was keeping an eye out for cars decorated with orange and blue and pointing them out when he saw one. To hear his dad or Mr. Rasco talk, you'd think we didn't need jet planes and atomic bombs to keep the Russians at bay. Just send the Yankees over and let them handle it. And even if what Mr. Rasco said was true, Dave didn't think it was right that ballplayers got paid oodles more than the doctors who'd helped him, but then, the Yankees weren't all that bad. He might even be for them if his dad wasn't. Mantle was Dad's guy.

"A clean cut farm kid and with those knees, he can hardly walk," Mr. Norris would say. "What he's accomplished, why, it's amazing."

Dave could repeat that refrain from memory. He liked Yogi Berra because Yogi cobbled words together into wacky phrases that sounded crazy but made sense in a twisted sort of a way. When you heard one of his "Yogi-isms" you were certain to screw up your face and shake your head. "It ain't over 'til it's over." "When you come to a fork in the road, take it."

Rafe and Gunner were keen on Elston Howard and spent most of their time talking about him.

"You boys have enough money?" Mr. Rasco asked, when he dropped them off.

They replied that they did.

"You're O.K. then?" he asked again.

"Sure," Rafe said, walking away.

Dave wondered. He'd never heard of this Lester character before. That seemed odd, but with eight thousand fans cramming into the cracker box arena the games were being held in, that was for later. Dave was a little more jittery than he had been, afraid some team would play way over its head and spoil Central's perfect season. His dad always said any team could beat any other team on a given night. It was a feeling he could never quite shake until Central had a sizable lead. That happened from the tip off. Central was out to a twelve point lead almost before the game started. The Elkhart Blue Blazers wouldn't be the Cinderella team today. The second game featured Plymouth and Pierston, two small towns located south of South Bend. They were scrappy competitors, but not of much interest to Dave and his pals. As far as they were concerned it was two hick teams fighting it out to see who'd lose to Central that night.

The place was a mad house when the games ended. It was hard for Dave and his friends to stay together.

"Where's the car?" Dave shouted, as he struggled to keep up.

"Hold on, I'm lookin'," Rafe snapped. "Said they'd park—wait up, over here," he yelled, pointing to a battered station wagon well back in the parking lot.

"We're taking that?" Ron exclaimed.

"Yep," Gunner smiled evasively.

"Yo, Lester," Rafe said, greeting the heavy set boy clutching a crumpled program.

"Move the stuff that's in your way," Lester said.

Looking in, Dave and Ron hesitated, then fired apprehensive glances at Rafe who acted like he didn't notice. The instant the door opened they'd been engulfed by an overpowering, extremely pungent odor.

"Go ahead, get in, it's all right," reassured the equally heavy set man behind the steering wheel. "We'll get all that cleaned out of there one of these days."

The seat furthest back was heaped with refuse and it took some doing just to make room for everyone. Once In, Dave took stock of what looked to be six months' trash: rumpled shopping bags, smashed cans, tons of old newspapers, rags and hundreds of empty bottles, and, something furry partially buried in a pile of dried leaves under the seat.

"Is it alive?" Ron mouthed.

Dave moved his head slightly after first stabbing it with a stick. Dave and Ron tried to get Rafe's attention with a nudge. He continued to gaze straight ahead with a stony stare, a slight twitch of an arm, his only response. They could see he was struggling mightily to maintain control and almost lost theirs.

"Y'all enjoy the games?"

"Sure did Dad," Lester replied enthusiastically, as he turned to look back from the front seat. "Beat 'em bad didn't we?"

"Tore 'em up," Rafe responded, with the same blank expression.

"Oh, sorry there," Lester's dad said to Gunner, who was starting to roll down a window from the middle seat. "You'll have to run that back up. Don't want anything blowing out, you know, littering."

At that Gunner started sputtering and put a hand over his face.

Lester's dad glanced up into the rear view mirror. "Anything wrong there?" he asked.

"No, I'm O.K.," Gunner hurriedly replied. "It's the cold air—makes my nose run."

Quick thinking, Dave thought.

Lester's dad pulled a disgusting, what had once been a white handkerchief, from his pants pocket.

"Here Junior, pass this back," he said, "and I'll turn up the heat."

Gunner looked horrified. "No, really, I'm fine!" he replied, a hint of panic in his voice.

Lester held out the filthy cloth. Gunner, still sputtering, waved him off. Lester persisted, held it out further and paused. Dave was squeezing his leg, digging in with his nails again. Rafe still gazing straight ahead, sat with fists and teeth clinched. Ron, petrified, looked ready to explode. Lester swished the hankie through the air for what seemed like hours, frowned and handed it back to his dad. His dad turned on some sappy music Lester knew all the words to. With him happily singing along, the tension eased. Not another word was spoken until the car reached the bus stop on Colfax Street.

"Thanks," Rafe said, raising a hand, as the rusty hulk left them at the curb.

"For what?" Dave scolded, "bringin' us in that piece a junk. Thought we were friends."

"What was that terrible smell?" Ron asked. "My eyes were watering."

"Mostly that was Lester," Gunner grinned and he and Rafe burst into a howl of laughter.

"I couldn't tell with all the trash," Ron said.

"Wouldina been so bad if someone hadn't lost it and ol' Dad cranked up the heat," Dave added. "I 'bout died."

"Hey," Gunner bristled, "how was I s'posed ta know there were rules 'bout the windows?"

"Yeah, you want as much fresh air as you can get when you're 'round Lester," Rafe cut in. "And ya don't wanna be downwind from 'im either. We call 'im Stanky at school."

Rafe and Gunner were rolling in laughter, the more so, because Dave was angry.

"Wonder why? And he's a friend a yours?" Dave snapped.

"Get off it," Rafe growled. "He thinks we're cool 'cause we play sports, that's all. Stanky hadina brung us, we'da missed the games."

"Still coulda told us," Dave said, sensing he'd made a mistake.

"Yeah, well, Monday it'll be all over school that Stanky's got new friends, that's gonna be fun."

"Sorry," Dave said.

"You'da jabbed me one more time, I'da exploded," Rafe smirked.

At that, they all laughed.

The O'Brien Street bus arrived. As they got on, Gunner poked Dave in the ribs. "Lester's gotta sister," he snickered.

After supper, the boys were back in Mr. Rasco's big Lincoln and very glad to be there.

"Unless I miss my guess," he said, "we'll be celebrating Central as Regional champs on the way home."

"That'll be neat Dad, for your first away game," Ron remarked.

"Be Pierceton's last," Dave chuckled. "Just hope they don't stall all night."

"Ball control is the only weapon these farm clubs have," Mr. Rasco commented. "Running with Central would be suicide. Slowing it down, looking for openings, it's their only chance."

Mr. Rasco was dead on. Even with the "B" team in most of the second half, Central couldn't keep from boosting up the score.

"It'll be much harder from here on out," he remarked, as the group walked through the parking lot. "All the weaker teams have been defeated." Mr. Rasco fumbled with his key ring a long time at the car. "Aw, here it is," he said, opening the door.

The dome light didn't come on. "It must have burnt out," he noted.

Dave froze. It was another of those moments.

"Gettin' in or not?" Rafe carped.

"Gimme a second," Dave barked. "I'm thinkin'."

"I thought your dad told you to quit doing that," Ron quipped.

Dave smiled. Ron didn't often enter into the give and take.

A clue, Dave had a real clue, something that might actually be important. He knew the dome light had been out in the Blue Beast. As they drove along he racked his brain, trying to recall when that was. Then he remembered it'd been out a couple times. Was there a connection between that and the bomb shelter project? You couldn't load in buckets of dirt after dark with the car's dome light coming on all the time. Your neighbors would know something was up the first night. Had they removed the bulb, then replaced it? Did they forget and leave it out? Dave knew the Beast's wiring was screwed up. Tim had told him that his dad once turned on the wipers and the radio came on, or maybe it was when they hit a bump. Dave wasn't for sure. He just knew he had a lead, a hot new lead that would make Blackie's mouth water and he was going to pursue it, if he could, and see where it led.

Dave felt something hit his shoulder.

"Hey! Hey! You awake over there?" Rafe asked.

"Huh, yeah, sure," Dave replied.

"Bet ya don't even know where we are?" Gunner challenged.

"Sure I do." Dave said, looked out the window. "I can read, Bonnie Doon."

"Did ya hear Mr. Rasco say he'd buy and we can order anything we want?"

"Really?"

"Hold on there," Mr. Rasco corrected. "That's all you can eat, but you must eat everything you order. We aren't wasting food."

Dave debated and debated then went for broke.

"Guess I'll have a banana boat," he ventured, a hint of uncertainty in his voice.

"And one more banana boat," Mr. Rasco said to the bubble gum chewing carhop who was anxiously waiting.

Rafe and Gunner jeered and pushed Dave around.

"You can't eat all that," Rafe snorted.

Banana boats were huge: three giant scoops of ice cream, a whole banana, all the extras; you could hardly hold the hull shaped dish in one hand. It was big even for Rafe and Gunner who snickered and laughed the whole time he ate. Dave got it down, but he didn't know how. Mr. Rasco dropped him off first. As the car pulled away, and with the Scanner brothers peering through the rear window, Dave almost heaved in the street. You could learn a lot from a banana boat.

It seemed Dave had hardly dropped off to sleep when he heard his mother's voice. When she called again, he practically leaped out of bed, knowing his dad would be in if he didn't. Even then, he nearly made his family late for church. There he was, listening to Reverend Gray's sermon on the power of prayer, inspecting the collection plate, just trying to stay awake, and extremely anxious to get home. On Sundays this time of year, there was always a shoot-around on his court in the time between church and the noon meal. Rafe and Gunner would already be playing when he got home and Ron and Doug would arrive shortly after that. Today, Pete was there.

Dave had the door open before the car stopped and was ready to sprint the forty or so feet to join in the fun.

"Hold on there," Mrs. Norris said, "your clothes first."

Dave's brace tore up pants and he wasn't always careful about changing when he was in a hurry. A two minute delay and he grabbed his first rebound.

"Where's Luke?" he asked.

"He's not coming," Pete said, sliding his foot along the pavement then firing in a ten footer. "He sent his mirror out to have the final grinding done and the silvering put on. It came in the mail yesterday. You won't see him for a while."

"Wow, that was fast," Dave remarked. "Think I'll go down and check it out after lunch."

"I wouldn't advise it," Pete said. "He doesn't want anybody hanging around. Everything's got to be perfect."

Rafe took a jump shot that careened off the rim. Gunner grabbed the rebound and took it out of bounds.

"Here they come," Pete said.

Ron and Doug were jogging down the alley toward them.

Sunday morning basketball was fast and furious. You didn't have that long to play. You didn't have to worry about being late for dinner either, because Holy Cross Church, located across from Muessel Park at the corner of Vassar and Wilber Streets, had Mass at eleven o'clock. A lot of pre-teens who wanted to sleep in, fulfilled their obligation at that time. Most walked past Dave's house alone, a few with a sibling or friend, all quietly reflective, neatly dressed and carrying a missal. As they walked along, they looked straight ahead as though they thought playing basketball on Sunday morning was irreverent and anybody involved must be a delinquent. After Mass they'd return. When about half had passed by, the game broke up. Dave thought his friends were very respectable, though at the moment he might be violating a commandment by gawking at the pretty girl in the white dress across the street. He didn't know how long he did that, but in an instant, any doubts these adolescents may have had about him and his friends vanished. There was a commotion behind him. As he turned he saw Rafe and Gunner going at it. Cussing and punching, Rafe finally pushed off and ran for it. A tall, skinny, red haired kid was coming by. They got their legs tangled up. The missal leaped out of his hand. Gunner jumped Rafe and downed him on the tree lawn next to the sidewalk, more punching. The boy regained his balance, dodged a flailing leg with a nifty bit of footwork, picked up his missal and barely breaking stride, walked on without looking back. Dave was amazed. Suddenly he heard a loud shrill voice in his ears.

"You two quit that scuflin right now!"

It sounded exactly like Mrs. Scanner's voice, but the words had come out of his mouth. A chill ran down his back. He was suddenly afraid, very afraid. So much for thinking before you act. Rafe somehow got away and with Gunner in hot pursuit, the two disappeared around the corner house on O'Brien. Dave wasn't sure, but he thought they might not have heard what he said.

"You're crazy!" Doug exclaimed. "They could've killed you."

"I didn't even know I said it," Dave replied, gesturing with his hands.

"I was going to ask how you felt after all that ice cream last night," Ron jabbed, "but your life expectancy is probably so short now, why bother."

On that encouraging note, Pete, Ron and Doug went home and Dave went in the house.

He was angry with himself. Here he'd been trying so hard and slipped so badly. He shuddered. What if those two had turned on him in a fit of rage?

Now what? There wouldn't be anything to do this afternoon, and he wasn't hiding out. The garage, he'd clean the garage: rearrange everything, sweep up all the dirt the car had brought in over winter. Cleaning, like raking, was fun, if no one made you do it. He moved some of the bigger items to the driveway then stacked smaller ones on them. Next, he brushed all the cobwebs from a back corner and lined up the broken ball bats lying around in case he got a lathe. He was doing that when he heard the mower handle clank into his grandma's old Hoosier cabinet. He looked up. There, silhouetted against the bright sunlight, standing side by side in the doorway, were two giants. It was Rafe and Gunner. Dave's heart started to pound.

"I thought..."

"You thought nothin'!" Rafe growled, taking a step toward him. Gunner followed suit. Rafe's face had two nasty welts on it and swelling around one eye. Gunner's didn't look any better. There was no escape. It was over. Dave began to tremble.

"We just got ta sit through an hour's lecture," Rafe gripped. "Our mom says if there's any more scufflin' we're grounded and she means business this time."

Dave gulped.

"Yeah," Gunner continued. "We get in another fight we won't be able ta do nothin'."

"That means ya can't hit me," Dave exclaimed, looking over his shoulder.

Rafe took another step. "Sure we can," he said. "It'd be worth it ta pound somebody who tried ta make a fool of us."

Rafe and Gunner were practically on top of him. He leaned backwards as far as he could. The table behind him collapsed. He fell hard on his back. Rafe lunged. Dave twisted to protect his face and smashed his nose against a flower pot. It started to bleed. Something struck him on the arm. It was the roll of paper towels he'd brought out to do the garage window. "Wha." There was laughing. Rafe and Gunner were gleefully hopping around, their puffy faces twisted into grotesque smiles. Ron and Doug were standing behind them.

"What are you guys doin' here?" Dave growled.

"Enjoyin' themselves same's we are," Rafe sputtered. "Mom says we can't play any more sports where we havta guard each other 'til school's out, so we're playin' whiffle ball. Stopped by Ron's on the way ta gettin' one. You get ta call the other guys."

"S'pose I could," Dave said, nervously wiping his nose.

Dave promised himself that the next time there was an altercation, he'd be a spectator, not a participant.

Whiffle ball was the spring and summer pastime in the neighborhood, at least until the boys got bored and moved on to something else. It was a perfect game for hot weather because it wasn't regular baseball. They played "over the line" behind Rafe's garage with a hollow plastic softball that had large holes in it. In over the line there were landmarks like the big "singles" rock behind Rafe's garage. Whichever one you hit the ball past, if it was on a fly and wasn't caught, it was the same as if you were on that base. If a teammate hit successfully, you advanced accordingly or were forced in. It was a game Dave could play because you didn't have to run, and when you stood in to bat, the pitcher had to throw the ball where you wanted it.

The minute that afternoon's game ended, Ron pulled Dave aside. "When are you going to ask him?"

"Tonight, if he's in a good mood." Dave replied.

"What happened to your nose?" Mr. Norris inquired at supper.

"I leaned against that wobbly table in the garage while I was cleanin' and it broke."

"Let's be more careful next time."

"Don't worry! I will!"

After supper Dave cornered his dad. "Can we take the other kids with us ta see Central play at Fort Wayne? They wanna go real bad."

"I've been wondering when you'd ask? I'm afraid six would make the car too crowded."

"Six?"

"Stu is riding along."

"Stu, why's he goin'?"

"He's good company on the long drives I have to make. You know that."

"But Central's undefeated."

"I'm sorry, I gave my word. We'll have room for two extra, no more, and that's only if I can find tickets."

Now what was he going to do? Even though they'd had problems lately, Rafe was a great friend who rode him all over on his bike. Gunner loved to talk sports with his dad. Ron was sort of a confidant because he didn't have nosy brothers snooping around and could keep a secret. How could he choose between them? He started to hope one of them would catch the flu or sprain an ankle during the week. Then he wondered if he'd even get to go. Tickets would be scarce as hen's teeth. He remembered the story about Milan. There was a thirteen mile long traffic jam when they won State in '54 and Milan barely qualified as a town. That's how it was at tournament time in Indiana. The next day he had to fend off a barrage of questions.

"Do'no," he fibbed, "depends if Dad can scrounge any tickets."

"When ya think ya'll know?" Rafe queried.

"I'm not askin' 'til Thursday, 'cause he's startin' on taxes. You know, 'cause he works for so many different companies."

"Thought he always waits 'til the last minute on that?" Gunner questioned.

"Does, but it caused lots of trouble with Mom last year, so now there's stacks of papers all over the dining room table. He's spendin' hours sortin'."

Dave's story about the tickets must have gone over because the subject turned to Fort Wayne South, the Bear's next opponent. They had a seven foot center who was supposed to be pretty good.

On Wednesday Mr. Norris pulled Dave aside.

"Three tickets, that's all I've been able to find. There probably isn't another one available in the state. Two are on an aisle, you can take a friend and sit there. Stu can have the other one and I'll slip in with a sportswriter I know."

Great, three friends, one ticket. Maybe it'd be better if he couldn't take anyone along. The decision didn't have to be made immediately. He was off to Luke's. The word was out that you could visit now. As he started down the alley he saw smoke ahead and caught wind of a foul odor. It was unlike anything he'd ever smelled and seemed to be coming from the next house past Leon's on his side of the street. He couldn't be sure because that garage was set back from the alley and his view was blocked. He assumed someone was burning trash and didn't give it a second thought.

Coming closer, he saw that a roaring wood fire had been built beneath a giant cauldron propped up on rocks. Crackling and spitting sparks, the flames licking its sides nearly engulfed the pot. Filled with steamy liquid, a thick frothy goo roiled on its surface. A short frumpy woman wearing a babushka and black hooded robe that obscured much of her face, was dancing around it. Humming and singing along as if mesmerized, she was apparently having the time of her life. As Dave started past, she picked up a long pole that had been leaning against the garage and began to wave it menacing through the air. He angled right to give her a wider berth.

She stopped waving the pole, looked his way momentarily, plunged it into the pot and began stirring the concoction. She withdrew it part way, slid a finger down until it was wet then touched it to her tongue. Dave, unable to look away, watched her every move. The woman remained motionless for a time, working her tongue against her lips. She slowly turned toward him, frowned and pulled the pole from the kettle. Dave lurched forward a few ungainly steps and continued down the alley. The pungent odor, unpleasant earlier, was overwhelming now. Dave quickened his pace in an attempt to escape it. When he was another house away, he glanced back. The pole must have been leaning against the garage again because the woman was pouring something into the cauldron from an old milk bottle.

If there were actually such things as witches, he'd just seen one and she was brewing up an elixir of some sort right there on his block. Thing is, he didn't believe in witches, at least he didn't think he did. When Dave rounded the corner of the Razyniak's garage still looking back over his shoulder, Pete and Tim were playing catch in the yard. The minute they saw the expression on his face, they started to laugh.

"It's soap," Tim said. "She's making soap."

"Didn't know ya could do that," Dave remarked. "We get ours at the store."

"It's only granny people who still do it, immigrants who came over from the old country," Pete explained. "She does it every year in the spring. Dad says soap's made from fat and ashes."

"Musta been I was gone then. Doesn't suck blood does she?" Dave grinned playfully.

"You should've asked her," Pete came back.

"Why was she tastin' it?"

"That's how you know if it's too sharp, if it'll burn your skin," Pete said, snagging a one hopper. "Mom told us her grandpa did the same thing years ago on the farm."

"Glad we don't get that smell at my house," Dave scowled.

"For some reason she always does it when the winds blowing our way."

"Where's Luke?" Dave asked.

"In the basement," Tim motioned. "Go on down."

No time to get cute, Dave thought to himself, as he went into the house. Just stay calm.

The telescope, a gleaming white aluminum tube four feet long and eight inches in diameter, was lying on a makeshift table cushioned by a blanket. It was big. There were wooden blocks on either side to keep it from rolling off. The mirror was secured to its bracket in back. The eye piece was in place.

"Whoa! That—is—really—cool!" Dave said in slow distinct words.

On the floor next to the table stood a beautiful, hardwood, heavy-duty tripod.

"Looks great," Dave said, as he walked around the table inspecting the instrument. "Ya do all this yourself?"

"Pretty much," Luke replied, "except for the eyepiece. Oh, and the mirror bracket, that's a casting."

Dave worked his way around the instrument again, examining each part as he went.

124

"I'm pretty sure I'll have it finished before the comet's visible," Luke continued. "It's called Arend-Roland. It will be the brightest one since Haley's in 1910. My big challenge now is machining the mounting pieces that hold the telescope on the tripod and getting the camera together. Everyone thinks astronomy is about looking at the stars but it's not. It's about getting all the neat things out there on film so you can study them later."

Dave listened carefully as Luke explained how you aligned the mirror and brought the object you were observing into focus once the camera was installed.

"There's a film pack that slips into the camera," he said. "You replace it with a piece of ground glass, focus the image on that, then, without moving anything, replace the film and you're ready to shoot. The camera's in the darkroom. You wanna see?"

Dave felt the words, "Why ya think I came over!" forming, but forced them back and answered with an offhand, "sure."

The small, framed-out enclosure was exactly where Dave expected it to be. Luke opened the sturdy door and Dave walked in. It was finished off nicely. A large piece of corrugated metal was bolted to the back wall—big surprise. Luke pointed out the various trays required, the bottles containing developer, fixer and other chemicals, the timer, thermometer and red light.

"You can leave that on when you're working. It won't damage your film. Otherwise, the place is light tight."

"Where'd ya get the cabinets?"

"From Auntie. She had some friends who were remodeling. The enlarger used to be my uncle's."

"What's this?" Dave asked, pointing to a wire stretched overhead.

"You hang your film and the prints there to dry. The metal piece on the wall is there to channel the air. That was my idea."

"Yeah," Dave said, fighting the urge to be clever.

Luke went into detail. Dave said uh-huh a lot while he investigated. There was no grit underfoot or on the stair treads. No gray concrete dust in the corners that he could see. All the bolts holding the "air channeling panel" to the back wall had the same heads and appeared to be tight. Everything was in order. He was getting nowhere. The Razyniak's hadn't left a single item to chance.

"Hey, thanks for showin' me your set up," Dave said, once Luke had concluded the tour. "Think I'll take the street side home. Still some muddy spots in the alley."

That was true enough but there was also a spooky, very creepy lady with a wicked long pole he'd have to get past. And no matter what anyone said, he wasn't at all sure a few spells weren't being conjured while the soap cooked up in that blackened kettle.

"Hey, what happened ta the cover over your light?" Dave asked, when he returned to the porch. "Just noticed it's missin'."

"Aw, the nut or something came loose," Tim said, as he took a hard pitch straight in. "It broke into smithereens when it hit and we haven't found a replacement that fits."

Another clue? Dave pondered. Your hauling out dirt on the sly, can't have the porch light on while you're doing it. O.K., that makes sense. Wouldn't you just unscrew the bulb? Wasn't that likely how the cover got broken? That was dumb. Why wouldn't you just switch the light off? Then he remembered that there were only two switches on the wall inside the Razyniak's back door. One was for the light in the kitchen. The other—wait, the basement steps and outside light must be on the same circuit. Sure, they were always looking for ways to save money on houses built during the depression. You couldn't lug pails of dirt up a flight of stairs in the dark. Nobody'd do that. He must have it right. They were unscrewing the bulb and bang, the cover got dropped. Now he was getting somewhere. Biding his time and being cool was working out.

He walked past the Blue Beast and looked in. Nothing In particular caught his eye except that it was way cleaner than the vehicles most people owned.

On the way home Dave found himself violating another commandment. He was envious. Luke had a heck of a layout. All his friends either had paper routes or their families had more money than his did. They could buy stuff. He had to scrimp for everything. He didn't much like himself when thoughts like this went through his head.

The investigation was really picking up. The red dirt in the yard had mysteriously disappeared. There was the more than suspect air channeling panel on the darkroom's back wall, the broken porch light and nobody, nobody with three kids had a car that clean. Dave skipped along with a big smile on his face.

Thursday, what to do about the tickets? While they played "horse," Dave explained the situation to his friends. He wasn't choosing one over the others.

"We can only take one extra," he said. "Even Dad doesn't have an actual ticket."

Dave didn't know what his friends would do. He thought they'd roll for it or draw straws. It didn't happen. In fact, no one said anything for the longest time.

"Take Ron," Rafe said unexpectedly. "Me and Gunner'll watch it on T.V."

Problem solved. Dave was elated.

Chapter 10
FOUR GAMES TO GO

It was a long ride to Fort Wayne, most of the way across the state. Once out of the city Mr. Norris stopped for gas and went in for a cigar.

"Watch," Dave whispered, as he and Ron waited outside the restroom.

Through the car's windshield they could see Stu pull a thin, silver container from an inside coat pocket. He unscrewed the cap, tipped it nearly to vertical with a single motion, dropped it back down, wiped his lips and as quickly as it appeared, it was gone.

"See, it's just like I said. He can only go so long. Mom calls it his medicine bottle."

"I thought you were joking around."

"Heck no. Ten, fifteen minutes down the road, he'll be out like a light."

Stu was older, like Mr. Norris, and lived with his mother. He spent his days working at Drewry's Brewery and his evenings at his brother's tavern. Alcohol dominated his world and set the pattern of his life. Dave found him to be likable and always willing to lend a hand when he needed to get to his seat in the bleachers. He also discovered that Stu was a more complex person than he'd expected. One moment he was alert, witty, knowledgeable, the next, he was a sad, sorry soul.

They were on the road again, more baseball, the Dodgers. Dave and Ron occupied themselves watching the scenery roll by. It was spring. People were out of their houses now, doing things in their yards. Somehow Stu and Mr. Norris got off on nicknames: "The Iron Horse," "Satchel," "Hit-'Em-Where-They-Ain't Keeler." That was a guy Dave had never heard of. Stu faded away. As he did, his head slid sideways across the seat and came to rest against the passenger's side window. It was quiet. Dave gave Ron a nudge and motioned with his head. Every time the car hit a bump in the road or a wheel dropped into a pot hole Stu's head banged against the glass. He was totally unresponsive. For Ron, at least, it was an eye opening experience. Eventually the car hit a wide gap in the pavement. It shuddered, and with a final violent impact, roused Stu from his stupor.

They were traveling through Amish country now. Amish people rode around in austere black buggies pulled by black horses with black blinders. The men wore wide suspenders and had full beards. The women dressed in long flowing gowns and wore boxy white bonnets on their heads. Amish people were supposed to be serious and hardly ever smiled. Their houses didn't have electricity either. Dave found that very strange.

Dave felt Ron pinch his leg.

"Ouch, that hurts."

Ron had a big grin on his face and was frantically pointing down by his knee at an Amish lady who was walking across her yard toward a small building. Dave lit up.

"Hey, Mr. Stu," he said without thinking, "you ever tip outhouses like Dad?"

He could hear the words ringing in his ears and knew he was in trouble. Mr. Norris' face was there in the rear view mirror. If he wasn't careful he'd get a backhander. His dad had laid one of those on him a while back and, well, you never forgot it when you got a backhander. He pushed back into the seat so he'd be out of range.

"I've warned you about instigating," Mr. Norris scolded.

"Sorry, just slipped," Dave replied. "Try not ta do it again."

"It's O.K.," Stu mumbled. "Kid's just havin' a little fun. No, I never did anything like that. Now, we did have this one boy in class. As I remember, he got it for backing one up on April Fool's Day—it was pitch black that night."

"Who'd he get?" Dave asked, knowing he was riding the edge.

"Nobody. He slipped while he was pushing and fell in. It seems the ground along one side gave-way under foot. I didn't know him. Around school they called him 'Splash'—he lost his shoes."

Dave had struck pay dirt of a sort on this one, he was beaming. Stu was cool. Even Mr. Norris laughed.

A car passed them with "GO CENTRAL" painted on the windows. Dave and Ron waved. The teens inside held out orange and blue streamers.

"Say Dad, ya think Big John can handle that McCoy kid from Fort Wayne? He's eight inches taller."

"That may be, but John's eight inches wider. Remember McCoy can't get rebounds if he can't get close to the basket, and you can rest assured Mr. Coleman will see to it that he doesn't."

The Fort Wayne Memorial Coliseum was a spacious, first-rate facility. Dave and Ron joined the ten thousand or so other ravenous fans entering the arena and were hardly in their seats when the fight song reverberated through the building. Central's players filed out onto the court, circled around and went into their precision warm up drill. Split second timing, the ball relentlessly in motion, it was choreographed to inspire confidence, and it did.

When South came out, Dave and Ron sized up McCoy. He was tall, much taller than South's other players.

"He's got more meat on 'im than I expected," Dave said.

"Yeah," Ron concurred. "I hope your dad was right."

"Big John's awful tough and Dad doesn't miss a call very often."

At that, the buzzer sounded and the two teams retired to the sidelines. Seconds later the game was underway, with Central immediately up two on a Sylvester Coleman field goal. Then Herbie Lee caught on with a series of jump shots.

"Why aren't their guys playin' man ta man?" Dave wondered out loud. "We're overloadin' their zone defense on every play. Lee's gettin' easy shots."

"They're trying to double up on Coleman down low," Ron remarked.

"S'pose," Dave said, "but it ain't workin'."

Big John was having his way in the lane and helped put Central up by eight at the end of the first quarter. In the second Herbie scored five more times without a miss. Dave was jubilant. Then disaster struck. Herbie went down on a fade away. For a second you could hear a pin drop. Dave couldn't see a thing. Everybody was standing up.

"It's his ankle," Ron said, standing on his seat.

Dave grimaced. "Is it broken?"

Ron shrugged.

Herbie was assisted off the floor. There was anxiety then panic, as South cut the spread from seventeen to eight. Their hopes were short lived. Central quickly regained its poise and rallied. In the second half Big John came out smoking. South was finished.

The second game was between Marion and Noblesville. Dave and Ron didn't think either could mount much of a challenge against Central.

"Hope they wear each other out," Dave said.

Ron let that comment pass. "How long has Stu been that way?" he asked.

"Do'no," Dave replied. "Long's I've known 'im."

As they talked, the scourge of alcoholism took on meaning it never had before. Drunks were always comical figures, people you laughed at, made fun of, not individuals to be understood and befriended. Minute by minute Stu's future was slipping away while theirs was expanding. Dave wondered how a person could wake up one morning and find himself in such a fix. Stu was intelligent, that's what made it so hard to comprehend.

It was Central and Noblesville in the night game. Could Central plug the gap left by Lee being out of the lineup? That was the nagging question Dave couldn't get off of his mind. Central, like always, came out as a force to be reckoned with. The winner of this game was a foregone conclusion. All was right with the world. Then Noblesville caught fire and the lead evaporated. This wasn't supposed to happen. Dave was biting his nails, trying with all his might to will the ball into the basket. In the third quarter Big John overpowered the defense and Central pulled away to an insurmountable lead. Dave was exhausted.

"Your dad really knows his stuff," Ron said, on the way to the car.

"When Dad played for LaPorte in the '20s, they made it this far in the tournament."

The Ford joined the procession of vehicles exiting the parking lot.

"I was really scared there for a while," Dave commented.

"Central's just too big and fast," Mr. Norris observed. "They can turn it on anytime they need to. That's the sign of a great team, and Central's a great team."

The occasional trip to Fort Wayne was never complete without a late dinner at the Green Grill in Churubusco. Twenty-one shrimp for ninety-nine cents and Dave ate every last one, a perfect ending to a perfect day.

Once back in the car for the last leg of the journey, Dave only recalled hearing his dad say two words, "remember when..." He wasn't aware that Stu had assumed his role of watching the spot where the headlights caught the white line at the edge of the road to guide the car through the intense fog they encountered. It was just as well.

Two more games. Two more wins. Dave repeated those sentences to himself over and over the next week.

Somewhere in there he had what he thought was a brilliant idea. In whiffle ball, especially over the line, it was hitting that counted. Dave couldn't swing like the other kids. His body wouldn't twist far enough, so he held the bat with just his right hand and swung that way. Regular bats were too heavy. The broom stick Rafe used was so spindly he couldn't make decent contact. That left a yellow plastic bat he could really whip, but it didn't deliver any power. Under the circumstances, the occasional single and rare extra base hit he got, weren't half bad. Still, most of his trips to the plate ended in "can-a-corn" pop ups or "automatic-out" grounders. It was frustrating. He needed his own bat. One especially designed for him. If he just had the right bat he was sure he could do better.

All the baseball bats he'd collected in the garage had broken handles, except for one, a fungo bat that was split at the end. Fungos were used for fielding practice before a game. He didn't know why but figured their thin barrels made it easier for coaches to place the ball where they wanted it. Dave sawed off the broken section. It was still unwieldy. He cut off more. The heft was perfect. He knew it the minute he picked it up. Better yet, he could get it around. The first time they played, he held out a finger to show the pitcher where he wanted the ball then golfed it up at a forty five degree angle to get the most distance. He knew about that from studying rockets but kept it to himself. The ball flew high into the air and careened off the second garage in left field for a triple. It had to be a fluke, but then, he got another solid hit the next time up. The bat made all the difference in the world. His friends were amazed. So was he. Dave was a hitter now. He could make things happen.

The piles of receipts, statements and shop orders on the dining room table grew taller every day. They, along with expenses, depreciation, donations and deductions, had to be converted into net income, and finally the tax owed. Mr. Norris spent a lot of time moving papers from here to there, mumbling and scratching his head. Dave took notice and stayed out of his way. Their only conversation in days had been about Fox Park and whether he wanted to sell pop there during the upcoming baseball games.

"The job's yours if you want it," Mr. Norris said, "but I'll have to know shortly one way or the other."

"Do'no," Dave replied. "The cart looks heavy and it'd be hard ta push. I haven't decided for sure, but I will—soon."

It was after that discussion, when Mr. Norris trekked out to the car for yet another box of papers that Dave asked his mother about Stu.

"Hey Mom, is Stu a drunk?" he inquired, mostly to see how she'd respond.

"He has a condition," she replied coolly.

"What does that mean?"

"Never you mind."

Dave could tell by the tone of her voice that no further explanation would be forthcoming. If it was a medical problem worse than a broken bone that was about all you could expect to get at his house.

The big day arrived. They were headed to Indianapolis. Mr. Norris was down to two tickets, one for Stu, one for Dave. The first order of business was for Central to defeat Lafayette Jefferson, a team they'd pummeled twice in the regular season.

"Think they'll stick ta their ball control strategy?" Dave asked.

"There's not a team in the state that can go head to head with Central on an open floor," Mr. Norris said.

"But Herbie's ankle's bound ta be sore."

"It will be until the game starts. Then, with what's at stake, he won't feel it."

Dave heard what his dad said, but he also remembered him saying that on a particular night any team could beat you.

The Bronco's, in fact, matched Central point for point into the second quarter, and didn't succumb until a scoring spurt demoralized them in the fourth. It was another great team effort: Denny Bishop in the back court, Lee McKnight the third man upfront. Still, it was Sylvester Coleman's game. He swept the boards at both ends, blocked shot after shot, even took scoring honors. Dave was drained. He looked at Stu wondering if he should ask for a nip then went to the concession stand and bought a Snickers bar. When he returned, Crispus Attucks finished off Gerstmeyer, but again, not until the fourth quarter. The stage was set. Central had just beaten last year's runner up. Now only the two-time defending State Champions stood between them and destiny. The time for analyzing strategies and tactics was over. It would either be a win and glory or the depths of despair. They couldn't have come all this way then lose the last game, they just couldn't.

Dave's stomach was churning. He'd be euphoric one second, panicky the next. Central had the ball. Attucks deflected a pass out of bounds.

Dave followed every dribble, every shot, every rebound. Central scored. He lurched forward with a start, momentarily lost his balance, felt a rush of fear and grabbed for the seat in front. Attucks scored. He was chewing his nails. Attucks had the ball again, Central stole it. He pushed forward. His heart was pounding. The Bears drove and scored, then scored again. Attucks was hopelessly over matched. Dave slid back and took a deep breath. He could finally relax.

At the final buzzer, ecstatic fans streamed onto the floor. The noise was deafening. Dave thought the building would burst. The spontaneous celebration seemed to go on forever. When order was restored, the nets were cut down. Then the gigantic trophy was awarded. The South Bend Central Bears were the undefeated Indiana State Basketball Champions for 1957. As two exuberant players held the trophy high over their heads, Dave and Stu left for the car.

"That was quite a performance," Mr. Norris said, as he got in.

Dave didn't hear the comment. He was taking one long last look over the car at the brightly lit Butler Field House, trying with all his might to fix the image in his mind.

On Monday, there was a big parade. Seventy-five thousand people lined Michigan Street to celebrate as a procession of open convertibles inched its way past. No one seemed to notice the spitting snow. Dave wasn't there to see it. Only high school students got the day off. He sat in Mrs. Pritchard's room somewhat dejected, imagined he was in the midst of the festivities and sang the fight song to himself about a hundred times. At supper, Mr. Norris said it was the biggest celebration South Bend had seen since the end of the war. Then, just like that, it was over. The anticipation, the excitement, was gone. Their place taken by a vague unpleasant emptiness that lasted for days.

Dave's hitting streak continued. He tried applying glue to the paper before he rolled aerial bomb tubes so they could hold more pressure, watched movies. He wasn't really back on track until he got a call from Luke. Luke wouldn't tell him why but asked him to come over. There were possibilities here, maybe more clues.

"Wow! Where'd ya get it?" Dave asked, as Luke rolled a large reel of wire out of the garage.

"The Salvage Company, down town, you were right."

"Really, I just threw that out there, musta cost a fortune."

"Nope, its Signal Corps wire, army surplus. It's steel, not copper, nobody wants it. And the insulation, we think that's nylon. It's tough stuff, exactly what we need. I was looking for a piece of steel to make into a counter weight bracket when I spotted it.

"Is there enough?"

"There's plenty. We're going to split it up three ways, one third for you, one third for Leon and one third for us."

"I made up diagrams on how we might wire it over Christmas," Dave said. "I'll dig 'em out."

Their own telephone system, science, engineering, another adventure, and with a long carefree summer ahead there were bound to be more. Dave just hoped none would be traumatic. It wasn't to be.

Chapter 11
PAYBACK

For a little better than two weeks Dave was a big time hitter, right up there with Rafe and Gunner. He gloried in every second. It was great being on top for once, especially since no one else could make his bat work as well as he did. Everyone tried, but switching to one hand after using two threw off their timing, so, after a few wasted swings, they all gave up.

He could be at school, supposedly working on a lesson, holding the ladder while lengths of cable they'd wound were fastened to trees along the alleyway, be splicing wires on Leon's garage roof, it didn't matter. All he could think about was batting, what else he might try. Maybe line drives. It'd be super cool if he could level out his swing and slash a few past Rafe, though Ron cautioned him not to tempt fate.

"Why not?" he countered. "Rafe's been makin' fun a my hittin' for as long as I can remember."

"You're not going to learn until you get a good pounding."

"Hey, I'd just be givin' 'im a taste of his own medicine so he can see how it feels."

"If you two are such good friends, why do you have to be so competitive?"

"And mouthy," Dave smirked.

"Ya, and mouthy."

"I do'no," Dave returned. "He starts most of it."

"O.K.," Ron relented, "but don't say I didn't warn ya."

That Saturday Dave's hitting streak came to an end. He was having another great game and laying it on especially thick whenever he got one in for extra bases or Rafe muffed a catch. Rafe was hot but under control. Then two ear splitting explosions drew everyone's attention to a fiery cloud of embers bellowing from Mr. Young's trash barrel.

"Dang, those were a lot louder than his usual," Ben said to Dave, while they awaited their turn at bat.

"Musta been they were M-80s or cherry bombs," Dave agreed.

"We're playin' that one over," Gunner glared, as he watched the ball he topped roll limply a few feet then stop.

"Rules say grounders are out," Leon observed from the mound.

"Yeah, well, you try meetin' the ball square when somethin' like that goes off," and Gunner stood in for another pitch.

As Leon reached for the ball Dave noticed Rafe trotting in from the field with an eye fixed directly on him. He couldn't figure why. He hadn't scored off Rafe with a wisecrack in at least two innings. Something was up though, something bad. The wicked smile on Rafe's face told him that. Hopefully, it wasn't Ron's prediction about to come true. Rafe kept coming. He closed in. Dave cringed but Rafe went on by, ignored him completely. What was going on? A second later Rafe turned on him, the smile replaced by an angry scowl, the fungo bat cocked ominously over his shoulder. Dave raised an arm and tried to yell "stop" but nothing came out of his mouth.

Rafe leaned in. "I oughta," he snarled, raising the bat even higher.

Dave was petrified. It was the nightmare in his garage all over again. Him, frozen in fear, Rafe towering over him like a giant, poised to strike. An eternity passed. Then, ever so slowly, the wicked smile returned. Rafe abruptly lowered the bat and without a word stalked back toward the pitcher's mound. Once the panic subsided, Dave took after him.

"Fork it over Bozo, that's mine," he said emphatically.

Rafe whirled around. Dave stopped dead in his tracks. Rafe held the bat out, dangling it like a pendulum in front of Dave's nose.

"Come get it if ya want it so bad," he taunted.

Dave lunged. Rafe pulled the bat away. Dave almost fell on his face. He tried to speed up. Rafe back pedaled, keeping pace. The bat was just hanging there inches from his finger tips, yet completely out of reach.

"Give it back. I mean it," Dave screamed.

As the bat swung lazily from side to side, Rafe's smile widened.

"Better not do it," Dave threatened.

Rafe began making crane like noises as he raised the bat in halting mechanical jerks high into the air next to the flames. Dave considered another lunge but didn't dare risk it.

"'Member when ya tried ta gas me? I told ya we weren't even. Well, now we are."

Plunk, in went the bat. Dave rushed up to the barrels edge and tried to look in. The fierce fire blazing inside drove him back.

"You rat!" he yelled. "I told ya that was an accident. I didn't mean it."

Dave tried looking in again. It was no use. The barrel was glowing red around the middle. His bat would be a cinder in seconds. He picked up some stones and threw them at Rafe. Rafe effortlessly slapped them away. He caught the "I told you so" look on Ron's face.

"Ha, ha, ha," he seethed but there was nothing he could do. Just minutes before he'd been a fearsome hitter. Now he looked the fool with everyone watching. He thought about quitting and going home but then he'd look even stupider. He was furious with no way to dispel his anger. He couldn't take it out on Rafe and he couldn't take it out on the ball, though he tried with all his might. He swung so ferociously the rest of the game that except for one squibber, he fouled the ball off or missed it every time. The squibber, spinning so fast it whipped up dust devils, kept changing directions as it skittered along the ground until it finally came to rest on the far side of the singles rock.

"Never seen a spinner go that long before," Pete said, scooping the ball out of the dirt. "Still an out though."

Dave had an overwhelming urge to yell, "And I s'pose ya think I don't know that," in his snottiest voice but before the phrase could escape his lips, he felt the anger draining away. It was too quiet. Where was the razzing? He wasn't hearing any of the catcalls someone hitting the ball that ugly could expect. No comments about killing worms or snuffing gophers, nothing about nubbers, no one asking if that was the best he could do. The deathly silence could mean only one thing. His friends thought he'd had enough for one day. He was sure of it.

Chapter 12
PROJECTS

D oug Pilarski was building a Soap Box Derby racer, a real one.
"I just brought it out from the basement now that it's nice," he
said. "I've been working on it since Christmas vacation started."

"Those official wheels?" Dave asked, inspecting the surfboard-shaped
piece of plywood they were attached to.

"Yep, they're the only ones you can use in the race. They come as a set
with the axles. It's called the 'running gear.'"

"Never seen one close up before," Dave said. "Heard they coast practically forever."

Doug lifted the front of the plywood onto a paint can. "Watch this," he
said, giving the closest shiny red wheel a flip.

"Wow, no wobble at all," Dave marveled, as he sighted down the spinning wheel's edge. "Really runs true."

"I can hardly wait to start cutting out bulkheads. I would have already if
Dad hadn't made me plan so much and make drawings. That wasn't any fun
at all, but now I'm glad I did it. The rule book's this thick," and Doug held
his thumb and index finger apart about a Quarter of an inch.

A big project to work on, that's what Dave needed, something to keep
his mind off his bat being burned so he could cool down. He'd seen the bat
changing his whole summer. Now it was gone and he'd never get his hands
on another one. Fungo bats were really rare and undoubtedly expensive.
He'd thought about whittling down a regular bat to replace it but that would
take forever and getting it the same shape as the one he'd had would be
next to impossible. He'd been over it he didn't know how many times and

it always came out the same way, his big mouth. That's what got Rafe in the igloo in the first place. That's what got his bat burned. He couldn't blame anyone but himself. What if Rafe hadn't busted through like he did so he could breathe or hit him instead of just terrorizing him? Then what? Rafe was huge, one blow and he'd be a goner. Na, Rafe wouldn't actually hit him, just like he hadn't meant any harm. It was different where he lived. There might be squabbles, on occasion an argument, but fight? Only Rafe and Gunner ever did that and then only when they were guarding each other. Still, anybody could be pushed too far and it was obvious that sooner or later his mouth was going to get him in real trouble. His dad was always on him about it. Ron could see it. Instigating, not doing that was something he needed to work on a lot harder. As soon as they got the loose ends wrapped up on the phone system, he'd start building a car of his own.

Crates, that's what Ron called the push cars kids in Dave's neighborhood built. The opposite of sleek, streamlined Derby Racers, crates were made from cast-off materials, discarded fruit boxes, broken furniture, wheels from old lawn mowers, whatever you could lay your hands on. You couldn't buy a crate in a store. Companies didn't make them, though Leon had a wrecked gas tank car in his garage that had once been an auxiliary "drop tank."

WW II fighters carried drop tanks under each wing on extended missions. Just before going into action pilots jettisoned them to reduce drag. Some quick thinking mechanical type, hot on making a buck, had bought up thousands after the war and, until the supply ran out, converted them into kids' toys. Dave guessed the one Leon had was about six foot end to end and two foot across at the widest point before it got crashed. Silvery aluminum, drop tanks were aerodynamic like a tear drop. Dave had only seen it used once. That was a long time ago when what looked like a giant guppy zoomed past him on the sidewalk, Ben crouched in behind the wheel, Leon pushing hard on the slender tail. It took welding to fabricate the automotive type steering that was the car's most advanced feature. After innumerable encounters with curbs and other obstacles the welds were what eventually gave out and no one around had the equipment or expertise to repair sheet aluminum. So, what had once been a youngster's pride and joy hung broken and forgotten from the rafters in the Cheske's garage, collecting dust.

Constructing a crate was a challenging, creative endeavor, a tribute to an individual's ingenuity. When the craze first hit the year before, everybody had to have one. Ron's was made from a heavy duty parts box left over from a crane his dad had sold. Doug's, much more stylish, was painted bright red.

Rafe and Gunner had a wide squarish car that seemed much too large for its tiny wheels. The Razyniaks converted a spoked pulley into a steering wheel that worked ropes when you turned. Leon and Ben's, the most innovative, was made from orange crates and two wide planks separated by auto-engine valve springs. The springs were a crude attempt to isolate the driver from the jarring the contraption took when it hit a chuck hole or uneven sidewalk slab. As it turned out, they were too stiff and transmitted every vision-blurring jolt undiminished. Dave's crate, the most primitive, was held together with rusty nails he'd had to straighten before using.

Crates had one glaring deficiency: decent brakes. A wooden lever you could force against a rear tire was the most common type. It would stop you but only if you had plenty of time. If not, veering off or crashing were your only alternatives to running down a pedestrian or sliding into an intersection. In an emergency the best thing to do was look for a shrub and plow into it. That way your car didn't get smashed and neither did you. Accidents were common but crates were great fun and no one was ever seriously injured. For weeks, taking turns pushing, repairing and rebuilding was all they did. Then, as the cars started falling apart and the novelty wore off, interest waned. Dave hoped the fad would catch on again this summer. If it didn't, he'd have the only car in the area and the other guys would push him around just to get a turn driving. It wouldn't be a junk car either. He was going for a fancy steering wheel covered with leather from an old jacket, brakes that really worked, and if his dad came through, wire wheels like the ones on the bag cart he rented when he went golfing with his sports buddies. In addition, he was planning on a front bumper made from thick rubber if he could get hold of any and tin can headlights, maybe even a horn.

Money for bulbs and batteries was what came to mind when his dad asked again if he wanted to sell pop at Fox Park.

"I'll need to know this time for sure, otherwise they'll give the job to someone else."

"Will I still get my allowance?" Dave asked.

"If I have it," Mr. Norris smiled.

"O.K., then I'll do it. When do I start?"

"The two LaPorte teams open the season on May 5th."

A paying job, Dave had never had one of those before. It'd be hard, he knew that, and he'd only make a measly two cents per bottle, but he wouldn't be destitute anymore.

April 14 was Palm Sunday, the day of Dave's Confirmation and the cul-
mination of two years instruction in church doctrine. Like any rite of passage
should be, it was commemorated with a special service. In white gown and
black bow tie, Dave felt more eyes than usual were on him, as he sat with
the other candidates in the front pew. When the time came, he nervously answered Reverend Gray's questions even though they'd rehearsed the answers
beforehand. Then he took his first Communion. It was a time for reflection,
serious introspection and reverence, after which, family, out of town relatives
and friends gathered to celebrate at his house.

There was food for all after the requisite pictures had been taken and
numerous cards for him, most with a few dollars inside. He wasn't at all sure
presents were appropriate on so solemn an occasion but then, he hadn't
thought much about that. Once everyone settled in, his father and mother
presented him with a small, heavy wrapped box. Their manner indicated
it held something special. Even so, he was totally unprepared for what he
found inside.

"A transistor radio," Dave said in awe, holding it up. "An Admiral!
Thanks! Wow!"

His parents had the same look on their faces he'd seen when they came
home from Chicago.

Dave turned it on. "Sounds as good as a regular radio! This is great!"

Later, his brother Will, home on leave, pulled him aside.

"This isn't new but it's yours," he said, unbuckling his watch. "It's a
chronograph. I picked it up on base before I left."

"Really?" Dave said, his mouth gaped open. "A chronograph?"

"It tells the time, day, date and it's a stop watch, and you don't have to
wind it, a weight inside does that automatically every time you move your
arm."

"Can't over wind it, can ya?" Dave asked.

"Nope, it has clutches inside to prevent that."

Dave thanked Will just like he had everyone else.

The watch went to school with him the very next day and the radio kept
up a rock and roll beat in the basement while he gathered together anything
that might be useful for a crate.

Dave couldn't speak for others, but in his neighborhood, chronographs, and especially transistor radios, had much higher status than letters from rocket scientists.

"Guess what?" Dave asked at supper the following day.

"Well, it was cloudy last night," Mr. Norris replied, "so it can't be the comet."

"Yeah, Luke was real disappointed. We got our telephone system done. It's all hooked up here at the house and it works just like a real one. I can call the Cheske's or the Razyniak's, whichever I want with the push of a button. Woulda been done sooner, 'cept Luke was busy and all the wires are the same so it was hard tellin' which was which at each end. Once we figured that out, it was easy as pie. It's very sophisticated."

"Sophisticated?" Mr. Norris repeated, meeting Mrs. Norris' eyes.

"Good one isn't it?" Dave grinned. "I been tryin' ta use my vocabulary words in sentences so's I'll remember 'em better."

"That's a wonderful idea," Mrs. Norris said approvingly.

"Yeah, I figure I can elevate my achievement that way."

"Let's not go overboard," Mr. Norris cautioned.

Dave frowned. "Luke's telescope's done too. It's really cool," he continued. "We're goin' for pictures tonight.

"Quiet! Sports is on. It's opening day."

"I was onl..."

"That's enough," Mr. Norris returned, more forcefully.

Dave stabbed a piece of ham with his fork. Opening day, what was the big deal? President Eisenhower throwing out the first pitch, whoopty-do. The Yankees beating the Senators? With all their money, they ought to win every game they played. Dave nudged his mother.

"Mom," he whispered. "Can I be excused ta Luke's?"

"Finish your cabbage first," she replied softly, pointing to the yellowish mass Dave had pushed to the edge of his plate.

Dave wondered. *Maybe Dad was so obsessed about baseball because he once played.* Dave didn't know. He couldn't play regular baseball.

When Dave got to the Razyniak's, a crowd had already gathered and was milling around.

Luke's telescope was very impressive, especially the big white aluminum tube that made up its body. Dave was certain that alone had cost a fortune. Then, there was the equatorial mount, counterweight, various shafts, brackets and the magnificent tripod the whole thing sat on. All in all it was a splendid instrument any professional would be proud to own. The telescope was backed up against the side of the garage pointed into the northwestern sky when he arrived and everyone was just waiting for it to get dark. Once it did, the show began.

"The view will be best right when twilight ends," Luke advised.

A line formed. Luke adjusted the telescope's position slightly.

"There, got it," he said, after a second and his mom and dad bent to look through the eyepiece.

The comet was spectacular. A long thin sliver of light in among the stars to the naked eye, it grew into a mammoth flying saucer trailing an immense tongue of flame, when highly magnified. Luke waited patiently until everyone had taken a turn, removed the eyepiece and installed the camera. He described the focusing process to the group huddled around and the picture taking began.

There was a gathering in Luke's backyard every clear night for the rest of the week. All agreed Luke's telescope was a singular, first-rate achievement. The Russians might have H-bombs and be working feverishly to spread their ideology around the world but America was still stronger, much stronger, and that was due, in no small part, to the resourcefulness of its people, people like Luke.

Over the weekend Dave's family set up his telescope at Muessel Park to observe the comet. Dave could immediately see that the image it produced was much less brilliant than the one Luke got. Still, using his telescope showed he appreciated the investment his parents had made and that was what really mattered.

"It's the primary mirror's diameter," Luke explained over their new telephone system. "Mine's twice as big as yours, so it collects four times the light."

"Didn't know it worked that way," Dave returned. "Say, how 'bout, could I help with the developin'?"

"Sure," Luke replied, "I've burned a whole box of film so far."

Dave had been looking for an excuse to get back into the Razyniak's basement and here it was. When you're on a mission, you have to stay cool and be observant, he said to himself, as he walked down the sidewalk.

Developing film was a more exacting process than he expected. There were any number of things to do: mix chemicals, check temperatures, run negatives, crop, enlarge. He was busy every minute and had no chance to check the metal panel attached to the darkroom's back wall. It was obviously there to cover the shelter's entrance and somehow you had to be able to move it.

Dave's search for crate materials was going nowhere. Most of what he'd found at home was junk. Until people got serious about spring cleaning, scrounging alleys, his main source of supply, was a waste of time.

He made another trip to Luke's and discovered nothing. On his third trip he caught a break. Luke went upstairs for snacks. While he was gone, Dave worked his hand along the panel's top edge, cutting a finger on a burr in the process. Now, instead of having time to sleuth out the hidden lever or button that must surely be there, he had to concoct an excuse Luke would buy and content himself with lending a hand and enjoying the music from his radio.

With pictures of the comet as detailed as any printed in astronomy journals, Luke moved on to planets and stars.

Dave was moving on too. He'd tired of playing detective. The Razyniak's had built a bomb shelter and they'd been slick about it, big deal. He'd keep on nosing around to see if anything turned up. If it did, fine, but he wasn't spending any more time on it. Why bother? The bomb shelter was like the coin. You got the scoop on something really hot, then, instead of being able to tell someone about it, you has to keep it secret. What was the fun in that?

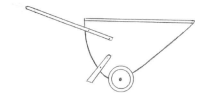

Chapter 13
SELLING POP

D ave was bored and having second thoughts about his "job" long before his dad turned on Truesdell Avenue, the road that separated Fox Park from Clear Lake. It was a nice day, way too nice to spend working.

Mr. Norris always arrived an hour before game time and parked on the far side of the path that went from the Pavilion into the park. "You can't have a game without umpires," he'd say. "And you never know when you'll be delayed on the road." Mr. Kaufner, equally devoted, arrived about the same time and parked next to the path on the near side. While Mr. Norris did his usual trunk rearrangement, puffed away and reminisced with friends, Mr. Kaufner set about unloading a table, chair, microphone, amplifier, numerous wires and a ladder from his panel truck that had California Orange Juice painted on the sides. He'd position the rickety table exactly in line with home plate behind the backstop, the three or so rows of benches and the path. That was the location of the "press facility." He'd place the electronic components on it, then, using the ladder, he'd hang a boxy speaker in an oak tree at each end of the backstop. He'd stretch wires overhead as he went along, run them across the path to the oak next to his table and finally down to the amplifier sitting on top. He'd connect power to the device and watch the exposed tubes glow red as they came to life.

"Testing, 1-2-3-4."

Satisfied that the system was operating as it should, he'd sit down with a magazine and begin to read. Dave, trying to rest, watched it all from one of the benches. Then, with time passing at a snail's pace, he leaned back to enjoy the spring weather and beautiful scenery.

The green "Park Department" stenciled benches, positioned here and there around the diamond, began to fill. He got up and walked to the domed, white columned Pavilion on the lake shore. The man who ran the concessions there looked skeptical.

"We'll only load in fifteen bottles and some ice to start," he said. "That'll make it lighter."

Lighter maybe, light no. Dave hadn't pushed the green garden cart ten feet before he began to question the wisdom of his decision. He'd been afraid the cart would be too heavy all along. Of course, the first forty feet to the road were slightly up hill. Then, with the path from the road past the press facility paved and more nearly level, his confidence grew. He noted that a few more fans had trickled in and counted three blankets spread out on the knoll that paralleled the first base line.

"Have a root beer in there?" Mr. Kaufner asked.

"Sure thing," Dave replied, enthusiastically digging through the ice then snapping off the cap.

His first sale; Dave dropped the dime into his pocket then backtracked a few steps so people coming in on the path would have to walk past his cart. He tallied three more sales. Fans continued to arrive. He did some mental calculations. Let's see, he thought, $50 / 9 = 5\frac{1}{2}$. If enough people came and he sold five and a half bottles per inning, at two cents a bottle, he'd make a whole dollar. A dollar would be twice his weekly allowance. He'd be rolling in dough. With extra innings, double headers coming up later in the season, there were possibilities here, real possibilities. There was also, now that he looked more carefully, hardly a spot in sight that didn't slope up or down at least a little.

The actual playing field in front of him had once been part of Clear Lake. Then, as he understood it, some overzealous citizen had proposed improving on nature by cutting channels between the numerous lakes around town to turn LaPorte into a sort of inland Venice. The idea, apparently not carefully thought through, went kafluey when the digging disrupted the underlying strata and the level of all the lakes dropped a few feet. That resulted in Clear Lake receding south through the shallows behind the player's bench on the third base side. The newly exposed, nearly level land, except for a low hill extending part way into left field, made a perfect natural ball field. Dave was, at that very moment, standing under the magnificent oaks that once graced the lake's shore. Now they shaded the makeshift press box and most of the benches provided for spectators. Some of the trees had tangled roots ringing their bases, obstacles he would, no doubt, have to contend with. This would, as usual, require a plan. Course then, everything he did required a plan.

The two teams arrived. Dave watched LaPorte Cubs, loaded down with equipment, make their way to one bench, LaPorte Sportsmen to the other. Most of the Sportsmen walked past him on the path. Their cleats clacking on the asphalt reminded him of Mrs. Pritchard's shoes and the wooden floors at school.

Dave felt a tug at his sleeve.

"You selling that soda, Sonny?"

Dave turned to find an old woman and two children peering into his cart. "Ah, yes ma'am," he responded.

"Take a Coke-Cola." She glanced at the older of the boys, "a grape—come come now, make up your mind," she coaxed, as the boys played in the ice. "One Coke-Cola, two grapes," she said, not waiting for a response.

Dave found the appropriate bottles and removed their caps.

"That will be thirty cents please."

The woman nodded, pulled out a small change purse and snapped it open.

"Thank you," Dave said politely, when she handed him the coins. He chuckled as she guided the children away. Both boys had a grape in one hand, ice in the other and their mouths packed so full they couldn't take a drink. He had to wonder if they'd ever seen ice before. This was working out. He sold five more bottles during batting practice, though his focus was on the fungo bats the coaches were using.

Mr. Kaufner, a usually reserved orange juice salesman in his late fifties with receding hair, laid his magazine aside and reached for the microphone. The instant his fingers touched it, he underwent a remarkable character transformation. No longer was he sitting in a forlorn kitchen chair between the last hurrah for unfulfilled athletes and a slowly deteriorating restroom building to his rear. He wasn't looking out on the mostly old coots who likely considered today's game "a little action." Now he was a mile above home plate in a bustling, air conditioned press box full of international reporters. Thousands of fans, arriving by every conveyance known to man, were crowding into the enormous, multi-decked stadium below for a pivotal game. They came by car, bus, train, steamship on the lake, rode in on horseback or camel, all intent on being part of the "spectacle." The "crowd," responding to the whimsical meanderings, played along with subdued smiles and, on occasion, a chuckle.

"The award winning staff of sportswriters, statisticians and the fine sponsors who make these presentations possible would like to welcome all our loyal fans and out of town guests to another slice of heaven, another rousing season of baseball, here at Fox Park."

Dave thought he'd puke.

Mr. Kaufner went on to list the eight teams in the league along with their managers. He previewed the schedule of upcoming games and praised the hard working ground crew. When he asked for a round of applause on their behalf a few people responded. Dave concluded they were the ones who actually thought there was a ground crew.

Mr. Norris called out "PLAY BALL," in a firm voice and the game began.

Dave hi-tailed it back to the Pavilion, stopping as usual, at the ornate stone drinking fountain just before he got to the road.

"Let's try twenty this time," he said, panting.

He raced back, decided to try his luck among the scattered benches and blankets on the knoll. It was hard pushing the cart through the grass, and, a waste of time. He waited a whole inning and only sold one Coke. He didn't sell a single bottle on the third base side where there were only two benches but learned that pulling his cart backwards through the roots surrounding the giant oak at the end of the backstop was a lot easier than trying to push it through. He also learned that people intent on watching a ballgame didn't want to be bothered by a pop vender, particularly when the first inning had been exciting and the Cubs and Sportsmen were hometown rivals. He went back to the path where it was shady. People were too comfortable that was the problem. He wouldn't make the really big money until it got hot and they were baking.

"That's two to nothing Cubs, bottom of the second coming up," the speakers announced.

It was quiet for a time. Then, Mr. Kaufner, possibly afraid the spectators were getting bored, began talking up the rookies and how much they'd learn from the seasoned veterans.

"They'll be picking it up from some of the best in the business," he noted.

Of course, it went without saying that the rookies all had the potential of a Ruth or Gehrig.

"They'll be set for the big time in a season or two. That is, if the major league teams can afford to buy out their current contracts and match the facilities we have here."

Smiles appeared here and there. A few eyes rolled.

"Oh, and this just in! The official attendance for today's game, 17,201. Correct me if I'm wrong," he deadpanned, "but that's down slightly from last year's opener. Don't know how long the front office can hold the line on tickets before going to a full ten dollars. Operating expenses and those hefty signing bonuses eat up the gate faster than ever these days."

That got laughs even from some of the players and a nod from Mr. Norris. Dave laughed too. He knew his dad barely made gas money on these trips, and facilities, heck, while the bathroom building here was certainly larger, Dad had probably tipped over better when he was a kid.

Dave sold a Coke, then a root beer. People were thirsty now. He'd sell a bottle, pick up an empty or two, sell a second then hurry on to where another hand was waving. He had to make change for a dollar bill and lost track of sales. He hauled a load of empties to the Pavilion. Empties were a pain. He reloaded and returned. Three more sales and the game was tied 4-4 going into the ninth. The last he'd remembered it was the 6th. The rush was over. The Cubs won 5-4 in ten on three consecutive walks. Dave settled up at the concession stand and walked away with sixty four cents in his pocket. Selling pop was hard work, just as he'd suspected, but worth it. One last stop and they'd be headed home.

Dave's uncle owned Wally's Bar, a block from the LaPorte County Courthouse down town. Mr. Norris stopped in after every game for a beer or two no matter what, even though the tavern couldn't legally be open on Sundays. Dave assumed it was all right so long as they came in the back way and sat behind the curtain that separated the table area from the actual tavern part. He got to play the jukebox with the wooden wheel over the speaker for free while his uncle took a break from restocking to relax with his dad. He drank a Coke, ate some chips and watched the records change through the glass. The records, stored in a round silver stack on the left, would swing out for each new play. When the song ended the turntable would drop down and the carrier would return the record to its original slot. Then, after a series of clicks and buzzes a new one moved into position. The jukebox was very cool. Uncle Wally always turned the sound down when Dave and his dad arrived so passersby on the street wouldn't wonder what was going on inside.

It played all the latest hits and Dave could have listened for hours, but after Dad polished off the beer they said their goodbyes and started for home.

Mr. Norris lit up and turned on the radio to see how the Yankees were doing as soon as they were in the car. They'd been battling the Chicago White Sox for first place in the American League since the season began. Dave could rile his dad just by saying something good about them, but not today. The Sox were in the process of dropping a pair at Comiskey and Mantle had already blasted a two-run homer. As long as Dave could rest up and analyze the day's events, he didn't much care. How could he improve his sales strategy? Where should he be at a particular time? Did he have the right mix of bottles in his cart? Was he friendly, polite enough? For him, trips to the park weren't about the games, they were strictly an economic proposition.

One lousy afternoon, that's all he'd been gone and he was already missing out. According to Rafe there'd been a terrific game of ditch-em and the Razyniak's had gone to the river with their cousins from Michigan to blow up ships. He got all the details from Tim over the phones.

"It started when Mom made us clean our room, the closet too. She said we had too much stuff and whatever was broken or we didn't use anymore had to go, especially our plastic ship models because they took up so much room. Some were in bad shape and there's no getting around Mom when she's on a clean. We hid two battleships and an aircraft carrier in the attic when she wasn't looking and boxed up the rest. Pete said we should blow them up so Luke rigged some bombs. We used "delayo" and launched them from upstream. When they floated by, Whamo! Pieces flew everywhere. It almost looked real except there wasn't enough smoke. We had fun. We're going back with the ones from the attic on Saturday before papers and Luke's working on smokier bombs."

Dave immediately put that on his calendar and asked Rafe to ride him down to the river.

"Hey, we got 'nother game of ditch-em planned," Rafe objected.

"So, we go see the ships get blasted first then come back and play while the Razyniaks are deliverin'."

"Um, O.K.," Rafe agreed. "But it's costin' ya a stop at the Morgue on the way home."

"All right," Dave replied reluctantly, "but only somethin' for a dime."

During that week Dave and Tim played their first chess match over the newly installed telephone system. They had each numbered the squares on their boards so they wouldn't have to mess with the rook to queen's bishop whatever. Chess was fun, a battle of wits they both enjoyed.

It was neat watching the ships float along with the current then, as though blown apart by torpedoes or bombs, hurl turrets and miniature planes out in all directions. Dave saw the flight deck on the aircraft carrier, torn from its mountings, spin erratically as it rose three feet or more into the air. With each explosion, waves would circle out from the condemned ship and wash, with a whisper, against the shore. The only unpleasant part was getting down the steep incline to the river bank. It must have been twenty feet high and was covered with thick undergrowth, some of which, Rafe thought, might be poison ivy. Dave had to all-four-it to keep from falling but wasn't much concerned.

"I'm 'bout positive I'm immune," he said.

Morie's Morgue was one of the countless small corner grocery stores that dotted neighborhoods all across America in the 1950s. Morie's was located across from Muessel School. Rafe and his buddies bought snacks there before sports practice and, if any of the stories Dave heard were true, at least some of them snatched candy bars while others created a diversion. Morie was on guard the minute Dave, Rafe and Gunner entered the store. That made Dave uncomfortable.

Rafe and Gunner each set a Double Cola, some sort of taffy thing and a bag of chips on the counter. Dave took an orange Popsicle from the freezer case and set it next to what they were buying. Rafe slid one of the Double Colas over next to the Popsicle and pointed at Dave.

"He's payin' for that."

Money changed hands and they left.

"Morie got a little nervous when you guys came in," Dave said.

"Do'no why," Rafe snickered.

Rafe and Gunner finished off their drinks in no time, all 16 ounces. If Dave tried that he'd be ducking into alleys all the way home.

Ditch-em was fun, scary most of the time but fun. One person, usually somebody fast, was chosen. He'd get a head start on his bike and try to ditch everyone behind him by cutting through yards, navigating openings between shrubs, whatever else he could think of. Whether a person got caught or not depended on how quick, how daring and how creative he was. Ben Cheske was particularly good at it, a real natural on a bike. Dave went with Rafe and was off then back on the bike's bar more times than he could count as Rafe hoisted the bike up steps, over fence rails Dave had to crawl under, through places too narrow to ride. By supper he was worn to a frazzle.

When Dave went to bed that night he knew he was in trouble. Red blotches had appeared all over his hands and arms. There were lines of tiny bumps mixed in that itched like crazy. When he undressed he found more around his ankles and on his right leg. In the morning they turned up on his cheek, neck and in other, more sensitive places. The most annoying were the ones between his fingers. They itched something terrible. When he scratched them they weeped and his fingers stuck together. He had poison ivy, his worst case ever. He tried but couldn't resist tearing away at the blisters.

"O.K. Where've you been this time?" Mrs. Norris asked, first thing at breakfast.

"The river," he replied warily.

"Again! You didn't learn anything from the last trip?"

"I hardly got it then. I thought I was immune."

"What do you think now?" she said, angrily raising his elbow almost to his nose. "Does this look immune?"

"No ma'am," he said softly. "It doesn't."

"Don't let me catch you scratching," she warned indignantly, "not even once!"

Mrs. Norris wasn't going to let Dave go to LaPorte on Sunday but Mr. Norris insisted.

"He's made a commitment to the concessionaire and unless it gets a lot worse he's seeing it through."

When Dave and his dad got to the park, Mr. Norris pulled an oversize sweatshirt from the trunk.

"Here, put this on," he said.

"It's too hot," Dave protested.

"You won't sell a bottle if people see those blisters. You're wearing it! That's final!"

Dave put the sweatshirt on. Whatever challenges he'd faced the week before were nothing compared to this. The sweatshirt felt like burlap. Every movement was agony. He spent the whole afternoon fighting the urge to throw it off and rip violently at his skin.

Selling pop was the furthest thing from his mind. He just wanted to sit in a shady spot and not move. Finally, Mr. Kaufner gave him a nod and pointed to the knoll; pushing the cart that far was torture. He stood there motionless, hoping no one would wave him over. While he counted off the seconds, one of the Cubs, a guy named Clisp, hit a home run. All the Wanatah right fielder could do was watch helplessly as the ball soared over his head and disappeared into the dense woods beyond the outfield fence. When he went around the barrier to find it Mr. Norris called "TIME OUT." The LaPorte fans were out of their seats cheering.

Within seconds the "tape measure" on it came over at 600 feet. More cheers, chortles. Even the Bambino couldn't hit one that far.

"Looks like another great year for the long ball hitter here at the park," Mr. Kaufner boomed.

By now two more players had joined the search. It was a jungle out there. The vines on some of the trees were so thick you couldn't see their trunks. Dave guessed a lot of them were an inch or more in diameter. If it'd been up to him, he'd have left the ball out there to rot, but contrary to what Mr. Kaufner said, this league couldn't afford to lose even one baseball.

Dave earned 42 cents that day, 52 to be exact but he treated himself to a candy bar for his suffering, figuring he'd get to wash it down with a free pop at his Uncle's. On the way home his dad castigated him for always having to learn the hard way and he got the "think before you act" lecture. Actually he got one of the three or four variants Dad used depending on the circumstance and the infraction. Dave said "yes sir" a lot and didn't dare get smart.

"I had to pull a few strings to get you that job," Mr. Norris chastised. "Don't let me down again."

Dave was out of circulation the whole next week. Except for something to do with his legs that was more school than he usually missed in an entire year, and there was no relief in sight. As soon as one area began to heal, he'd break out somewhere else. He couldn't go anywhere because he'd missed school and Mom was dogging his every step with a pair of stiff leather gloves at the ready. He'd messed up bad this time. Heck, it wasn't even noon on Monday when his dad dropped off his books. He knew what was up the minute he saw slips of paper slid in under their covers. Then, there was one further note listing additional assignments he could do to get ahead.

"You'll have plenty of time. Plan on doing them all," Mrs. Norris said sternly.

For a second there Dave thought about trying to bargain her down but by now it was pretty clear that on something self-inflicted there were no deals to be had at his house.

On Saturday, Dave finally got to go to Doug's to see how the racer was progressing. Rafe, Gunner and Ron were already there watching Doug glue curved wooden strips, one atop the other, to the front section of its plywood frame. When they saw him, they burst out laughing. Rafe pulled a make believe six shooter from its holster and shot himself in the foot then danced around on his other leg blowing imaginary smoke from the gun barrel. Moments later he flung himself to the ground and was doubled up scratching like a maniac

"Look, I'm immune! I'm immune!" he shrieked.

Bet he spent the whole week workin' that up, Dave thought to himself, but what could he say, standing there with crusty scabs and splotches of pink ointment covering half his body.

"Buyin' that by the case are ya?" Gunner sputtered.

"Go away," Doug motioned. "I can't concentrate."

"We're leavin'. We're leavin'." Rafe howled while he inspected Dave's arm with a non-existent magnifying glass.

"Why were those two here?" Dave hissed after Rafe and Gunner left.

"Rafe said they were on the way to buy a new inner tube for Gunner's bike," Ron replied, "but I think they were just hanging around to see if my dad would take off work early and get the motor bikes out. I told them he was behind on the mid-month books but they didn't listen."

It was nearly Memorial Day before the last of Dave's blisters disappeared. Even so, he'd been lucky. A rain out at the park saved him from a second encounter with the sweatshirt and Dad worked a game in Michigan City the following week. That meant no one attending the big family get together Thursday after the game would have to know anything about his unfortunate little mishap at the river. Well, Uncle Wally knew, but he wouldn't say anything.

Dave was back on track. He felt great, had a pile of money socked away in the closet. He even joked around with his dad some about the Yankees, but only to a point.

Chapter 14
THE STRANGER

Baseball was always a part of Memorial Day in LaPorte. So was paying respect to deceased relatives. In the past, Dave, Mom and Ann did that with his Uncle Virgil, Aunt Martha and Cousin Christine while Dad umpired. Then, after the game, there was the big doings on the hill adjacent to left field where the picnic tables were located. This year it was different. Dave had a job now, a commitment, like his dad said. That meant after the first stop at St. John's Cemetery, he would need to be dropped off at the Pavilion to load his cart. Things got off on the wrong foot from the start when Uncle Virgil drove into the cemetery through an entrance they hadn't used before. None of the landmarks that directed them to the grave sites were where they were supposed to be. The one lane inter-connecting roads went every which way and nobody could get their bearings straight.

"I think we should have taken the right fork back there."

"What direction are we going?"

"You suppose the tree with the split trunk came down in last winter's ice storm?"

"It's around the water fountain, I'm sure of that."

Finally, Uncle Virgil drove back out onto the street and came in the usual way. It was a real gut buster, would have been even funnier if Dave could have laughed.

All the confusion made Dave late for work. He was still filling his cart when the game started. There was a huge crowd. All the benches were filled. Rows of blankets lined the crest of the knoll. It wasn't the mainly geezers wearing suspenders with bellies so big the buttons on their shirts were about to pop and they couldn't sit straight. Today there were families, lots of kids. It was warm, exactly what Dave had been waiting for, and people were still arriving. They stopped him on the path, signaled from the benches behind the backstop. The lady with the two kids was there, so were the other regulars. He could scarcely keep up. They hailed him from the knoll. Five minutes there and he was out of drinks. He hurried back to the Pavilion. As soon as he returned, more bottles disappeared. Twenty three sales, just like that. Then the rush was over. He was glad. If that pace had continued much longer he'd either be a millionaire or dead from exhaustion.

He took a minute to catch his breath and concentrate on the two men who were sitting behind the player's bench across the field on the third base side. He'd been catching glimpses of then since he'd first gotten to the knoll. For some reason they were using hand signals to communicate. It was weird, like they couldn't talk to each other. One was a player. The other, about the same age, who looked strong as an ox, Dave hadn't seen before. The player seemed to be trying to explain the game as it went along. Once Dave rested up a bit he was going over to investigate.

Mr. Kaufner was pulling out all the stops today, Dave assumed because of the large holiday crowd. The steamships on the lake had been replaced with ultra modern hover craft, a dozen of which were at that very moment ferrying hundreds of excited passengers, decked out in their trendiest spring finery, into the park. Scores of pro scouts and pricy agents with note pads and binoculars were packed shoulder to shoulder in the box seats. Player's autographs were going for $500 a pop before the game. The State Police had a new radar-equipped squad car on hand.

"Folks, you're witnessing baseball history being made here at the park today. For the first time ever, in any ball park, anywhere, the fireballs hurled by today's starters have been accurately clocked coming in at over 130 miles per hour."

Dave saw his dad shake his head. He was doing the same, laughing too.

Empties littered the ground everywhere. Dave started collecting them, sold a lemon-lime, pushed a bunch of dead soldiers in under the ice, sold two Cokes. By the time he was back behind the backstop his cart weighed a ton. Making it through the snarl of roots to check out the hand signals with that load was out of the question. He'd have to drop them off first. As he crossed the road Mr. Kaufner was recapping the third inning. When he returned the stranger was gone and the player had moved over to the team bench. Dave couldn't be bothered with that now, not with sales this brisk. A half dozen bottles later the two were sitting together again. Dave started working his way over for a second time when someone tapped him on the shoulder. It was Little Harlan.

"Don't do that," Dave protested.

"Sorry," Little Harlan said." My dad sent me down to tell ya we got the last table."

"Great, I was afraid ya wouldn't get here in time."

"Selling a lot?"

"Am today," Dave returned, coming off the knoll toward the backstop.

"I been thinkin' about you."

"Oh, yeah, why's that?" Dave inquired.

"Your brother. 'Member last fall when you were telling me about the A-bomb test he was in."

"Hang on," Dave said—"was that two root beers and one grape?" he asked the gentlemen standing a few feet from his cart. A thumbs up and Dave handed him the bottles.

"Well," Little Harlan went on, "they're shooting off lots more now. It's on T.V."

"I seen it," Dave nodded, "at Yucca Flats."

"The British are doin' it too. They're testing H-bombs in the Pacific at Christmas Island."

"Didn't know 'bout that," Dave said.

"First one was two weeks ago. Anyway, I had this dream. Everything was peaceful. Then blamn, there was this flash of light so bright, it was like day. My window's wide open. I'm standing in front of it lookin' out. I don't even know how I got there but this gigantic mushroom cloud's rollin' up off in the distance behind our house. All those colors are mixed in. Streaks of sunlight are shootin' off the top like you said. I could practically touch it. My skin's burnin'. It hurt terrible. I couldn't move. And 'member you said about how birds flyin' by burst into flame when it went off."

"Yeah"

"Well, they were there too. There were flashes everywhere like cameras goin' off, and where the birds used to be, there were just puffs of smoke hangin' still in the air, just hangin' there, not movin'. When I woke up I was shakin'."

"Whoa! That's way scarier than any I've had."

"Now I'm afraid to go to sleep at night."

"Can see why. Sure hope ya don't have that nightmare again." Dave said, responding to another hand. "Gotta keep at it."

"Right. Tell ya more later," Little Harlan said, walking away. "Just wanted ya to know."

Dave eventually made it to where the stranger and player sat. Both were watching the game like regular spectators when he pulled up to their bench. Without saying a word the player reached into his cart, searched out a Coke, wiped off the ice and held it out in front of the stranger. The stranger, hardly looking away from the game, said "Coke, yeah."

"Make it two," the player said.

While Dave dug for the second bottle he noticed the player's left hand. It was grotesque, swelled up something awful. The stranger, in comparison, looked ready to suit up at a moment's notice. He was concentrating so hard there were lines of wrinkles running across his forehead. The player, with a nudge, handed over the bottle. Dave took the dime and two nickels. As he started to leave, there came a resounding, "STEEE-RIKE THREE, YOU'RE OUTTA THERE." That meant a batter had just gone down, probably looking, as one of those fireballs blazed across and his dad had given him the thumb. The call seemed to confuse the stranger so the player held out three fingers on his good hand and drew the injured one across his neck. The stranger repeated the motion and, with a smile, said, "Strikd out."

When he did, Dave spotted the watch on his wrist. Actually he noticed the watch band. It was a Spidel Twist-O-Flex, only the coolest watch band on Earth. Silvery gold with embossed links, a Twist-O-Flex was so stretchy you could tie it in a knot. Dave had been dreaming about buying one for his chronograph every since he'd gotten it, would've already if they weren't so expensive.

The lull when he got a break, never materialized that afternoon. Whatever he made today, and it was going to be plenty, he was earning. Even so, he kept an eye on the player and stranger in case they started up signaling again. He didn't know why they'd been doing it, only that the stranger must have come from somewhere far away, like China, not to know about baseball. He was asking his dad about that first thing after the game.

"He's a freedom fighter," Mr. Norris explained, while he packed his chest protector and shin guards in the trunk. "His name is Johannas Kovach. They call him John."

"He's from Hungary?" Dave asked.

"Yes, and lucky to be alive. He escaped just before the Russians crushed the uprising last October."

"Tanks blowin' up buildings in Budapest," Dave said. "I know 'bout that. But what's he doin' here, in LaPorte?"

"President Eisenhower had some of the young men who made it out brought to this country. It shows we support their struggle."

"He doesn't understand English, right?"

"Hardly a word, he hasn't been here long enough but I hear he's quick on the uptake, a good athlete too. He's rooming with a Hungarian couple and the government arranged for him to work at the new Castinal plant. This was the first baseball game he's ever seen."

Knew it, Dave thought to himself.

"And the player with the busted up hand was trying to explain it?"

"That's a nasty sprain he's got. It'll keep him out of the line up for a couple more weeks and he needed something to do. It was Manager Bradley's idea. Nothing's worse than having to sit the bench and watch someone else play your position."

"It won't be easy teachin' 'im with Mr. Kaufner helpin' out."

"You can say that again," Mr. Norris chuckled. "Used his whole repartee today, didn't he?"

"Guess," Dave shrugged.

"Timing pitches with radar, who ever heard of such a thing? The batter missed the ball by four inches when he laid that one on. It's crazy. Nobody can throw a ball 130 miles per hour."

Maybe not, but Dave still had this vision of his dad glancing down through his mask to see if there weren't wisps of smoke mixed in with the dust the ball blasted out of the catcher's mitt.

While the car was moved down the road to the picnic area, Dave marveled at how fast Dad had gotten the low-down on the stranger. Then, in an instant, a smile forced him to turn away. It had just occurred to him that his dad was as good at keeping up on the latest as his mom, maybe better.

It took Dave a while to climb the hill. By the time he reached the picnic tables Dad andUncle Gilbert from Michigan City were deep into a discussion and, as usual, talking past each other. They almost always did that when they got together. Dave loved history and liked listening to adults talk politics, except maybe in this case. Uncle Gilbert was a WW II veteran. He saw the world through the eyes of a foot soldier who'd fought his way from the coast of France into Germany. Mr. Norris saw it through the prism of athletics.

Dave assumed that was why when they talked, things didn't mesh very well. As Dave slid onto the bench next to his dad they were exchanging segments of unrelated stories and trying, with limited success, to keep the conversation going by making connections at the fringe.

Dave was wolfing down a hot dog he'd snatched from the grill on the way and contemplating a second. Being that hungry reminded him of how hard he'd worked and how good it felt to sit down. The double slide his sister and cousins were playing on didn't look the least bit inviting. All he wanted to do was sit and rest until it came time to go home, and that's what he was doing unless the conversation got so zany he couldn't stand it. Then, he had two choices. He could go watch Uncle Virgil and Uncle Harlan pitch horseshoes or slide down to the other end of the table and eavesdrop on the women. Watching horseshoes required getting up while the women would almost certainly be discussing somebody's friend who'd just been diagnosed with a dreadful, incurable disease. If he heard about that he'd be up half the night trying to remember if he'd ever had any of the symptoms. So, unless his dad and Uncle Gilbert somehow concluded that Ted Williams hitting .400 had prevented WW III he was staying right where he was.

"Mom, do we have time to go over to the roller rink?" Dave's out of breath cousin Paula shouted from the slide.

"No," Aunt Betty replied, "we'll be cutting the cakes soon."

In four days, on June third, Dave would be fourteen, in five his cousin Christine would be fifteen, so Memorial Day, already hectic, always ended in a birthday party with two cakes. His was butterscotch, made from a war-time recipe. It was squat, no more than half the height of Christine's and scrumptious, especially the caramelized icing. Once everyone had gathered, he and Christine would close their eyes, make a wish then blow out all the candles with one huge breath. You had to do that or the wish wouldn't come true.

"Bet you'll still be able to do that when you're sixty," Little Harlan joked.

Dave didn't look up. He knew everybody'd agree with that statement.

While they ate, Dave's relatives passed him birthday cards. He made sure to say thanks for each one. After that they packed the car and went home.

Dave could hardly wait to tell Ron about the stranger and all the money he made.

"Dad says he barely got out alive."

"A freedom fighter! You met a freedom fighter?" Ron exclaimed.

"Well, sorta...."

"Darn," Ron interrupted, after he flipped the tarp off the "buckboard" parked in the extra stall of his garage. "Spiders, and this thing's only been here two days. You talk to him?" he continued, whisking away cob webs with his hand.

"Couldn't, he and this other guy were using hand signals. He doesn't know any English yet."

"Oh, yeah, there's one like him in town here too. They had him on the radio the second he stepped off the plane. You couldn't made out a word he said either."

"Huh, hadn't heard 'bout him," Dave returned.

"Mind you don't scratch in there," Mr. Rasco cautioned, over the putt-putt-putt of a motorbike, whose carburetor he was adjusting, in the alley.

"I'm being careful," Ron replied, raising his voice. "He's real fussy about the paint."

It was easy to understand why. What everybody called the buckboard, did somewhat resemble the horse drawn carriages seen in T.V. westerns. Its body was a row of varnished oak slats. It had chromed wire wheels, thin, bright red fenders and two laminated bucket seats. Similarities to the simpler rig ended with the addition of a steering column angling up from the floor in front of the driver and a fifth motorized wheel hanging off the back. They transformed the little vehicle into what it really was, an open air 1920s sports car. With glossy finishes and fancy pin striping, the buckboard was a hit wherever it went. Until Dave had seen it, he hadn't known Briggs and Stratton, a company famous for lawn mower engines, ever made a sports car. Course, it wasn't a modern sports car, nothing like a Corvette or T-Bird. Still, it was cool, and Mr. Rasco loved to tinker with it. In fact, other than working, tinkering with his antique vehicles and two old motorbikes was about all he did.

"Man, that's sweet," Dave noted, rubbing a finger lightly over a fender.

"Smooth as silk," Ron replied. "Dad had it repainted over winter, buffed out too, that's what brings up the shine."

"Yeah, so what's he doin' home on a Friday?"

"They've had work at the shop the past two Saturdays. They're taking today off to make up for it."

"Your Mom drivin' it in the Fourth of July parade again?"

"Yep, same as last year, that's why Dad brought it home. We're going over every inch, then I'm waxing it."

"Sounds like a lot of work."

"I don't mind. He said I could drive it some this year."

"What's your dad doin' to the bike?" Dave asked, watching Mr. Rasco kneel down to tighten something on the Johnson.

"At the moment? I don't know," Ron shrugged. "Earlier he changed out the spark plugs because it was running rough."

"Seems like Rafe and Gunner should be here by now the way they been itchin' ta ride."

"They are," Ron said, looking past Dave into the alley.

Sure enough. Before Dave could turn his head Rafe and Gunner stepped in the garage next to him.

"Woulda been here sooner, 'cept Mom made us mow this mornin'," Rafe grumbled.

"Didn't see ya when I came past," Dave puzzled.

"Had ta go for gas," Gunner quipped. "'Cause someone left the tank dry last time."

"We ridin' today?" Rafe asked, ignoring the comment.

"As soon as Dad checks over the Smith," Ron replied.

On those rare Saturdays, in this case a Friday, when Mr. Rasco squeezed out a few hours for his hobby, he treated the neighborhood boys to motor bike rides in the alley behind his house. While he readied the machines, they'd appear like magic, seemingly out of nowhere. In no time at all the air reverberated with the sounds of engines straining and excited teenager's joy-riding, all but Dave, that is. He couldn't handle a regular bike, let alone one carrying the added weight of a motor. It wasn't so bad. He got to watch and give advice if he spotted something that went unnoticed. It was even entertaining on occasion. His friends, half of them scared silly, acting brave when they started out, then, afraid the bike would get away from them, slowing to a crawl before attempting the big round house curve at the end of Rafe's garage. Ron, panicky every time Rafe and Gunner tore out like maniacs, shifting his eyes back and forth between them and his dad, in hopes his dad, busy with the buckboard, wouldn't look up from what he was doing to see what they were doing. Mr. Rasco did, of course, but only when Ron wouldn't notice. That elicited a big grin and a restrained snicker from Dave. By this time Ron would be standing at the alley's edge watching with dismay as the Scanner brothers spun out in the narrows just past where everybody else turned then streaked back. As they did, Ron's hands would unconsciously drift forward, palms out in a rhythmic slow down motion that if seen, was purposely ignored. Only when the two screeched to a halt next to him, skidding in with brakes locked and cinders flying, did he exhibit a measure of relief and revert to normal.

"Thought that vein in your neck was gonna burst their last trip," Dave chuckled, when he and Ron had a chance to talk.

"Me too," Ron winced, feeling for the spot. "Lunatics, gotta race every darn time. You watch, one of them's gonna wreck out and Dad'll put everything away for the summer."

"Na, don't worry 'bout that," Dave consoled. "Your dad's on ta 'em."

"Just wish he was," Ron groaned.

Eventually, after Ron had had several more near death experiences, Mr. Rasco rolled the buckboard into the alley, gassed it up and started its engine. That put a stop to Rafe and Gunner's antics and got Dave thinking again about motorizing his crate. He was still building one, no way had he given up on that. He'd thought about a motor too, any number of times. Not seriously though, but now, with a job, if he could get his hands on, say, something used, an old lawn mower engine, there'd be nothing to it. Rig up some sort of clutch, a brake that operated off a lever instead of a pedal and he could be feeling the wind in his face the same as his friends. He bent down to examine the buckboard more carefully. The usual rope loop connected to the front axle would do for steering. To stop, he could connect wooden brake shoes to a board that pressed against the rear tires. It didn't have to look like anything. He just needed something that would get him where he wanted to go, get him from A to B without always having to walk or finagle a ride on someone's bike.

"Hey! Hey!"

He heard a voice then pushed aside the annoying hand waving in his face.

"What!" he demanded.

"Snap out of it," Rafe said, clapping his hands. "Mr. Rasco said we're done ridin' for the day so we're goin' ta the Morgue. You comin'?" he grinned. "Gunner and I are buyin'."

"Ah," Dave thought for a minute, "um, don't think so, got an errand ta run."

"An errand," Rafe scoffed. He turned to Ron. "You?" he said.

"Sure, as soon as these bikes cool down and I get them put away."

"Well, don't be all day 'bout it," Gunner groused. "We ain't waitin' there forever."

"I'll catch up, only be a minute," Ron shouted, as Rafe and Gunner rounded the bushes next to the garage and disappeared.

"I never actually been to the Morgue," Ron confessed while he and Dave watched Mr. Rasco straighten his corduroy cap, then, with a delicate release of the clutch, ease the buckboard down the alley for a test drive.

"Are all those stories Rafe tells true?" he asked.

"Do'no," Dave replied, "I only been there once. Be good for ya ta get acquainted with the place though, the way that vein was throbbin' out."

"Hey, get off it," Ron grimaced, rubbing his neck. "So they make me nervous, so what."

"Best not be nervous at the Morgue. Rafe says Morie can slab out a guy your size in fifteen minutes."

"And what does Rafe know about anything?"

"Hey, just tellin' ya in case it blows while you're there," Dave teased.

"That why you're not going, can't stand the sight of blood?" Ron shot back.

"Nope. Got somethin' special ta take care of, that's all."

"Must be if you're passing up free stuff."

"It is," Dave smiled. "The Morgue's too far anyway."

"You decided on it then, right?" Ron asked.

"I mighta," Dave replied evasively, taking note of the clock on the wall. "So, you letting me in on it or not?" Ron prodded.

"Tomorrow," Dave said abruptly, as he hurried out the door.

Seconds later Ron was trotting down the alley on his way to the Morgue and Dave was walking briskly through his backyard toward the sidewalk on O'Brien Street. Part way along he heard a scraping sound coming from Doug's yard and paused to peer over Ron's fence. The racer body, with the wheels removed, was propped up on saw horses just outside the garage and Doug was tearing away at the car's front end with a wood rasp. The hood area looked like half an oval layer cake with each succeeding layer slightly smaller than the one beneath it. Working the unattractive steps down, one by one, with only rasps and sandpaper, to produce the sweeping curves of a racer, now that would be one mean feat and take a whole lot of hours.

"Wish I could help out," Dave said.

"You're not the only one," Doug replied, straightening up to wipe the sweat from his forehead. "I've already had about ten offers, but the rules say..."

"I know," Dave cut in, "All work must be performed by entrant."

"Right, but thanks anyway." Doug smiled.

"Gonna have it done in time?"

"Not the way I'm going," Doug sighed. "Once school's out though, and I have all day to work on it, yeah, I'll make it."

"When's the race?"

"July 4th, but it has to be ready for inspection before that."

"Good luck," Dave encouraged, knowing the pile of shavings accumulating around Doug's feet would have to grow into a great heap before the racer was finished.

Dave was on the path again trundling his portable concession stand up the rise toward the road, his enthusiasm for selling pop all but gone. In the three days since he'd worked, except for the stranger, he hadn't thought about the park even once. Now he felt like he'd never left it. Did he have too much ice on? Was he still tired from running his errand? Whatever the cause, he had to force himself to take each step. What about when you got to be an adult? They didn't just work once a week, twice at most, like he did. They had to get themselves up and going every single day. It was baffling, another of life's mysteries he hadn't as yet unraveled.

What had become clear over the past weeks was that a job consisted of two not particularly equal parts: the actual work part he'd thought he was prepared for but wasn't, and the much more important getting paid part. The work seemed to last longer each time, while giving up a whole afternoon's freedom for what you could spend in the blink of an eye, what kind of deal was that? And what about all the other lousy jobs out there? What if you got stuck with one of those the rest of your life?

As he closed in on the backstop, mulling over his latest insight, a voice called out, "Mighty fine day, isn't it?" Turning, he found Mr. Kaufner loaded down with equipment coming up behind him.

"Sure is," he replied, and it was, now that he took notice, a stunningly vibrant spring day. Puffy white clouds against a vivid blue sky, brilliant sunshine flickering through the oaks, an aromatic scent on the breeze, Dave drank it all in. It lifted his spirits.

"Help ya with those?" he asked.

"These speakers?" Mr. Kaufner returned, "You bet. They're awkward when I climb."

And heavy Dave discovered when he handed the first one up.

While Mr.Kaufner hung it from the hook screwed into the tree's trunk and Dave held the ladder, his eyes swept across the park. There were kids in the distance waiting for the roller rink on McClung to open, others at the merry-go-round and the monkey cage up the hill behind the bathroom building. On the knoll a scraggly little dog was leashed to a spindly old gent so wobbly a good sized squirrel could have carried either off if the other hadn't been there. When he saw a squirrel watching the pair from an overhanging branch, he broke a big grin. A hint of crispness wafted through on the next breeze. Nobody was going to waste a whole afternoon watching baseball in this weather. Today was one of those rare days when you just had to be active.

Mr. Kaufner repositioned the ladder for the second speaker. Dave took note of the fishermen on the lake. He might be wrong about that wasting time thing.

What was it with fishing anyway? Sitting, hunched over, all alone in a rowboat, staring at your bobber for hours on end, hoping a twitch, a ripple would bring the thing to life so you could spring your trap? What if your bait was dead or nothing wanted it? You couldn't be pulling your line every five minutes to check, and what were you supposed to do the other 99% of the time, meditate, ponder the meaning of life? Fishing was hard. You had to concentrate every second. Slip up, let your mind wander off, and bingo, before you could set the hook, the big one'd be gone. You couldn't win either way. Catch a slew, you got lucky, they were feeding. Get skunked, and no matter what you said, you were lame.

As Dave watched he realized the fishermen were in mortal danger.

Mr. Kaufner would be switching over any minute now. If the hovercraft were operating today, those anglers were done for. When one of those thundering monsters came cruising past, the wash would swamp every boat on the lake. Dave chuckled then frowned. He was bored silly. Mr. Kaufner moved over to the press box. Dave slumped onto an empty bench, watched the water dripping from the bottom of his cart form into a tiny rivulet. At least the fishermen were in for some excitement. He sucked in some more air, went back to watching the squirrel then dropped his head and closed his eyes. He heard the clicking of cleats. The squirrel was gone. The rivulet was meandering aimlessly through the roots at the far end of his bench. His butt hurt. He got up to stretch. He looked around for the stranger or a signal someone wanted to buy, neither materialized. He moved over to the path. Doing nothing was worse than working hard. Mr. Kaufner wouldn't be wasting his good stuff on this meager crowd. The fishermen were safe.

Right off with the first crack of the bat Dave made two sales. That doubled his take so far for the day. He pushed off, made a pass along the knoll and started back. So much for the stranger, then there he was, crossing the path on his way to the bench he'd occupied earlier. Dave followed him over and held out a Coke. The stranger responded with a hesitant but firm, "Ya-es—please'" and went for his pocket. Seconds later the transaction was complete. There were no incomprehensible foreign phrases, no cryptic signs to decipher, but then, Dave didn't really know what to expect from a man who'd cheated death, probably more than once; maybe some indication of what he'd been through, a wary shifting of his eyes.

Mr. Kovach quickly refocused on the game. A hitter smacked a double. He was on his feet waving the runners around, his shiny watch band streaking through the air. Dave rolled away. As he did, one of the Cubs relievers sat down next to Mr. Kovach. Dave found a spot behind the backstop and watched the two, using gestures and pointing, start up another conversation. No doubt about it, LaPorte was looking out for their newest and arguably most heroic citizen.

Dave wondered, *why was it that time passed so slowly when there was nothing to do, but flew by like crazy when you were having fun?* And why did people have to spread out all over creation? Why couldn't they sit closer together? Then he wouldn't have to work so hard. There were even two blankets at the base of the hill next to the foul line in left field. He decided to take a chance on them. It was a long haul to be sure but he wasn't making any money standing around. On the way he passed Mr. Kovach who looked to be on his way to the necessary building. It was comforting to know there were other people around without a spare tank.

The foray was a success, his best stop of the day, three more sales. When he came back, Mr. Kovach, who had returned, held out his empty. As Dave reached for it, he heard a deep agonizing groan and looked up. His dad was doubled over, grimacing in pain. Mr. Kovach must have missed seeing what

169

happened because he had a bewildered look on his face. The player sitting to his left raised his arm and gave his elbow a sharp slap. Dave knew what that meant. Dad had just gotten thumped by a foul ball and by the looks of it, he got hit hard. Both managers rushed to his aid. One steadied him while the other pressed gently around the joint with a finger. In a while Mr. Norris made a fist then slowly began working his arm back and forth to determine the extent of the injury.

Getting smacked by foul balls was a hazard all umpires faced and Mr. Norris got smacked a lot. Dave couldn't remember a time when he didn't have at least one fading bruise. Dad called then "blue-blacks" and threatened him with one on occasion when he misbehaved. After Mr. Norris bent his arm a few more times, he motioned the hitter back into the batter's box. Everyone clapped. He kept making a fist and flexing every time a side was retired. Wouldn't you know, after nine it was tied 4-4. Fortunately in the tenth the Cubs pulled off a spectacular squeeze play to win. Minutes later Dave and his dad were on their way home, straight home. It was serious when Mr. Norris didn't stop at the tavern after a game to take on coolant.

"Think it's broken?" Dave asked, along the way.

"No, but it's plenty sore and it will be for some time."

As soon as the car stopped Dave sped down to Ron's to tell him about his dad getting hit.

"Really got walloped, doubled right over. I had ta help load his equipment in the trunk."

"I can imagine," Ron chuckled. "Wait a minute," he added, abruptly raising a finger then disappearing off his front porch into the house. "What do you think of this?" he said, when he returned.

"Never seen one a these before. It really work?" Dave asked

"Yep, try it," and Ron handed Dave a clear plastic yo-yo.

Dave gave the yo-yo a flip. As it whirled down the string, colored lights came on. It spun at the bottom a few seconds then Dave snapped it back up. "Cool," he said, looking through at the mechanism inside. "Where'd ya get it?"

"From my cousin, Mr. Sensational, for my birthday. Remember I'm Ron 3:16, like in John 3:16."

"Ya had it since March?"

"No, Only since Thursday. Our family always has a picnic at the farm on Memorial Day. I hadn't seen him for months before that. I didn't bring it out when we were riding because if Rafe gets hold of it, he'll run the battery down."

"Can ya do anything with it?"

"Not much, I've been practicing 'walking the dog.' I've got that down pretty good."

"Ya oughta go for 'rock-a-by-baby,' be neat all lit up."

"Nobody can do that one. Wait a minute. My cousin, sort of forgot, he ate a frog," Ron said, matter of factly.

"What!" Dave frowned."

"Well, not exactly," and Ron's expression widened into a broad grin. "See, he and some of his buddies were down at the swamp pond in the woods trying to catch frogs and he pinned this giant croaker. He said it was big as a baseball. Anyway, he perched it on the heel of his hand facing toward him and lifted it up eye high to stare it down. Someone said it'd be a whole mouthful so he lowered it, said let's see and opened up real wide. I guess he did it without thinking."

"It didn't?" Dave snickered.

"Sure did. Jumped right in, all the way. The only things sticking out were the back flippers. That's when his friends gasped and busted out. They said he was trying to spit, then the expression on his face turned to panic."

"Come on," Dave snorted, giving Ron a shove, "you're makin' this up."

"Am not! The best part is he couldn't get it out."

"No way?" Dave said, with a look of disbelief.

"He couldn't spit the thing out. It was stuck, you know, because of the slime sauce."

Dave and Ron looked at each other and burst into laughter. After Ron recovered sufficiently he said, "Hang on, there's more. He went for a flipper but it was slippery and the frog pulled it in. He said he was afraid to grab the other one so he went back to spitting. See, the frog's back was the same shape as the roof of his mouth. It was suctioned up there tight and wouldn't budge. About a whole minute went by before he worked a finger in around it and popped it out. It fell back into the pond. Nobody saw it after that," Ron hacked. "Bet it died."

"Can see why," Dave roared.

"We better stop laughing," Ron cautioned, "or we'll get sick. One of his friends did, got to coughing and chucked all over himself."

"That's what I'm 'bout ta do," Dave shrieked.

"We better move off the porch, Mom would have a fit."

"She knows 'bout it?" Dave howled.

"Yes, now quit. I knew I shouldn't have told ya."

"And you were gonna keep one this good ta yourself?"

"I tried."

"Hang on," Dave said, after the laughter died away, "I got somethin', too. Whatcha thinka this?" and he pulled the chronograph complete with a sparkly new Twist-O-Flex watch band from his pocket. "Got it at Robertson's yesterday. Took the bus uptown after you went ta the Morgue."

"Knew it! knew it! Knew it!" Ron repeated, slapping the railing with his hand. "You show it to her yet?"

"Show who?" Dave said, raising his voice.

"Marcie, that's why you bought it, right, to show her?"

"No, well, partly, maybe."

Marcie was the girl who lived next door to Dave. She was very nice and getting cuter by the day.

"She's been sunbathin' in a lounge chair outside my window for weeks."

"So, what'd she say when you showed it to her?" Ron asked quickly, "and how'd you get it past your parents?"

"My parents don't know 'bout it and I haven't seen her yet."

"Let me know what she says when you do," and Ron wrapped the band around a finger. "Are these things as expensive as I think?"

"Yep."

"You're in trouble aren't ya?"

"Yep, but what the heck, I haven't heard a word from Dad 'bout gettin' crate wheels and I work hard so I figured I'd spend some a my money on a watch band—your cousin really told ya all that stuff 'bout the frog?"

"He told everybody."

"Man, that warn't too bright," Dave snickered. "Wonder what woulda happened if the frog backed in?" And the two cracked up again.

"Probably the same thing that happened after it jumped in," Ron hacked. "I think he swallowed some of it."

The two, their faces screwed up in disgust, were doubled over in agony laughing.

It was Monday, June 3rd, Dave's birthday. He wasn't just a teenager any more. On Wednesday, at exactly three thirty, when school let out for summer vacation, being fourteen would start paying off. It'd be official; he'd be a high school freshman. If anybody asked, he'd say he attended South Bend Central, the best school in town. That's what he was thinking about while he shot baskets before supper. Then the big surprise came. Mr. Norris called him over to the car and there, neatly laid out in the trunk on his dad's inventory, was the snazziest set of wire wheels he'd ever seen.

"They're the ones from the golf bag carts!" Dave exclaimed.

"They are," Mr. Norris grinned.

"I thought ya forgot."

"I did. Last year after you noticed them I stopped in to see Mr. Skilerak. He's the pro where we usually go. Mike's been a friend of mine for years. I told him what you had in mind. He said he couldn't help me then but that the carts they rented out had defective handles and I should just hold tight. Well, the decision was finally made. Seems they were getting too many complaints so they junked the lot and had no use for these replacement wheels. That's when I got a call."

"They're new!" Dave said in disbelief. "Whoa! Thanks! Think the guys could have the ones off the carts?"

"They're gone," Mr. Norris replied. "The bearings were shot. They weren't worth saving."

"They got bearings!" Dave said, picking up one of the wheels. "Wow! I'm takin' these down stairs for safe keepin'," he said, reaching for a second wheel.

Mr. Norris held up a hand. "There's more," he smiled and pulled two shiny steel bars from alongside some boxes. "It's ground stock for axles, fits the wheels perfectly. I stopped by a tool and die shop where they use it on the way home."

Dave was speechless. After they carried the running gear into the house he said. "Dad, you're the greatest."

"I'm glad you're listening this time," Mr. Norris remarked. "See how saving your money and being patient can pay off?"

"Sure do," Dave replied squeamishly, glad his chronograph was safely hidden away. If Dad saw it, he'd be back to square one on his crate.

Dave scrounged alleys for blocks around the rest of the week looking for building materials. There was plenty of stuff now but with cool wheels, he was being a lot more particular. Fancy wheels on a junk crate just wouldn't do.

On Thursday, Dave decided to make his move. With his dad at work and his mom busy cleaning, he slipped the chronograph into his pocket, took a stack of magazines out to the front porch, plunked them down on the plant stand and went to reading. Pushing off with his right foot, he rocked gently back and forth and watched for Marcie out the side window. He waited; nothing. It was cloudy, she wouldn't be tanning. He read some more. If he sat there much longer Mom would get suspicious. Just as that thought went through, Marcie appeared on her porch with a book under her arm. Dave hurriedly looked into the living room. Seconds later he was out the door so he could "accidentally" meet up with her on the sidewalk between their houses. Along the way he managed to get his watch on without her noticing.

"Where ya off to?" he inquired casually.

"The library," she replied, holding out the book, "to return this or it'll be overdue."

"My mom usually returns mine downtown," Dave said, attempting to connect. "Whatcha thinka my new watch band?" he asked nervously. "It's one a the ones ya can tie in a knot."

"It's nice," she smiled, giving it but a passing glance. "You want to come along?"

"Sure do," Dave responded, with possibly more enthusiasm than was necessary.

As he turned to walk with her, Dave saw his mother busy with something on the porch. She had a clear view of his arm. He spun around and pulled it up tight against his body so she couldn't see the watch.

"Er—sorry—wish I could," he stammered. "Gotta go ta Luke's."

"O.K.," she said, looking baffled, "but I hate to walk alone."

The two parted without another word.

This watch thing was turning into a total nightmare. Here he'd had his best chance with Marcie in weeks and completely blown it. A walk to the library and back, they could have spent an hour together, maybe more. Now he'd have to figure a way to talk himself out of looking like an imbecile. Then there was the little matter of Mom. What had she seen? What might be in store for him when supper time rolled around?

"Hey!" Dave jumped about a foot. Leon, Ben and their friend Johnny Zooker were right behind him.

"Where'd you guys come from?" he asked, astonished.

"The pass," Leon smiled.

"What pass?"

"Lykowski's Pass, ya don't know about it?"

Dave shook his head.

"We come out our back door, go down the alley a house, cut between the garages on your side, come out the driveway you just passed and we're on O'Brien. Lykowski's Pass. Slipped in right behind ya, didn't we?"

"Had no idea you were back there."

"We're going ta Isidor's for popsicles," Ben stated.

"And baseball cards," Leon tacked on.

"Me too," Dave added. "'Cept I'm gettin' a candy bar and maybe a pop."

"Splurgin' are we?" Leon quipped. "What's the big occasion?"

"There's no big occasion," Dave said defensively. "And it's none a your business anyway."

Isidor's was the store on the corner of O'Brien and Humbolt and the closest place where you could get anything.

"I don't buy cards there anymore," Dave remarked. "The gum it comes with tastes like cardboard and I never get anybody good."

"I got Yogi Berra and Stan Musial last week," Leon countered.

"Maybe so," Dave replies, "but I still think somethin' fishy's goin' on there."

The motor bikes came out again that Saturday. So did the yo-yo and just as Ron predicted there was no getting it away from Rafe until he'd done a whole series of tricks, most ones no one else could do.

"Look, I'll cruise over ta the Morgue later and buy a new battery for it," he dodged, not wanting to relinquish control.

Dave was concentrating hard on the buckboard. He'd decided one thing already. He wasn't having no fifth wheel hanging off the back of his crate. The pavement would grind the rubber down in nothing flat. His crate would have a drive belt that went slack for a clutch, that way he could precisely control the transfer of power from the motor to the rear wheel and guarantee a smooth, steady take-off every time. The big problem was designing a suspension system. If he was going to go all out, a suspension system that

175

worked was a must, otherwise with those new wheels, his back teeth would get knocked out. How to go about it? He had ideas, plenty of those, but not the materials and the tools needed to carry them through. It was always the same old story.

After the novelty of the yo-yo wore off and Mr. Rasco curtailed Rafe and Gunner's racing, it was time for the usual jaunt to the Morgue. Dave hung back with Ron to put the bikes away.

"So, what happened with Marcie?" he asked.

"She barely noticed. Then she asked me ta come with her but Mom was there on the porch." And Dave explained how his plan had gone awry. "I made a complete fool a myself. Got no idea if Mom saw the watchband but I'm positive she knows I'm up ta somethin'."

"You're always up to something," Ron laughed.

"Yeah, but she doesn't havta know about it every time. Anyway, after that, I met up with Leon, Ben and Johnny Zooker. Ever get any decent baseball cards at Isidor's?"

"Na," Ron replied, "Twillers' Drugs on Lincolnway's closer for me."

Dave sighed. "I was gonna take Marcie there for a phosphate after we went ta the library."

"Too bad about that," Ron consoled. "There's a baseball card story about my cousin," he smiled mischievously. "You want to hear it?"

"Sure, why not," Dave groaned. "What'd he do this time?"

"Well, somebody he knew had this Superman comic."

"So."

"It was the 3-D version from when we were kids. It had the "Origin of Superman" story in the middle so he thought it was valuable. He said the images jumped right off the page at ya."

"And?"

"The guy wouldn't sell, as if my cousin ever had any money. So he hit up my other cousin, his older brother for some of his baseball cards. That didn't work either. He took the cards anyway, just to show the guy, figuring he could talk his brother into the deal later. Then, I don't know why, but he left the cards in his pants pocket and my aunt ran them through the washer."

"Ouch," Dave cringed. "Hearda that hap'nin."

"Anyway, the cards were still rubber banded together when he got them back but the corners were gone and he couldn't get them apart."

"How many he lose?"

"I don't know, ten, fifteen."

"Good ones?"

"Let's see, Kaline, Musial, Vergil Trucks, Brooks Robinson, two Mantles, I think from his first year. That's all I—no wait, a Willy Mays too."

"Them's good ones," Dave shrugged. "Got beat up didn't he?"

"Pretty bad from what I heard. I think he had to make restitution."

Dave frowned, smacked Ron playfully on the shoulder. "Come on," he scoffed.

"Hey, we do vocabulary words too," Ron said pushing back.

Chapter 15
A CHANCE DISCOVERY

Dave was bubbling over with excitement. He had purpose again. He might be driving soon, even if it would only be down alleys and on side streets. He had his cart loaded, ice and all, in under five minutes. When he came past the orange juice truck, his dad and Mr. Kaufner were leaning against its front fender talking.

"Seems we have a game or two with a turn out like that every year," he overheard Mr. Kaufner say.

"And it was easily the best game so far," Mr. Norris added.

"How's the elbow?"

"It started coming around Thursday," Mr. Norris said, working his arm to show its range of motion.

Word must have gotten out that the last game was a thriller because people were arriving ahead of schedule for this one, but then the Cubs were tied for first place in the league and it was muggy. Dave made a pass along the knoll and was back at the path to take care of fans coming in long before the game started. With sales in the bag this early, things were looking good. He was happy about that because the list of items he wanted to buy for his crate kept growing, little things: bolts, screws, cotter pins. There wouldn't be any bent nails holding the wheels on his crate. The main thing, of course, was finding a good used motor. Three, three and a half horsepower would be about right. He'd even upped his wish list to include a centrifugal clutch, though that was a long shot. They cost about as much as his watchband and he'd never put that much money together before at one time in his whole life.

There was magic in the press box again. Today's addition was rickshaws. Fans were being shuttled to the game in rickshaws powered by bare-chested, under-nourished Chinese men in cone shaped straw hats. "Aw-so," Dave said to himself, as he conjured up images from old Charlie Chan movies. Number two son off to blankets at base of hill.

Mr. Kovach had arrived earlier for this game and was taking in the last minutes of fielding practice from his usual seat. He had one foot crossed over the other knee, his left arm stretched out on the top rail of the park bench where the Twist-O-Flex caught the sun's rays. Dave hardly noticed. Now that he had fancy wheels there were more important things than watchbands. Except for the hand signals, Mr. Kovach hadn't turned out to be all that interesting anyway. Dave thought about stopping then decided to go for the sale on the way back. As he passed behind the bench he heard, "Coke please."

Somehow he'd missed seeing the dime Mr. Kovach held between his thumb and forefinger. He backtracked and dug out the bottle. Then he got a shock. The watchband, so dazzling in the sunlight, was scratched right there on the next to last link by the twelve. It wasn't much of a scratch but something sharp had cut into the metal and left a pin prick at the far end. It was disheartening to see so cool an object defaced, even if no one else would notice. Dave continued on toward the blankets. When there was a big play and his dad was occupied he pulled out his chronograph and examined the band to be sure it wasn't scratched. He was very careful about that, wiped his pocket clean before he put it in and never carried anything with it when he had it along.

Mr. Kovack's arm was still stretched out when Dave came back, giving him a chance to check out the scratch more closely. He guessed it was a little longer than the width of a pin head and a bit deeper than what he'd first thought.

The early innings rush carried Dave into a second cartload of pop. He wasn't complaining about that. The fans were losing out, though. With the Cubs pounding the Argos Merchants into the ground, they'd gone dead silent. The wind was out of Mr. Kaufner's sails too. He sounded like any other announcer now. It was just as well, there was no way he could top rickshaws.

Dave usually went around for empties in the fourth or fifth inning. There was almost always a lull then he could take advantage of. He hated collecting them. They were strewn all over after a sales spurt and hauling them just added weight to his cart. When he came to collect Mr. Kovach's bottle, it was laying on the ground next to his bench and Mr. Kovach was sitting there alone, intent on the game. Dave reached down to retrieve it. When he straightened up his eyes almost popped out of his head. He stood there staring. The bottle slipped through his fingers. He never felt it fall. It hit the ground, bounced and clanked into the metal on his brace. Mr. Kovach turned around. Dave realized his mouth was hanging open and with an audible click, snapped it shut.

"Real nice—mister watch, ya got there," he blurted out, as he pointed to it.

There was a penetrating look in Mr. Kovach's eyes.

A second or two passed. Dave abruptly dropped to the ground, grabbed the bottle and put it in his cart. He started to get up then sat back down, unlaced his shoe, upended it as if to remove a stone and began rubbing the bottom of his foot. He could feel Mr. Kovach's eyes on him the whole time. He slipped his foot into his shoe, laced it, stood and without looking back, hurried away. His head was spinning. He knew what he'd seen and he knew what it meant. The distant struggle with the Russians wasn't distant anymore. The Cold War had come to the American midwest, to a rather nondescript small town in Indiana, to LaPorte. Mr. Kovach was a spy.

Dave found a spot on a bench in among the old codgers behind the backstop. He sat rigid and stared motionless at home plate, His brain was racing. *How?* He wondered. *Why? Why here? What could they possibly be after?* He tried to get a sense of who was around him in case he was under surveillance. Nothing seemed amiss. He forced himself to relax, felt the tension ease and noticed how quiet it was. Mr. Kaufner was out passing the hat through the crowd, collecting donations. Dave picked up a few pebbles and started pitching them at a twig a few feet away, thinking that's what a bored kid should probably be doing. His mind was going a mile a minute. Maybe he hadn't seen what he'd seen. Maybe it was all in his head. No, just like with the coin, he had seen it, clear as day in the mid afternoon sun. He was positive. He tried making mental sketches. Maybe Mr. Kovach just had his watch on backwards. That wouldn't work because then the winding stem would be on the wrong side and it wasn't. Maybe he had a second watch exactly like the one he was wearing in his—that was stupid. Dave glanced around to see if anybody was looking his way. A geezer two benches over was but then he mimicked taking a drink. A few minutes ago that would have been important and Mr. Kovach didn't matter. Now, Mr. Kovach and the intrigue he was a part of, were all that did matter.

Dave started peppering his dad with questions about Mr. Kovach the minute they were in the car. Where exactly had he come from? What part had he played in the uprising? What did Dad know about the people he lived with, his friends, what he did, where he went?

"Whoa there," Mr. Norris said, raising a hand. "Why the sudden interest in our newest citizen?"

"I just wanted ta know more 'bout him," Dave fibbed, in as calm a voice as he could manage.

Dave went silent while he tried to figure out his next move. At his uncle's he played the jukebox and sang along as if nothing had happened.

When they were back on the road and reached the newly constructed building at the edge of town, Dave remembered that Mr. Kovach worked there.

"What's his job?" Dave asked.

"I believe metal finishing, yep, that's where they started him. Pretty classy for a factory," Mr. Norris noted, as they passed the red brick facade. "I've made some good sales there already and the plant's not in full production yet. I'll sell them a lot more tools in the future, yes indeedee," he said confidently, as much to himself as to Dave.

"What does Castinal make?" Dave inquired.

"Buckets."

"Buckets," Dave repeated, with a frown. "Ya mean pails?"

"No," Mr. Norris laughed. "They make engine buckets."

"What kind a engine uses buckets?" Dave asked, perplexed.

"Well, they're not really buckets. That's just shop talk. Castinal makes turbine blades for jet engines."

"Oh, no!" Dave gasped out loud.

"They're one of the largest producers in the country. Most all of our front line fighters and bombers use engines with Castinal turbine blades inside."

"Isn't all that stuff top secret?" Dave probed.

"Some is, some isn't," Mr. Norris explained. "To make a turbine blade they first make a model of it out of wax, that's the pattern. They suspend the pattern in an empty container then pour in a special material that hardens around it. That makes a mold. After the mold has cured, the wax is melted out and molten metal is poured into the cavity left behind. After it solidifies they break the mold and the blade is ready for machining. Then it's polished, inspected and sent out for service. They subcontract a lot of work for G.E. out of Cincinnati."

The J-79, Dave thought.

"It's called the lost wax process. It's been around for centuries."

"So everybody knows how ta do it?" Dave asked, apprehension in his voice.

"Not exactly," Mr. Norris chuckled. "The theory's well known but putting it into practice, now that's an altogether different matter. It takes a lot of know-how to turn a lump of metal into a turbine blade. Turbine blades are the most critical parts in a jet engine. They're subject to great stress and extremely high temperatures. It's the sophisticated techniques Castinal has developed that makes the process work. That's what's classified. That's what's top secret. Nobody knows exactly how they do it."

"Well, somebody's tryin' ta find out," Dave said, bracing himself and taking the chronograph out of his pocket. "Mr. Kovach is a spy."

Mr. Norris took the cigar out of his mouth and turned toward Dave. When he did the car edged off the road onto the berm. Mr. Norris guided it back. To say he had a skeptical look on his face would be more than charitable.

"What on earth put that crazy idea in your head?" he said sternly.

"This," Dave replied hesitantly, handing his watch to his dad. "Mr. Kovach's got a watch band just like that one. I been keeping an eye on it since he first showed up."

"This is new, isn't it?"

"Yes sir," Dave said, swallowing hard.

"And expensive?"

"Yes sir," Dave replied, his stomach doing a flip.

"I thought I told you not to let money burn a hole in your pocket like this."

"Ya did, and I know I shouldn't have bought it but my leather one, well, it was so shabby. When I saw Mr. Kovach had a Twist-O-Flex for his watch and how cool it looked, I couldn't resist buying one for mine. But I'll give Mom half what I make for the rest of the summer ta put in my bank account, if that's all right, that is, promise," Dave added.

"I don't suppose Marcie had anything to do with this?" Mr. Norris asked firmly.

Brother, does everybody know, Dave thought.

"A little maybe," he stammered.

"Uh huh, and now, for the sixty-four thousand dollar question, what does this watch have to do with spying?" Mr. Norris interrogated, giving it a good shake.

"It's not the watch," Dave corrected. "It's the watch band."

"All right," Mr. Norris said, his patience waning, "what does the watch-band have to do with spying?"

Dave laid out what he'd seen one step at a time.

"See, his arm was stretched out on the backa the bench and the sun was blazin' in on the band. The scratch was right there, plain as day. Then, when I came back for his empty, bang, it was gone, I'm positive. Now the scratch, it's real small and if ya didn't catch it in the li..."

"Let me see if I've got this straight," Mr. Norris broke in. "There was a scratch, then there wasn't, but it's nearly impossible to see. That about it?" he said, shaking the watch with his right hand while he steered the car with his left.

"Yes sir," Dave answered. "It's just that ya havta know where ta look. It's right here on this link," he said, trying to synchronize his finger with the moving timepiece.

"And you can only see the scratch when the sun's on it," Mr. Norris repeated to himself.

Dave nodded.

"Now, If you could just make a connection here for me I'd appreciate it," Mr. Norris said in a forced calm.

"See, they're switchin' watches. I don't know exactly how or when but they havta be. It was all in this movie I saw on the late show."

Dave realized saying that was a mistake before the words were out of his mouth. This time the look was exasperation and the butt end of Dad's cigar was all but chomped off.

Somehow Dave found the strength to go on.

"See the spy had a camera that took super tiny pictures. He developed 'em in his basement like Luke does for his telescope. Then he cut 'em inta squares and put 'em inside the back cover of his watch. After that, he and this other guy switched at what they called "a drop." It was in a phone booth right out on the street. The watches were exactly the same and they hid the extra one in the same place every time. The spy would go in, exchange his, then later, the first guy returned, picked up the one with the film and walked away."

"So, from a scratch that's practically invisible you've concluded Mr. Kovach is a spy. You're really out in space on this one," Mr. Norris said, shaking his head and taking a deep breath. "Do you have any idea how much trouble saying something like that could cause? I do business in this town! Our relatives live here! You can't be calling the local hero a spy unless you have incontrovertible evidence!" and he banged on the steering wheel with his fist.

"Aww..." Mr. Norris uttered a few choice words, pitched his mutilated cigar out the window, lit up a new one and continued the lecture.

"People look up to this man; he's been on the front line of freedom, something they can only dream about. Making a charge like that, if it's not true, it's against the law. You could ruin his reputation, destroy his character. People go to jail," he bellowed. "Are you listening?"

"Yes sir, but I did see it," Dave replied. "I looked at it so hard, when I walked away I had shivers goin' up and down my spine."

"Why would a man who fought for liberty turn against the very country that gave it to him? He has a new lease on life here."

"I do'no, maybe he was a spy all along and just slipped in with the other guys they brought over. I mean, how could ya be sure? What about the government guy they sent ta sort 'em out? Maybe he made a mistake. I saw the scratch. It was there. I'm tellin' the truth."

That was it. Dave had made his case as best he could and gotten the reaction he'd expected. If he couldn't convince his dad, there was nothing more he could do. But there had to be. He had to find proof, no matter what.

Mr. Norris made the left turn off of Lincolnway onto O'Brien then turned right onto Vassar.

"So ya believe me?" Dave asked hesitantly, once the car had stopped.

Mr. Norris just sat there for what seemed an eternity then pointed a finger directly at Dave.

"Don't be spreading this cock and bull story around...an accusation like that."

Lines formed across Mr. Norris' brow.

With the finger still there he said," I don't want to hear another word about this unless you have incontrovertible proof, first! And to refresh your memory, the man they sent over, his name's Zavatski. You met him at Kiwanis field when we picked up the books last fall. He's Meyer's friend."

Proof, that's what Dave needed. His dad was right about that. If he had proof Dad would have to believe him. They could go to the police and get Mr. Kovach and whoever else was involved put away, hopefully, before any real damage was done. But how was he going to get it? Even if the scratch appeared and disappeared every Sunday for the rest of the summer, his dad wasn't about to go over and inspect it. If he wasn't fourteen, if the scratch was bigger and easier to see, he'd stand a chance. But then, Mr. Kovach would notice it too. He might be able to finger the other guy, the guy Mr. Kovach was switching with. What good would that do? Dad would say the two were friends, played golf together, fished the same lake and just got their watches mixed up. Then there was the matter of his mouth dropping open and the stupid look on his face. Was Mr. Kovach wise to him? How many others were involved? Was he in danger?

After supper Dave went to Ron's, a regular occurrence of late.

"Look," he said, after explaining what had happened at the park, "These guys play for keeps. I screw up again, they'll be on ta me sure, if they aren't already."

"But your dad, you can't go against what he said."

"Looks like I already have," Dave said with a shrug. "There's just too much at stake."

Both Dave and Ron thought for a while.

"Is this for real?" Ron asked eventually. "I mean, you absolutely sure?"

"So you don't believe me either!" Dave shot back.

"I'm just saying, this one's pretty farfetched."

"You're tellin' me? I didn't go lookin' for this, ya know. It woulda been just fine with me if someone else had stumbled on their operation. Then breakin' up the ring would be their problem. I'd be off the hook. What I need ta know now is whether you're with me or not."

Ron studied Dave's face.

"You're positive?"

Dave shook his head. "I can't do this alone. They'll probably have somebody watchin' every move I make. That's why I need you. Our dads are friends; they trust each other. So I figure it'll be O.K.... It might be risky."

Ron didn't respond. Then in a measured tone he said, "All right, I'm in."

"Ya mean it? Ya sure?" Dave challenged.

"I said I'm in, didn't I?" Ron answered firmly. "So what's the plan?"

"There is no plan, that's why I'm here."

"You must have some ideas. You always have ideas," Ron prodded.

"I got a few. First, somebody else has ta see the scratch then see it disappear. That gives me a witness; that's number one. That's where you come in. Once I got a witness, people will know I'm not lyin'."

"How are we supposed to pull that off if he's already suspicious?"

"Got no idea. Well, there's one thing. He's nuts 'bout baseball, watches every play like a hawk. We might be able ta use that against 'im but we'd havta be careful or the other guy'll pick up on what we're doin'."

"That's the accomplice, the other guy." Ron said.

"Knew that's what they call 'em," Dave returned. "If we both tell Dad we saw the scratch disappear he might go for it."

"He might," Ron replied. "Then again, he might just go for you."

"Yeah, he might, but if we knew exactly how they were doin' it?"

"How about if I just hang around and keep my eyes open until I see something?"

"That ain't much."

"What if we have to talk?"

"Won't work, the park's not that big. Ya can see all the way across."

"O.K., then I'll write a note on a gum wrapper, crinkle it up and leave it..."

"On the ground next ta the front wheel of our car," Dave said, finishing the sentence. "I can keep an eye out for it when I'm goin' ta the Pavilion."

"I still can't get over how you thought of faking a stone in your shoe, man that was some quick thinking."

"No it wasn't. I just knew in another second he'd know if I didn't do somethin', simple as that. I do'no how I thought of it. I was scared, real scared. The way he looked at me, it was like he could read my mind. I do'no what was worse, that or havin' ta tell Dad. He used the word 'crazy' in the very first sentence. His face was all twisted up."

Ron couldn't keep from smiling.

"The minute I said I saw it in a movie he said I was havin' a brainstorm. That's what he calls it when I have an idea that's different."

"This one's a real doozie, your best ever," Ron chuckled. "Was it something like that?"

"Yeah, kinda, 'cept he said humdinger instead a doozie and he thought I bought the Twist-O-Flex just ta impress Marcie. So now I getta put most a what I make this summer in the bank. Do'no what I'm gonna do for my crate."

"Did he believe any of it?"

"Ya mean before or after he called me a space cadet? Na, I don't think so. He chewed the end right off his cigar, never seen 'im do that before. Then he started givin' me the business about sayin' stuff. Said he didn't wanna hear another word 'bout it unless I had "inconvertable" proof. Would you wanna havta tell your dad a story like that?"

"No," Ron replied.

"I best get goin'," Dave said. "Tim's gonna call me on the phones. We're playin' chess 'fore bed tonight. Be back in the mornin'."

Dave had just started for home when he realized the rudimentary plan they'd fashioned was just that, rudimentary. Ron didn't know what Mr. Kovach looked like, might not be able to spot the scratch. They didn't know where the switch was being made, how many people were involved. They didn't even know if the culprits followed the same procedure each week or altered their routine to throw off suspicion. All they had was what Dave had seen and six days. Once they were in the car next Sunday, they were on their own. Getting together at the park to compare notes was out of the question.

Moonlight flooded into Dave's bedroom that night. When it was this strong he usually lay there studying the shadowy outlines it produced. Not this time. He kept looking out his windows, searching for movement then quickly pulled back into the corner at the head of his bed where it was dark. He'd even played chess with the lights off and figured that was why Tim won. His mind was abuzz with activity. He couldn't get it to slow down. Normally that was fine. He did some of his best thinking before dropping off. On this occasion, the thoughts just kept coming. He couldn't make them stop. Hours drifted by. He started to panic. If he got to sleep after midnight he'd pay big the next day and here it was, already two in the morning.

Dave heard the vacuum cleaner's whine from the kitchen and tried to ignore the not so subtle reminder that it was time to get up. It worked for a few minutes but then his mind started going again. He managed to stay out of his mother's way just long enough to wash up, eat breakfast and zip out the back door.

"You sick or something?" Ron asked.

"Really tired," Dave yawned. "Couldn't getta sleep last night, too much on my mind."

"Same here," Ron concurred. "But I figured some stuff out."

"Me too," Dave said, rubbing his eyes. "You go first."

"Well, if they stick to the same plan this week, you don't have anything to worry about. They don't know you know. If they aren't there or they don't make the switch then..."

"Then I'm in trouble." Dave groaned

"We're in trouble," Ron supported. "But even if they think you saw something, they won't think anyone will believe you."

"They'd be right 'bout that," Dave frowned. "Thing is, none of this helps us catch them."

"I'm getting to that," Ron persisted. "O.K., to start with, you go over everything that happened from when you first saw that Kovach guy, from the very beginning. We write it all down, everything in order."

"And I'll draw up a diagram of the park," Dave said. "So's you'll know where everything's at 'fore ya get there."

"Shhh," Dave said, raising a finger to his lips. Rafe and Gunner stepped onto Ron's porch from the walkway that ran between his house and Doug's.

"All right, out with it," Rafe said. "I saw that."

"What you guys up to?" Gunner asked.

Dave pulled his finger away from his mouth. "Not much," he returned.

"Come on," Rafe grinned, "you can tell us. We're best friends."

"If ya must know, I'm tryin' ta figure a way ta get my hands on another fungo bat."

"Hope ya do," Rafe said, the grin now a cheesy smile.

"Where are you two going?" Ron asked.

"Twillers', for a new whiffle ball," Gunner explained.

"Here," Dave said testily and he and Ron each handed Gunner a dime.

"Thanks," Gunner replied. "'Member, game's on at one sharp."

Dave and Ron watched the Scanner brothers walk up O'Brien then disappear around the corner on Lincolnway.

"And that fungo bat comment just popped into your head, right?"

"Had ta say somethin'," Dave shrugged. "I'm dead tired. I'm goin' home ta read for a while. Come over after supper, we'll work up a plan in the basement. Nobody'll bug us there."

Dave was lying on the ledge nailing a piece of plywood over the second of the two small windows that admitted light into the basement when he heard footsteps on the stairs.

"What the heck are you doing up there?" Ron asked, moments later.

"Just playin' it safe."

"You afraid the bogeyman's going to get you?" Ron jeered.

"I'm not takin' any chances."

"LaPorte's miles from here, plus the way you were hitting today..."

"Yeah, I know, who's gonna bother with me? Now that you've had your fun, let's get ta work." Dave pointed to the notebook on his chemistry table. "You get the stool," he said, "I'll make do with the tool box."

The two sat down. Ron started to laugh. "You've got cobwebs in your hair."

Dave brushed them out, then, before Ron could say anything more, he raised a hand, reached across and turned on his radio.

"That's too loud," Ron complained. "I can hardly hear."

"Means nobody else can either," Dave said, adjusting the volume down slightly.

"O.K., first, before I forget, I looked it up." Ron said.

"Ya looked what up?" Dave questioned.

"What your dad said. It's incontrovertible. It means indisputable. We've got to have them dead to rights or we can't do anything."

"Yeah, I knew that."

Dave stood and pulled a roll of paper from behind his chemical rack on the ledge.

"I drew this up 'fore supper. It's a map of the park, shows the Pavilion, the path. Here's where Mr. Kovach sits."

Ron looked it over. "What we have to do is show patterns," he said. "Adults like that and they like it when stuff's written down. If we can show on paper when they make each move, what they do and if they're doing it over and over the same way each time, I think we'll have them."

Ron took a pencil from his pocket. "So when did you first spot him?"

"That was Memorial Day. We had the picnic then, but I didn't get over 'til late 'cause there was a big crowd and there were lots a bottles scattered around on the knoll. I didn't get much of a look at the watch either because the Sportsman player with the mangled hand was sittin' between me and Mr. Kovach. After that, with all the haulin' I had ta do, it's kind of a blur."

"Think he was switching with the player?"

"The player? Na, that guy was only there the one time."

"Is there a calendar I could see?" Ron asked.

"This year's?" Dave said, propping his head up on his hand. "Beats me."

"Cancel that," Ron directed. "I'm putting down the dates since Memorial Day then we'll work backwards. Maybe that'll jog your memory. Now, when do you think they made the switch?"

"Wait, I can't," Dave said, shaking his head. "I've had it. I gotta get some sleep. Let's do this tomorrow."

"Same way?" Ron asked.

"Same way," Dave replied.

Dave was in bed ten minutes after Ron left, this time with better results.

"How'd it go?" Ron asked the next morning when he and Dave met up on his porch.

"Better, not great. This time I only got half my breakfast."

Ron looked puzzled.

"My mom. I had ta get outta the house 'fore she got a look at my face. You know how she's always checkin' up on me. Last time I couldn't sleep she accused me a stayin' up all hours. Grabbed hold of my mouth so tight I couldn't talk."

"Praise the Lord," Ron snickered.

"Yeah, yeah, anyway, I shook my head that I hadn't then she thought I was lyin'. I was afraid she'd have Dad take my T.V. out and jerk my phone wires."

"Forget about that. The watch, they're doing it in the bathroom." Ron said

"That's where I do it," Dave hooted.

Ron frowned, "They're switching watches in the restroom. It's the only place where no one can see."

"They could be switchin' at the Pavilion or in the woods, even at a car," Dave said, "but I think you're right. The bathroom building makes the most sense. We should do this later. Soon's we start takin' stuff down somebody'll come around the corner again. Anyway, I'm wide awake now, so I'm goin' home for lunch. Then, Ben's got this giant rocket, 'bout a foot tall. We're gonna fire it at the gravel pit this afternoon. If it works, we're putting furnace bombs on 'em and lightin' a bunch off on the 4th of July."

"You two are going to blow each other up some day."

"If we do, we'll be in the hall a flame," Dave grinned. "How 'bout we plan for Sunday at my house tonight?"

"If you're still alive," Ron smirked.

The gravel pit was located a mile or so from Dave's neighborhood on a long strip of land near the South Bend Airport. When Dave and Ben came to where the street they took ended, they hid Ben's bike in the bushes behind the "NO TRESPASSING" sign. Then they proceeded to fight their way through the brambles to where the gravel had been dug out. Instead of one big hole like might be expected, this gravel pit was a hodgepodge of irregularly shaped craters and deep interconnected valleys separated by narrow ridges. On these ridges, where the earth hadn't been disturbed, an impenetrable thicket of scrubby trees and tangled undergrowth thrived. The dirt road that snaked through the property at the bottom was once used to remove aggregate from the "pits" at the north end. It had long since been rendered impassible by landslides and erosion. Isolated, inaccessible, mostly barren, once inside this abandoned labyrinth, it was easy to imagine yourself on another planet. It was the perfect place to launch rockets.

Dave and Ben had visited their "Peenemunde" test site many times before and long ago made friends with the faded orange cab of an abandoned Bantam Crane, their only companion. Scavenged for parts, its windows broken, the rusting skeleton that lay on its side had transported them to the moon and distant planets more than once. They were younger then. Now with pedals missing and levers gone, it silently awaited its fate. Each year it was less orange, more brown, the weeds around it more profuse. Nature was slowly, inexorably reclaiming the land, obliterating the scars left by man. For the moment this real estate belonged to David W. Norris and Benjamin W. Cheske but, being a gravel pit, it was still a dangerous place and Dave knew it. Every time he was there he thought about the boy who'd dug out a cave in a gravel pit, climbed in, and when the hill side above him collapsed, suffocated. They didn't find him for days. Anytime Dave heard stories like that, he tried to learn from them. He stayed away from hillsides that were steep or undercut.

Ben's rocket was a fabulous success. It blasted off the pad with a roar, accelerated as it climbed, then, still going strong, streaked out of sight. Behind it a tell-tale gray line extended skywards into the heavens. Slender, straight as an arrow, it looked like the finest of ropes beckoning to be climbed.

"Wow!" Ben shouted. "Did you see that!"

"What'd ya put in that thing?" Dave asked, an astonished look on his face.

"Just the regular stuff," Ben said gleefully.

They looked at each other in shock then looked up at the wispy trail of smoke slowly being deformed by the breeze.

"Wish the other guys had been here ta see this," Dave remarked.

"Quiet," Ben said, "I want that one back."

The boys listened intently and scanned the skies for a long time.

"See anything?" Ben asked.

"Na," Dave answered. "That one mighta come down miles from here."

Ben's rocket was like a carnival ride: a few moments of wild excitement, a letdown, then only memories.

"Think back," Dave quizzed on the way home. "Ya musta done somethin' different. We never had one fly like that before."

"I'm tryin'," Ben said, "The only thing was the wire. Paper clips weren't big enough so I used newspaper bundle wire instead. I wrapped on three turns just like always and squeezed the paper in real tight. Darn, I wish we'da found it."

"Yeah," Dave agreed, as Ben shook his head in dismay. "Then we coulda taken it apart ta see what happened."

When Ron came downstairs that night he found Dave pulling staples out of thick insurance forms.

"Got these from Ben," Dave explained. "His dad gets piles from work. You shoulda gone today," and he told Ron all about his experience at the gravel pit and how marvelously Ben's rocket had flown. "It was sensational," he grinned. "I never seen one zoom like that before. This is the paper he used. I'm gonna make up tubes while we talk." And Dave began rolling pieces of paper around a large dowel rod. "It was the third inning."

"Hold on," Ron said, opening his note pad. "What day are we on?"

"It's still Memorial Day. Think I got it straight now. There was a big crowd. I already had a load of empties on, so while Mr. Kaufner was recappin' the second inning I whipped over ta the Pavilion. When I came back, 'bout five minutes later, Mr. Kovach was gone."

"To the restroom?"

"Do'no, prob'ly."

"We'll put that down as a maybe."

"Then, coulda been in the sixth, I know I didn't get a break. That's when I sold 'im a pop and first saw the watch."

"O.K., this Sunday?"

"Mr. Kovach got there early. I was gonna go on by ta the blankets further down but he called me over. That's when I saw the scratch. Saw it again when I came back. Then, 'bout the fifth, the scratch was gone."

"What'd he do in between?"

"No idea. I was real busy."

"And on the Sunday in between, June second?"

"That was the day Dad got smacked. I was tired. Let's see, soon's he got there in the first or second I sold 'im a Coke—he always buys Cokes. Then for a while there he was jumpin' up and down like a crazy man. Later I went on past ta the blankets. Usually do that once a game. On the way back I grabbed his empty. That's when Dad got nailed."

"Then what?"

"Then nothin'."

"Hum, that's not much."

"Wait up! When I went on past ta the blankets he was goin' the other way, ta the bathroom! I'm sure of it!"

Dave and Ron looked at each other. An ear to ear grin appeared on both their faces.

"They're switching in the third or fourth and they're doing it the same way every game," Ron said, astonished.

"That warn't smart at all," Dave snickered. "They're really bein' stupid. If we're right, it's a pattern, 'cause they're repeatin' it, so we got 'em."

"We might, if they keep doing it and someone else sees the scratch disappear," Ron reasoned.

"I could steal the film outta the watch this Sunday after Mr. Kovach switches," Dave said. "Know I could find it in there but what if I got caught? Or, I could just take the watch, but if I stole it, they'd know 'fore I could do anything with it 'cause Dad'd still be umpin' and Mr. Kovach would still have a watch. He'd say he didn't know anything 'bout the other one and they'd come lookin' for us. Don't know 'bout you but I'm not plannin' on endin' up in the river with buckets of cement on my feet. We gotta go slow, take it one step at a time 'til we get it rock solid."

"Not to change the subject but is this place going to be a war zone on the Fourth?" Ron asked.

"Nope," Dave replied. "Not after that lady 'cross from Young's went berserk last winter. We're not chancin' anything like that hap'nin again. If we get Ben's rockets perfected and I mean they fly straight every time and blow up at the very top, then, maybe. We don't want any trouble and we don't want anybody gettin' hurt." At that, Dave dropped a third precisely rolled tube into the jar beside his radio.

"That's good to hear."

"We best stick with it," Dave said.

"Right."

"You're new ta the park and no matter what ya say you're gonna be nervous, real nervous, so we only go for two things. First, ya see if you can get a look at the watch while you're keepin' an eye on the restroom buildin', maybe if his arm's laid out. There shouldn't be a scratch."

"Is that one thing or two?" Ron asked.

"Quit goofin' off."

"I wasn't."

"Then, later, ya make another pass. This time the scratch should be there. I'll work my route around so I can do the same. Next, ya stake out the bathroom and try ta spot the accomplice, um, I'd say from a ways back on the knoll where ya can see everything from one spot. Ya can work all that out when ya get there. Oh, and whatever ya do, don't look 'em straight in the eye, that's important. It's a dead giveaway. I know. I did it. Turn your head and take a passin' glance or look outta the corner of your eye. Later, we'll get together here and compare notes 'fore we forget or it gets jumbled up."

"You forgot something."

"What's that?"

"Not getting caught," Ron said.

"Yeah, not gettin' caught," Dave repeated. "Guess that's number one."

"Everything set for Sunday?" Ron asked on Thursday.

"Almost," Dave replied, "except for one thing. I haven't asked Dad if you can go yet."

"What?" Ron exclaimed. "Why not?"

"'Cause I don't know how, I mean, if I just say, 'can Ron come along' for no reason, he might blow. He's bound ta know you're in on it. 'Member, he said I couldn't tell anyone. I been hopin' I'd come up with somethin' clever all week but I haven't."

Ron scowled but didn't say anything.

"All right, all right, I'll ask him." Dave frowned.

Ron continued to scowl.

"Tomorrow. I'll do it tomorrow afternoon, soon's he parks in after work."

"Well, if I never see you again, it's been nice knowing ya," Ron smirked, holding out a hand.

Dave pushed it away. "This is serious," he snapped.

When Dave saw his dad pull up the next afternoon, he came barreling out of the alley like he was just coming home.

"Can Ron go with us Sunday?" he said, out of breath. "I been tellin' 'im all about the old roller rink on McClung across from the park. He really wants ta see it."

Dave got the eye.

"Well, if you mind what I said," Mr. Norris replied firmly, "I suppose, but we're starting double headers this weekend."

"I will, promise."

"Stu is going too." Mr. Norris noted.

"Stu?" Dave questioned. "I didn't know he liked baseball."

"Of course he likes baseball. Why else would he have asked to come along?"

"It's all set," Dave told Ron when they met in his basement that night. "You can go. I told Dad ya wanted ta check out the roller rink next ta the park, it's here," he said, pointing to the spot on the sketch he'd made. "So don't forget ta ask 'bout it when we're in the car. Now, in the first or second inning, if somethin's hap'nin, ya know, a team's threatenin', got a couple guys on, ya could probably come down from the slide and stop behind Mr. Kovach's bench ta watch. Ya wouldn't block anybody 'cause there's no benches further back and he's gonna be tunnelin' in on the game."

"What if I can't see the scratch?"

"Just hang around. If he spots ya, ignore 'im. Don't panic. You're just a fan, and whatever ya do, don't look 'im straight and don't leave, at least not for a while. O.K., now, let's try it out. I penciled a mark on my watchband. I'll sit here with my arm out. You go back by the stairs, walk toward me and try ta spot it."

Ron did and couldn't see the mark. They tried again. He still couldn't see it.

"That's 'cause a the sun," Dave explained. "The scratch is only visible when the sun catches in the groove. Ya gotta get it at just the right angle."

"I hope it works better at the park than it is here," Ron said, a dubious expression on his face. "Let me take the drawing you made. I can study it at home."

Chapter 16
SPUD

R on pulled Dave aside before they got in the car that Sunday.
"Look here," he whispered, slipping his hand into his pants pocket then withdrawing it only far enough to expose half a dozen gum wrappers. "Just in case."

"Too risky," Dave mouthed, and he pushed Ron's hand back in.

When they stopped to pick up Stu, Mr. Norris got out to check a tire.

"Why are you wearing the old band on your watch?" Ron asked. "Where's the Twist-O-Flex?"

"I switched back ta the leather strap this mornin', figured if Mr. Kovach saw I had a watch, he'd think that's why I noticed his."

"Good idea," Ron replied.

Stu was more alert than normal. But then, it was just noon and a Sunday. He and Mr. Norris started discussing the latest Yankee brawls the minute he got in the car: the fights, the fines. It went back and forth. Both men knew their stuff, you could tell. Stu went from one extreme to the other as he so often did; making a brilliant observation one minute, fading out the next.

Dave and Ron, mentally walking their way through the plans they'd made, sat quietly in the back seat.

"Will Harridge was at the game Thursday when it broke loose," Mr. Norris said.

"Who's Will Harridge?" Stu asked.

"He's the president of the American League. He gave me my start in '39 when I worked the Northern League. He's a pretty tough cookie."

"Fighting like that sets a bad example for the kids," Stu remarked. "That's what riles me."

"Very true," Mr. Norris agreed. "I like their competitiveness though, can't fault them for that, but thousands of dollars in fines, the publicity, it's bad for the game. They're all a bunch of crybabies and sissies nowadays."

Were Dave's ears deceiving him? Were these the same Yankees who up until a few days ago could do no wrong? He desperately wanted to get his two cents into this conversation but for once kept his big mouth shut. If there was ever a no-win situation this had to be it.

"It's not like in the old days. It was the game back then. The game's what mattered, not the money. Give you a good example: Pikey Schwartz. When he played for us, gloves were little more than pancakes. He cut the center out of his just to toughen up. We hit line drives at him for hours. He never flinched once."

"Ouch," Dave cringed, twisting up his face.

Ron did the same

"By the middle of the season you could hit the palm of his hand with a hammer and he wouldn't blink. He was a ballplayer's ballplayer."

Stu groggily shook his head in agreement. "I tell you," Mr. Norris continued, "ninety feet between bases is the closest man has ever come to perfection."

Dave looked at Ron thinking that was the corniest thing he'd ever heard. The conversation became more and more one-sided as they drove along but Mr. Norris didn't seem to notice.

"Sure, the 'greats' got their money. They earned it. The 'Babe' got a fair shake but he loved the game too. That's what counts. That's what's important. The money was secondary."

"How far did the Babe's longest home run go?" Dave asked.

"Would you like Mr. Kaufner's estimate or the actual distance?"

"Mr. Kaufner's would probably say ten thousand miles," Dave joked.

"Actually, one went further. Ruth's wasn't officially measured but it was over five hundred feet."

"Where's the ten thousand miles come in?" Dave smirked, looking at Ron.

"That's the longest distance a baseball has ever been known to go before it was found."

Dave and Ron were snickering now.

"A home run was hit out of the park in Baltimore. It landed on a steamer in the harbor and wasn't discovered until weeks later when the ship docked in Japan."

Dave and Ron laughed.

Mr. Norris, encouraged by the reaction, went on.

"There was a shortest home run, too," he smiled, the boys in the palm of his hand. "It only went a few feet. Nobody knows for sure."

Dave had no idea where his dad came up with all these crazy stories.

"It was in the 1800s," Mr. Norris said. "Most of the infield was a bog. A ball was hit hard into the mud in front of home plate and the soup not only swallowed it up, it splashed back into the catcher's eyes, blinding him. He tried to rub it out then dropped to his knees and started digging around but he couldn't find the ball. Two other players came in to help. All three were up to their elbows when the runner slid in behind them. One of them claimed to have put on the tag, but the umpire didn't get a clean look so he awarded the run."

Dave and Ron were in stitches.

"Didn't get a clean look, that was a good one," Dave howled.

"It's in the books. You can look it up."

The boys rolled their eyes. *Sure it is,* Dave thought.

For a few minutes the two had forgotten how serious their mission was. With the return of silence, their stomachs began to churn, their minds began to race. They nudged each other and crossed their fingers. Dave concentrated on the scenery zipping past his window, hoping it would take his mind off of spies and spying. It's what he always did when the pain started. He was glad he wasn't alone. When they passed the Castinal plant Dave poked Ron, nodded slightly and twisted his thumb. Ron, following his lead, looked out in silent response. A few minutes later they turned on Truesdell and entered the park grounds. As the car slowly followed the curve of the lake shore, Dave saw horse droppings at the edge of the road. Up ahead beyond the Pavilion, three horses with riders were trotting along. Ron started to snicker.

"Hey," Dave said. "That's right where I havta take my cart across. Somebody should clean that mess up."

"That was one of my chores, way back when I was young," Mr. Norris remarked. "There were very few cars then. Horse carts would stop all along the street we lived on making deliveries. They brought us our milk, our ice. When the ice cream wagon came past we'd take bowls out, I remember, it was a nickel a scoop. Most people had carriages too. I had to shovel the manure up and bury it in the garden after school each day. If Grandpa came along and saw any that wasn't fresh I might be in for a thrashing. We had the best garden around."

"Bet those veggies were yummy," Dave said, rubbing his stomach and smacking his lips.

"Everyone said they were," Mr. Norris continued, ignoring the interruption. "Our plants were at least half again taller than anyone else's in the neighborhood. The tomatoes they produced were big as softballs. Grandma canned them for the winter. We ate well. Didn't do me a bit of harm either," he said, a yearning in his voice. "But boy, did I hate having to spread it."

Dave looked at Ron thinking his dad was still plenty good at that.

Dave was scared of horses. They were too big. He was always afraid one would spook and run over him before he could get out of the way. In the movies they went galloping off with riders or buggies all the time. If it was with a pretty girl, the good guy would race on ahead, slow the horse and pull her to safety at the very last minute. If it was the bad guy, he'd get clotheslined by a low hanging branch, or the wagon would catch a wheel on a rock, fly up into the air, flip over and be dragged away. The villain, thrown free in the process, would roll down a steep embankment like a rag doll, fling out his arms, and die.

"You think we should be sitting here together?" Ron asked nervously, after he and Dave took the path into the park and found a spot on one of the benches.

"Don't see why not. Dad says Mr. Kovach and the family he lives with always go ta late church then have a big Sunday dinner. Nobody else'll be here for at least half an hour, well, 'cept for Stu."

"Why's he hanging around the bathroom?"

"He's got a nipper in his pocket. Told ya, he never goes anywhere without one."

"Right," Ron said, raising a finger. "This is a beautiful park."

"Yep," Dave replied, looking up into the green canopy above them. "I think it's the big trees and the way the land slopes, makes me feel closer ta the action."

"You're always telling me there is no action in baseball."

"Well, it makes me feel closer ta what little there is."

"Does he do that every week?" Ron asked, looking over his shoulder as Mr. Kaufner set up the press facility.

"Yep, he's the 'nouncer I told ya 'bout. He had hovercraft ferrying people across the lake a couple weeks ago."

"That lake?" Ron pointed, with a laugh.

"That's the lake all right." Dave smiled.

"I could hit a ball across it," Ron frowned.

"Sure you could," Dave grinned.

"Rafe could."

"He was clockin' pitches with radar too, really had the crowd jumpin'."

"TESTING, TESTING," the speakers blared.

"I made up this little game," Dave said. "I try ta guess what he's gonna have bringin' people in before he announces it. Figure it'll be flyin' carpets today. The other thing, when we send up the first satellite, he's gonna have cameras mounted on it ta beam the games right into people's living rooms from space."

"That's impossible," Ron laughed. "He's nuts."

The speakers came alive again.

"Our featured sponsor today is Cavanaugh Flowers, home of the finest, freshest flowers at the lowest price. When the opportunity presents itself, say it with flowers, Cavanaugh Flowers, and if you appreciate this commentary, mention us when you do."

"Just rehearsin' his spiel," Dave said. "Does it 'fore every game."

"What's he mean by 'when the opportunity presents itself'?" Ron asked.

"You're jokin', right?" Dave returned, with a nudge and a look of disbelief. "Just kiddin'," he teased. "Took me a while too."

"Oh, yeah," Ron said, the light going on. "Guess he can't come right out and say it."

"When Granny kicks off," Dave mimicked, "pay your respects with flowers, Cavanaugh Flowers."

Mr. Kaufner put his microphone down and leaned back to rest.

"Dad told me he was at a poker game in the twenties. After Mr. Kaufner folded, he picked up something for a prop and bang, started 'nouncin' just like he was on the radio. Says he's been doin' it ever since. If the visitin' team's got a rookie, nobody puts him wise. It's like an initiation. When Mr. Kaufner had rickshaws goin', one of the new guys kept scoutin' for 'em out on the road, cracked everybody up. The manager was none too happy."

Dave heard kids chattering, looked around, saw the elderly lady and checked his watch.

"We best split up," he said. "Forty-five minutes 'til game time."

Dave's eyes met Ron's, each felt the weight of the world resting on his shoulders.

Ron stood up. "I think the best vantage point is up by the slide."

Dave nodded, took a deep breath, turned and walked toward the Pavilion. On the way he dodged the manure. When he returned, thousands of fans were assaulting the turnstiles; thousands more packed the bleachers and box seats. There were people here and there, but fans, he counted maybe eight so far, smiled, shook his head, and laughed.

He positioned himself at the edge of the path. The lady and the two kids converged on the spot. She pulled out her coin purse. Dave reminded himself that everyone, even a shriveled old lady, was a suspect.

The players arrived. It was the Cubs verses the Sportsmen again. Spectators began to file in. Dave sold a lemon-lime, then a root beer. Minutes later he was swamped. Had he just served up a pop to one of the conspirators? How many were there?

Mr. Kovach didn't show for batting practice. The game started. Dave was on the knoll getting more nervous by the minute. If this turned out to be a wild goose chase, he'd never live it down. The initial surge subsided. He saw that Ron had moved closer to the foul line in left field. Lounging against the hillside, his legs crossed one over the other, he was just another kid watching the game. Dave dug through the ice. He had two Cokes and one orange left. He started back toward the backstop collecting empties as he went. Mr. Kovach was there behind the fence, bent over a bench, tying his shoe. A minute later he was on his way to his accustomed spot. Dave heaved a sigh of relief. It was interesting. No one ever sat on that bench but him. It was out of the way and he figured Mr. Kovach liked it because he didn't want to be bothered while he watched the game. Dave considered. Should he wait until he reloaded or hit Mr. Kovach up right then? He'd been making his move early and decided not to alter his routine. You couldn't script this sort of thing. He'd just have to take his chances. On the way, he noted that

Ron was angled slightly so he could see Mr. Kovach out of the corner of his eye; so far, so good.

As Dave approached Mr. Kovach's bench, the Sportsman player he'd first noticed on Memorial Day walked over and sat down, blocking Ron's view. Dave told himself to stay calm, stick to the plan.

Dave produced a coke. The usual dime changed hands. Mr. Kovach took the bottle without even looking his way. Whatever suspicions he thought Mr. Kovach might have had, must all have been in his head. Cool. He relaxed. As obsessed as this guy was, LaPorte was the perfect place for him. He decided Mr. Kovach was thinking of signing on with one of the local teams and the Sportsmen player was there to help him make the "proper" selection.

"STEEE-RIKE TWO," Mr. Norris called, with the usual ring of authority.

Dave had momentarily allowed himself to be distracted. It wouldn't happen again.

Mr. Kovach's left hand was grasping the front of the bench next to his buddy's leg. Dave wasn't going to get a look at the watchband unless he moved it.

"STREEE-RIKE THREE, YOU'RE OUTTA THERE."

Dave knew that with those words, his dad's right arm would instinctively shoot up in a fist. He'd give it a firm shake, then bang it down as the deflated hitter sulked away.

Dave impulsively thrust his left arm out in front of Mr. Kovach's face.

"Look," he said, pointing to his watch, I've got one t..."

Wham! Mr. Kovach's fist came flying up. It hit Dave's arm inches below his elbow, throwing him off balance. As he fell backwards, two strong arms reached out and grabbed him.

"Okey-dokey! You okey-dokey?" Mr. Kovach asked, holding him steady.

Dave shook his head. Mr. Kovach held on a little longer then, confident Dave wasn't hurt, slowly released his grip. As Mr. Kovach turned to see what he'd missed, Dave glanced at his watch. It was turned wrong. While Dave trundled his cart along to refill it at the Pavilion, he pondered. Something wasn't right here. He could feel it. There was genuine compassion in those eyes. How could a person have that and still be a spy? He liked Mr. Kovach. He was afraid of him, but he liked him.

Dave was snapping off caps left and right now. Another home town face-off—hot, muggy—the "opportunity" Mr. Kaufner was always talking about might have just presented itself and he was making the most of it. His hands were freezing, he was roasting. Between customers he wet his hair and his shirt. This was the day to score. Until he got a break, Ron was on his own, but with the player hopping benches again, their plan looked to be coming apart at the seams. His showing up was their first serious glitch. Ron might get shut out.

They were in the fourth. Dave was out of pop, another dilemma. Mr. Kovach would make his move anytime now. Should he break for the Pavilion or try to hold off? He worked his way over to the knoll where he could see the privacy panel outside the entrance to the men's room. Ron hadn't moved. Maybe they could salvage something from this mess yet. The second Mr. Kovach set foot in the door one of their suspicions would be confirmed and missing out seeing the watchband wouldn't be such a big setback. If, per chance, another guy, wearing the same watch went in with him—*na, that ain't hap'nin* Dave thought. Nobody could be that stupid. He sat down on the ground next to his cart; put his elbows on his knees and his head in his hands. That way he could look up every so often to see what was going on but no one could get his attention. His hair was dripping, his shirt sopping. He was exhausted. Too bad this wasn't the week hardly anybody came. It'd be easy to identify the accomplice then.

Minutes went by. The pitcher was locked in a duel with a Cub intent on stealing second and Dave was getting signals from a bald guy three blankets down. The runner would lead off as far as he dared. The pitcher would throw to first to hold him on. This could go on forever; what luck? The man on the blanket waved. Dave ignored him. Mr. Kovach, alone now, stretched out his arm on the back of the bench. Ron saw his chance and started toward him. The runner got caught in a run down between first and second. Mr. Kovach moved his arm. Ron veered off toward the drinking fountain. The runner went for second. The throw went wild. The runner raced on for third. He and the throw arrived simultaneously. The base umpire's arms flew out. "SAFE," he yelled. The Sportsmen manager bolted for third to engage the umpire. Dave felt a tap on his shoulder. It was the man who wanted the pop. Dave told him he was just leaving for another load. He took a few steps then tried the stone in the shoe ploy. It was no good. The manager and the umpire were going heavy at it, his dad standing by in case things got out of hand. This wouldn't be resolved for a while. When he saw Ron coming his way on the path he shrugged. Ron whispered, "I got it," as he passed.

There was a hold-up at the Pavilion. The man who ran it was dealing with a line and trying to fill the mustard dispenser at the same time. Dave had to wait. Eventually the man told him to load up and they'd sort it out later.

Dave knew what he'd find when he got back and he was right. Play had resumed, apparently without the Sportsmen's manager being ejected. Mr. Kovach's friend was in the field and he was gone, so much for having a ring side seat. Ron was sitting against a tree where the knoll met the woods. There was only one place Mr. Kovach could be. Dave smiled smugly as he passed the press facility. A step later Mr. Kovach came bounding down from the restroom right in front of him, turned his way, stopped abruptly and asked for a Coke. Dave uncapped it. Mr. Kovach was standing to his left. When he raised the bottle to take a swig the scratch stuck out like a sore thumb. Dave waited for the dime but Mr. Kovach asked for a second Coke instead and handed him a quarter. Dave uncapped it. Mr. Kovach raised a hand as Dave held out a nickel and walked away. Dave figured the second Coke was for his player friend.

Dave was happy but sad too. The switcheroo had come off exactly as they'd thought it would. That was good, but Mr. Kovach was a spy. There was no doubt about that. The next question, had Ron gotten a line on the accomplice?

Dave delivered the soda to the man who'd tapped him on the shoulder, all the while fighting the urge to glance up at Ron. There were empties everywhere and there'd be plenty of time later to share what they'd learned. Ron moved from place to place on the knoll for the rest of the game. Eventually Dave forgot about him. He had a business to run and at the moment, business was good. Between games Dave took up station beside the path. With a fan shaped array of colorfully labeled bottles protruding from a frosty snow white background, he was ready to intercept spectators going to the Pavilion or drinking fountain. There was nothing like a little temptation, he'd learned, to help people make "good choices." Some of the players went for the bait, then found seats in the shade, took off their caps and wiped their brows with handkerchiefs. From what Dave could see, they didn't exactly look to be enjoying the "National Pastime."

During the second game sales remained strong. When people were hot and sticky they wanted to be waited on. You could make money.

Ron was back on the third base side looking for openings. Dave wondered why he wasn't still staking out the bathroom. Stu, sequestered at the end of a bench near the press box, looked droopier than ever. Dave sat down next to him. Stu bought a root beer. Dave wasn't sure, if, at this time of day, Stu knew root beer wasn't real beer.

"I'm sure glad your dad asked me to come along today," Stu said. "It breaks up the week, gives a person a chance to get away for a while."

Dave didn't know what Stu was getting away from, but if sitting in this heat for hours was better, he was in trouble. Before moving on, Dave got a paper cup from Mr. Kaufner and filled it with ice so Stu could keep cool.

In the sixth inning Ron disappeared. Dave didn't think much of it for a time but then began to worry. He left his cart with Mr. Kaufner, checked the restroom, the merry-go-round and monkey cage area. He went to the Pavilion, looked both ways along the lake shore. Ron was nowhere to be seen. Ugly thoughts began to go through his mind. He told himself there were too many people around for anything bad to have happened, but then, where was Ron?

Settling up at the Pavilion took forever. The concessionaire had been behind all afternoon and was looking a lot like Stu. Dave, desperate to find Ron, finally started sorting bottles into their wooden cases and totaling up sales himself. When he was paid and reached the road he expected to find Ron leaning against the car. Ron wasn't and the park was nearly empty.

"Dad," he said, in a voice just short of panic, "ya seen Ron?"

"He's in the car," Mr. Norris returned.

"In the car!" Dave exclaimed.

"He was in the car when I got here," Mr. Norris replied, closing the trunk.

Dave opened the car door. There was Ron slumped against the back seat. He hadn't thought of looking in the car when he'd come by.

"Where ya been?" he said sharply, as he got in. "I looked all over for ya."

"I was at the roller rink like we talked about."

"The roller rink," Dave flung his head back. "Never thoughta that."

Mr. Norris and Stu got in.

"Did ya find...I mean, did ya think the rink was cool?" Dave asked.

"I used to spend hours there," Mr. Norris interjected, "when I could scrape enough money together."

They were moving now. The windows wide open, the breeze flooding in, this is what Dave had been waiting for. He cupped his hand in the air to funnel more of it onto his face. He was dying to know what Ron had found out and mouthed a question. Ron turned away. He always did make good decisions. He was right too. Not much escaped Mr. Norris if he was watching for it. After all, watching was the main thing umpires did.

"Dad, why we goin' this way?" Dave asked, when instead of leaving the park through the main entrance they drove ahead on Truesdell then turned up the west side of Clear Lake on Hoelocker Drive.

"I have to drop off something at Leonard's for the Old Timers get together next month."

Old guys again, Dave thought.

"Look!" Dave said, pointing past Ron as they neared the south end of the lake, "Are those hobos?"

"I would say," Mr. Norris responded.

"I never seen any from this close. What they doin'?"

"Probably cooking fish," Mr. Norris suggested.

"They clean 'em first?" Dave asked excitedly.

"How should I know?" Mr. Norris replied, shaking his head.

The two men tending the stick and twig fire next to the lake were indeed cooking something. Seated on weathered wooden boxes, their attire shabby and worn, each proclaimed his independence in his own way. The bigger of the two, wearing a leather vest with silver medallions and a misshapen black hat, stood out the most. Dave figured him for a blacksmith, maybe a cowboy.

"Bet he was in the movies once," he said, to no one in particular.

The other man, thinner, wiry, with sunken cheeks, had a large dragon tattooed on his right arm, a cigarette dangling from his mouth. He looked agitated as he poked randomly at the fire. Neither man noticed them pass by. Occupied with their meal, surrounded by refuse, it was exactly the image one would envision.

"Why they campin' in that trash?" Dave asked. "Why don't they clean it up?"

"Couldn't say," Mr. Norris replied, "but that's one reason people don't want them around."

The second Mr. Norris entered the restaurant Dave looked over the front seat to see if Stu had zonked out. Just when he decided Stu was still awake something hit his leg. It was Ron's fist. Dave slid back. Ron grinned, turned his hand up and opened it. A folded gum wrapper appeared. Dave took it, opened it and read, *Cardinal's cap yellow shirt.* Dave made a writing motion. Ron produced a stubby pencil and handed Dave *The Baseball Bible* from the box of books on his left. Dave starred out the windshield momentarily then wrote, *first base side under maple.* Ron nodded. Dave made the "you're outta there" clinched fist and wrote, *lumpy head.* They both snickered and shook theirs. He thought again and added, *Mr. Potato.* Ron crossed it out and wrote, *Mr. Spud.* They both grinned. Dave nudged Ron for another wrapper. Ron reached into his pocket. Mr. Norris was there. That ended that; another close call.

The best part of the trip for Stu was Wally's Bar. The instant bottle chinked against glass,he was alert, chatty, even funny. Dave was hoping his dad and Stu would chat and drink quickly so they could be on their way. Then disaster struck. Uncle Wally asked the forbidden question.

"Hey Gadg," he said, "when are those Yankees of yours going to clean up their act? Three brawls in a row! They're giving baseball a bad name."

Dave's eyes rolled up into his head. He looked at Ron then reached for some peanuts. He wanted to show Ron the jukebox but was too tired to move. By the time they left the bar he was out of patience. He had to know what else Ron might have learned, if they had enough between them to put the spies out of business. He leaned forward and started pestering his dad with questions about hobos. At the same time, he prodded Ron for more wrappers. Ron resisted. Dave persisted. Eventually a clean wrapper and the pencil appeared.

"How do they get rid of 'em?" Dave asked, as he and Ron slid the "bible" back and forth across their knees. *Ya see watchband before switch?*

"When the police get complaints," Mr. Norris explained, "they arrest the vagabonds for littering or vagrancy. If they've been a problem before, it's the county jail or a work detail. If not, it's a one way bus ride out of town."

Dave read Ron's response.

No.

"Where do they send 'em?"

Afterwords?

"They were sending them to Michigan City until the police there got wise and started sending them back. Now they both send them down state. It's called Greyhound therapy."

Yes.

"Those two at the lake won't be around much longer. LaPorte does a sweep about this time every year to clean them out before the big 4th of July celebration."

They go in together?"

"Most of them are savvy enough to have moved on by now. These two must not have gotten the message."

No.

"Doesn't seem fair ta kick people outta town who aren't doin" anything wrong."

Ya sure it's him?

"There's a few things you don't understand. When people own property or have a link to a community they usually behave themselves. With transients you can never be sure. If there's vandalism or a break-in, people want something done about it. They want the derelicts rounded up. They work hard and they want to feel safe."

Pretty.

"Then there's the tunnel."

"Tunnel?" Dave and Ron repeated, looking at each other.

"There's a storm drain under the railroad tracks that carries run-off from town out into the lake."

Dave read the note again and wrote, *How ya no?*

"It's been there for years. When people see hobos about it frightens them. Then someone remembers the tunnel. Rumors start circulating that tramps are using it to get around and commit crimes. It's probably not true, but the police have to do something."

Hobos poppin' up out of manholes all over town in the middle of the night, Dave could picture it.

No tan.

Dave drew a question mark on the wrapper and slid it over to Ron. When he glanced up his dad's face was there in the rear view mirror with a telling look on it. The wrapper disappeared. The rest of his questions about hobos, where they went when it got cold or rained, what they did when they were hungry, why they didn't just get a job and live regular like everybody else, Dave wasn't asking any of these. He was in the clear at the park. Ron had a line on the accomplice. It was time to check out.

When the Ford pulled to a stop on Vassar Street it was so late Mrs. Norris had to reheat dinner. After two long hot games, hours of surveillance, dissertations on baseball etiquette, Dave ate his supper, took a bath and went to bed.

Dave was standing on the precipice again looking out on the desolate moonscape of sand and gravel stretched before him. He should have been at Ron's discussing strategy but he wasn't. He was with Leon and Ben, a prospect altogether unthinkable before he'd gotten what had to be one of his best nights' sleep ever. He'd expected to wake up a zombie again, the day's success contingent on his dodging his mother long enough to get a decent breakfast. Instead he and the Cheske's were about to fire six big rockets, three designed to end their lives in a brilliant white flash and thunderous crash high in the sky.

Before he started the climb down to the "launch pad," he took a second to look back over his shoulder. The contrast between what lay behind and what was in front always set him to thinking. What had gone through the minds of the early explorers when they first laid eyes on the Great Lakes or reached the rim of the Grand Canyon? Were they struck rigid by its magnificence? Did they take it in stride? How must it have felt not to know your fate beyond the next valley, the next obscuring ridge and still go on?

Dave lived in an age of exploration too. Not of far distant lands, continents away, but the very heavens above. A new breed of explorer, infinitely more knowledgeable than the last, would soon leave the safety of earth and venture into this vast unknown. What would these modern day seekers encounter on their wondrous journeys through space: untold wealth, strange new beings, death? No one could say for sure but a lot of Americans wanted to be part of the adventure. Only science could make it possible. Only science could solve the complex problems posed by this extraordinary new means of travel.

Learning its ways was the objective of the three teenage boys intent on improving the reliability of their home made rockets. They couldn't have told you that. They didn't know it themselves, but that was what they were about. Threads of gray smoke rising high into the air, explosive bursts hundreds of feet above the ground, these would be the measure of success today. Seeing these would bring jubilation, a sense of accomplishment.

Unfortunately science wasn't just about success; it was also about failure. In fact, it was mostly about failure: living with it, learning from it, moving on when it happened. If you were going to accomplish anything, you had to understand that. Whether today's expedition went well or not didn't really matter. Science would be served either way, because either way, they'd learn something. They'd see what they could make of it then forge ahead. There was no guarantee anything they tried would work. That's how it was with science, and though today's results weren't at all encouraging, one thing was certain—they'd be back.

"Don't ya get tired of doin' that?" Dave asked, when he finally rounded into Ron's garage after lunch.

"What?"

"Dusting off the buckboard."

"Sure, if it's hot like this I do. But Dad says having something of ours in the parade that looks sharp brings extra business into the shop and, re-member, I get to drive it this summer.... I was worried. Where've you been? I thought we were supposed to be catching spies," Ron said. "—never mind, I can guess."

"I woulda been here way sooner, 'cept Leon and Ben showed up just as I was leavin' ta come. They wanted ta go ta the gravel pit. I tried ta get out of it by tellin' 'em I had ta clean my room, but then I put my watch on and that last note of yours made sense. So I figured, it's not that hot yet, what the heck."

"Didn't you see me pointing to my wrist in the car?

"I was tired. Anyway, what'd ya do with the wrappers?"

"I was going to burn them. Then I decided not to, so I hid them."

"Not where someone's gonna find 'em, I hope."

"Nope, they're upstairs in that heavy baseball bank I got from Grand. How'd you do at breakfast today?" Ron asked.

"Great, slept like a log last night."

"How about your trip, was it worth it?"

"Not hardly," Dave replied, dejected. "It's the fuel, same's before. Nothin' we try makes any difference. We almost blew up our space ship this time," he grinned. "One slammed into the ground and went off right next ta it. Gravel flew everywhere. Look," he said, showing Ron the red spot on his neck. "We got pelted good."

"So what are you going to do if one comes down right where you're standing?"

"The way I can move?" Dave smirked.

Ron frowned.

Dave shrugged, "I haven't exactly thought that through yet."

Ron laid down on his back to inspect the underside of the buckboard. Dave sat down beside him and removed his shoe.

"Now what are you doing?" Ron asked.

"I got a sore on the side a my foot from my dog tag. I had it in my sock yesterday when we were at the park. I didn't notice then, but it musta been rubbin' 'ganst my skin. It hurts," he grimaced.

Ron slid out, put his hands under his head and lay there starring up at the garage roof. Dave rubbed his foot. The gravity of what they were involved in was slowly sinking in. They looked at each other in silence.

"You're crazy," Ron said. "You know that don't you?"

"And you're gonna tell me you're not afraid of these guys?"

"I wasn't, at least not until I saw it was like you said. Then I was. That Spud guy, he really creeps me out. I've never seen a head that shape before. Why do you suppose it's like that?"

"Who knows," Dave replied. "Coulda been he was in the war and got blasted. Maybe he got it squished in somethin'."

"Yeah," Ron said, contemplating. "It had to be something bad that happened to him."

Dave didn't respond. He was concentrating on his foot. "Aw," he winced as he gingerly pulled on his sock. "I ain't takin' that thing along this week, that's for sure."

"Don't worry," Ron quipped. "If they rub ya out, I'll identify your corpse."

"Ho, ho, ho," Dave chortled. "We got a regular Milton Berle here."

While Ron chased down the last specks of dust on the buckboard, Dave slouched on the tarp used to cover it. Propping his sore foot up on Mr. Rasco's tool box, he too folded his hands behind his head and leaned back to think.

"Ya know," he said quietly after a while. "We're past the point of no return on this."

"What does that mean?" Ron puzzled.

"It means we're expendable," Dave said gravely. "It was 'bout this plane comin' 'cross the Pacific. John Wayne was in it, can't 'member the name though, but everything was goin' great 'til they passed the point of no return, where they couldn't make it back ta Hawaii if somethin' went wrong. The camera went back and forth between the passengers so ya could listen in on what they were sayin'. Mostly it was boring, stupid stuff, but then, things did go wrong, engines caught fire, gas leaked out. There was a real bad storm raging down below so they couldn't ditch. It was then, when they all thought they were going to die, that's when the people tried ta sort out what was really important in their lives. Made ya think a lot. Pretty good movie. I 'member now, it was called *The High and the Mighty*.

"Did they make it?" Ron asked.

"Barely, they cleared inta San Francisco by 'bout two feet over the trees and with only a couple gallons left in their tanks. That's where we're at. Now that we're for sure they're doin' it, we can't go back either. We havta stop 'em no matter what and whatever happens ta us along the way doesn't matter."

"O.K. then, so what's our next move?"

"That's another reason I wasn't 'round earlier. I was hopin' I'd come up with somethin' while we were shootin' rockets."

"Here," Ron said, passing Dave a chamois, "you want to polish while I wax? I'm done under here."

"Sure," Dave replied, taking the cloth.

"You could talk to your dad again."

"And get a replay on the, 'we got relatives, I do business' lecture, no way for that. What I can't figure is how you knew it was him."

"Spud you mean?"

"Yeah."

"I told ya. The outline of the watch was there on his wrist, right in plain sight. He must spend a lot of time in the sun. I'm surprised you didn't see it."

"That's 'causea where he sits on the knoll. My cart's too heavy. I never get up that far. But that's not what I mean. What made ya think it was him in the first place?"

"He went in. I kept track of everyone who went into the bathroom after Mr. Kovach came out. Spud was one of the first. Later, when I walked past behind where he was sitting, bingo, there it was, a perfect watch outline on his wrist and just the right shape. Most likely he's carrying the second watch around in his pocket while he's there at the park."

"But ya saw the scratch after the switch, right?"

"I thought I did—na, I didn't see it. I never got a good look at the watch before he went in either. Every time his arm was in the right position his

Sportsmen buddy would show up to give pointers or there'd be a close play and he'd go wild."

"Told ya, he's a fanatic. They did switch though. I saw the scratch again," and Dave told Ron about selling Mr. Kovach the Cokes on the path.

"The one time I thought I had him, he turned around just as I came past his bench," Ron said. "My heart almost stopped. It turned out it was the horses going by on the road behind me. He must have heard their hooves clicking on the pavement. One other thing, the way Spud went strutting in there, it was like he was asking to get caught. That means they think they're safe, which means we're safe."

"Yeah," Dave agreed, "I thoughta that too. What bugs me is they're doin' it right in plain sight, right under our noses and we can't do a thing 'bout it."

"You'd think they'd be smarter," Ron remarked.

"Ya'd think," Dave grumbled.

"Look, your dad said Mr. Kovach's first game was on Memorial Day and that Castinal was still tooling up. Maybe they're just testing out their system and haven't gotten anything going yet."

"Yeah, maybe," Dave shrugged, "but they will."

Dave only knew of one way to keep unpleasant thoughts at bay. That was to stay busy. So that's what he did. He spent hours that week trying out his latest "bat," a broken off chunk of branch. It improved his hitting to where he was almost an asset to the team he was on. He drew crate plans, did experiments, cashed in his rain check at the Morgue, played chess with Tim. When frightful scenarios did creep in, he told himself the nasty business in LaPorte was just another game, a bit more serious maybe, but nobody was actually going to get hurt.

About the only time Mr. Kovach and Spud were completely off his mind was when he and Ben went to ride the trail alongside the railroad tracks at the east end of Muessel Park. That was a real adventure, dangerous too. The tracks crossed Vassar at street level then cut steadily down into the earth. A quarter mile north they went under the big wooden trestle at Portage Avenue. The trail ran between the two in the narrow space next to the Drewrys' Brewery fence on the ridge and the steep drop off adjacent to it. As you rode along, the gorge beside you got deeper and deeper. That would have been scary enough, but the area inside the fence was paved and in places water puddled after a rain then flowed under the wire. Once you passed the corner post where the fence started, a series of deep washouts crossing your path lay in wait. That's when the real fun began. Working up enough nerve to make the attempt in the first place was the hardest part because once on your way, there was no turning back. To successfully navigate the sinks you had to be going full blast and stay perfect in the groove. You'd be tearing along and bang, the ground beneath you would fall away. A split second later you'd fly up the crater's far side. You'd suck in a breath and drop into the next one. Up ahead a huge chasm loomed. The second you spotted it your stomach flipped, you gasped, tried to swallow, knew you were insane and shot down. Only when you pulled up next to the trestle's heavy plank decking, when you heard the sounds of traffic rumbling past, could you heave a sigh of relief and relax. What seemed to last forever while you were doing it was over in the blink of an eye. Ben would collapse against a wooden beam to rest. After he recovered he'd turn the bike around, they'd buck themselves up a second time, pray their luck held and start back.

Sometimes, if it was cool, they made the trip twice. Today they didn't. Once safe, Dave always relived the ride. Going toward the trestle, he had to keep his feet from digging into the washout's high side and throwing them over. On the way back, he'd be looking bug eyed down the chutes at the tracks. He could imagine the earth caving in under a wheel, them splattered unconscious across the rails. He'd shudder, think what might have happened, vow never to tempt fate again and promise, this time, to really mean it. He thought of Ben too. Giving the trail a go took a tremendous amount of energy. With him along, riding double, he didn't know where Ben found the strength.

By the time Dave got home the trail was ancient history. He'd seen two kids bouncing up and down on a teeter-totter and made a break through.

All the crates he and his friends had constructed so far were stiff rigid structures built on the stronger is better principle. They tore you up. The buckboard, on the other hand, flexible to the point of being flimsy, smoothed bumps out. Flexibility wasn't a design flaw, it was the key, a simple, elegant solution to a baffling problem, and it was doable. A few, just the right sized planks and you were there. His whole mind set had changed in an instant.

Dave went into the garage to find some paper. What he found were wet pamphlets and folders laid out to dry on every flat surface around.

"Dad," he asked at lunch. "How'd all that stuff in the garage get wet?"

"The trunk lid on the car was leaking. I misplaced some tool orders and discovered it while I was searching for them. The man at the dealership said the seal had a rip in it. If I get it in by two thirty, they can install a new one today."

Dave thought that was a good idea. Half of what his family owned was stored in the Ford's trunk.

"Think I could have one of the baseball scorer's books?" he asked. "Ron would like ta learn how ta score a game."

"Ron seems to have a new interest every week," Mr. Norris noted.

"Yeah Dad, he's like me, always tryin' ta better himself. Is Stu goin' this week?"

"Yes," Mr. Norris replied, "but Ron can come along too."

Dave asked to be excused and made for the back door. His parents looked at each other, cracked a smile, and shook their heads slightly.

Dave picked out the best scorers book of the lot and went to Ron's. No one was home but he heard voices. Ron, Rafe and Gunner were sitting in Doug's garage watching him put a coat of primer on the racer. The progress he'd made was phenomenal. The ragged steps were gone. A lean, sleek, streamlined machine sat in front of them.

"Where ya been?" Rafe asked.

"Probably at the gravel pit shooting off more rockets," Ron remarked.

"Was not," Dave corrected. "Went ta ride the trail with Ben."

"We do that sometimes on our way ta the Morgue," Gunner said. "Pretty scary isn't it?"

"Yeah. And the washouts are gettin' deeper. You're 'bout below ground on the big one. Think we went weightless droppin' in."

"We're playin' soon's Doug's done," Rafe said. "What ya got there?"

"Scorer's book. Trunk lid was leakin' so Dad said I could have it. Thought I'd be neat to look through."

Except for Doug, each of the boys did.

"Somebody spent a lot of time figurin' all this out," Gunner commented.

"Hey Rafe," Dave said, "while we're waitin', how's 'bout we go ta Ron's. I need ya ta help me with somethin'."

"Why ya need me ta do it?" Rafe asked warily.

"'Cause it's gotta be somebody big. It's an experiment."

"I almost died on your last experiment."

"That wasn't an experiment, it was a dare," Dave smirked.

"You're askin' for it again," Rafe said, jabbing Dave in the side. "Got a new bat, don't ya?"

"It's not like that. All ya gotta do is sit in the buckboard so I can make a measurement. Take 'bout two minutes."

Dave and Rafe followed Ron around to his garage.

"Take off your shoes before ya get in," he instructed, as he opened the door. "Dad can spot a scratch a mile away."

"O.K., now what?" Rafe asked, holding the steering wheel with both hands.

"Nothin'. I just havta measure how much it sags in the middle, that's all."

"Always gotta be smart don't ya?" Rafe growled.

" Am not," Dave answered, and he asked Ron to sit in the passenger's seat.

Dave went on measuring then had them bounce to simulate a bump. While he scribbled on a scrap of paper, he explained how his new plan had clicked in when he saw the kids on the teeter-totter.

"Been thinkin' a goin' with you two on Sunday," Rafe grinned. "Games any good?"

Dave looked at Ron. "Depends," he said. "Can't work it out this week though, Dad's takin' Stu again and the car's packed so tight we can barely squeeze in."

Later in the day, after they'd finished playing Whiffle ball, Dave told Ron the scorer's book was for him to take along.

"That way ya can get down what they're doin' inning by inning."

Ron started reading. Dave studied the buckboard.

"Ya see that big guy, plaid shirt, was hangin' 'round last week?" Dave asked. "Saw 'im glance my way when he was at the drinkin' fountain."

"So, people do that all the time," Ron shrugged, not bothering to look up.

"Yeah, s'pose," Dave pondered.

"There's a lot in here," Ron said, flipping pages. "It tells you how to do everything. You can log in each pitch."

"Uh huh."

A loud clap of thunder stirred Dave to life Saturday morning. It looked like an indoor day. He went downstairs for a while then after lunch walked to Doug's. Doug was upholstering the car's seat.

"At least ya don't havta worry about bumps," Dave said.

"Only two things are important in the Derby," Doug replied, "staying within what the rules allow and getting to the finish line as fast as you can. I'm doing great on the first one. Can't say how I'll make out on race day."

Ron made an appearance, nodded and gave Dave the eye. They talked a few more minutes then left for Ron's garage.

"What's up?" Dave asked.

"I was," Ron replied, "half the night. I made up a code so we can keep track of what they're doing. It uses the same symbols and numbers as the book, but I changed the meanings around, that way if they get a hold of it, they won't be able to figure it out. Here goes," he said and he started explaining.

"I converted outs into numbers. 6 is the last out in the first inning. 10 is the first out in the bottom half of the second."

"Got it so far," Dave said, following along.

"Kovach and Spud are abbreviations."

"Ya didn't use 'K' for Kovach I hope?"

"Nope," Ron replied, dismissing the comment." He's 'HR', home run. Hungarian Refugee."

"Yeah, O.K.," Dave nodded.

"Spud's double play, 'DP', Dumb Potato."

"Bound ta be a place for you in the C.I.A.," Dave chuckled.

"Wait there's more. If Spud leaves his watch in the bathroom before the game, it's 'DPBG'. Then if I see the scratch, say late in the third, it's 'HRSS', and I put a—let's see, a 17 in the circle on that diagram. The rest I'm making up as I go along.

"Heck, I can hardly remember people's names," Dave responded. "All that mumbo-jumbo, do it any way ya want," he shrugged. "Ya can decipher it for me when we get back. Main thing though, we got Spud tagged. Now we need ya ta get good looks at the watch band. Try comin' off his left side, worked great for me on the path. Gotta get somethin' this week though; somehow we gotta force their hand."

Ron continued to study the scorer's book as if he wasn't listening. Dave got up to leave.

"Hey," Ron snickered, "when your trunk sprung a leak, did your dad have boxes lined up all along the curb?"

Dave shot Ron a nasty look, "Hey, it's not like with your dad, ya know," he said defensively. "Our car has ta double as my dad's office and be a delivery truck at the same time."

"I didn't mean anything by it," Ron said, aware that he'd hurt Dave's feelings.

Chapter 17
A HELPING HAND

This trip to LaPorte was far less exciting than the last one. There was no baseball lore, no stories of youthful chores in the "good ol' days."

"We were almost rained out today," Mr. Norris said.

"How's that?" Dave returned. "It's sunny. I don't see a cloud anywhere."

"The rain we had yesterday. The field at the park doesn't drain well. Anymore and we wouldn't be able to play. It won't be much of a game anyway. It's the Merchants and Sportsmen again."

Dave looked at Ron and shrugged. Lovely, more bench hopping.

"Now next week, the Michigan City Prison team and the House of David will be coming in to play the Sportsmen at the park. Those games should be much more interesting. You might want to bring another book along so you can both try your hand at scoring."

Dave knew anytime the "Davids" were playing the park would be jumping.

"Think I'll just stick ta sellin' pop for now," he replied, "if that's O.K.?"

"Why they let prisoners outta jail ta play baseball?" he asked. "What if one of 'em sneaks off into the woods or does somethin' ta somebody?"

"That's always a possibility," Mr. Norris conceded. "But almost all of these men will eventually serve out their sentences and be released back into society. If involving them in organized sports where there are rules everyone has to follow helps rehabilitate them, everybody wins."

"That really big guy still play first base for 'em?" Dave asked.

"I believe he'll be playing first base for a number of years yet," Mr. Norris replied.

"Isn't it only trustees they allow outside the walls?" Stu mumbled.

"That's correct," Mr. Norris confirmed. "And they've only had one minor incident since the program started."

After Mr. Norris parked next to the path, Dave steered Ron toward the Pavilion.

"Come on," he said, "I found a spot." He led Ron through the columns to a park bench hidden by a row of bushes on the other side. "Can't be seen here 'cept from the lake."

The two hunched down. Ron wanted to talk about his code. Dave wasn't interested. He looked out over the lake while Ron made notes in the scorer's book.

"That first baseman for the prison, wait 'til ya see him," Dave rambled. "He's 'bout four, five times bigger than Rafe and he doesn't hit the ball, he crushes it. I spect he's gonna rip the cover off every time he comes up, gets lots a walks. Pitchers are scared of 'im. Ya can tell."

"Does the prison team win much?"

"Na, they bungle plays all the time. Think Dad said they've won two so far. He asked me once if I wanted ta go along when he was umpin' a game in there. I said heck no. Hard tellin' what those guys might do if they got hold of a kid, me for instance, and tried ta ransom 'im out. I get goose bumps just thinkin' 'bout it."

Dave rose up and looked over the bushes. There were three cars parked next to his dad's, four more on down toward the picnic area.

"Must be big doin's scheduled there for later," he said. "You ready? Gotta get somethin' today ya know."

"Yeah," Ron said, acknowledging the comment. "I know."

Dave loaded up, rolled into the park then plopped down on the usual bench behind the backstop. He didn't see Ron anywhere. Then there he was, off to the right, across McClung, in the roller rink's parking lot. It was a ways away but he had a clear shot at the restroom building and wouldn't be noticed. Ron was getting pretty good at this stake out stuff. The next forty-five minutes unfolded as they always did. Mr. Kaufner cobbled together the press box. The teams appeared. Batting practice started. Spud made the "drop." Ron recorded it. The game began and Mr. Kovach showed up to spur on the runners. Dave made the loop on the knoll so he wouldn't appear too anxious, fought his way through the roots then started toward Mr. Kovach's bench. Up ahead, Ron was in position on the hillside near the picnic tables. Dave figured the people there outnumbered the spectators around the diamond by two to one.

Something was different. As he approached, Mr. Kovach shook his head sideways and continued watching the game. Dave hesitated a moment then turned back for the path. Once there, he noted that Ron was gone.

Mr. Kaufner had hardly said two words so far. He was sitting back from his table with a magazine laid open across his lap. Though the hapless Merchants were trying mightily not to embarrass themselves, one could see they didn't have much of a club. It was strictly balls and strikes when they visited. Players whose team record started with a zero might not see the humor in talk of bonuses or references to big league scouts scrutinizing their every move.

Dave sold a pop, then two more, big deal. Three truly ugly strike outs in the top of the second and the Merchants were retired. The Sportsmen player, fresh in from fielding, moved over to Mr. Kovach's bench. Dave frowned, looked around for Ron. Mr. Kovach and his buddy began an animated discussion about something then the player left to bat. A hand went up on the rise where the knoll began. Dave made the sale then took inventory. He wasn't about to get caught empty a second time, not, at least, until after the switch took place. When he looked up Ron was standing next to Mr. Kovach's bench eating from a box of popcorn. *Hum*, Dave thought, *what was that all about?* A minute later, Ron, still shoveling, sat down as though he was wrapped up in the game and offered the box to Mr. Kovach. Dave panicked, recovered, resisted the urge to look at Spud, reorganized his load and responded to another hand a few feet away. He had to be behind the backstop when Mr. Kovach made his move. That happened before he got there. Darn. He'd missed out on a "Kaufner." He started to snicker and rolled his eyes. Nobody bought a pop on their way into a bathroom. Unfortunately, a man with a small boy went in at the same time. Now what? Dave waited nervously. Ron was still sitting on Mr. Kovach's bench. The man and the boy came out. Seconds later Mr. Kovach came out. Dave made the sale. Mr. Kovach's arms were red as beets. He had one nasty sunburn and wasn't wearing his watch. *Whoa*, Dave thought, *those are gonna peel sure.* Mr. Kovach trotted back to his seat. Ron sat there next to him.

By the fourth the Merchants were in the hole six-zip and looked to be finished. Then, as improbable as it seems, they sandwiched two runs in between three more ugly strike outs. In the fifth, Spud made the pick-up. Once he'd returned to his seat Mr. Kovach left. Dave, on his way to refill, watched him, rubbing his arms, leave the park. That closed the deal on the watches for the day. Dave settled in to just selling and retrieving empties. He did note however, that the big guy he'd spotted earlier at the drinking fountain was never far away; as time went on that started to bother him.

Dave completely forgot that the Sportsmen, ahead 12-5, wouldn't bat in the last of the ninth. That put him behind setting up his between games display. He might have caught a break, though. Lots more people had congregated for the reunion. He'd noted men lugging coolers out of car trunks, ladies spreading colorful cloths on every table in sight. Now that they'd gotten things situated, many were descending the hill to watch the second game.

Dave didn't know what caused it—the enhanced audience, an imagination held too long in check, something—because just as the lead off batter stepped into the box, Mr. Kaufner really cut loose.

"Let's all extend a big league welcome to our special guests," he boomed over the speakers. "And congratulations on seventeen consecutive years with us here at Fox Park. Nothing like sharing an exciting afternoon of baseball with beloved family and friends on a glorious summer day."

Not again, Dave thought.

"We hope your journey, by whatever conveyance—ouch, that one took a nasty hop. Merchant runner safe at first, the catcher due up next."

Dave busily levered off two lids.

"For our out of town visitors, the management has asked us to acquaint you with our new stratospheric, satellite seating. Located directly below this press facility, these exclusive, luxury box seats, the latest refinement in stadium design, combine a panoramic view of the diamond with all the amenities of a first class hotel. Bastions of baseball bliss, a limited number, on a first come first served basis, are still available for the "Fall Classic." To arrange a professional, complimentary tour or to purchase tickets please contact the front office or any of our courteous ushers."

Dave was cracking up. He knew his dad was too. "STEEE-RIKE THREE", eight and a half innings to go.

"That's no runs, one hit, one error, two left for the Merchants, Sportsmen half of the first coming up. And now, in keeping with the broadcaster's code and for those of you who have not as yet read Friday's Herald Argus, it is my duty to report that the three men so conspicuously engaged in a scientific pursuit on the lake last week were not, I repeat, not searching for the large fish residents have recently reported seeing. It was simply a plotting expedition to map the lake bottom using sound waves, nothing more. Sightings of the fish some believe to be a sturgeon are at this point only rumor, although the visiting Scottish ichthyologist interviewed by this public servant, certain of the creature's existence, cautioned that it was likely a much larger, more primitive animal."

The pitcher lost concentration midway through his windup and stepped off the rubber. The Sportsmen manager threw up his hands in protest. The crowd went wild. Mr. Norris called "TIME." He casually bent over and brushed off the plate. He took the ball from the catcher, examined it, looked around, handed it back and barked, "PLAY BALL."

At the end of the fourth, Mr. Norris and the Merchant manager got into it over something and Dave made one last run for pop. As he approached the drinking fountain he heard two ear splitting discharges from behind. He whirled around in sheer panic to find himself starring down the barrel of a pistol. There, practically on top of him, in hat, boots, kerchief and chaps, was a pint sized cowboy who didn't come much past his waist.

"Got ya mister," he drawled. "You're dead."

Dave was speechless. A huge lump blocked his throat. The cowboy stood motionless, glaring. Dave swallowed hard, attempted to growl, "You little twerp," and reached for the gun. He was cut off in mid sentence by a man over to his left whose raised index fingers were clutched tightly in the fists of a toddler balanced across his shoulders.

"Chuckie! Get over here. Now!" he ordered. "Or we're not going to the slide."

The woman at his side, motioning in support, tried to hurry the child along. Dave pulled his hand back. The wrangler scowled, leaving Dave dumbstruck once more. Chuckie squinted. The gaze turned to an ever meaner sneer; he worked around what Dave assumed was an imaginary chaw in his cheek, snorted up something vile, leaned over, spit it on the ground next to Dave's shoe and ran off. Seconds later, Ron, who had observed the whole affair from behind walked up splitting a gut.

"You see the size of the buckers on that kid?" he roared.

"Who cares about his teeth?" Dave snarled. "I thought I'd been shot. Those suckers were loud."

"I know, I was watching," Ron said, wiping tears from his eyes. "You almost jumped."

"Real funny," Dave shouted. "And what the heck," he caught himself. "And what the heck were you doin' sittin' over there with your box of popcorn?" he whispered. "You lose your mind or somethin'?"

"Hey, we talked about that," Ron returned quietly. "You said we had to force their hand."

"Yeah, their's, not ours."

Ron bent down for a drink.

"Have your dad pick me up at the roller rink," he said under his breath and walked away.

Dave continued on to the Pavilion, came back looking out for Chuckie and sat down next to Stu. Mr. Kaufner did a promo for the House of Davids bearded band of baseball vagabonds. Dave didn't care. He was a wreck.

"Art really had the place hopping today," Mr. Norris said cheerfully to Uncle Wally at the bar. "You should've come out. Those seats, what'd he call them?"

"Bastions of baseball bliss," Dave responded, while he watched Stu wash down his last beer with his current one.

"He got the crowd going with that just as the second game started. Then he brought down the house with his version of the mapping expedition on the lake."

"That's been the buzz around town all week," Uncle Wally commented.

"Not his interviewing a Scottish scientist who claimed some sort of wild beast lived there?"

"Hardly," Uncle Wally laughed.

"It'll be interesting to see how many people swallow that line," Mr. Norris chuckled.

"Loch Ness Monster," Ron whispered into Dave's ear.

Dave hung his head. He didn't much like it when something that obvious got by him.

"The pitcher flat out lost control. I had to call time until things settled down," Mr. Norris explained. "It was too quiet. I should have seen it coming."

If Dave had cared, he would have asked his dad why they made a stop at Uncle Harlan's on the way home. As it was, the extra ten minutes just gave him more time to sleep.

After supper he was off to Ron's to compare notes.

"Sorry 'bout blowin' up," he said.

"Me too," Ron returned. "I shouldn't have been making fun."

"Can you believe that kid?" Dave grumbled. "Tellin' ya, that's one evil little dude. Be a delinquent someday sure. Where'd he come from anyway?" Dave asked.

"He came down from up by the monkey cage with his parents. When they crossed the path he saw you," Ron started to snicker. "Guess you know the rest."

"Guess I do," Dave seethed.

"You weren't really going to grab his gun away from him, were ya?"

"Damn right. Sawed off little runt, he shouldn't be drawin' on people like that."

"Are you listening to yourself?" Ron chuckled. "He was what, six, seven?"

"Snotty kid. He's mean. You could see it in his eyes."

"I don't know what you're so worried about," Ron laughed. "At his height the best he could do be'd shoot you in the knee."

"In case you haven't noticed, I can't afford a knee," Dave fumed.

"They were just caps. They really weren't that loud."

"They were loud," Dave insisted. "So'd ya get anything with that stunt ya pulled?" he challenged, changing the subject.

"I saw the scratch if that's what ya mean. See, the way he was fidgeting, there was no chance I'd get in for a look. Then I saw this kid scooping out from a box of popcorn and there it was, so I bought one. I acted like I was all interested in the game. Then, when that blooper dropped in and the runner on third took off for home, I sat down and offered the box to Mr. Kovach. It was nearly empty and he's got big hands. I figured he'd tip it up and pour some out because that's what I always do. Anyway, there it was, the scratch, all sparkly in the sun. But you're right, it's hard to see. In case you're wondering, I left the scoring book at the Pavilion so he wouldn't go nosing through it."

"Gotta say, that was pretty slick," Dave complimented.

"The way I figured it, we weren't going to get anything. I had to try something."

"Yeah, sometimes ya havta make your own opportunities, know that," Dave remarked. "How 'bout later?"

"Well, since I was already there, I decided to hang around but he must have pocketed the watch on the way back. Then he left. Those arms, he's in for it."

"Yeah," Dave agreed. "He is."

"How'd you do?" Ron asked.

"He waved me off when I first came over and he wasn't wearing his watch when he came out of the bathroom. That did it for me."

"So now that I've seen the scratch, we go to your dad, right."

"Yeah, well, we're gonna havta think that one over some," Dave cautioned.

"What do you mean?" Ron protested. "We've got the evidence you said we needed."

"It's—it's the 'we got relatives, I do business' thing. That's the problem."

"No it's not. We just tell him what we know and hand over the ledger. He passes it along to the police and we're off the hook. It's their problem."

"Right, he goes in there sayin' the kid who pushes the pop cart around the park on Sundays, his kid, has uncovered a spy ring 'cause there's this itsy-bitsy scratch, he thinks he saw disappear on the local hero's watchband. Ya think that ain't gonna be 'round town in five minutes. They'd be callin' for the white coats ta haul him off ta the funny farm."

"Not when they see what's in the watch."

"S'pose we're wrong on that, and 'nother thing, we've never seen Spud with a watch."

"If that's how it's gonna be I could go a hundred times," Ron balked. "What difference would it make? What happened to all the big talk about the movie, priorities, us not mattering, saving the country?"

"All that still counts. I'm just sayin' we give it a little more time, that's all."

"Before you were saying the opposite."

"I know. I know. O.K., we give it another week, then, whether we get anything new or not, we go ta Dad."

"One more week," Ron said firmly. "No more."

"I almost flipped when I saw ya sittin' there nexta Mr. Kovach," Dave said.

"My dad says doing stuff like that builds character."

"Mine would too. I'm sick a character buildin'. Don't think I can take much more. All I wanted was a quiet, peaceful summer so's I could relax and look what I got. Why these things keep hap'nin ta me?" Dave griped.

"Guess you're just lucky," Ron shrugged.

"How 'bout the big guy?" Dave asked.

"Yeah, I saw him. He's around. I didn't see him doing anything. You sure your imagination isn't just running wild again?"

"S'pose it could be."

Dave poured some potato chips into a bowl, grabbed a glass of milk from the fridge and went into his room to watch a movie. Shortly after it started Mr. Norris pushed the curtain aside and leaned in. Dave slipped off his earphones.

"Here," Mr. Norris said, gently pitching a small box onto the bed. "Take care of this. It's expensive."

Dave went to speak. Before he could, Dad said, "Your Mr. Spud's an ex-con." With that the curtain closed and he was gone. Dave stared at the fluttering strip of cloth for a second then looked down at the box, hardly able to believe what he'd just heard. He removed the lid. A booklet fell out. Minox, the letters on it red. Dave carefully took the instrument from its leather case, slowly rolled it around in his fingers. His dad had just given him a spy camera. What did it mean and how the heck did he know about Spud? Dave clicked off the T.V. The dilemma, the urgency, engulfed him again. Another long night lay ahead.

Chapter 18
GAME PLAN

"**M**y basement. Seven sharp. Be there." Dave whispered to Ron in passing during the next afternoon's whiffle ball game.

"Did you come up with something new?" Ron asked, when he arrived.

"Kinda," Dave replied, handing him the Minox.

"It's a—" Ron looked up.

Dave shook his head. "I know, it's a spy camera," he said, completing the sentence.

"Wa—where'd ya get it?" Ron asked.

"Dad. He tossed it in on my bed last night."

"Where'd he get it?"

"Spect from my Uncle Harlan. 'Member, we stopped by his house on the way home yesterday."

Ron studied the camera.

"Then," Dave continued, "'fore I could say anything, Dad said, 'your Mr. Spud's an ex-con.' A second later he was gone."

"How'd? Oh! No! I!" Ron said, turning white.

Dave was shaking his head again.

"I left the first wrapper we wrote on in *The Baseball Bible*, didn't I?"

"Musta," Dave returned. "Only way he could know."

"When he came out of that restaurant and almost caught us, I quick stuck it under the cover. Then I forgot about it. Sorry."

"No, no. Look, it worked out great," Dave asserted. "See, Dad lost track of a tool order, was diggin' all over for it. Then, when he found the wrapper, he checked out Spud. We wouldina known he was a jailbird otherwise."

"Yeah, O.K., so that's why we got the camera?" Ron said.

"No," Dave explained. "It's like this. Everybody thinks umpires can only see straight ahead. That's wrong. Dad's been watchin' every move we make. We didn't get the camera 'cause he found the wrapper, we got it 'cause he trusts us. He's convinced we won't do anything stupid. He's with us now—sorta. So we just stay cool, let him decide when it's time ta pull the plug on these guys."

"But we're still taking the book to him after Sunday, right?"

"Half a witness won't do. I told ya, somebody else has ta see that the scratch is gone. Then, yeah. Pull the popcorn stunt again 'fore Kovach goes in and we'll have 'em."

Ron looked skeptical. "So what are we supposed to do with the camera?" he asked.

"No idea," Dave replied. "Dad didn't say. Guess that's for us ta figure out."

"Well, we're obviously supposed to do something with it," Ron pondered. "We'll have to conceal it somehow."

"Good thinkin' Sherlock," Dave teased.

"All right then, what do you say?" Ron came back.

"I say we try for pictures of the watchband and the outline on Spud's wrist. That plus the ledger should make our case."

"Do you think the camera can pick up the scratch?"

"We need a picture of it gone. The lens is super high quality but we'd havta get in close and the watch would havta be laid out just right."

Ron's face showed frustration.

"I know," Dave responded, "that'd be nexta impossible. Anyway, we can't do it alone. I'll be sellin' and you'll be workin' in for looks so we're gonna need help. I cornered Dad 'fore we played today. He said Stu was off ta his brother's in Ohio and we can take two of the guys along. I figure Rafe and Leon and we meet here tomorrow night ta plan. Gotta limit the number of people who know."

"Why them?"

"The Razyniaks go visiting Sunday afternoons and Doug's tied up 'til after the Fourth. Rafe looks like a ballplayer and Leon can handle the camera."

"What happens when the rest find out we didn't trust them enough to let them in on it?" Ron objected. "They will ya know. You think about that? And how are you going to get the film developed? You can't just run it down to

Greene's Camera like it's from a Brownie. Luke's the one you want for that. He's got the chemicals and the enlarger."

"Ten people. Man, I don' know," Dave vacillated.

"Look," Ron reasoned, "you've been able to keep it secret, right?"

"Barely," Dave replied, "but yeah, so far."

"Well then, if you can do it, they certainly can."

"Thanks, I think," Dave said.

"We always do things together around here. It doesn't make sense to stop now, just when we need fresh ideas."

"This best be good, quick too," Rafe said, taking the basement steps two at a time. "I'm missin' *Lone Ranger* and *Gangbusters* comes on at nine."

Dave shot Ron a "we should've done it my way" glance.

"Where's Gunner?" Ron asked.

"He'll be here," Rafe replied."

"Five more minutes then," Dave replied.

"We're here," Leon gasped, as he, Ben and Gunner filed into the room.

"That's everybody," Pete said. "Now what's so important that we all had to be here?"

"That's 'you can't tell a soul,'" Tim corrected.

"Yeah," Rafe chimed in, "what's the big secret?"

"All right, all right, just keep it down," Dave whispered. "First thing, whatever's said in this room has to stay in this room. No exceptions."

"Oooh," Ben quipped.

"Listen," Ron said sharply. "This is serious, real serious."

Eyes met all around. No one had ever seen Ron irritated before. The room went dead silent.

"Now everybody's gotta promise not ta tell. Not anybody," Dave emphasized, "parents, friends, nobody."

He looked at each of his friends in turn until he was satisfied.

"Now spill it," Rafe said.

Dave looked at each of his friends again, then at Ron.

"Almost afraid to," he sighed. "O.K. here goes. There's a spy ring operating outta Fox Park in LaPorte where my dad umpires games on Sundays."

"Ghastly," Rafe hooted. "Mystery's afoot."

"Stop," Ron snarled.

Ron was getting scary. Dave put out a hand. It was quiet again.

"Let's hear the rest," Luke said, with an air of authority.

Dave continued. "Well, ya know how I go ta sell pop there each week?" and he told them about his chance discovery, Mr. Kovach's new job, the turbine blade connection. How the switch with Spud likely started the film on its journey out of the country.

"I've gone along twice now and it's just like he says," Ron confirmed. "We've got everything coded in here, inning by inning," he continued, opening the scorer's book.

Dave looked at Rafe. It was real gangbusters tonight.

"How do we fit into this?" Pete asked.

"Gettin' ta that," Dave replied, taking the Minox from his pocket to explain how an overlooked gum wrapper had put them in possession of an expensive spy camera. "Bet Mr. Kovach uses one same's this ta get the pictures," Dave speculated. "Anyway, Dad says we can take two more along on Sunday."

"Pass it over," Leon said, motioning to Dave.

"We need proof ta back up what we've seen."

"Wait a minute," Rafe countered, "we don't even know what these bums look like."

Dave set up the rickety card table. Ron laid out the map of the park on top.

"Mr. Kovack always sits here," Dave said, pointing to a spot off at an angle and a few feet behind the player's bench on the third base side. "He's got big muscles and he's nuts about baseball. Now Spud..."

"He the dopey one?" Tim interrupted.

"Check," Dave sighed, not breaking stride. "He'll be a ways back up on the knoll, 'bout here.

You can't miss him," Ron snickered. "His head's lumpy."

"And the switch?" Doug pursued.

"Goes down here," Dave said, laying a finger on the entrance to the men's room.

"How's this thing work?" Leon asked.

"Pull it apart," Luke pantomimed. "Each time you do, you advance the film one frame. Other than that it works like a regular camera."

"Best be right on this," Rafe said. "A spy ring in Indiana?"

"He is," Ron assured.

"Shhh," Dave whispered, at once alert.

Leon closed his hand around the camera and slipped it into his pocket. Ron laid the ledger on the map.

"Hi, Mom," Dave said cheerfully, "What's up?"

"I thought a snack and some juice might be in order."

Mrs. Norris passed around a tray of cookies, glasses and a pitcher.

"And what devious schemes are in the works tonight?" she asked.

"Just the usual," Dave smirked.

"And that's supposed to bring me comfort?" she winced as she turned. "Not too late now."

"She know?" Gunner mouthed, when Mrs. Norris started up the stairs.

"Do'no," Dave shrugged, "might. Best get movin'."

"What if Mr. Kovach doesn't come Sunday or he doesn't wear his watch?" Tim asked.

"We make the best of it," Dave replied. "That's all we can do."

"They haven't missed a game yet," Ron noted.

"How are we going to hide this?" Pete questioned, taking his turn examining the camera.

"Hang on," Leon broke in, "I got it. You said they switch in the restroom?"

"We're positive," Dave responded.

"Where at?"

"Not absolutely sure."

"Yes we are," Ron corrected. "I checked it out. There's a flat ledge, like around the basement here, that goes from the top of the walls out to the eaves. If you stand on the toilet seat you can set things on it. The other spot is the urinal. It's not like regular ones. It's a trough. Actually, it's a long sink and the way it's shaped you could wedge something up against the wall behind it."

"Think that's where the scratch came from?" Rafe asked.

Ron shrugged. "I don't know, but there's this panel outside they put up because the door's always wedged open. When the light reflecting off it dims, you've got about two seconds before someone walks in.

"O.K., two places, what's the big deal," Leon scoffed. "Kovach hides the watch with the film, we steal it—they're done for."

Dave looked at Ron in frustration, "We woulda done that weeks ago 'cept Dad said we couldn't do anything that might cause trouble. Remember, LaPorte's not just any town for my family. What would happen if somethin' went wrong, seems like it always does?"

"What could go wrong?" Rafe challenged.

"Only 'bout a million things," Dave came back. "You watch movies, don't ya?"

"Yeah."

"Well, when's last time ya saw one came out exactly the way ya expected?"

"That's just in the movies," Rafe rejected.

"No it's not."

"So then they've won," Pete said. "We've lost."

"Not yet," Dave countered. "We still got our eyes and we got this," he said, holding up the Minox.

"We can't get them with just that," Leon rebuffed.

"Look," Dave said firmly, "my dad always says *there's no such word as can't*. He's been tellin' me that for as long as I can remember. Whenever it gets really tough, when somethin' 'bout impossible comes along, he pulls me aside and says *there's no such word as can't, we're just gonna do it*. I ain't sayin' it'll be easy, it's never been easy. Only thing I know is it works for me and if we stick together I'm bettin' it'll work this time too, so unless somebody's got a better idea..."

For a few interminable seconds Dave's pitch was met with stony silence. The faces around him were non committal. He looked away dejected.

"I say we give it a try," Luke said.

No one objected.

The next afternoon the newly assembled "task force" met in Dave's garage. A full range of ideas was discussed, though Dave got the impression everyone hoped the person next in line had come up with something better than he had. Hide the camera in a hat, a paper cup, popcorn box, someone's pocket, a candy bar wrapper...

"I like the candy bar idea," Ben cut in.

"Me too," Dave supported. "It'd fit perfect."

"Who carries a candy bar around all afternoon when it's hot and doesn't eat it?" Gunner scoffed.

"Yeah," Dave agreed. "On second thought, that'd be kinda stupid."

When scrutinized, none of their ideas held up long.

"Why not use one a those," Rafe said, pointing to the line of broken bats leaning against the wall. "Camera'd fit easy in there and we could carry it around with our mitts like we planned ta play catch or scoop grounders if we got bored with the game. See kids doin' it all the time. We could walk by, take a picture whenever we wanted, nobody'd spect nothin'."

"Chisel out a cavity that deep? Baseball bat wood's hard," Dave objected. "We'd havta rig a plunger ta trip the shutter, get it all aligned, only got a couple days."

"I just think 'em up," Rafe quipped. "Buildin' 'em's your job."

No one could hold back a laugh on that.

"That would be a big hole," Tim said.

"And you'd need another smaller one for the lens," Doug added. "How would we hide them?"

"Aw—do this," Rafe replied, his eyes flashing around the room. "Pack a wad of paper in behind the camera then, wrap the bat with this black athletic tape," he grinned, obviously delighted that the thought had come to him in such a timely manner. "It'd look like the bat broke and we fixed it up."

"That's not athletic tape. That's friction tape for covering electrical wires," Ben corrected.

"Still work," Rafe returned

"I like it," Dave said. "Just no way we can get it done by Sunday."

"Sure we can," Luke stated. "We'll chain drill it on my dad's drill press."

"What's chain drillin'?" Gunner asked.

"That's where you lay out your box shape and drill a row of small holes inside your guide lines. Once you've gone around, you put in a bigger drill and go around again. Pretty soon the holes come together like in a chain. You break out the block in the middle then square it up. It goes along fast if you do it right. Shouldn't take more than a couple hours."

"Then we'll rub dirt into the tape and scuff it up," Pete added.

"Hold on," Leon said. "How are we supposed ta line it up if we can't use the view finder?"

That question stumped everyone.

"Put a mark on the bat so when it's facing up the lens points sideways," Doug suggested.

"We snap a picture then go slide or play rundown so we can move up the film and we're ready for another pass. Simple," Rafe smirked. "Now you two get ta work," and he pointed at Dave and Luke.

Rafe stood and picked up the basketball he'd been sitting on, his forbearance for meetings at an end.

"Hold on," Ron said firmly. "This is important. No looking them straight in the eye."

"Yeah," Dave emphasized, "whatever ya do, don't look 'em level in the eye. It's a dead giveaway. And 'member, these guys play for keeps. We gotta get the goods on 'em without 'em knowin' we got it. Then the police can swoop in and round up the lot 'fore they come after us."

"We haven't decided who's going yet," Pete said.

"I think since it was Rafe's idea, he should," Dave replied. "And Leon can take the pictures."

"O.K. by me," Rafe said.

Leon nodded. They were set.

"Either of you know how they're smuggling the film out?" Doug asked.

Dave shot Ron a glance.

"Not sure on that," he said.

"Maybe this Kovach guy isn't really a spy," Gunner speculated. "Maybe they brainwashed 'im then snuck 'im in with the others comin' over."

"That ain't real," Rafe scoffed.

"I'm not so sure," Leon countered. "I heard some of our pilots they nabbed in Korea got it and now they think the commies are the good guys."

"Think maybe they used truth serum on 'em," Ben theorized.

Dave shuddered.

Chapter 19
THWARTED

The bat, the mitts, a ball, the boys and the scorer's book were waiting at the curb when Mr. Norris came out to the car. He looked them over momentarily then got in. They followed his lead. Before they could pull away Luke appeared.

"Just wondered if maybe..."

Mr. Norris nodded and Luke got in.

An extra man, an uneventful trip, plenty of time to think, the team was as ready as could be when Mr. Norris eased the car into its customary parking spot at the park. He snuffed out his cigar in the ashtray as the doors swung open.

"Not so fast," he decreed, turning to examine his charges. "We all know the rules today?" he asked, over drooping glasses and raised finger. "I've got to have your word on it," he pressed, through the uncomfortable silence.

Dave nodded and was sure his friends had as well.

"All right," Mr. Norris said, satisfied his message had been unambiguously received. "Let's enjoy the games today."

There was a collective sigh of relief. Mr. Norris stepped out of the car. Dave and his friends did too. Mr. Norris took in a breath of the fragrant air and raised his arms to stretch. The boys split up. Dave and Ron walked toward the backstop on the path.

"Be O.K. today," Dave said, "'cause it's early."

Dave heard his dad say, "The sun's shining and they're fighting to get in."

"Almost always does that when it's nice," Dave remarked as he and Ron sat down. "Think 'cause he's stiff from sittin' in the car so long."

"Since you were busy with the camera, I'm supposed to bring you up on the plan," Ron said. "Rafe and Leon are looking out by the merry-go-round. When they spot Spud or Mr. Kovach, they'll alert Luke on the knoll. We're O.K. here until he moves. Then we have to split up."

"Really glad he could come," Dave said.

"I was surprised your dad let him."

"Wouldina, 'cept the timin' was perfect. Five's a load."

"How's come the prisoners aren't here?" Ron questioned. "You said they always come early."

"They do," Dave affirmed. "That's why we had ta leave early. Heck, they're usually done with battin' practice 'fore most people finish lunch; s'pose 'cause it's easier for the guards ta keep tabs on 'em that way. There's rules 'bout everything. They havta stay in the field area, can't go ta the Pavilion or be out by the road. If they need ta use the restroom a guard waits outside next ta the panel the whole time."

"Really."

"Sure," Dave continued, "and the game can't go past three fifteen or they miss curfew. That's the reason why, if there's a double header like today, another team comes in for the second game. Uniforms are cool, all white with I.S.P. on the front—Indiana State Prison," Dave grinned.

"I'd have gotten it, if you'd have given me a minute," Ron frowned.

"It's in big red letters right here," Dave said, drawing a finger across his chest. "Dad says the prisoners are always on their best behavior when they're here, that gettin' outside the walls is a really big deal for 'em and they're not 'bout ta blow their chance ta breathe free air by doin' somethin' stupid. Plus, if they did, the other players would kill 'em when they got back inside—I spect they'll show anytime now."

"You ready for the plan now?" Ron asked.

"Shoot," Dave said. "On second thought, make that go ahead."

"Well, you know what I'm doing. Now Rafe and Leon..."

"They're here," Dave said, as two cars and a bus stopped along the road. See, there's a car load a guards, the bus with players and more guards in the middle then another car full a guards in back."

Ron barely noticed. He was watching Mr. Kaufner strong-arm a speaker onto a hook.

"Those things look heavy."

"Pssst, there he is," Dave whispered, as he eyed the enormous man stepping off the bus.

"Whoa! He is big," Ron exclaimed. "Looks scary."

"Told ya," Dave said. "I heard the other prisoners call him Gorilla."

"To his face?" Ron asked staring.

"No, stupid, not to his face."

"Bet he'd break your legs if he didn't like ya. That what he's in for?"

"You're jokin', right?" Dave sputtered.

"Maybe," Ron replied, unable to take his eyes off the looming hulk bearing down on them.

Ron abruptly turned his head toward the diamond. "Luke," he burst out, jumping to his feet.

Dave looked toward the knoll. Luke had moved down from where he'd been sitting. Ron was trotting along the third base line toward the outfield, zeroed in on Luke. He didn't look back even once, Dave thought to compensate for missing the signal. Mr. Kovach was there too, jogging in from the road. He apparently hadn't noticed the prisoners in the shade behind the backstop because he was gawking over his shoulder at the last few stragglers and guards leaving the bus. He and Ron didn't see each other and nearly collided. Ron stumbled backwards, regained his balance and continued on. Mr. Kovach, startled as well, stopped momentarily to let him pass then took his seat. Dave laughed. The only two people in the whole area and they crack into each other. What were the odds on that?

After the prisoners and their "escorts" had reached the visitor's bench on the first base side of the diamond Dave left for the Pavilion. He'd bet money Mr. Kovach had come early because he couldn't believe prisoners in America got out of jail to play baseball and had to see for himself. *Probably shoot 'em where he comes from*, Dave surmised.

Mr. Kaufner was rehearsing plugs for his sponsors when Dave returned. The convicts were into their warm up drills and the first Sportsmen players were walking in on the path. The park was beginning to fill. Convict's and Davids were a big draw. Dave would be bellying up to that trough all afternoon. With the primary responsibility for collecting evidence resting with his friends, this could be the best day of the season. A dollar and a quarter, even a dollar and a half wasn't out of the question. Dave positioned his cart and within minutes bagged six sales. It wouldn't be hard getting used to all the new faces he was seeing. With the first break at the turnstiles, he shot a glance toward the knoll. Spud hadn't arrived yet. He caught Ron's eye in the distance. Ron stood to stretch and grasped his left wrist with his right hand. Dave felt a sinking feeling and moved to where his view was unimpeded. Their worst fear realized; Mr. Kovach wasn't wearing his watch. How had he missed that? Maybe Mr. Kovach had just pocketed it while he hiked into the park and it would reappear once he got situated.

The game started. Gorilla stepped into the batter's box. The pitcher, a pinnacle of confidence, wound up. The first pitch blazed in. "Crack," the first pitch flew back out. It was a line shot to the second baseman. He took it straight in then, instantly ashen, recoiled in pain. The ball popped out of his mitt and fell to the ground at his feet. Looking bewildered he slowly reached to pick it up. As he did, Gorilla stepped lightly on first. This was gonna be a fun afternoon.

"I.S.P. runner on first," Mr. Kaufner announced, "error charged on the play, right fielder to bat next, no outs."

Dave felt a tap on the shoulder. It was Spud. "One of those," he said gruffly, pointing to a Coke protruding from the ice.

"Yes'ir, right away," Dave stammered, pulling on the cord that attached his bottle opener to the cart's handle.

Spud took the bottle, paid up and ambled off toward the knoll. As he passed behind the prisoner's bench, one of them acknowledged his presence with a barely perceptible nod.

Birds of a feather, Dave said to himself. *Bet he knows every last one of 'em.*

Dave had ridden the initial wave of sales into a second cart load and was back on the knoll when it subsided. He was getting to like convicts. He saw Rafe and Leon walk past the prison bus on the road. Minutes later when he crossed over it with a load of empties, they were at the slide with Ron, and Luke was coming his way.

"How about a root beer?" he said, looking down into the cart.

"Got one in here somewhere," Dave said, shaking ice off his fingers.

"What's with Mr. Kovach not wearing his watch?" Luke whispered.

Dave shrugged. "Thinkin' it's in his pocket," he answered, trying to keep his lips from moving. "Goin' over there soon's I get back. Did Spud make the drop?"

"Yep," Luke replied, "just before you sold him the pop."

"They must still be gonna switch then," Dave surmised. "How 'bout pictures?"

"Rafe and Leon are starting that now. Thanks," Luke said in his normal voice. He tipped the top of the bottle toward Dave and walked away.

Tangled roots and a full cart were a bad mix. Unfortunately, traversing them was the only way Dave could get to Mr. Kovach. He struggled through then stopped cold. Gorilla was standing in the on-deck circle twirling three bats over his shoulder like they were toothpicks. Dave wasn't stepping one foot past the backstop with him coming up. Getting the low-down on Mr. Kovach would have to wait.

A perfectly placed bunt and the pitcher, more aware of his mortality now than before, was forced to consider his options. There were trickles of sweat coursing down his temples. Gorilla stood in. A hush settled over the crowd. With everybody in the park watching, the pitcher nervously checked the lead runner at second, shook off a sign then, looking out of the corner of his eye checked the runner again. He abruptly reared back and fired. The pitch crossed the plate low. Mr. Norris, deep in his crouch, rose slightly but said nothing. That meant it was a ball. The second pitch hit the dirt. The catcher, twisting away, knocked it down. A second later, mask flying, he was up, ball in hand, ready to throw. *Good reflexes* Dave thought. The Sportsmen's manager didn't blink an eye. Hand clamped to chin, he sat expressionless at the end of the player's bench as if in a trance. Gorilla wasn't getting anything decent from these guys. The runners lengthened their leads. The next delivery broke outside at the knees. Gorilla reached, got hold of it and drove it deep to left. The left fielder, climbing as fast as he could, raced up the hill with outstretched glove. At the last instant he lunged, stabbing at the ball. What could have been a spectacularly memorable catch ended in humiliation when he fell in a heap to the ground. The ball, careening off the mitts' lacing, smacked into the outfield fence then ricocheted erratically into left center. By the time the center fielder ran it down, both runners had scored and Gorilla, seemingly unaware of the devastation he'd just wreaked, stood dusting himself off at second. Dave pushed off for Mr. Kovach's bench.

Tracks of crusty blisters, tiny mountain chains running up and down his arms, Mr. Kovach's sunburn had been the onset of poison ivy. Nobody scratches a sunburn Dave reminded himself. Another one had slipped past him and he was practically an expert on contact dermatitis. No wonder Mr. Kovach wasn't wearing his watch. Dave fought to keep a straight face when he handed Mr. Kovach his Coke. Another setback. Would Mr. Kovach and

Spud still switch watches? Would he come out wearing the one with the scratch? Had all the effort they'd put into hiding the camera been for naught?

"5-3 Michigan City," Mr. Kaufner updated. "One duck left on the pond, Sportsmen half of the second."

On the way back to the path Dave bemoaned their run of bad luck. Rafe and Leon, certainly aware of the situation, were sitting back in the trees on the first base side, watching the duck, that is, Gorilla, lope in from second. Luke, behind the backstop, was doing the same. It looked like a picture of the watch outline on Spud's wrist was all they could hope for today.

The innings rolled by. Dave busied himself selling. Gorilla came up again. This time the Sportsmen weren't taking any chances. They pitched out, obviously figuring a gorilla on first posed less of a threat than a gorilla in the box, swinging away. After seeing him in action, Dave couldn't fault that decision. *Better safe than sorry,* he thought.

The Sportsmen, on the strength of a triple, a single and a pop fly lost in the sun, managed to tie the game 5-5 in the fifth. Mr. Kovach, reinvigorated by the action, sat at the edge of his seat. Leaving a pricey watch, especially this watch, secreted away in a bathroom so long seemed foolish to Dave. He began to worry. What if somebody found it? Spud, for his part, was still trying to connect with his old convict buddies. They weren't having any of it. *Bet he's been in on every kind of caper imaginable,* Dave speculated. A little delay in pullin' off another isn't gonna faze him.

In the sixth, while the prisoners fanned out across the field, Mr. Kovach, walking with purpose, slipped into the restroom. A few minutes later he came out. No watch. They were sunk. Ron would be scratching a big S.O., struck out, in the scorer's book that very second. Dejected, Dave decided to try his luck with the people on the freshly spread blankets down past Spud. They hadn't brought coolers. As he started along the knoll, Rafe and Leon trooped down from the woods further up to his right, walked in front of Spud and looking straight ahead, continued past him. No eye contact, that was good. He glanced over his shoulder. The pair stopped at the path but Rafe went on, rounded the panel outside the men's room and disappeared inside. His heart skipped a beat.

"He wouldn't," Dave stammered in a panic.

His cart twisted violently to the left. He almost fell. A foot was wedged against its right wheel.

"Better watch where you're going," an unfamiliar voice said.

The foot belonged to a young man whose outstretched arm was shielding the small child to his right.

"Er, sorry," Dave said, pulling back off the blanket. "Wasn't payin' attention, won't happen again."

Dave altered his course slightly to go around.

"Hold it," the man ordered.

Dave stopped cold.

"We'll take a lemon-lime and," hesitating, he turned toward the young woman on the other side of the child.

"And a cream soda," she said.

"Walking inta people," Dave groused, once the sale was complete, "real swift move."

Rafe joined back up with Leon. They waited. Dave began to retrace his steps. Suddenly, for no apparent reason, Spud jumped up and made a bee line for the bathroom. Rafe and Leon walked toward him. Leon turned the bat slightly. They crossed paths behind the prisoner's bench. Bingo, Dave smiled, a photo run. He knew all about it and for a moment there hadn't even realized. Cool.

Walks interspersed with timely hits; a call for a new pitcher, Mr. Kaufner had more than enough time to cajole the crowd in preparation for passing the hat during the 7th inning stretch.

"Captivating contests of this caliber, why you're enjoying the best bargain in baseball. On a par with any facility anywhere, nationally acclaimed, ardent fans visit our fair town from every corner of this great nation to experience the extravaganza you enjoy each week. This afternoon's special guest is a zoologist from Syracuse University. Brought here by recent, peculiar scientific discoveries on the lake, he's extended his stay just to be with us today. 'Professor,' would you please stand and be recognized?"

At that, a man, seated with a friend on the bench Spud had occupied the previous week, stood and waved.

"Let's extend a warm LaPorte welcome to the man from upstate New York," Mr. Kaufner said.

The professor thrust his hands into the air above his head, clasped them together, shook them and smiled broadly.

"Sir, would you like to show your support for our 'Sunday Spectacular' by starting off today's collection with say, twenty dollars?" Mr. Kaufner asked.

The professor's demeanor suddenly changed. He turned out his empty pockets, shook his head from side to side and frowned. The crowd roared.

"That guy's a plant, sure," Dave groaned, laughing along.

Mr. Kaufner pulled a concealed ten gallon hat from beneath the "nerve center" and started his rounds. Dave laughed again, doubting the not so subtle hint would appreciably increase the collection.

At the end of regulation the Sportsmen and the Prison were tied. That prompted Mr. Norris to hustle the players along in hopes of completing the contest before curfew. Dave's team of investigators with nothing to investigate, were mere spectators now.

Dave looked across at Mr. Kovach, then at Spud.

"Spies, what a joke," he snickered. One didn't look smart enough to know the time of day and the other, Mr. Rosy Rash, what could you say about an adult being that dumb? Could you be that stupid and still be a spy? It didn't make sense. Spies were suave, outwitted their adversaries at every turn and never lost their cool, even when cornered. In the movies women dripped off them and the good guys always won. Here it wasn't so simple. Dave felt a wave of apprehension. Catching spies, the whole business was slipping out of their grasp. He could feel it. Why couldn't life be more like the movies? Why'd it have to be so complicated? He made for the Pavilion.

The prison tallied two in the eleventh with the tail end of the order supplying the spark. Not to be out-done the Sportsmen shortstop scored an out later. Then, with a man on first and two gone, the center fielder lofted a well hit ball into right. The man on first waved around by the coach and Mr. Kovach dug hard for home. The catcher, holding his position, put on the tag. "CRUNCH! THUD!" Both players, arms and legs intertwined, pancaked atop the plate. There was a moment's indecision while Mr. Norris, bent low inches away, determined if the catcher retained possession of the ball. Finally, a thumb shot up through the obscuring dust. The home town crowd, holding its breath, let out a collective groan as the familiar "YOU'RE OUTTA THERE" dashed their hopes. The Sportsmen manager, livid, descended on the plate. The Prison manager followed suit.

"It's been called," Mr. Norris barked in a threatening voice.

Neither manager backed down. It was toe to toe. Someone was about to get the boot. Dirt got kicked on Mr. Norris' shoes. You were gone for sure when that happened. Instead, Mr. Norris did an about face and walked away.

The managers were speechless. With no way to plead their case they stood there dumbfounded.

That's how it ended, peacefully and in silence. The prisoners, feeling free as birds, if only for the moment, packed up and jubilant all the way to their bus, departed. The Sportsmen, many cradling their heads in their hands, sat quietly for a time on their bench. Mr. Norris had been magnificent. Dave didn't think many other umpires could have defused the situation so easily. It seemed effortless. The game was always under control when Mr. Norris held court behind the plate and any thought that a decision might be reversed on appeal was a complete waste of time.

The first thing you noticed about the Davids, other than their beards and uncut hair, was their over-sized hats. Part of each player's pre-game ritual involved manipulating the sometimes waist length locks into a shape suitable for stowing beneath the headgear and each player had his own unique way of going about it. Some leaned forward, twisted, bundled, and stuffed. Others leaned back then worked it into a ball. One used a crazy swaying motion that threw the hair out to the side. One swing, another, a precisely timed grab, mysterious contortions Dave couldn't begin to explain and presto, a neat coil of rope sat perched atop his head.

No matter the technique, what emerged was a relatively normal looking ballplayer ready for action and with the Davids, action was the name of the game. Non-stop motion, speed, intensity, daring, the Davids played a fiery brand of baseball most other teams didn't understand and tried to avoid. It wasn't just a come-on shill either, it carried over into regulation. Drop your guard for even a second and you paid dearly. Delayed steals, double steals, hit and run, squeeze plays, ridiculously long lead offs, you had no idea what they'd do next. Where most teams tried to conserve energy, the Davids seemed to relish expending it, and there was no letup. The ball streaked here, flashed there. They whipped it like lightning. Most times they threw it. Sometimes you only thought they did. Even if you were watching you couldn't always be sure who had it. It was all psychology. The fear of being overwhelmed debilitated opponents. They made foolish mistakes, flinched in the clutch. Teams in the Negro Leagues called it "shadow ball." The Davids' version, "pepper ball," was very similar and equally effective. Other similarities existed too. Both clubs had had their glory days between the World Wars when they criss-crossed the country in jalopies and broken down buses. Barnstorming was a way of life then. Bouncing from town to town, you played baseball when the sun shined and traveled when it didn't.

Fans flocked to the games. A show not to be missed, it was the best entertainment for miles around. The team playing today was only a remnant of that by-gone era. When Dave had asked his dad about it he'd answered with one word: television.

Dave knew television changed people's lives. He remembered how it was before his family owned one. You read after supper, imagined the scenes portrayed on the radio. You built things, played games together. You controlled your life. Then, overnight, all that changed. Instead of you deciding what you did and when you did it, somebody far away, somebody you didn't know and would never meet, decided for you. Everything revolved around the T.V. listings in the newspaper. "Gotta go, my program's coming on. Tell me about it later." That's how people phrased it. Why venture out after a hard day on the job when with a twist of a knob, you had the world at your finger tips? So quick, so easy, so subtly controlling, in a way it was scary.

Mr. Kovach not wearing his watch was scary too. Who knew? Today might just be the day something crucial fell into enemy hands. Dave put Mr. Kovach out of his mind. Watching the Davids was fun.

With his cart parked next to the press box so people would think he was in the bathroom, Dave wedged himself between two tobacco chewing old coots, each needing an arm rest for support. Here, free from beckoning waves that required immediate attention, he took his first real break of the afternoon. Sure, he was passing up sales, what of it? Traipsing back and forth to the Pavilion wasn't exactly his idea of a good time.

The Davids' razzle-dazzle, whether manifest on the field or in the batter's box, confounded the Sportsmen and mesmerized the crowd. Spectacular feats reduced to the routine, if a way had been devised to get a leg up on the opposition, the Davids employed it. The Sportsmen, sullen to a man, didn't need to be told the hoots and howls emanating from the usually supportive crowd weren't for them. After the way the last game ended, everybody knew this wasn't their finest hour. Mr. Kovach, if enthusiastic before, was downright ecstatic now. Eyes locked, muscles tensed, from what Dave could see spying was the furthest thing from his mind. A Davids' outfielder scrambling, pin wheeling into a pirouette, the ball coming from behind, falling past his face into a waiting mitt—Mr. Kovach, looking over his shoulder, his hand cupped open in front like a glove; a Davids' player raced for second—Mr. Kovach reaching, ready to sacrifice his body in a head long slide;

on practically every play, a leg shifted position, a shoulder tightened involuntarily. Even if the movements were subtle, not instantly recognizable, you knew Mr. Kovach, attired in dandy Davids' uniform and puffy cap, was on the field giving his all. He wasn't out there physically, of course, but he was there none-the-less. How had he survived all these years without baseball? For him Fox Park wasn't in America. Blissfully detached from reality, he was in heaven. Dave would have been there too, if a row of adolescent detectives wasn't sitting a short distance away. How could he enjoy himself, the stakes being what they were?

"Benton Harbor's House of David 5, LaPorte Sportsmen 0," the speakers announced.

With the Sportsmen piling up strike outs like cord wood, it didn't take long for the crowd to grow restive. The bathroom ruse was played out too. Dave went back to work.

In the bottom of the fifth the Sportsmen lodged their first hit, a single off an anemic blooper lollipopped over the shortstop's head. About three people cheered. Another game like this and the Sportsmen would be battling Argos for the cellar.

Dave sold out to the last bottle. Hurrying to reload, he passed a pair of disgruntled Sportsmen on the path. *There's lots worse things in life than losing a ballgame,* he told himself.

Mr. Kaufner had the crowd eating out of his hand when Dave returned.

"And in response to the more adventuresome, our concessionaire at the Pavilion has put on additional glass-bottomed boats. From this vantage point I can see scores of curious citizens peering expectantly through the clear panels into the murky depths below."

Dave wanted to scream. *There's no scientist! No professor! There's no glass bottom boats! And there's no monster!* Instead, he parked his cart and went to the bathroom. This time he really did have to go.

Mr. Kaufner was still at it when he came out.

"With thousands expected again this year, only early birds will garner the most preferential spots: a carnival at the fairgrounds, baseball here in the afternoon, spectacular fireworks at dusk to cap off the evening. Celebrate the nation's birthday with us on Thursday. Come out for a picnic. Make it a day."

For once, Mr. Kaufner was playing it straight. On Thursday, the 4th of July, LaPorte really did come alive. Sometimes people stood six or seven deep to watch the parade inch its way past the Courthouse. At least for one day, LaPorte was what Mr. Norris always said it was, the biggest small town in America.

"The House of David 7, LaPorte Sportsmen 0. That concludes our program for today. Hope to see you all Thursday."

The Sportsmen and Davids had only gone 7 innings. It was an exhibition game.

Uncle Wally treated the "sleuths" to snacks and cold drinks. Dave gathered with them around the Wurlitzer for a while then sat down to rest, another long disappointing Sunday.

In the car, the discussion was lively.

"Man, those Davids are good," Rafe commented. "Be great ta play for them someday."

"Soon as you can grow a beard," Ron quipped.

"Got more than you do," Rafe scoffed.

"The way they move the ball, that's what gets me," Luke said.

"A couple times there I didn't even know who had it," Leon agreed.

"Dad, is it really like Mr. Kaufner said? Did the House of David team travel all across the country in the twenties?"

"Yes indeedee," Mr. Norris responded. "They took on all comers too and won most every game they played. The House of David players were religious emissaries. Every time one of them took the field he put a human face on the sect. It was how they got their message out to the people and recruited new members. It was slick marketing. Everyone likes baseball."

"They get paid a lot?" Rafe inquired.

"No," Mr. Norris chuckled. "Competition, love of the game, being on the road with their family, that was their reward."

"Their families went along?" Dave asked, surprised.

"In a manner of speaking," Mr. Norris continued. "Most of these men didn't have family of their own. They weren't allowed to marry or even have girl friends. Their family was their team. Some of the men played together for years."

"Hey Rafe, still want to join up?" Ron snickered.

"Prob'ly not," Rafe frowned.

"Playing all those games, is that why they're so smooth?" Luke asked.

"Well, there's the raw talent, of course, they had plenty of that and good baseball sense but you're right. Barnstorming with the same teammates certainly gives you an edge. It hones your reactions. Eventually they become second nature. Remember though, the team you saw today wasn't the team of old."

"They're still lot's better than the ones playin' at the park." Dave said.

"That's to be expected," Mr. Norris explained. "Northern Indiana baseball teams usually only play one game per week. This House of David club is chasing a legend."

"What about that first sacker for the prison?" Leon asked. "He's a bruiser."

"That's Gorilla," Dave noted proudly. "Overheard a player say it."

"But not to his face," Ron reminded.

"Right," Dave snickered. "Not to his face."

"I don't care what they call him," Leon stated. "He really slams the ball."

"Coulda made the 'bigs' sure," Rafe speculated.

"I'd say so," Mr. Norris commented, "if he hadn't developed a taste for fast cars along the way."

"What's wrong with fast cars?" Dave asked.

"Nothing, if they're yours," Mr. Norris said.

"He threw away the chance of a life time ta joyride in stolen cars?" Dave exclaimed.

"With some people it doesn't sink in very fast. Had his talents been discovered before he went astray, thing's would be different today," Mr. Norris mused. "He could have had it all."

"Be battin' .400 easy," Rafe added.

"We'll never know," Mr. Norris continued. "He'll be locked up for a number of years yet. By then, his playing days will be over. Life's a one way street. You can't go back and undo the past."

What a waste, Dave thought.

"Ya see the second baseman take that liner?" Rafe remarked. "Thought he was gonna pass out."

"How 'bout the pitcher?" Dave chimed in. "Facin' down Gorilla, man, he hits a 'come-backer,' you're dead."

"Bierwagon could have handled him," Mr. Norris stated.

"Who's he?" Rafe sputtered.

"Ike Bierwagon," Mr. Norris clarified. "He pitched for us when I coached with the Bendix Brakes in '41. We were Softball World Champs that year. Ike was the fastest underhand pitcher I ever saw. Phenomenal speed, steady as a rock, he went thirty and one that season. They said he was the best ever."

"Yeah Dad," Dave scoffed, "but we're talkin' baseball here, the big leagues."

"It doesn't get any bigger than being World Champions," Mr. Norris said proudly. "When we played Zollner's out of Fort Wayne, almost twenty thousand fans turned out to watch. Ike broke two catcher's hands that year. They said they could feel every bone up to their elbow when the ball hit. That big enough? We had to draft an outfielder, Chuck Goldfreid, to do the job going into the tournament. He was black and blue from his ankles up; took guts to carry out that assignment. In softball the pitcher's mound is only forty-three feet from home plate. Being a catcher, that's no job for the faint of heart."

Dave knew his friends behind him were exchanging skeptical glances and he had to admit that this sounded a lot like one of Mr. Kaufner's tall tales but then, he'd heard the story before and knew it was true. He closed his eyes, felt the cool breeze on his face and began to fade away. The radio clicked on. The Yankees were pulling away from the Sox. His dad had been right about that too.

"Hold on," Dave exclaimed, minutes later. "Mr. Kovach, he's an adult, s'posed ta be cool. How'd he get himself in a patch a poison ivy?"

"Art and I were discussing that between games," Mr. Norris replied. "It seems poison ivy is native to North America and doesn't exist in Europe. Mr. Kovach had never seen it before and didn't know to look out for it."

"What!" Dave said, shocked. "No poison ivy! He didn't know!"

"He was clearing a thicket for the people he lives with and tore out the vines with the rest of the underbrush," Mr. Norris explained, "I suppose they just assumed he knew. Once the rash developed and they realized what happened, they showed him pictures of the leaves."

Rafe reached over from the back seat and tapped Dave on the shoulder.

"You best be studyin' up on those 'fore our next trip ta the river," he snorted.

Dave pulled away.

"There won't be any more trips to the river," Mr. Norris said firmly, in a raised voice.

Dave closed his eyes. No poison ivy. No watch. No witness. He was hot, tired, sore and for the moment at least, he'd given up.

Dave lay on his bed staring up at the ceiling, apprehensively contemplating. It was first light and deathly silent. Mr. Kovach not knowing about poison ivy, that had to be a one in a million. It was also a fact and not something he could change. If he just hadn't gone to clearing brush right when they were closing in, right when they got the camera. Dave closed his eyes and forced himself to relax. It was much too early to get up. Even if Rafe and Leon did get a picture of Spud's wrist, what good would it do? He turned one way, then another, banged his pillow into a more comfortable shape. The minutes ticked off. Finally, he got dressed and went to Luke's.

The dark room door was closed when he went downstairs. He knocked. The door opened. Leon and Ben came out.

"Kinda got it," Leon shrugged.

Dave went in. Luke showed him the narrow strip of film

"Didn't realize it'd be so small," he groaned. "Pictures aren't much bigger than the end of an eraser."

Luke motioned and the two stepped over to the enlarger.

"You can't make anything out unless you use this."

Dave pored over the magnified images the instrument projected. Luke slowly slid the negative along to bring each succeeding frame into view. There was a picture of Mr. Kovach scratching his arms, one of trees, Spud cut off at the eyeballs sitting with his legs crossed, a long shot of Mr. Kovach entering the men's room, Spud's hideous face and Gorilla standing in to bat. Dave looked at each picture twice hoping something would magically jump out at him. A vague watch outline was the only thing that did.

"It's just a mish-mash," he said.

"That's why I didn't make prints," Luke remarked. "You want to take the film with ya?"

"Take the 'evidence'?" Dave frowned. "Na—no wait, actually I do," he replied.

When Dave got back upstairs, the Scanner brothers and Ron were waiting.

"We didn't get…"

"We know," Gunner said. "Leon told us."

"So, what you guys doin' now?" Dave asked.

"Kid we know from school got a new ping pong table," Rafe replied. "We're goin' over ta play."

"Stanky?" Dave snickered.

"You're cruisin'," Rafe warned. "You two wanna come?"

Dave looked at Ron.

"Can't," he said, "Dad brought the Reo home. It's got to be ready for the parade on Thursday."

"You?" Rafe asked, turning toward Dave.

"Think I'll stick with Ron on this one," Dave returned. "Got lots ta sort through."

"Looks like they've won out," Dave grumbled, as he and Ron made their way up the alley. "It's been at least a month they been doin' it, prob'ly more. That's a life time for spies."

"Listen, earlier you were saying it's always the details that trip them up, that no one thinks of everything."

"Yeah, well, it's not workin' out that way is it?"

"Look, you'll be at the parade with your family in LaPorte Thursday and I'll be at the one here after the Derby," Ron noted. "Sunday, I'll buy a box of popcorn and work in on Mr. Kovach like before. He knows me now and the poison ivy will have cleared up. We'll get 'em," Ron encouraged.

"S'pose," Dave said, dejected.

A shaft of brilliant sunlight flooded the previously dark garage when Ron raised the door.

"I always forget how big the wheels are on this thing," Dave remarked, sliding his hand over the massive chunk of solid rubber that served as one of the truck's rear tires. "Stuff's hard as a rock."

"Has to be to carry the weight," Ron replied.

"What we doin' to it?" Dave asked.

"Waxing the wood and cleaning the chain."

Dave climbed up to the elevated stage coach style driver's seat.

"What's this thing do?"

"Top speed's about ten," Ron answered.

The Reo truck, like the shiny buckboard sitting next to it, came out of that early twentieth century transition period when vehicles weren't modern cars and trucks yet but weren't farm wagons or carriages anymore, either. And where the buckboard was delicate, the Reo was heavily built with a huge radiator jutting out in front. At the time, the two marked the latest advance in man's quest to harness nature.

"Why'd Leon and Rafe take a picture a Gorilla battin'?" Dave grumbled.

"Just Rafe being Rafe I guess," Ron shrugged. "He said he couldn't get over the size of Gorilla's biceps. The rag for buffing's on the seat."

"Shouldina been takin' dumb chances like that."

"Let it go," Ron said firmly. "You owe him."

"How ya figure?" Dave challenged.

Ron put down the can of wax he was holding.

"Well, I wasn't supposed to say but he saw Spud's watch. He told me all about it at Luke's."

Dave had a look of disbelief on his face. Before he could speak, Ron cut him off.

"It's O.K. There's nothing to worry about."

"Out with it," Dave ordered.

"Well, Leon and Rafe left their mitts and the bat with Luke and were standing on the knoll a ways back behind Spud."

"I saw that," Dave interrupted. "It was in the second game when the Davids blasted those back-to-back doubles."

"Anyway, Rafe told Leon they should move in closer. So there they were, watching the Davids pile up runs like everybody else. Rafe's munching down a bag of peanuts. Then, wham, out of nowhere, he ups and asks Spud for the time. Leon said he couldn't believe it. He said Rafe never blinked, didn't move a muscle or turn away from the game, just kept chomping away. Next, Spud gives them the once over and Leon reaches for some nuts because he's about to lose it. Rafe's still crunching away. Spud dips a hand into his pocket, pulls out the watch just enough and looks down. When he does, Rafe does too. Then, they hang around awhile so he doesn't get suspicious."

"So the watch looks like Mr. Kovach's?"

"From what he said, he only barely saw it. Now don't go getting all steamed up over this. We were going to tell you about it later. If I see that the scratch is gone Sunday, we've got 'em."

Dave was delighted and went home for lunch with a spring in his step. He'd settled on a plan too. If Ron didn't see that the scratch was gone Sunday before Mr. Kovach went to the restroom, he was taking matters into his own hands. In spite of what his dad had said, he'd steal the film if he could and replace it with blank pieces from the end of the roll Luke developed. That might buy a little time. If not, he'd just take the watch and hope for the best. He'd waited as long as he could. Time was running out.

Chapter 20
THE DUEL

When the prisoners arrived, this time to play the Cubs, Dave was seated on a bench behind the backstop with his feet laid across a corner of his cart. He'd been standing most of the morning at the parade downtown and, was, for the moment, perfectly content listening to the leaves rustle and the birds twitter. Gorilla, towering over the rest of the team and wearing his usual scowl, appeared with the other convicts. As they started in on the path, the birds flew away. Rafe was right on about the muscles.

Dave was doing one thing for himself today. When Gorilla stepped up to the plate he was watching, no matter what. Even now, during batting practice, Gorilla's half swings sent the ball screeching into the outfield. Dave could only guess at how far one would go if he really laid into it and there was a tail wind. The Cubs took notice too, especially the pitchers. Dave conjured an image of the terrified starter making a frantic call, just before taking the mound, to bump up his life insurance. As he watched Gorilla take his remaining swings he kept repeating to himself, *What a waste, what a waste.*

Dave caught sight of Spud walking behind the prisoner's bench on the first base side. *Right on schedule*, he thought.

He felt someone tap him on the shoulder.

"Hey there Sonny, wake up, you're losing money."

He stood and did a one-eighty. It was the diminutive schoolmarm lady and the ice crushing kids. They were right on schedule too. All the available parking places were filled. He hadn't noticed the throng of people converging on the path. "Whoa," he gulped.

Before he knew it there was a line along-side the asphalt behind his cart. When it finally dispersed, he had three bottles left and his hands were freezing; the ends of his fingers were numb. While he made fists against his shirt to warm them, he looked around. A hand was raised just where the knoll started. He was out of pop and the game hadn't even started. While Mr. Kaufner hawked orange juice and flowers for that special occasion, he tore out for the Pavilion, more freezing ice. He was worn out already. People continued to stream in. The path was blocked. Mr. Kaufner's turnstiles were being ripped from the ground. It was Gorilla. The word on him must have spread like wild fire. Dave could hear it.

"He almost killed the second baseman." "He's huge." "His bat's as big as Paul Bunyan's ax."

Dave politely worked his way through the crowd. On the way he made four more sales.

Mr. Norris called "PLAY BALL." Dave ripped his cart through the roots and edged up to the corner post of the backstop. From there he could see clearly without the risk of being hit by a bone shattering foul ball, should one, per chance, come his way.

Gorilla was standing in the batter's box banging dirt off his cleats with his bat. Dave was just trying to catch his breath. Gorilla took the pitcher's measure. The pitcher took his. The crowd hushed. All eyes were on the dueling pair. The pitcher shook off the first two signs then settled on a pitch. It whizzed in slightly below the letters. Gorilla swung, Dave thought a hair late. "STREEE-RIKE ONE." A perfect pitch and Gorilla missed it. Dave figured because he'd never seen one before. More signs, the next pitch, another one down the middle. "CRACK!" So much for that theory. What a hit!

"It's going, going," came Mr. Kaufner's excited voice over the speakers.

The ball curved at the last minute and crashed through the windshield of a car parked just to the right of the home run fence. The crowd groaned. A middle aged man on the knoll jumped up, threw his hands against the sides of his head, stumbled and charged off at a dead run toward the damaged vehicle.

"FOUL BALL," Mr. Norris called.

Gorilla and the pitcher stared each other down. The pitcher's lower lip quivered ever so slightly. Dave pulled back half a step. The third pitch came in low and outside. Gorilla lunged for it but missed.

"YOU'RE OUTTA THERE," Mr. Norris bellowed.

Gorilla looked none too pleased but turned and ambled off the field. Dave couldn't believe it. The crowd was stunned. Wiggins, the Cubs pitcher, was on his game. Dave would've sworn he saw a fleeting smile wash across his face.

Where was Mr. Kovach? With the prisoners visiting again, he should have arrived long ago. Clocking in late was completely out of character for a man who went bonkers every time a big hitter came up. Dave was worried. He was also being worked to a frazzle. There were people everywhere. He'd never seen the park this crowded. He sold five bottles as fast as he could snap off their caps then sat down next to his cart. A few minutes rest and he was back to the grind. The convicts went down on three consecutive strike outs, Gorilla leading the way. The Cubs put on two in their half of the first. "CRACK!" A long fly, both men scored. The hitting continued. They tallied two more: 4-zip Cubs. Dave looked for Mr. Kovach. No luck. Wiggins bagged two more strike-outs. The next hitter slipped a bouncer between third and short to end the streak. Wiggins kicked at the rubber in disgust. He beaned the next batter. Dave hoped the prisoners would keep the rally going long enough for Gorilla to bat again. It didn't happen. They went down three pitches later on a pop fly.

"Michigan City 0, your LaPorte Cubs 4, bottom of the second," Mr. Kaufner announced without the customary fanfare. He was, as usual, treading lightly on the prisoners sensibilities.

Gorilla would be the second man up in the third. Dave had four outs to complete the circuit on the knoll, race to the Pavilion and reload. With the Cub's hitters blasting away, he was back behind the backstop in two.

The next Cub hit a towering shot which rose nearly straight up into the air. Mr. Norris called "TIME." Mr. Kaufner and the fans behind the backstop readied themselves. Those timid or sensible hunkered down with both arms crossed over their heads. The more assertive scanned the branches above hoping for a chance to display their mettle. Mr.Kaufner, ready to sacrifice all, bent forward to shield his beloved microphone and amplifier. Foul balls terrorized spectators all the time. This one, however, seemed to have Mr. Kaufner's name on it from the start. Ricocheting from branch to branch like a pinball, it clanked here, caromed there. Finally it clunked off a burl on the tree trunk next to the press box and plummeted straight down. Mr. Kaufner, a study in concentration, sat poised to react. Seeing disaster as unavoidable, he took a calculated, last second swipe at the ball—and missed. The ball caught the lip of his coffee cup sending coffee flying in all directions, the cup straight toward him. He instinctively drew up a hand in front of his face and threw himself back. When he did a rear chair leg unexpectedly plunged into what Dave guessed was a subterranean gopher hole. The chair lurched sideways taking Mr. Kaufner with it. He lay there twisted and prostrate across the seat desperately trying to retain his balance and dignity. A helping hand from the closest by-stander, ungainly twists and turns on his part and he stood unharmed, though shaken, next to his table. The riveted spectators in his grasp, he calmly wiped his face with a handkerchief, ran his fingers through his hair and reached for the microphone. Looking toward home plate then leaning into the instrument, he said, "Y-whooo-dirty," just loud enough to be heard. The crowd, previously unsure as to the proper response, began to clap loudly then burst into a howl of laughter. Dave joined in. Mr. Kaufner was great. Even under pressure his sense of timing was impeccable.

The offending baseball, having come to rest at the edge of the path, was returned to Mr. Norris. He wiped the dirt and coffee from it, rolled it in his hands and dropped it into the catcher's mitt. Mr. Kaufner, by now seated on a repositioned chair and blotting the remaining liquid off his paperwork, whispered softly into his mike, "Gadg, what's the count?" Mr. Norris, without turning, held out one finger on each hand.

"For those of you who might presently have been distracted, that's one ball, one strike on the batter, Cub runners at second and third, two outs in the last of the second."

The crowd responded with another round of applause.

"PLAY BALL," Mr. Norris decreed.

The game resumed. Four balls sandwiched around a strike and the dazed pitcher had loaded the bases. Dave glanced at the prisoner's bench. The prison manager, obviously dismayed by the turn of events, pushed his hat back and scratched his head. He sighed and motioned for a reliever. The pitcher, hanging his head, shuffled off the field. *What luck,* Dave thought, hardly anybody went to the bull pen in the second inning. With the warm up throws the prison's new pitcher had coming, he could haul a load of empties to the Pavilion and be back with time to spare before Gorilla was due up. *A Kaufner,* he said to himself. Where was Mr. Kovach? What was going on?

The stage was set. The main characters were in position. It was show time again. Dave placed his right hand against the silver fence post and peered around it, ready, in an instant, to push back, if necessary.

Gorilla was in the box. Wiggins fidgeted nervously with the ball. Mr. Norris was set to go into his crouch. The crowd stood fixated. The pitch came in. Gorilla jerked back hard as the ball passed inches below his chin.

"Whoa!" Dave exclaimed. This Wiggins character had courage, not a lot of brains, but courage. The fans gasped. Suspense deepened. Gorilla stepped out of the box, glared at Wiggins and drew the back of his hand across his lips. No response from Mr. Norris, ball one. The second pitch, chest high, was way outside. Gorilla let it pass. More fidgeting. Wiggins abruptly went top side again. The ball almost hit Gorilla in the cheek. He twisted wildly to avoid it, nearly losing his balance in the process. The crowd issued another gasp. Dave detected the hint of a smirk. He swallowed hard.

"No way," he said stunned. It wasn't a control problem. Wiggins was trying to brush Gorilla back, throw off his timing. Those grazers weren't accidental. They were deliberate. Wiggins was trying to make a name for himself at Gorilla's expense. Was he crazy or something? Gorilla was gigantic. He had a bat in his hand, a very large bat. If he took umbrage, he'd be on you in a heartbeat.

"TIME!" Mr. Norris slipped past the catcher to put himself between Gorilla and the mound. Gorilla regained his footing. After momentarily accessing the situation and watching Gorilla coolly bang more dirt off his cleats, Mr. Norris bent down to dust off the plate. Dave noticed that the closest two guards had taken a step onto the field. Mr. Norris turned toward Wiggins, gave him a stern, unambiguous scowl then returned to his position behind the catcher.

Intentionally throwing at a batter, no way would Mr. Norris tolerate that sort of thing. You played fair, by the rules when he umped. You might cut it close here and there but you played fair.

Wiggins looked toward his bench. Dave could almost read the expressionless manager's thoughts.

"Son, you'll have to work your way out of this one alone. I can't help you."

"PLAY BALL."

Gorilla stepped in. He and Wiggins squared off. With apprehension peaked, it was as quiet as if the park were empty. Gorilla worked his bat through its motion. Wiggins leaned in, got the sign, sighed, stretched, went into his windup, came off it and with every ounce of strength he could muster, delivered a smoking fast ball that was slightly high—a cream puff. "THWACK!"

"Ha! Ho! Say good bye to that one," Mr. Kaufner shouted, jumping from his chair. "There's a ball that would clear the fence at any park in America.

Dave's mouth dropped. His eyes bulged out. The ball was still climbing when it slammed into the trees beyond the home run fence.

"A Ruthian blast if ever there was one," the speakers proclaimed.

The straining crowd, seeing the ball disappear into the vegetation, rose collectively in a thunderous, ravenous cheer then clapped wildly, as Gorilla, taking it all in stride, circled the bases. Wiggins, acknowledging defeat, threw his mitt to the ground. Mr. Norris called "TIME."

The right and left fielders rounded the ends of the outfield fence. Seconds later, they disappeared.

"Findin' that ball's gonna be fun," Dave chuckled.

Gorilla, upon reaching the prisoner's bench, was besieged by ecstatic teammates. Players jumping, clapping, slapping him on the back, it was a raucous, joyous, spontaneous celebration. *Prisoners celebrating, that's gotta be a first,* Dave thought as he wrested his cart from the roots. Watching Gorilla made you forget unpleasant things, at least for a while.

Once Dave regained the path, hands shot up all around. It might be twenty minutes before those hayseeds combing through the woods found the ball. Did he hear opportunity knocking again, another Kaufner? He began snapping off caps. Chips of ice dripped from his fingers. There was a momentary hiss indicating a seal had broken, then another, then another.

Chapter 21
SIRENS

The left fielder, frantically waving his arms, ran up behind the home run fence.

"Hey, hey, there's a guy out here," he yelled, turning to point.

Everything stopped. The crowd's attention was instantly focused. A second later the right fielder shouted, "There's another one over here." Dave's stomach flipped. He was suddenly very frightened. He searched the park for Mr. Kovach but knew he wouldn't find him. It was like he'd had a premonition, like he'd known something terrible had happened all along. Mr. Kovach was lying out there in the woods dead. It was the only explanation that made sense. He'd been watching Mr. Kovach for weeks. Mr. Kovach was a baseball nut. He wouldn't miss seeing Gorilla hit for anything.

A few of the younger boys who retrieved foul balls had gathered at the ends of the fence but none ventured past. Mr. Norris raised a hand. Then, with his cumbersome chest protector tucked under his left arm, his mask in his right hand, he dashed off toward the outfield. He climbed the hill in left, went around the corner post and with the animated players, was swallowed up by the foliage. The guards were tense, on alert; the people in the seats and those standing, jittery. There was a buzz of hushed speculation. In the press box, Mr. Kaufner nervously fingered his mike. Dave, trying to convince himself he was all wrong, scanned the area once more and noted that Spud had vanished. That Bozo's in on it sure, he said to himself.

Mr. Norris was in the woods a long time. When he reappeared he motioned for the managers. With a guard and Mr. Kaufner joining in, a conference was convened in the outfield. Presently, the Cubs manager gestured to his players. They rose, and upon receiving instructions, cordoned off the area. Mr. Norris pulled one aside, a speedster, and dispatched him to the roller rink where there was a telephone.

On the hill, preparations for the after game picnic were at a standstill. The people there and at the slide were caught up in the drama like everyone else. Some had their hands over their mouths, others, a look of foreboding on their face. Mrs. Norris had Ann pulled up close to her side. Dave wondered if they could see into the woods or hear any of what was being said.

Mr. Norris, Mr. Kaufner, the prison manager and the guard started back toward the infield. At the pitcher's mound the latter two split off to confer with the remaining guards. Mr. Norris and Mr. Kaufner shared a parting word then Mr. Kaufner returned to the press box. The crowd, in anticipation, followed his every move.

He picked up the microphone and said, "Due to extenuating circumstances the remainder of today's game has been canceled. You are asked, however, to remain seated until the Michigan City team has boarded their bus and left the park."

People clinging to whatever security could be found in uncertainty had nowhere to turn. Obscure possibility, remote probability, the unthinkable had just become reality. The prospect that their secure little hamlet would continue to be a refuge from big city woes was abruptly shattered. Two victims, almost certainly murdered, had just been discovered in one of the town's favorite haunts, in sleepy, out of the way LaPorte. Disbelief lingered on a few faces. Everyone else knew they were experiencing a moment that would be locked fast, vivid in their memories for the rest of their days, that they were being carried along by a tide of grim events, both impossible to foresee and impossible to deny.

The park suddenly reverberated with the sounds of screaming sirens. They came from both directions on Truesdell, and from McClung.

Dave looked toward the prisoners. They were seated in a tight row on their bench with guards standing at each end and behind. The burst of euphoria following Gorilla's home run, likely the high point of their year, maybe their lives, was now but a distant memory.

Flashing lights, regular squad cars, one from the sheriff's department, unmarked cruisers, they pulled up to the end of the home run fence, behind the orange juice truck and at the roller rink. In minutes the park was swarming with police. There was pointing, gesturing. A line of wary officers entered the woods. Dave saw drawn guns. Reality was a lot scarier than T.V. Patrolmen coming in on the path, immediately began to clear it. The crowd, transfixed by each new development, watched as the melodrama unfolded around them. The Cubs manager joined Mr. Norris on the field. More patrol cars arrived. From what Dave could see, nobody but Spud had left the park.

The prisoners were approaching. Police officers on each side of the path pushed people back. Dave found himself in a crush of bodies. He looked around. The big man, the one he'd been sure was watching him earlier, was standing just off to his left, next to the bench behind him. A rush of acid flooded into the back of his mouth. He almost pitched on the spot. He grabbed onto the cart handle and forced down a swallow then found himself methodically taking long, slow, deep breaths. Where had this guy come from? Dave hadn't seen him earlier. Actually, he'd forgotten about him. He was sweating. His hands were shaking. Dad was too far away. Mr. Kaufner was across the path. There were policemen close by but they were busy and he was just a kid. He thought he'd scream, then, at the same instant, decided he was safe as long as he stayed where he was. He edged away so more of the bench was between him and the man, knowing he was as white as a freshly laundered I.S.P. jersey.

The fans, just inches from the convicts, stared poker faced as they walked, single file, through the opening. It was all part of the show. They were actors. None of this was real. The prisoners, glum, knew it didn't matter if they'd been involved in the killings or not, once a felon, always a suspect. Dave, positive they were innocent, hoped they'd still be let out to play.

For the fans, the prisoners' departure brought the curtain down on the matinee. No one was getting close to the home run fence or the woods beyond, so what else was there to do but leave and, of course, tune in the evening's newscast? Tomorrow, with the gory details splashed across the front page of the Herald Argus, you could feast at your leisure. Who knew? Two dastardly murders, updates might trickle in for weeks.

Dave had more somber concerns at the moment. As soon as he could, he moved his cart across the path and parked it and himself next to Mr. Kaufner's table. When he did, the big guy fell in with the fans strung out behind the prisoners and from what he could see, left the park. O.K., that worked, he thought, feeling more in control.

With patrolmen still scurrying around he waited until most everyone was gone then scavenged the last of the bottles and settled up. After what seemed like hours, Mr. Norris broke off with the Cubs manager, got the inside on evidence collected in the woods and moved on to trunk packing.

"Was it him?" Dave asked hesitantly. "Was it Mr. Kovach?"

"Yes," Mr. Norris confirmed.

"And..."

"And the other man was one of the hobos we saw along the lake, the bigger of the two, the one wearing the vest."

Dave couldn't, for the life of him, see how drifters who cooked minnows over twigs might figure into a sophisticated spy ring.

"I thought all the bums had been run outta town." he remarked.

"The police thought so too," Mr. Norris replied. "Now it appears those two moved into the woods where they wouldn't be seen."

"What happened ta the other guy, the one with the dragon on his arm?"

"Nobody knows but he was at the scene and likely had a hand in the murders," Mr. Norris answered, positioning his chest protector just so on top of the boxes in the trunk then cautiously closing the lid.

None of what Dave had just heard squared with his theory, though now that he thought about it, he didn't actually have a theory. If he did, hobos and killings weren't part of it.

"How do the police know he was there?" Dave asked pointedly.

"Shoes," Mr. Norris replied.

"Shoes?" Dave repeated.

"When Mr. Kovach was brought to this country he was given a new pair of shoes, pretty snazzy ones too."

"Saw those," Dave noted. "They were neat."

"Well, they're gone. That's why the police think the other tramp killed him."

"I don't get it."

"A hobo's life can depend on his shoes," Mr. Norris explained. "Without good shoes he can't get around. He can't find food. Most importantly, he can't protect his feet from cuts and scrapes. Hobos don't go to doctors. If he picks up an infection, the penicillin that could easily save his life might as well be on the moon."

Dave knew about penicillin. It was whitish and thick and a shot of it hurt like the dickens.

Mr. Norris and Dave drove the short distance to the picnic area. When Dave reached for the door handle his Dad took hold of his arm.

"Who else knows of your suspicions?"

"Everybody," Dave replied in a faltering voice. "I mean just us guys," he hurriedly clarified.

"Anyone else?" Mr. Norris probed over his glasses.

"No sir," Dave answered resolutely. "We all promised."

There was a moment's silence.

"I want everything you've got on this tomorrow," Mr. Norris instructed, "everything. Now move to the back seat, we'll be heading home as soon as we pick up your mother and sister."

For some reason, missing the fireworks at the fairgrounds that traditionally capped off the day didn't seem very important.

Dave's morning began with light taps on the wall next to his curtain.

"Time to get going," Mrs. Norris directed. "Ralph and George are on their way over."

Dave was instantly in gear. He got dressed and quickly ate breakfast. He had a long day ahead of him.

"Mom, when the guys get here, tell 'em I'm downstairs," he said, as he went through the kitchen door.

Minutes later, Rafe, Gunner and Ron, charged down the steps to join him in the basement.

"What's the ruckus about?" Gunner asked. "Our parents said we couldn't go places alone today."

"Had ta run escort for this light weight," Rafe added, mussing Ron's hair.

Ron pulled away and rolled his eyes. "Body guards," he quipped, pointing at the pair.

"Yeah, we're hirin' out now," Gunner grinned.

"And if somebody gets bumped off while we're guardin' 'em, we're takin' the corpse ta the Morgue," Rafe snorted. "Morie slabs 'em out, he's cuttin' us in on the take."

"Means we come out either way," Gunner beamed and the two brothers complimented each other on being so witty.

Dave frowned. He wasn't in the mood for frivolity. "This is serious," he said.

"We know that," Gunner returned. "Just kiddin' 'round."

"Well, don't," Dave snapped. "Not now."

"So what happened?" Rafe asked, responding to the anxiety in Dave's voice. "We went for fireworks last night. Heard your dad was makin' the rounds though. Called Mom way early this mornin', 'fore we were even up but she didn't say."

"Musta, he didn't want to disturb our beauty sleep," Gunner said, lightly sliding his hand down his cheek.

"He and my dad spent almost an hour on the front porch," Ron added. "Then Dad said we should come here today."

"Come down here?" Dave returned, surprised.

"Yep," Gunner confirmed. "Same for us."

"Don't exactly know where ta start," Dave said.

"Just tell us what happened from when you got to the park," Ron advised.

"Well, first off, Mr. Kovach wasn't there, well, actually he was," and Dave went on to tell them about the standoff between Wiggins and Gorilla, how Gorilla's fabulous home run had resulted in Mr. Kovach and the hobo being found dead in the woods, the connection with the shoes, Spud's leaving, the big man.

Dave noticed that his friends were looking at one another with strained expressions on their faces.

"Thought you guys knew 'bout the murders."

The response to that comment was searching looks and shaking heads.

"Well, the police were swarmin' all over the place. Some of 'em back in the woods had their guns drawn. It's not anything like on T.V. It was scary, real scary."

"When we got home I had ta stay in the house. Mom locked both doors. We never do that. Then Dad got inta the trunk and strapped on the bag that holds baseballs for games. I'm bettin' he was usin' it as a holster. Next thing, he's gone."

"'Fore we left the park yesterday he said he wanted all the stuff we had on Kovach and Spud and ta give it ta 'im this afternoon. Spect he'll pass it along ta the police, do'no what'll happen then."

Dave had finished the story and was fielding questions when Leon and Ben showed up. Half way through repeating it for them, he had to start over for the Razyniaks. The minute he said the word "murdered" all the boys were on board. It couldn't be true but it was.

"'Member now," he underscored. "We can't breathe a word a this ta anyone, not a soul."

A break for lunch and the "security detail" returned Ron to Dave's basement.

"We're gonna shoot around awhile then we're goin' ta the Morgue," Rafe said. "Be back later."

Ron was all business and well prepared. He had the scorer's book, a writing tablet, pens, accounts of what Rafe, Leon and Luke had seen.

"Stuff only happens on Sundays and holidays," he said, "so I'm doing one page for each day. To make it look official I'm putting the date right at the top then who went along and what they saw—and I'm doing it in order, by inning."

"Don't see where any of it's gonna matter," Dave grumbled. "The cops are pinnin' it on the hobos. I was layin' there thinkin' 'bout it for hours last night and that's how it goes down. LaPorte's a hick town in the middle of nowhere. I wouldn't even know it exists 'cept for my relatives. Probably hasn't been a murder there since that Gunness lady chopped up all those love sick loners and fed 'em ta the hogs and that's been what, like fifty years ago. Tellin' ya, the cops, they're not gonna have a clue. They're gonna go with the evidence that's obvious. They'll make a quick arrest if they can. The citizens payin' their salaries will think they're Johnny-on-the-spot and bang, that'll be it. Case closed."

With the way Ron was concentrating, Dave might as well have been talking to himself.

"Thing is, none of it makes any sense," he continued. "We don't even know if Mr. Kovach was killed there. Coulda been he got it somewheres else and was just dumped off behind the fence 'cause of the underbrush. The hobos coulda done it but with all the other bums run outta town they've got the place ta themselves. They're eatin' outta barrels back a the best restaurants in town, got a hideout safe in the woods, the secret tunnel ta go back and forth in, no competition, no responsibilities. For hobos they're living like kings. Why they wanna blow all that over a pair a shoes? And even if Mr. Kovach was joggin' through the park and they knew he was comin', he's a strong dude. They go for him, what if he gets the best of 'em? It's not worth it. They're not chancin' it. A bum in LaPorte? A scrufty bag a bones facin' a clean cut jury bent on avengin' the murder a their number one citizen? Heck, one look at that dragon on his arm, he's dead. Even a hobo's gotta know that. I never seen anybody in LaPorte got a tattoo. They're mostly like farm..."

"O.K., hold up," Ron said. "It was June ninth when you saw the scratch, then saw it disappear, right?"

"Yeah, sure," Dave replied.

"What about Spud and the big guy? They could have done it."

"Coulda. I know Spud was in on it. When the bodies were discovered, everybody was gawkin', strainin' ta see. I don't think a soul left the park 'cept Spud."

"That's not actual proof," Ron remarked.

"Come on," Dave frowned. "Two murders in LaPorte? Bet he made it to his car and was gone before the police ever got there. But why? Mr. Kovach was their meal ticket. Without him they wouldn't have anything ta sell. Where's the motive?"

"Do we know how Mr. Kovach was killed?"

"No idea," Dave replied. "Never thought ta ask Dad 'bout it. They musta had rain at the park though, 'cause with all that went on and the soggy ground I had ta push through, I was so wiped when we left, I didn't care.

"Are we sending the film along?" Ron inquired.

"Why bother," Dave scoffed. "There's nothin' on it gonna help. I 'bout trashed it when I passed the barrel on the way ta countin' out at the Pavilion."

Another hour crosschecking details and the boys were confident all the pertinent information had been recorded and a clear time line established. That accomplished, the subject turned to Doug and the Derby race.

"Too bad he didn't win," Dave said. "He put in one heck of a lot of work on that car."

When Mr. Norris returned home they handed over the tablet and ledger then went through each, step by step. Once Mr. Norris mastered the code, which Dave gathered he thought was of questionable value, the "evidence" found its way into the Ford's trunk. Nobody's findin' it there, Dave smirked, as Mr. Norris closed the lid then turned to go into the house.

"Almost forgot. Dad, how was Mr. Kovach killed?"

"Knifed," Mr. Norris replied, continuing toward the back door. "They were both knifed."

Dave looked at Ron. The two were thinking the same thing. The big guy they mouthed simultaneously.

With that Sunday's game rained out, Dave didn't get any news from LaPorte for over a week, meaning each day was a roller coaster of emotion. He was up, down. It was on his mind, off his mind. He couldn't understand why, when adults did things, it always took so long. The waiting would have been practically unbearable had the paranoia not subsided as quickly as it took hold. That circumstance put the Scanner brother's and Morie's little business venture on the rocks before they had their first paying "customer" and allowed Dave to roam free again.

Finally, the next Saturday, after Mr. Norris had been gone all day and Dave was as antsy as he could ever remember being, the word came down.

"Did we get 'em?" he asked, the minute his dad stepped out of the car. Are they in the slammer?"

Mr. Norris didn't immediately reply. He didn't have to. The answer was there on his face.

"But—" Dave went to protest.

Mr. Norris raised a hand. "I spent most of the afternoon with the detective assigned to the case. We went over everything you sent along. He showed me the evidence they collected. Foot prints from Mr. Kovach's shoes led directly through the woods to the railroad tracks leading out of town. The tramp that got away hopped a freight there and was long gone before the killings came to light. He could be anywhere in the country by now."

Dave had tried to brace himself for such a revelation but couldn't hide his disappointment. Mr. Norris put a hand on his shoulder.

"I'm sorry, son," he said. "The damning evidence was the rusty kitchen knife," Mr. Norris explained. "It was still in the bigger tramp's back when the police rolled him over. The other tramps fingerprints were on the handle. That's what took so long. The police had to wait for the lab reports to come back. The personal items they recovered from the hobo's camp site indicated that no one else had been there."

Dave was devastated. The others in on the spying were going to get away scot-free.

"If your Mr. Spud had a motive, if we had something concrete, a tie in of some sort that placed him at the scene of the crime, at the moment there's nothing the police can do. Their hands are tied. In this country people have rights. The police can't act without probable cause. That's the law."

Dave couldn't think of anything to say. He was angry, wished he'd stolen the watch weeks ago but then, his dad had forbidden that. How was it you could find yourself in a predicament such as this? You knew a mistake was being made yet couldn't do anything about it.

Supper passed with hardly a word spoken. After Dave finished eating, he delivered the "good news" to Rafe and Gunner then went on to Ron's. He'd fill the others in later.

"This ain't gonna stop 'em ya know," he groused. "Soon's this blows over they'll work another guy in and pick up right where they left off; wouldn't be a bit surprised if they go back ta switchin' at the park like nothin' happened—hey, sorry I'm grumpy. This spy stuff, what we been on it, like two months?"

"O.K. on that. Now tell me about Gorilla's hitting," Ron said, changing the subject.

"It was somethin'," and Dave recounted each pitch in order. "Can't believe Wiggins tried ta brush 'im back. Woulda pegged 'im square in the temple if he hadn't practically fallen down. I thought a fight was gonna break out sure, and Dad woulda been smack in the middle of it.... The cops are supposed to follow the evidence no matter where it leads, right?"

"So?" Ron returned.

"So, that's a bunch of hooey," Dave sneered. "We gave 'em evidence, tons of it and what'd they do, nothin', 'cause we're kids that's why."

Dave was still talking to himself when he left for home. Once there he continued unloading his frustrations over the phones with Luke and Leon. Then, before turning in, he took them out on the canister containing the microfilm that was sitting on the bookcase next to his bed. He picked it up and in a rage hurled it at the wall next to his T.V. When it hit the lid spun off, the strip of negative spiraled out and rolled under his bed. As far as he was concerned it could stay there forever.

Chapter 22
AS CLEAR AS MUD

The Nickols' Ducks, the other Michigan City club, was the visiting team at the park this Sunday. A baseball team sponsored by a duck farm, how many of those could there be? The opportunities this presented for Mr. Kaufner were practically endless: flocks of succulent mallards noisily cavorting on the lake one day, gone with barely a trace the next, wariness, unexplained agitation, reports of mysterious thrashing sounds in the night, clumps of bloody feathers inexplicably found floating in amongst the reeds near shore at daybreak. There'd be subtle suggestions that ladies wear bonnets, avoid looking up, oblique references to slipping. With a lively crowd Mr. Kaufner would be on a tear and Dave would be fighting back laughs every time a hoodwinked fan missed a gotcha moment, a circumstance likely to repeat itself all afternoon.

That wasn't the world Dave entered when he walked into the park today. It wasn't a festive holiday. There was no hometown rivalry to whip up enthusiasm. Gorilla wasn't around to bash homers. The "Fancy Dan" Davids weren't on hand to mesmerize the crowd. There wasn't, in fact, anything out of the ordinary to draw in spectators and with a persuasive, intangible apprehension hanging heavy in the air, a fair share of the regulars probably wouldn't show either. Hot, humid, muggy, it was a thoroughly unpleasant day, the sort best spent in a cool basement. And that's where Dave would be if it wasn't for the commitment thing.

Thirty-eight cents, that's what Dave had in his pocket when he and his dad left the park. He wanted to go straight home, salvage what little was left of the day. He didn't suggest it though, why bother? Unless injury, murder or an act of God prevented it, a stop at Uncle Wally's Bar was inevitable.

Parking off the alley, as usual, Dave followed his dad toward the unmarked service door. Once identified, they entered the narrow hallway. Up ahead, in the family area, Dave was surprised to see a slightly built, thin faced man, seated at the small center table. A thumb to his chin, a lit cigarette between the index and middle finger of his other hand, he was gazing, deep in thought, through the ribbon of smoke rising in front of his face. Dave watched the smoke crinkle into waves above his head then float away. *Casablanca.* A scene from Rick's Cafe sprang to mind. Uncle Wally returned to filling the beer cooler. The man, suddenly aware of Dave and his dad's presence, turned, flicked the cigarette against the rim of the glass ashtray beside his drink, smiled and extended his hand.

"So, this is the young man," he said.

Dave puzzled, looked up at his dad.

"Yes sir," Mr. Norris replied. "This is David."

Dave returned the smile, shook hands and said, "Glad ta meet ya."

"Sergeant Scruggs has been assigned to the case," Mr. Norris continued, "He's the detective I spent most of yesterday with."

"That was good work you and your friends did," Detective Scruggs said. "I wanted to tell you how much we appreciate it."

"Thank you," Dave returned, as he sat down. Then, hesitantly, he added, "I don't think the hobos killed Mr. Kovach."

"Maybe not," the detective replied, "but at this point the trail leads straight to them."

Dave couldn't think of a way around that answer so he didn't say anything more.

Uncle Wally set a bottle of beer next to the bowl of potato chips on the table and handed him a Coke.

"Thinking of becoming an investigator are you?" Detective Scruggs winked.

"Not plannin' on it," Dave grinned.

For the next fifteen minutes, the three adults engaged in small talk and Mr. Norris gave an account of the day's game. Dave didn't think it was anywhere's near as interesting as his dad made it out to be. From his perspective, it was hardly worth mentioning.

"Where do ya keep the evidence ya collected from the woods?" he inquired, once he'd drained his glass down to the ice.

"We have a special room for it at the station."

"Could I see it?" Dave asked, knowing his request was a long shot before he opened his mouth.

Detective Scruggs and Mr. Norris looked at each other. Dave was certain either or both would K.O. that idea on the spot. Mr. Norris went to speak. Detective Scruggs cut him off.

"With all the time you've put in on this," he replied haltingly, "I think we could do that."

Dave was amazed, first that Detective Scruggs said he could see the evidence then, that his dad had gone along with the proposal.

Dave and his dad followed the brown unmarked cruiser he'd seen at the park on the 4th to the police station.

"How do ya know him?" Dave asked.

"Kinne's an umpire. I broke him into officiating Little League years ago. He does a nice job. Kinne has a good eye."

Off a short, well lit hallway, Detective Scruggs, Mr. Norris and Dave approached a plain gray steel door, next to which a sign on the wall read, EVIDENCE ROOM. Detective Scruggs unlocked it and holding onto the door knob said, "Remember now, no one is allowed to touch anything inside. We're bending a few rules here."

The words AUTHORIZED PERSONNEL ONLY stenciled on the metal directly in front of him made that clear enough. The door swung open to reveal a most interesting sight. Though not particularly large, the room reminded Dave of a department store, albeit one in which the stock had been hopelessly mixed. Items of every conceivable description were leaning, stacked, filed, shelved and locked in drawers, their placement seemingly determined almost exclusively by size. The various goods, mostly what one would expect to find in such a place, included the latest electric tools, bicycles, cameras, transistor radios, television sets and a large safe. Interspersed, were more mundane articles whose significance wasn't at a glance apparent: a sturdy stick, a cement-encrusted work boot, a nearly new whitewall tire. Each object or box was labeled. Some had hang tags affixed. All carried a case number and date. Dave and his dad proceeded to a table in the back of the room. Detective Scruggs followed along behind.

"If its physical evidence related to a recent felony, this is where it'll be. We've found that spreading it out in a quiet area where one can think advances a case. Insights and connections overlooked in the field often times become obvious when an officer isn't distracted by his surroundings."

All right already, Dave chafed. If Mr. Detective here would just step aside so he could get a look at what had been removed from the woods, maybe he'd have an insight or could made a connection.

Trash. Dave was starring down at a pile of smelly trash that appeared to have been transported lock, stock and in this case wooden boxes from the hobos' last encampment to this table and a portion of the next: filthy blackened cookware, a partially collapsed tea kettle, handle-less cups, reclaimed dinnerware, two wallets, one new, one old, two pairs of broken down shoes. A quick overview of the items in front of him and Dave had no idea why he'd wanted to see the evidence, no clue as to what it might be he was looking for.

"Was that nicer wallet Mr. Kovach's?" he inquired.

"Yes," Detective Scruggs replied. "We found it empty along with the brown shoes a ways back in the woods where they'd been thrown. The other wallet was cleaned out too. It and the black shoes, there next to the plastics they used when it rained, those were with the larger tramp's body."

"Uh, huh," Dave nodded, trying to appear interested. "What happened to the knife?" he asked, after taking a step toward the second table.

"Sorry, I can't show you that. It's locked up in the vault. There wasn't anything special about it though. You probably have one just like it in your kitchen at home. Now, the clothes," Detective Scruggs continued, "They're on the drying rack next to your dad there just as they were found."

Dave noted the big hobo's blood stained vest hung askew on the end hanger. The slit made by the knife was clearly visible in the back panel. He cringed.

"Were there any tire tracks?" he asked. "Did anyone see a car in the area?"

"We have no witnesses," Detective Scruggs returned. "And we only get tire tracks if a vehicle slips off the pavement or it's parked in an area soft enough to leave an impression."

"Hey, that's from one of Mr. Kovach's new sneakers." Dave said, pointing to a white plaster cast of a shoe print.

"Right you are," Detective Scruggs smiled. "We found that beauty on the far side of the woods where the railroad tracks run up next to the cemetery. The pattern, the size, it's a perfect match for the left shoe Mr. Kovach was given when he first came to town."

That about did it: means, motive and opportunity.

"How 'bout these others?"

"Well, that one's your dad's" Detective Scruggs said, pointing, "The ones with the cleats belong to the ballplayers that went looking for the ball. The tramp's shoes left the ones down at the end of the table. We've identified them all except for the one next to your hand."

Dave examined it carefully then shifted position and looked it over again.

"That print was found near Mr. Kovach's body. As you can see someone slipped in the mud. Unfortunately it's so distorted we can't determine the shoe size. We don't believe it will be of any use but we have to follow every lead not just those that look promising. Very little of what we recover from a crime scene ever proves useful. Arriving at the truth is almost always a slow, tedious process."

"Are we about done here?" Mr. Norris asked in a tone signaling impatience.

"Finishin' up right now," Dave returned, looking back at the array of items on the tables.

Dave had a lot filling his head when he and his dad left the police station. Getting home topped the list, that and trying to take in all of what he'd just seen. For one thing, the police, his trip through the evidence room had completely changed his opinion of them. The way things were carefully stored, tagged, laid out so exactly on the tables and matching up Mr. Kovach's sneaker with the foot print left alongside the rail line that was great police work. Those tracks were darn near half a mile from the park.

Dave was impressed, hot too. Even with both front windows cranked down he was roasting. His Uncle's tavern was nice and cool, so was the evidence room. Maybe, if his parents ever bought another new car, it'd be air conditioned, course then, the windows wouldn't be closed just in winter but most all summer too. *There ya go,* he thought, *an idea sounds good first off and then...*

Dave was in his bedroom, flat on the floor, seconds after the car braked to a stop. It was dark beneath his bed. Where was the film? He couldn't see it anywhere. He twisted his head to one side and scooched under, nothing. He swept his arm around in an arc, still nothing. He waited for his eyes to adjust, reminded himself that the strip of celluloid wasn't much wider than a pencil and not nearly as long. He could barely move. Then, a vague outline against the back wall. There it was. He caught a finger in a curl and pulled it out. He returned it to its canister, put the canister in his pocket and went into the kitchen for supper.

275

Mr. Norris pointed at his head.

"Aw, sorry," Dave said, pulling clumps of dust from his hair. "Can I go ta Luke's after dinner?"

"As long as you're home by dark," Mr. Norris replied.

Dave ate fast then asked to be excused.

Luke was busy in the darkroom preparing his camera for another night's observing when Dave arrived. He tapped lightly on the door.

"Yeah," Luke responded, "in a minute."

Dave leaned against the wall panting. "Got here quick as I could," he gasped when the door opened.

"What's the big hurry?" Luke asked.

"Not sure, maybe this," and Dave pulling the canister from his pocket. "Can we run it through the enlarger again? Can't 'member if it was there or not."

Luke dutifully uncovered the enlarger, turned it on, positioned the film and brought it into focus.

"It's not going to look any different now than it did before," he remarked.

"I'm thinkin' it might." Dave returned. "Move it down," he said hurriedly. "One more. Wait! Stop!" he yelled, pointing frantically. "The curve! He wear's 'em! You can see the curve! It was there all the time. When Detective Scruggs showed—I didn't dare get my hopes up." Dave put a hand on his head. "I can't believe it, never thought ta look. The tie in, we got the tie in. Spud was there behind the fence when Mr. Kovach was killed. I can prove it. We had it all along. We just didn't know it."

Luke, studying the image intently, had a bewildered look on his face.

"All I see is Spud's legs and part of the bench."

Dave could tell he was a million miles away.

"That's why I wasn't sure," Dave said excitedly. "Rafe and Leon were goin' for the watch outline on his wrist when they snapped that one. When it wasn't there, I more-less skipped over ta the next frame. Couldn't 'member if they got the bottom of his shoe or not."

Luke's expression hadn't changed. He was as perplexed as ever.

Dave dropped to the floor.

"It's the heel," he exclaimed, twisting around so Luke could see the bottom of his shoe. "Spud wears orthopedic heels same's me. He's the only other person 'round I know has 'em. They're called Thomas Heels. The inside part sticks way out toward the front of the shoe," he said, tracing the heel's serpentine forward edge with a finger. "They're s'posed ta give ya better support, more stability when ya walk."

Luke looked at the image again.

"Curve's there all right," he said. "Matches up perfect."

"Once I saw the plaster cast..."

"Slow down, will ya," Luke interrupted. "You're going too fast. I've got how the heel's curved. Now what's this tie-in you're talking about?"

"It places Spud—see the ground was wet and he slipped, that's why they didn't know."

Dave realized he hadn't told Luke about his trip to the evidence room or how the plaster cast tied Spud to the crime, so he gave a brief account of his experience.

"I saw the curve the heel made right away but it was all stretched out from how he slid in the mud. Look, I havta watch every step I take, you know that. My brace leg slips out, bang, I'm on the ground and there it is, the curve cuttin' through the muck, same's I saw on the plaster. Tell ya, it was starin' me straight in the face. Thing I didn't know, was whether Rafe and Leon got Spud's heel when they took the picture. See, the curve's only there where the line starts out and if ya didn't know ta look for it, you'd miss it sure.

"Somethin' 'bout Spud always bugged me. It was the way he walked. I seen it before, at Shriners maybe, do'no, can't explain it. I just 'membered he sometimes sits with his legs crossed, so I thought, who knows, maybe. Anyway, could ya whip up a nice big print for Dad?"

"No problem," Luke replied, "but hang on, we've already sent everything else and they've got the finger prints. What makes you think this will do it?"

That brought Dave back down to earth.

"Gotta try," he shrugged, as he walked toward the steps.

On the way home, Dave convinced himself, that this time, he really did have Spud. *Got 'im sure*, he thought to himself, then an instant later he wasn't nearly as confident. He went into his bedroom to take off his brace, relax and read a magazine. His phone buzzer sounded. It was Luke.

"We've been talking it over down here and we think you'll need more pictures."

"Of what?" Dave asked.

"One of the heel on your shoe and one that's the same as what Spud's made in the muck. There's a place across the alley by Biever's garage where that black slippery stuff collects after it rains."

"Couple feet from the downspout, by the rock," Dave sighed. "Know where that is."

"Tomorrow?" Luke queried.

"Right," Dave replied. "Be over soon's I finish breakfast."

Dave was all set to make his slide in the muck when Luke stopped him.

"We've got to do this step by step," he said. "First we need a picture of your heel."

Dave sat down, unbuckled his brace and wiped off the bottom of his shoe. Luke had Tim position it just so in the sun and took pictures. That accomplished, Dave put his hand through the brace into the shoe, forced it into the ooze and dragged it off at an angle.

"Looks good," he said, "but Spuds shoe dug in deeper."

"Because they were fighting, right?" Tim remarked.

"Musta been," Dave replied.

"Bet he was pushing off," Pete remarked, "and that's why he slipped."

"Yeah, he was pushin' all right," Dave frowned, thinking of the bloody vest.

For their next attempt they found a new spot. Dave put his brace back on, held tight to Luke's arm, and with his weight on that leg, Pete pulled it sideways.

"That's far enough," Dave exclaimed, "or I'm goin' over."

The boys bent down to examine the indentation the shoe made, particularly the ridge the heel left.

"It's perfect," Dave beamed. "A plaster cast of that would be a dead ringer for the one I saw."

The four boys looked at each other.

"O.K., so let's make one," Pete said.

"Not so fast," Luke cautioned. "We need to get it on film first."

He knelt beside the depression. "It's too dark," he said. "We don't have enough contrast." A flashlight set nearly flat to the ground and presto, like magic, the all important ridge line stood out plain as day. They took pictures then poured in the plaster. While it cured and Luke made prints, Ron recorded the details. When the process was complete, they presented the lot to Mr. Norris.

"Let's not be getting ourselves in an uproar over this. The police can't build a case overnight. These are very serious accusations that have to be carefully considered."

Dave listened politely but didn't comment. To his way of thinking, the photos and plaster cast needed to be on Detective Scruggs desk when he came on duty the next morning.

It was the waiting game again, anticipation in the morning, disappointment at night.

On Friday, Dave's curiosity got the best of him. He couldn't stand the suspense any longer.

"Dad, how's it goin' with the pictures?" he asked.

"The police are looking at them," Mr. Norris replied.

That was it, one sentence. What did "lookin' at 'em" mean?

Saturday morning Dave went to Ron's, mostly to complain.

"Dad didn't say they're lookin' into it or they're sweatin' Spud. He said they're lookin' at the pictures. What they doin', sittin' there starin'?"

"Cool off," Ron said, "your dad's right. This stuff takes time. It's not like in the movies, you know. You said Detective Scruggs was cool."

"He is. Tell ya one thing though, when we were in the evidence room and he was talkin' 'bout how a clue could go unnoticed then all of a sudden jump out at ya...."

"Yeah."

"Well, 'bout a minute later, wham-o, the shoe print was right there under my nose. It was eerie."

Dave thought Fox Park must be caught in a time warp of some kind. Either that or people's memories had been selectively erased. Not that many days had passed since two bodies had been discovered on the premises, since two lives had been snuffed out, and here came people cheerfully sauntering in on the path, buoyant, carefree, as if nothing had happened. It was as if the gristly murders had never taken place and the isolation myth about big city troubles ending at the edge of town remained intact. Dave assumed the citizens had laid it on the hobos. They killed Mr. Kovach then got into a fight. The survivor beat it out of town and was long gone. Essentially, it was the same story Dad had gotten. People must have convinced themselves it was a crime of opportunity, a random act unlikely to be repeated so there was no cause for alarm. In any case Dave had learned something. People for the most part believe what they want to believe. He'd learned something else too. If you were going to have to work the rest of your life you'd better be doing something you liked, otherwise you were stuck.

He sighed heavily and pushed off for the knoll.

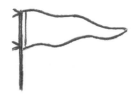

Chapter 23
A SILVER LINING

Tuesday.

"Time to rise and shine," Mr. Norris said. "Get dressed. You and I are going to LaPorte."

"Really?" Dave returned, rubbing his eyes. "Did we get 'em?"

"You'll see," and Mr. Norris disappeared into the kitchen.

Dave noticed that his dad had the same look on his face he'd seen months earlier. He was dressed, ready to go in a flash and aching to bust out with questions, an endless stream of questions. Who? What? Why? When? Where? They were all jumbled up in his head. Unfortunately, his dad had a certain way of doing things and you just had to go along, so, for all intents and purposes, father and son were simply taking a quiet drive through the country on a crystal clear, summer day.

The excursion ended in the parking lot next to Wally's Bar.

"Am I allowed? Kin I go in?" Dave asked.

"We'll sit at one of the back tables like we do on Sundays," Mr. Norris replied. "Everything will be fine."

Dave looked ahead and saw Detective Scruggs one table over from where he'd been before. Next to him sat another, heavier man.

"I see you're back again," Detective Scruggs grinned.

"Yes sir," Dave replied.

"This is Agent Burrows. He's with the Bureau."

An F.B.I. agent? Dave looked at his dad and was greeted with a giveaway smile.

Agent Burrows extended his hand.

"Quite a feat you and your friends pulled off," he said, "Helping us break up a spy ring we didn't know existed. That doesn't happen every day."

"Ya got 'em?" Dave stammered, reaching out to shake.

"Yes sir," Agent Burrows continued. "Except for a few loose ends this case is closed. Your dad's been working with us for the past week."

Dave looked at his dad again. He didn't know what to say.

"Turns out you're an investigator after all," Uncle Wally winked, while he distributed beverages. Then he raised a finger as some workmen took the table next to theirs. "And what will we be ordering today?" he asked.

"It's over?" Dave whispered.

Mr. Norris waved him off, "Later," he smiled.

Agent Burrows stood and checked his watch.

"I'm running on a tight schedule here," he said. "I'll have to be moving along."

There were handshakes all around and he departed.

"You helped the police nab 'em?" Dave asked, when he and his dad were back in the car.

"That might be overstating it a bit," Mr. Norris replied. "Let's just say they kept me informed. The big break came Thursday when the police interrogated Spud."

"And you helped, right?"

"I knew he lost his spot on the prison team because he had bad ankles. That might have saved a step or two. The confessions yesterday were what clinched it, but Agent Burrows wanted to meet you in person, so we held off telling you until today. Outside of the authorities and a few others, no one knows the real reason these homicides occurred. It's important things stay that way. The government usually has to put out a cover story in cases like this. If people think the murders resulted from a robbery gone wrong it's better all around.

"So then the pictures we took worked?" Dave exclaimed.

"They're what did it," Mr. Norris replied. "The pictures provided the probable cause that got the ball rolling. The way the killings were carried out had a hand in it, too. If a person is stabbed near the spine down from the left shoulder with a long enough knife, the blade will pierce the heart. Hitting the exact spot isn't something your average Joe on the street would know how to do. An ex-con, on the other hand, just might. Persuading Spud to talk was the only way the plot could be brought to light in a timely fashion and the higher-ups identified. An interrogation in town wouldn't have been wise so the police rousted him at night and took him to the prison. He, of course, didn't know anything about anything. The watch in question had conveniently been lost. He'd bought new shoes because his old ones wore out. It was the usual rigmarole. The police would lay out the evidence and point out the discrepancies in his story. He'd say it was all a big mistake and they'd go over it again. All the while a warrant was being executed on his apartment. For some reason people think the freezer compartment in the refrigerator is a great place to hide things."

"In the refrigerator?" Dave frowned.

"It's one of the first places the police search. Spud must not have known that because he capped the two watches in a bottle and buried it in a carton of ice cream. Frozen food doesn't usually rattle when you shake it."

"That's stupid," Dave laughed.

"Spud's not very smart, just willing if a buck or two's involved."

"The police had 'em cold," Dave grinned.

"And Spud had a captive audience. For a while there he was the center of attention. He was somebody. Eventually, the police got tired of playing games and told him he'd better come clean, name names or they'd see to it that he got a date with Ol' Sparky.

"The electric chair?" Dave asked.

"Yes sir," Mr. Norris replied. "Saving that lever until he was softened up worked like a charm. They walked him past that 'special room' on the way in. When Spud was in prison, his job included distributing books and magazines to prisoners confined in the cell blocks. He knew men on death row and some that were electrocuted. Once he started singing, the whole story was out by daybreak, signed, sealed, and delivered. Do you remember Meyer introducing you to a Mr. Zavatsky last fall?"

"I think," Dave replied.

"He was the one behind the whole thing. This spy operation was all his idea. It started when the revolution in Hungary collapsed last fall and some of the freedom fighters escaped. Once the men were cleared by the authorities, private citizens escorted them from Europe across to America. Speaking fluent Hungarian was the only requirement for the job. Miklos grew up in Hungary. He knew people there, including some who'd become communists and the freedom fighters trusted him because he worked for the government. When three of the refugees assigned to him were given jobs in defense plants, he saw it as a once-in-a-life-time opportunity to get rich. It was about the money from the very beginning. There are hundreds of factories doing defense work in the country. Each one has a contract to build equipment for the military. These contracts are awarded to the lowest bidders so costs have to be controlled. One way to cut corners is on plant security. The government requires that companies have it but leaves the details to them."

"But why would Mr. Kovach wanna spy on us?"

"Just listen," Mr. Norris continued. "To ensure that these factories are secure, the government has its own team of spies, people who take jobs in these plants and try to smuggle information out. If they succeed it's brought to the companies' attention. It's very serious business. If the abuses aren't corrected immediately, the companies can be heavily fined or disqualified from bidding on future contracts. One visit from an agent usually does the trick. That's what Mr. Kovach thought he was being enlisted to do. He thought he was being patriotic when, in fact, he was being duped."

"But the pictures, they were goin' ta the Russians, right?"

"There never were any pictures. You were wrong about that."

"No pictures?" Dave gasped. "Then what was in the watches?"

"Ceramic materials," Mr. Norris answered. "The Russians know what metals our turbine blades are made from because a few of our Sabre Jets were shot down in the Korean War. What they don't have access to is the specialty, high temperature mold materials that are used in the casting process. Different blades require different formulations. Once Mr. Zavatsky collected enough of the various types and shipped them out, he was in for a big payoff. He figured that if he stayed away from the day to day operations he wouldn't get caught. You can guess where the watch idea came from. And running three spies, as long as the men thought they were on a secret mission for the government, well, he might have been able to keep the racket going for some time. Eventually, when he'd wrung it dry, he'd tell the men the government appreciated their service, to stay quiet, and he'd keep the money. The damage could have been extensive. Then two things went wrong. You noticed that the scratch disappeared and Mr. Kovach started asking questions. He couldn't understand why it was only the refractory materials that Mr. Zavatsky wanted. That led to the meeting and the confrontation in the woods behind the outfield fence. Mr. Zavatsky warned Mr. Kovach that if he didn't toe the line he'd be deported back to Hungary, where, of course, he'd be killed. The two argued in Hungarian, the shoving started and Spud panicked. A bit later they heard noises in the woods. That's when the tramp got it."

"Did we get 'em in time?" Dave asked.

"Agent Burrows thinks so but the government hasn't decided yet how best to take advantage of the situation. At this point Miklos will do anything they ask."

"Where'd the fingerprints on the knife come from?"

"Those came about once it quieted down and the second tramp, the one who stole Mr. Kovach' shoes, went to check on his friend."

"How 'bout Spud? How did he get involved?

"That's a story in its own right," Mr. Norris chuckled. "Spud's a small time hood who's been in trouble most all of his life. Burglary's what got him sent up this time. They nicknamed him 'schemer' in prison after a big time Chicago gangster from the thirties because he was always coming up with harebrained, cockamamie schemes. He'd tell anybody who'd listen that he was just waiting for his ship to come in. This particular scheme involved breaking into expensive vacation homes along Lake Michigan during the off season. He and his buddies would steal T.V.'s, radios, jewelry, anything valuable they could lay their hands on. They were brazen, sometimes hitting two or three places at once. Spud got tripped up when he pawned a cello."

"That's like a really big violin ya sit next ta, right?"

"That's the one," Mr. Norris said, with another chuckle. "The man who owned it discovered the theft almost immediately and called police. Apparently the cello was a family heirloom. The police found it almost immediately at one of the local pawn shops, discovered Spud had given a fictitious name but used his correct address."

"You're jokin'," Dave sputtered.

"No," Mr. Norris replied. "Mr. Zavatsky knew Spud because he sold magazines and Spud worked in the prison library. That's where he was fitted with the orthopedic shoes. They helped him walk better but he still couldn't run very well. He was just a one year sub on their baseball team. He put effort into it but mostly it was just an excuse to get outside the walls. His parole came through about the time the refugees arrived and, of course, he was going nowhere. That made it easy for Mr. Zavatsky to procure his services as a go-between."

"But Spud's dumb?"

"He was also available, and willing, and for the most part he kept to himself."

"How 'bout the big guy at the park whose been hangin' 'round? Is he in on it?"

"You noticed Herb, too? Huh," Mr. Norris said. "That's Herb Trembler. He played first base for us in high school. I asked him to keep an eye on you in case you fell and hurt yourself."

"I hardly ever get hurt when I fall," Dave puzzled.

"I know that," Mr. Norris replied.

"What happens now?"

"Well, the tramp doesn't know about the spy ring and no one would believe him if he did."

Tell me about it, Dave thought.

"He's a pair of shoes richer and won't likely be seen in these parts again. The other two have both confessed and will serve very long sentences in a federal penitentiary. The government will want to keep all this quiet. As far as the local people are concerned, the tramp did it."

"But all my friends know 'bout it," Dave said.

"Their parents will be contacted—I want you to know I'm proud of you," Mr. Norris said. "It took a lot of nerve to stick with this the way you did."

There was a pause.

"Dad, I been thinkin' for a while now. I know it would be awful hard, but after I graduate Central, I think I wanna go on ta college, maybe be a teacher or somethin'."

Mr. Norris shook his head approvingly. He puffed out a huge rolling smoke ring and said," You know what I always say."

"Yeah, Dad, I know," Dave replied. *"There's no such word as can't."*

Dave leaned back into the seat, took a deep breath, and looked out his window.

"Let's see if we can catch some early scores," Mr. Norris remarked, reaching for the radio.

Dave smiled. With most of the summer yet to go and wire wheels, he'd build the best crate ever.

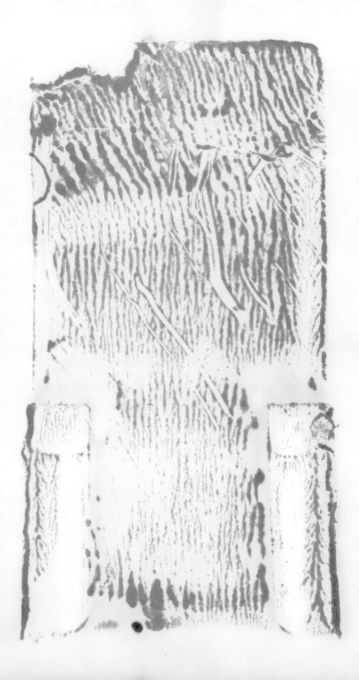

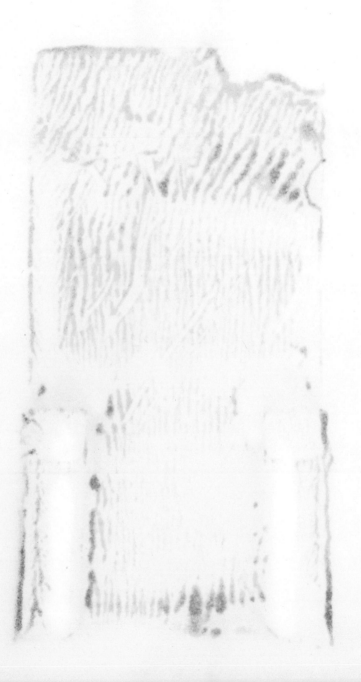